Lock Down Publications and Ca$h
Presents

Baby I'm Wintertime Cold 3

Meesha

First Edition 2023

Printed in the United States of America

Lock Down Publications
P.O. Box 944
Stockbridge, GA 30281
www.lockdownpublications.com

Like our page on Facebook: Lock Down Publications
www.facebook.com/lockdownpublications.ldp

Stay Connected with Us!

Text **LOCKDOWN** to 22828 to stay up-to-date with new releases, sneak peaks, contests and more…

Like our page on Facebook:
Lock Down Publications

Join Lock Down Publications/The New Era Reading Group

Visit our website:
www.lockdownpublications.com

Follow us on Instagram:
Lock Down Publications

Email Us: We want to hear from you!

Previously on Baby, I'm Wintertime Cold...

Blaze didn't have a set time for them to leave Aruba. He had been lying awake for hours thinking about the time he'd had with Icy. They had yet to have sex and he loved the shit out of her. Blaze had never loved a woman he had never been physically with. Icy was different from any woman he'd ever had a relationship with. Her drive was through the roof, she had her own money and thrived at running her business, family was everything to her, and she didn't need a man to be by her side every minute of the day. He could talk to Icy about anything and she would listen. Blaze just didn't want too many of his thoughts to add on to the stress she was already going through.

Icy brought her leg up and turned over on her side. The motion caused the covers to slide from her body revealing her nakedness. Blaze ran his hand up her exposed thigh and eased between her legs. He was waiting for Icy to make the first move, but in a couple hours they would be returning to the states, and he wasn't leaving until she felt the physical connection they had. It was already established that they had the mental connection on lock, now it was time for him to lock her fine ass down completely.

Lying on his stomach, he parted Icy's legs and came face-to-face with her shaved kitty. Blaze ran his tongue over his lips and blew on her pearl. Icy moved slightly and turned onto her back. Blaze in turn opened her lower lips with his hands before burying his face into her center. She started to moan in her sleep, making music for only Blaze to hear. He grasped her bud between his lips and sucked on it gently.

"Harder," Icy purred as she thrust her hips into his mouth. She was well aware of what was going on at that point and didn't want Blaze to stop.

Doing as she requested, Icy squealed, grabbing his locs with both hands. She was feeding him the pussy and he loved every bit of it. Blaze inserted two fingers into her love box and her muscles clenched down on them instantly. Finger fucking her while eating her pussy like a gourmet meal, Icy couldn't hold back a minute longer. He hit *that* spot and she erupted like a busted pipe. Blaze kept going as he drank every ounce of essence she squirted down his throat.

Blaze wiped his mouth and ran his hand down his beard as he used Icy's natural lubricant to wet up his wood. Icy was stuck as she released his hair, allowing him to get on his knees. Blaze ran his hands down her inner thighs before getting comfortable between her legs. Running the tip up and down her slick center, Icy couldn't take a minute more of his teasing. She grabbed his dick and placed it at her entry and pushed forward.

"Oh shit," she murmured.

"See, what you've been holding out on? We could've been enjoying this shit. This pussy mine now, beautiful."

"Take what belongs to you then," she challenged.

"You ain't said shit but a word."

Blaze captured both of Icy's legs and held them together. Slowly stroking in and out of her. He picked up the pace and pushed her legs towards her head until her feet touched the headboard. Icy was at his mercy and he had no plans of letting up.

"Fuck! You hitting my spot and I'm about to cum," she moaned.

"Cum on this dick then. That's what you supposed to do, Icy."

Looking down, the cum coating his dick as it moved in and out of Icy only made him harder. The sight alone was threatening to make him cum prematurely. Letting one of her legs go, Blaze pushed down on Icy's lower stomach and she started singing in a falsetto tone. He didn't give a damn who heard them, he was enjoying every minute of what he'd only had dreams about.

"Here it comes, baby. Hit that shit!" Icy instructed.

Blaze loved the fact that there was no limit to how far he could go. Icy was matching him stroke for stroke and taking all his dick. He'd met his match in the bedroom and he wasn't letting the shit go. Icy's inner walls clenched down on his member, and he was on the brink of nuttin'. There was no way to stop the inevitable because she had his shit in a chokehold.

"Oh, my God, I'm cummin'!" she screamed at the top of her lungs.

Blaze hit her with strong strokes and once again, Icy squirted hard. She pushed him all the way out of her silky cave, but he dived right back in because he was going to cum too. Tossing her leg to the side, Blaze held on to her hip and wore that ass out. Sweat beaded up on his forehead and slid down his face. At that moment, his nuts tightened and his future kids coated her vaginal walls and Blaze hoped one made it to her fallopian tubes.

"Grrrrrr. Shit. Oooooouuu," Blaze laughed as his dick slipped out. Smacking Icy on the ass, he got up to get a soapy towel to clean her up.

Soon as Blaze entered the bathroom, Icy's phone rang. She reached blindly for her phone, but it stopped ringing by the time she could answer it. When it rang a second time, Icy sat up, answering it without looking to see who was calling.

"Hello."

"Icy, I need you to get to Ingalls Memorial in Harvey. Your mother was hit with a car and she was rushed into surgery yesterday. Her pelvic bone is fractured, and she has a concussion. I wanted to make sure she was alright before I called." The words Staci's neighbor and good friend Fanny said didn't register right away. "Icy, are you there?"

"Fanny, what happened?" Icy asked, jumping from the bed with tears running down her face.

"We went to the Caribbean Jerk Restaurant in Harvey. Staci went to the driver's side of her car and when she was about to open the door, another came speeding down the street and hit her straight on. They didn't even stop."

"I'm in Aruba, Fanny. I'm about to leave in the next thirty minutes and I'll be there soon as I can. Don't leave my mama! She is to have no visitors unless it's me and you. Do you understand?"

"I'm not going anywhere, baby. Get here when you can. Staci's going to be alright."

"Thank you. I'm coming, Fanny. Tell my mama I love her and I'm on my way." Icy sobbed loudly as she leaned against the wall. Blaze raced back into the room and hugged her.

"What's wrong, Icy?"

"My mama was hit by a car. I know that muthafucka did it, Akoni! I have to go home. Now!"

"Get yourself together. I'm about to go tell the others we have to roll out soon as possible. I also have to make sure the plane is ready for takeoff. I'll be right back."

Icy grabbed an outfit and ran to take a shower. She washed the important parts of her body and got out. She had to get home to her mother. The thought of losing her had Icy's mind fucked up. She had already lost one parent and she wouldn't be able to go on with life if she lost the only one she had left.

The pilot had a sedative that caused Icy to sleep because her anxiety was through the roof. Kia and Julz were drinking and smoking to get by, while the guys talked amongst themselves about dealing with Leo. The nigga was doing anything he possibly could to hurt Icy. It was time to stop playing with his ass and tackle it head on. The situation was one big game to the bastard, but there was going to be one wrong move and he was going to get buried. Blaze just didn't know how much longer that would take.

"Do you really think Leo ran her mama off the road?" Joe asked.

"I wouldn't put shit past him, to be honest. All of a sudden, Icy finds out the muthafucka is alive after he was presumed dead, Kia's house gets shot up, Icy gets shot and the nigga was tracking her moves, then her mother gets ran off the road. That shit is not coincidental, Joe. It has his ass written all over it."

"Let me know if you need my help. I still have connections in the streets, I'll have muthafuckas lookin' out for his ass. Niggas was throwing parties when they heard Leo got knocked off. He's a fraud and I don't like that shit," Bryan snapped. "He could be out to hurt Julz next and I'm not going to let that happen."

"I was worried about that shit too. Julz is the only one he hasn't come for and it's a matter of time before he does. We have to protect all of them with our lives until we can eliminate the problem."

They all agreed and got up to smoke in the back of the plane. For most of the flight, they thought about different ways to bring Leo out of hiding. Sleep was the furthest thing from Blaze's mind, so he listened to music through his AirPods as he watched Icy closely. Time flew by and Blaze knew just how fast when he felt the plane descending in the air. About thirty minutes later, the wheels connected with the pavement. Icy was already awake, ready to bolt off the plane. Blaze was glad she decided to leave her car at the airport, because he could get them to the hospital in record time on his own.

The moment the doors opened, Blaze and Icy were the first to get off the plane. Bryan had parked in the garage too, so they were all going to pile in the cars and head to the hospital together. Kia and Joe followed Blaze once they entered the garage. Icy spotted her car first and tried to walk in front of Blaze but he held on tight to her hand. As they got closer to the car, Blaze hit the key fob to unlock the doors.

Julz and Bryan had just reached his truck when a loud explosion caught their attention. They went running in the direction of the blast but fire was blocking their path. There were no movements, and Julz started screaming at the top of her lungs.

"Nooooooooo! Icy, Kia, somebody answer me!" she cried falling to her knees.

Chapter 1

The fire was hotter than six shades of hell. Julz was screaming while running back and forth, looking for a way to get closer to Icy and Kia. The thought of either one of them being hurt damn near crippled her. Julz was in fear of losing the only family she was able to call her own. She would be nothing without them. It was bad enough Staci was laid up in the hospital, now here they were with another dilemma in the process of seeing about her.

"Icy! Kia! Answer me, bitches," Julz hollered so loud her voice echoed off the walls of the garage. The sounds of sirens could be heard in the distance as the authorities and emergency help neared. Julz wasn't worried about any of that, she just needed to make sure her people were good. She rushed in the direction of the blaze and was snatched back by Bryan.

"The fuck you doing?" he barked. "Getting yourself hurt won't make this shit better! You gotta think, Julz. Right now, we need to find an exit before the fire reaches other cars."

"I'm not leaving them! If they die, we going out together!" Julz said, fighting to get out of the grip Bryan had on her.

It was a good thing the garage wasn't closed in because they would've been fucked. The smoke was going out into the air, but the fire wasn't dying out. Julz couldn't leave her family behind to get to safety. Bryan grabbed Julz by the hand, searching for a way out. As he rushed to get away from the area, she continued to pull back. The crackling of the blaze was a huge concern for Bryan and he wanted to get far away from it.

"Come on, Julz, we gotta get out of here."

Reluctantly, Julz followed him in the direction he led. As they rounded the corner, there was another loud explosion and Julz fell to her knees, screaming in agony. Bryan lifted her off her feet and raced to the door with the exit sign above it. Carrying Julz down the three flights of stairs, they were met by a scene out of an action-packed movie. There were officers, everywhere in the lobby. Tears ran down Julz's face as she looked around for Icy or Kia. A door opened and Joe raced out with Kia in his arms. Blood covered one side of her face and she didn't appear to be moving at all.

"I need help over here!" Joe yelled.

Paramedics quickly went to aid and assist Kia. Julz ran across the lobby and was immediately stopped by the police. She struggled to get past, but the officer wouldn't budge.

"This is a serious situation. I can't allow you to go any further."

"That's my family! I need to make sure she's okay," Julz exclaimed.

"Ma'am, you can't proceed. I need you to step back so we can do our job."

"Your job is to make sure my friend is alright! I'm not injured, she is!"

Bryan knew the situation could possibly turn ugly if he didn't get Julz under control. He pulled her by the arm and placed his hands on her shoulder. Julz turned her head, looking in the direction where everyone stood with Kia. She was put on a stretcher and rushed out of the building. The police were talking to Icy, Blaze, and Joe while Julz couldn't go any further than she was across the room.

"I need you to calm down. Once the police are finished with them, they gon' come to you. Kia is going to be alright. I saw her moving on the stretcher so she's going to be fine."

"Bryan, did you see the blood on her face? That does not equate to her being okay. I need Icy or somebody to tell me that because we are all the way over here and don't know shit!"

At that moment, Icy was able to come over and talk to Julz. She walked right into Julz's arms and hugged her close. Bryan stepped back to give them a bit of privacy.

"Icy, is Kia going to be alright?" Julz asked, moving out of Icy's embrace.

"Yes, she has a gash on her forehead from a piece of metal that hit her. She may need a few stitches, but the wound isn't life threatening. We are lucky as fuck to come out of there without a scratch," Icy said. "This was not a coincidence. This shit was set up to happen."

"So, this wasn't an accident?" Bryan asked, walking over.

"No, my car was the one that exploded. Joe scooped Kia up and we ran into the stairwell right before the second explosion. I was supposed to die today, and I believe with everything in me, Leo had something to do with this."

"Yeah, I believe that's exactly what the plan was. The ignition had to be wired because I hit the button to unlock the car and start the engine." Blaze walked up, shaking his head. "The police won't be able to get the footage until they access the entire scene. The funny part about it all, they are trying to say the shit was caused by a faulty wire in the car. That's far from the truth because that muthafucka is new! Plus, the car went up soon as I hit the button. Had we been a little bit closer, all of us would've been fucked up."

"It's gon' take the police forever to get that footage. I'm on it and they won't be able to access shit fuckin' with me. We don't have time to wait and have them holding back lucrative information we're definitely going to need," Bryan said, pulling out his phone. Waiting for the call to connect, Bryan turned his back and the rest of the group watched out for the pigs.

"Aye, I need you to pull the cameras in the private garage at Midway Airport. Section 3C. Once you obtain the footage, wipe that shit clean. I need that info ASAP. Send J.R. to come through with the truck because I can't get to my whip. I'm dropping my location now." Bryan listened to whatever was being said on the other end, nodding his head as if the person could see him.

One of the officers walked over just as Bryan ended the call. Joe pulled him a few feet away to holla at him away from the others. Looking at Bryan through slit eyes, Joe folded his arms over his chest.

"For a nigga who's no longer in the street, you can still get shit done. How?" Joe asked.

"One doesn't have to physically be in the street to make shit shake. But since you asked, my money is still out there, I'm not. That's what I pay other muthafuckas to take care of. In the public eye, I own the Boys and Girls Club. In the background, I'm still the muthafuckin' boss. By the time our ride gets here, we will know everything that transpired in that garage. I'm seeing this shit through to the end."

"Bet. This shit is a tough one. I believe we are going to go through hell before we can even get to the point of being happy. I'm ready to dance with the devil or die trying."

"Ain't nobody dying on this end, nigga. Don't even speak that shit into existence."

Blaze waved them over as Joe dapped up Bryan. The officer let them know what hospital Kia was taken to and he wanted to hurry up and get his girl out of that muthafucka. Holy Cross wasn't a place anybody that knew better wanted to be. Bryan's phone chimed and J.R. was outside the main entrance waiting for them.

"Let's go, our ride outside," Bryan said, leading the way through the airport.

It took them about ten minutes to make their way to the pickup area, and J.R. was standing outside of an all-black SUV smoking a blunt. Everybody jumped in the back as

Bryan got comfortable in the front. Making his way to the driver's side, J.R. took one more pull before he put his blunt out on the sidewalk and got in. Pulling away from the curb, he made his way through traffic and put the pedal to the metal all the way to the hospital after being told where to go.

Nas' "Beef" was flowing through the speakers. Icy nodded her head while focusing on the lyrics. Nas was saying everything she was thinking. Why the fuck was she being dragged into some shit that she didn't ask to be in? Leo didn't really love her but didn't want to see her with anyone else either. Everything that had taken place was because of Leo's selfishness which turned into jealousy. Now, he wanted to kill everyone close to Icy while trying to kill her in the midst of it all. In her mind, Leo was a coward. He was throwing stones and hiding his hands while doing it. A real muthafucka would bring his ass out in the open and deal with this shit head on. Not Leo, he was having fun playing a cat and mouse game, but eventually the rat would come out to get the cheese.

The truck pulled up to the entrance of the hospital and Joe didn't hesitate to jump out. He went inside and straight to the counter, but Kia was walking out of the automatic doors from the back. One wouldn't be able to tell she'd been hit with a piece of metal because the murderous look in her eyes told a different story. Joe waved the nurse off and met Kia halfway across the room. Embracing her like he hadn't just seen her an hour prior, Kia moved out of his arms and took a step toward the door.

"Before you think you going out on the prowl, I'm here to let you know it's not happening. That's a serious cut you have on your head and rest is what you need."

"Yeah, aight. That won't happen. Somebody tried to end my sister's life and I just so happened to get caught in the crossfire. I'll rest when I'm dead. For now, I'm beating the streets until I find my beloved brother-in-law. This is the bitch I never wanted you to meet in action. Stay the fuck outta my way, Joe. There's no stopping me."

Kia didn't raise her voice and that alone bothered Joe more than the words she had spoken. All he could do was wait for the chips to fall because there was no way he could stop Kia from going on the tirade he was sure to come. When Joe stepped outside of the hospital Kia was climbing into the back of the SUV. Bryan stood outside of the vehicle with his phone in his hand.

"What's going on?"

"I just got the footage from the garage. Should we watch it now, or wait until we get to a bigger screen?"

Joe thought about it for a second before responding. "I think we should wait. Blaze for sure would want to be able to see everything unfold, and standing around watching on a phone is not the best way to do that. Plus, I think we need to be away from the women, so they won't know the outcome of what we find out. Especially that damn Kia."

"Is she alright?"

"Yeah, physically she will be good. I don't know the extent of her wound, but mentally, Kia is fucked up. Not in the usual way a female would be after something like this. It's like she has turned into a whole nigga, who can't wait to get back at the muthafucka behind this shit. With everything that has taken place, I don't blame her for wanting to get to the bottom of it all. It's going to be hard to convince her to let us men take care of the problem."

"We can figure all of this out at a later time. Let's get them to the hospital so Icy can check on her mama. That is the reason we came back from the trip early. All this other shit kind of just happened and put more on their plate to deal with."

Once they were back in the truck, Blaze gave the address to the hospital Staci was in and pulled Icy into him. She rested her head on his chest, thinking about how her life went from sugar to shit in a matter of months. Leo was trying to make Icy's life a living hell and he fucked up bringing her mother into the mix. Whatever qualm he had with her, Leo needed to keep that shit between them. The truck was quiet and Icy's thoughts were strictly on seeing Staci and making sure she was okay. Knowing her mother was laid up in the hospital behind some shit that was meant for Icy was really bothering her. She never meant for Staci to be caught up in the bullshit Leo had in store for her, but Icy knew his grimy ass was going to pay for hurting her mother. Out of all the years her father had been gone, nothing ever happened to Icy and Staci until the present day. The shit had Leo's name written all over it.

"What are you thinking about, baby?" Blaze whispered in Icy's ear.

"My mama."

"Staci is good," Kia said, reaching over the seat to pat her cousin's shoulder. "Soon as we see her, I'm going to the house to change. Then I'm tuckin' my Glock and hitting the block because these niggas gon' see me."

"Kia, what did we just talk about?" Joe asked, turning around in his seat.

"And what the fuck did I say in return, muthafucka? I'm not trying to hear none of that shit! These niggas violated and it's time to eliminate the virus off the streets of Chicago!" Kia was fuming. "Staci didn't have shit to do with what's going on and Leo's bitch ass tried to kill her! Nah, not on my watch."

Joe shook his head and turned back around. There was no use trying to talk Kia down. He was done with it. If she wanted to go out and play "Captain Shoot A Nigga," he wasn't going to stop her. Kia wasn't his woman *yet,* and Joe knew she had been through a lot in the past few weeks, but he was going to show her better than he could tell her. Kia may have run the relationship with every nigga she fucked with, but that shit wasn't happening with Joe.

"Kia, just leave it alone. We're not going to look for anybody because we don't know where to even start searching. Leo knows where we are. We don't have a clue where he may be or who he has on his team. We need a strategy to get to him because he's two steps ahead of us."

"I agree with Icy. Leo may be two steps ahead but he gon' get blown ten steps back," Blaze replied. "The more time you spend trying to find his ass is only going to frustrate you more when he's not sighted. Go back to your daily routines and watch your surroundings, that's all any of you can do. That alone will bring his ass out of hiding."

Kia huffed as she sat back with her arms crossed over her chest. She wasn't going to be a sitting duck, waiting to be shot dead by anybody. Kia opted to shut up while formulating a plan in her head. She knew more about how Leo and his crew ran than Icy did, thanks to Stack. There was no way she was going to sit back and let shit ride out the way Blaze and Joe wanted. Like she said, she was going to find them niggas and the shit wasn't going to be pretty.

J.R. pulled into the parking lot of the hospital and Icy started biting her bottom lip nervously. Blaze noticed the change in her body language and squeezed her thigh. She looked over at him with tears in her eyes.

"She's okay, baby. Go in and see your mother. I'll be right here waiting for you." Blaze kissed Icy's lips, then wiped the tears that fell from her eyes with his thumbs. "Take your time. There's no rush."

Icy nodded her head as she wiped her face with her hands. Exiting the truck, Kia and Julz followed behind quietly. Making their way to the counter to get Staci's room number, the nurse behind the desk was all smiles.

"How may I help you?" she asked.

"We're here to see Staci Winters."

The nurse pecked away on the keyboard and looked up after a few seconds. "Yes, she is in room 319, but only one of you can go up. There are only two visitors at a time," she explained while printing out a pass.

"Well, there's three of us and we're all going up," Kia snarled. "There are no rules when it comes to this family, so print out three passes so we can go up."

"I can't allow all of you to go up at once——"

"Did I ask you what you would allow? I *said* we're all going up. It's either you print the passes or get yo' ass whooped in this muthafuckin' lobby, bitch. You are at the point of catching this fade you ain't got shit to do with, so I'd advise you to just bend the rules today!"

"Kia——"

"No, no, it's okay. I know how it is when the family wants to see about a loved one. There won't be a problem allowing all of you up." The nurse's face turned beet red as she rushed to print out the other two passes. When she handed them across the counter, Kia snatched them up and headed across the lobby. Doubling back, she leaned over the counter.

"Which way do we go?" The nurse pointed to the left and Kia eased up out of her face with a frown.

"I'm so sorry," Icy said before walking off toward the elevators.

Kia was speed walking while Icy and Julz tried to keep up. When they got to the elevator, Kia was pressing the button as if the doors would open automatically for her. Icy took the opportunity to address her attitude while they waited.

"Kia, you have to calm down. That woman isn't the one that pissed you off."

"Icy, you got one more time to apologize on my behalf and we gon' have a muthafuckin' problem! See, the shit that's going on is partially yo' fault!"

"Whoa, let me stop you right there, cuz. I didn't make this shit happen and you won't blame me for anything Leo did on his own. I would never knowingly put my family in harm's way so you can stop spilling that false narrative. I'm not Joe, you won't talk to me any type of way because you already know we can tear this bitch up if that's what you want to do. You may scare a lot of people but, bitch, I'm not one of 'em."

Julz stepped between the two of them, shaking her head. "Nah, we not about to do this shit. Ain't nobody to blame except Leo. Kia, you wrong."

The elevator doors opened, and Kia stalked inside, pressing the button for the third floor. When they were all on and the doors closed, Julz finished what she was saying. "We all know you're pissed off and guess what, you not the only one. Blaming Icy for something that nigga did is out of pocket. Check yo' muthafuckin' self because the world didn't do this, Leo did!"

Kia knew what Julz and Icy was true, but her nostrils still flamed at how the two of them were coming at her. She didn't even consider the way she snapped at them as being a problem. Instead of a rebuttal, Kia gave them silence and exited soon as the elevator doors opened. Being upset caused her to walk right past Staci's room and Icy had to call her back without being too loud. When Icy knocked on the door and entered, her mother was lying in bed sleeping. Fanny looked up from her Kindle and smiled when she saw the women and jumped to her feet.

"How's she doing?" Icy asked after the tight embrace Fanny gave her.

"She's doing okay after being administered some morphine. Staci's recovery is going to be extensive. The doctor said she was very lucky to be alive. They had to stop the internal bleeding that occurred when the bone nicked her intestines. Her femur bone was broken in three places. Other than that, pins and plates were inserted to help the bone heal. Staci will have to go through rehabilitation and physical therapy to learn how to use that leg again."

Icy listened to Fanny but her eyes were on Staci. She walked slowly to the bed and dragged a chair along with her and sat down. Taking hold of her mother's hand, Icy ran her fingers along the back of her hands, to let her mother know she was there. Seeing the woman she grew up idolizing lying helplessly in the hospital bed weakened Icy. Before she knew it, the sobs Icy was trying to hold in escaped out of her mouth. Staci opened her eyes and licked her dry lips.

"We both can't be weak at this time, Icy. Clean your face because I'm going to walk out of this damn hospital. It may not be tomorrow, next week, or next month, but I will be walking out of this muthafucka."

Staci closed her eyes as she took deep breaths to get through the small amount of pain she was enduring. She looked at Kia noticing the bandage on her head. Staci tried to move but a sharp pain shot up her leg. Wincing, Icy stood to call for the nurse.

"Nah, I'm okay. I don't need them in here right now," Staci said, without taking her eyes off Kia. "What happened to your head?"

Everybody turned to look in Kia's direction because they were thinking the same thing, nobody wanted Staci to know what they had been through. The silence told the story nobody wanted to tell and that only pissed Staci off. Slamming her fist on the bed, Staci asked the question again.

"What the fuck happened to your head, Kia?"

"I had a minor fall getting off the plane," Kia lied effortlessly. "I'm alright. I just needed a couple stitches, but that's nothing compared to you being in a hospital bed."

"Look," Staci said clearing her throat. "I need y'all to be careful out there. What happened to me wasn't an accident. That shit had my name written all over it. When I say be careful, that doesn't mean go out looking for trouble, *Kia.* Prepare yourselves for what's going to find you. Leo isn't picking and choosing his prey. He's out to get all of us. His karma is going to hit him at the right time. Don't force it."

"Staci, I'm not sitting back waiting for anybody to come for me. I'm going out to find Leo and put a stop to this shit," Kia snapped.

"No, the fuck you not! You're going to take your ass back to work and act as if this shit isn't bothering you. That's bait in itself. You have to make Leo think shit is sweet. Stay strapped and blow his muthafuckin' head off if need be. But don't lose yourself in all of this. A nigga like Leo can smell fear a mile away. Don't give him the satisfaction."

Icy changed the subject before Kia could get started because she didn't want her and Staci to go back and forth in her condition. They stayed another thirty minutes before Staci told them to go home and rest. Icy didn't want to leave but she knew she wasn't going to win that argument with her mother. After giving her mother a kiss and a long hug, Icy led the way out of the room. She stopped at the nurse's station and put a lock code on Staci's chart. She wasn't taking any chances for Leo to come and do bodily harm to her mother.

Outside, the men were looking at the footage on Bryan's phone. They watched as a woman in a dark wig and sunglasses walked slowly towards Icy's car as she glanced around the parking lot. Pointing what appeared to be a key fob, she opened the door and kneeled inside for a few minutes. After taking something from her oversized bag, the woman continued to fiddle under the dash until she had completed the tasks she set out to do. Closing the door and hitting the fob, she walked away with a somber expression on her face.

"Go back and zoom in on her face," Blaze said aggressively. Bryan did as he was told, and everyone concentrated on the woman's features.

"You know that bitch, Blaze?" Joe asked.

"I don't know her personally, but that's the detective who locked Icy up for the bogus ass murder she was slapped with. I can't believe she hates Icy so much to try and kill her.

Everybody assumes Leo is dead, so what's her reason for taking Icy out? This shit doesn't make sense."

"It makes a lot of sense," Bryan cut in. "There is only one explanation as to why she placed that bomb on the car. Leo paid her ass a visit."

"He strong armed that hoe! Leo probably made her do it to put Icy's blood on her hands and not draw attention to himself."

"Exactly, Joe. That nigga is dragging anybody he can into this shit to throw Icy off. We on his ass though. I'm glad I got ahold of this before the police. We need to find this detective bitch and make her tell us Leo's plan. It's the only way we're going to get one up on him."

"And once we talk to her, we're gonna have to put her ass to sleep. She played a part in trying to take my lifeline away from me," Blaze said as he sat back and opened the door and got out.

Thinking about how close he was to losing Icy only made him madder than he already was. Detective Scott was going to make national news after he shot her ass in the back of her head. In his mind, Blaze already had a plan of making her death look like an execution-style killing. As he was about to spark the blunt in his hand, Icy emerged from the building. Rounding the back of the vehicle, Blaze stood waiting for his woman with opened arms and Icy fell right into them. No words needed to be spoken because he had given her just what she needed.

Chapter 2

Cynthia was on pins and needles since she was forced to put the explosive device on Icy's car. Every time she attempted to leave her home, there was someone outside the door with a gun pointed in her face. Cynthia felt like a prisoner in her own home and regretted every day she allowed the mistreatment of an arrestee as an officer.

It wasn't hard to find the expensive ass Porsche Leo sent to her phone. The difficulty came when Cynthia had to persuade the attendant that she was a detective on duty. Since she was stripped of her badge and gun, she had to dig in the crate to find her old badge and use one of her personal weapons to get the job done. Cynthia hoped the disguise she used to conceal herself worked in her favor, because she couldn't afford to get locked up for the treacherous act she was forced into. The alias she used to sign the log was one she had come up with while working undercover. The good thing about it, she never actually used the name in her line of work.

Cynthia sat on the couch watching the morning news in horror as the reporter talked about the investigation the police were conducting on the explosion. They were praying the incident wasn't another attack on the United States and wanted to investigate it thoroughly. Cynthia became paranoid once the reporter revealed there weren't any casualties. Jumping to her feet, she ran to the back door and opened it just enough to see if there was anyone lurking. Leo made sure the guards were on point, but that day, somebody was going to lose their life for sleeping on the job.

Not worrying about a coat, she made a beeline for the gate leading to the alley. Cynthia had one chance to get away and she was going for it. Making her way to the gate, she walked briskly through the cold air. Cynthia fumbled with the latch and cursed with every tug because it was frozen.

"Fuck! Not now. Come on. I need you to let me out of this muthafucka," she whined on the verge of tears as she looked over her shoulder to make sure she was still alone.

God must've heard her cries because the latch started to move, and it finally gave way after much pulling and tugging. Cynthia swung the gate open with her mind focused on running for her life. Instead, she was stopped in her tracks and frozen in place like a deer caught in headlights when someone she didn't expect blocked her escape.

"Damn, baby, where you trying to run off to?" Leo asked with an evil grin. "You had one muthafuckin' job and you couldn't do that shit right. You the law, Cynthia, y'all get away with everything. Get yo' stupid ass back in the house."

When Cynthia didn't move, Leo pulled his gun from his back and waved it in the direction of her house. That alone put a spark in her movements. She ran toward the house faster than Sonic the Hedgehog, hoping Leo didn't shoot her in the back. He was right on her ass. She tried to close the door before he could come in, but he forced it open, and it smacked her in the face.

"Bitch, stop playing with ya life. There's no way Icy or anybody with her should still be breathing. You were on the bomb squad before you hit the streets, for Christ sakes. That tells me you spared her muthafuckin' ass on purpose!"

'I did exactly what I was told!" Cynthia screamed. "You could've taken care of the shit yourself, since you're alive and well."

Leo hit her upside the head with the butt of his Glock and she fell into the wall. Cynthia's vision blurred as she tried to stand up on her feet. Snatching Cynthia by her hair, Leo assisted her in standing upright.

"Who the fuck you call yo'self hollerin' at? Where's all that hoorah shit you used in the streets? Try that bullshit on me!" he growled, punching her in the face. "A dead nigga punch hard as hell, huh?" he laughed. Here's your opportunity to get the revenge you were talking in the investigation room. Yeah, I heard about all that shit. Speak yo' mind or is it the dick that got yo' musty ass salty as fuck?"

Cynthia hated the fact of Leo having one up on her. The way he was handling her abolished the initial shock of seeing him in the flesh. Knowing the day would be her last on earth, Cynthia mustered up the nerve to fight back. Grabbing the antique vase her late grandma had given her by the handle, she swung with all her might, hitting Leo in the arm which held the gun. Groaning in pain, Leo immediately released the grip he had on her hair. Using the defensive training she'd learned in the academy, Cynthia commenced to beating the fuck out of him.

"You should've killed me the moment you laid eyes on me, pussy ass nigga."

Hitting Leo anywhere the vase landed while screaming insults and obscenities, Cynthia never heard the front door open then close. Watching the scene taking place before her only made Julian cackle a little bit but pissed her off in the next second. Shaking her head, Julian aimed her silenced weapon and sent a single shot to the back of Cynthia's head. Her body fell sideways and hit the table with a thud, knocking glass onto the floor. Julian walked further into the house with her eyes trained on Leo. He was balled up in a fetal position from the beating Cynthia had put on his punk ass.

"How the fuck you allow this bitch to beat yo' ass?" Julian laughed. "Being dead weakened you in the worst way. Get the fuck up!"

"Fuck you, Julian!" Leo hissed as he snatched his gun from under the table. "Who told you to shoot her? I wanted some pussy."

Aiming her gun at him, Julian wanted to splatter Leo's brains against the wall for disrespecting her. It was bad enough he had been fuckin' on Icy for years while hiding her in the cut. She'd be damned if he outright expressed what he'd planned to do to Cynthia's pickle-head ass.

"Come on so we can get out of here," Julian said, turning the thermostat up far as it would go. By the time anybody noticed Cynthia hadn't been heard from, her body would be decomposed and unrecognizable.

"I'll meet you at the house. I have something to take care of," Leo said, leaving out the way he had entered.

Julian wasn't going to let him dismiss her like she was some type of random bitch. Walking swiftly to the door she snatched it open and yelled, "Don't get yo' ass beat again, bitch ass nigga. I won't be there to save yo' ass next time."

Leo stuck his middle finger up at her and disappeared through the gate.

***

Leo had the right mind to fuck Julian up soon as he got back to the crib. He was pissed because Cynthia didn't kill Icy and yeah, he had put his hands on her, but he wanted to fuck her in every hole in her body. Hell, even her muthafuckin' ears. One thing he remembered was the bitch had some pussy that would make a nigga slap their mama if he couldn't get it when he wanted. Julian had to shoot her before he could apologize his way into Cynthia's bed. The thought of feeling her tunnel had him bricking up as he drove to his destination.

Taking a blunt from the armrest, Leo thought about all the shit that transpired in just a few months. Leo knew he wouldn't have a care in the world, knowing Icy was in heaven getting fitted for angel wings. That shit was short lived because her ass was still alive. Handling situations on his own was his main objective from that point on because muthafuckas couldn't do shit right.

"How hard is it to kill a muthafucka nowadays?" he shouted angrily, taking a pull on his blunt.

Leo turned onto 63rd Street and made his way to King Drive. He was going to Parkway Gardens, better known as O Block, to holla at Black. Leo had sent his ass on a mission to eliminate Zan and he fucked the shit up by missing. Everybody thought that shit stemmed from Leo killing Rico. Nope, Leo paid to have his brother killed, which led to Demon eating dirt. Leo's death had Black believing he got away with twenty stacks for something he didn't see through. Now, Leo wasn't hiding anymore, Black had to see him.

He parked across the street from the complex because Leo knew better than to park in the lot. The lil niggas over there didn't take lightly to anyone coming on their turf on the time Leo was on with Black. Tucking his Glock in the waist of his pants, he got out of his whip. Looking both ways, Leo made a dash across the busy street. As he got closer to the entrance, there were a group of niggas bundled up, fighting the cold. It didn't matter the weather, there was always a pack of wolves standing around doing nothing. When Leo approached, all eyes were on him.

"I know that ain't who I think it is!" a youngin' named Top exclaimed.

Leo laughed but kept his eyes trained on the whole picture before him. Poppin' back on the scene like Hans did in the Fast and Furious franchise had Leo feeling like a legend. Taking his hood fully off his head, Leo stood tall as he revealed himself.

"It is Leo! Man, they said you was gone!" a teen named Crip yelled, dappin' Leo up. "Shit been crazy out here. It's dry as fuck and we need work."

"I'm working on it. That's why I'm here, to holla at Black. Is he around?" Leo asked as the lie rolled off his tongue.

"That's what the fuck I'm talking 'bout! Black in the crib wit a lil shorty. You want me to buzz him?"

"Nah, I'm gon' surprise that nigga. Don't worry, y'all about to eat again. Be easy."

"I don't trust that nigga," Boots said he watched Leo walk away.

Leo strolled toward the building Black lived in and pulled the entry door open. The locks were broken, and the intercom system didn't even exist. Some of the mailboxes were secured and the hall reeked of urine. Leo took the steps two at a time and made sure he didn't touch the railing in the process. When he got to the second floor, Leo went to the right of the hall and stopped in front of Black's apartment door. Knocking hard, he waited patiently for someone to answer. It took longer than anticipated, so Leo used his fist, banging louder.

"Who the fuck is it?" Black's voice bellowed from the other side. "I told you niggas to hit my line, damn!"

Without confirming who was at his shit, Black unlocked the door swinging it open. One would've thought the Grim Reaper himself came to snatch his soul the way he jumped back. Leo entered smoothly, closing the door behind him. Black stood still, dressed in a pair of boxers and socks.

"Put some clothes on and let's roll," Leo commanded. When Black didn't move, Leo upped that thang on his ass to get his feet moving. "This ain't the time for procrastination, muthafucka. And don't try no slick shit."

Back pedaling toward the bedroom, Black turned slowly to close the door behind him. Entering, he tried to separate himself from Leo because his presence was intimidating. Not knowing Leo was on his ass, the door bounced back, almost hitting Black in the face. With his hand palming his eye, he looked down and saw Leo's foot was the reason the door didn't shut. His shoulders slumped in defeat knowing he wouldn't be able to do anything privately. Leo wanted to monitor Black's every move.

"All you got to do is get dressed. Won't be none of that extra shit. Do I look stupid to you, nigga?"

The female sat up in the bed with the sheet pulled over her chest. Confusion was written over her face as her orbs bounced in her head from Black to Leo. Licking his lips, Leo took in Shawty's beauty, and she fucked up making eye contact with him.

"What up, ma?"

"I wish you would," Black hissed, pulling a hoodie over his head.

"Stop wasting time. I got other shit to do while you stalling," Leo snapped, never taking his sights off the woman in the bed. "Lil mama, ya man will be back in about an hour. Don't move out of this apartment."

Winking at her, Leo knew Black wouldn't be returning, but she didn't need to know that. Her sexy ass was smitten and fought hard not to show it. Leo cupped his dick so she could see the python he was working with.

"Bitch, I will split yo' muthafuckin' wig!" Black spazzed. "We gon' talk about this shit when I get back! Let's go, nigga."

Leo didn't move on Black's command. Instead, he licked his lips and winked at the woman again, before he walked out of the bedroom. Black was fuming but didn't say anything else. His mind didn't register why Leo wanted him to leave his home. He just wanted to get Leo away from his girl fast as he could, because he knew how smooth the nigga could be with the ladies. Leo knew exactly what he was doing to force Black out of the apartment voluntarily and the shit worked like a charm. The two men made their way out of the building without saying anything until they got to Leo's whip.

"Where the hell we going?" Black asked the moment Leo sat in the driver's seat.

"You taking a ride with me. The streets are dry and I'm gon' make sure my shit get back out there. Y'all out here starving, per the niggas I talked to before coming up to your crib. You need me."

Leo pulled out into traffic and turned into the parking lot of Family Dollar to turn around. Once he was clear to turn, he made a left onto King Drive and cruised down the street. The inside of the car was quiet as Leo drove. Black thought about what Leo said when they got in the car and decided to pick the conversation back up.

"Word on the street is yo' plug was killed. How do you still have dope for me?"

Leo looked over at Black before answering. "Yeah, he was," he sighed, putting his attention back on the road. "I got keys hand over fist stored away though. Enough to hold me over until I can find another connect."

Black stared at the side of Leo's face to see if he could detect any signs of him lying. He couldn't tell, but that didn't stop him from speaking his mind. Black needed to know where Leo's head really was at that moment. One thing he didn't expect was Leo coming back from the dead and Black knew he was going to ask for his money back. So, before Leo could bring it to him, Black decided to clear the air himself.

"Look, I know I missed my target. Demon——"

"Ain't here to confirm what went down that day. Save that shit because I'm on to more important things like, getting this money."

Leo was laughing on the inside at the way Black attempted to throw a dead man under the bus. The shit didn't matter one way or another, because Black was the muthafucka that took the payment, eager to kill. Now, he was nervous trying to figure out what was about to happen to him. Leo loved the smell of fear and Black was saturated in the scent.

"Did you do yo' thang with the twenty stacks though?"

Black's body went rigid at the mention of the money as he contemplated how he was going to respond. Leo asking about the money caused his stomach to clench and he suddenly had the urge to shit. Running his hand down his face, Black let out a nervous cough, then cleared his throat before answering.

"I um, *cough*, *cough*, I still have all except five grand of it. It ain't nothing for me to give it back." Black threw that last part in there for good measures. There was no way he was coming off twenty G's.

Pulling up to the storage facility on 83rd and South Chicago, Leo threw his car in park outside of his unit without acknowledging what Black said and exited his vehicle. Fumbling through his keys, Leo unlocked and removed the padlock off the unit which was located in the far back of the facility. Black didn't move from the passenger seat as he watched Leo maneuver about in the frigid cold. He figured Leo would go inside and bring the packages to the car.

"What you sitting there like a bump on a log for? Get the fuck out, nigga! I know you don't think I'm luggin' this shit by myself."

In spite of the cold weather, Black was sweating bullets. Slowly exiting the car, he followed Leo into the unit. There were at least five wooden crates loaded with kilos of coke. Black got excited because he was about to eat in the streets again. Leo's interrogation was a thought of the past and money was his focal point. That was the wrong move on his part because Leo's mind was still on the fact of Black not completing the hit and pocketing the money. As he closed the door to escape the cold Chicago air. Leo watched as Black rubbed his hands together with his eyes fixated on the pure white sitting in front of him. Laughing lowly, Leo walked past him and retrieved a heavy tarp from the top of one of the crates and placed it on the ground.

"Wh-what's that for?" Black stammered once he realized what Leo was doing.

"I have to kneel on this cold ass concrete, nigga. Why you all nervous and shit?"

"Leo, I've been in the game a long time. I can feel the animosity you have for me about the hit I didn't complete. Deep down I believe I'm going to die behind that shit."

Leo laughed in Black's face because he was absolutely correct. The unit was going to be the last place he visited before taking his last breath. But not before he told Leo where the rest of his money was. Instead of verbally responding, Leo placed the tarp on the ground in front of the crate he planned to open and grabbed a crowbar from the shelf on the wall.

"Come lift this lid once I pry it off," Leo directed. Black walked slowly across the small space from the door as if he was approaching the electric chair. "Hurry the fuck up! It's colder than a muthafucka in this bitch!"

Waiting for Leo to pry the crate open, Black couldn't control the shakes in his hands. Leo inserted the crowbar slowly and without looking in Black's direction, he worked on popping the crate open when he decided to find out what needed to be known.

"So, where's the rest of my money?"

"I thought you said we was cool on that, Leo," Black huffed.

"At the time I was. Now, I want my shit back. You didn't do what you were supposed to do but expect to reap the benefits. Nigga, please! Where's my shit and you bet not lie!" Leo snarled as he rose to his feet.

"When you drop me off, I'll give you it to you," Black said, backing away from Leo.

"Nah, I want you to tell me where the fuck it's at! I didn't say nothing about you giving me shit!"

Black's eyes shifted as he tried to find a way out of the unit. He would have to turn his back in order to get to the door and he wasn't trying to risk being shot in the process.

Dropping his chin to his chest, Black mumbled his response lowly.

"Speak up, muthafucka!" Leo bellowed.

"It's in a safe hidden in the back of my bedroom closet."

"What's the code?"

"Come on, man. I told you I was going to give it to you. Don't do me like this, Leo."

"What's the muthafuckin' code, Black? I want you to be straight up because I will split ya mama shit and choke the fuck outta ya daughter. In other words, my money ain't something you want to play with. I don't have an ounce of care in my body since I was killed," Leo smirked.

"Two-two-seven-four."

Soon as Black closed his mouth, Leo swung the crowbar, hitting him with the hook end of the tool. Black's body was paralyzed for a few seconds before Leo pulled so he would land on the tarp. Leo snatched the object from Black's forehead and blood oozed out of the wound. He gave the corpse a swift kick in the ass.

"Punk muthafucka! Can't stand niggas like you!"

Leo rolled Black's body in the tarp as he shouted out expletives. After tying the twine to secure the package, Leo opened the door and peered out. The coast was clear, giving him the opportunity to jump in his whip to make his move. Backing the rear of his car closer to the entrance, Leo got out quickly while mentally preparing himself to throw Black's body in the trunk. He lifted the dead weight with a bit of a struggle but held on with all of his might. Leo tossed the cargo into the trunk and slammed it shut just in time. Luck was on his side because a security truck came around the corner at that precise moment. Leo secured his unit and walked to the driver's door of his vehicle.

"Aye, you good?" the security guard asked. "Oh shit! What's up, Leo? I heard you got shot, my nigga."

Leo was confused because he didn't know the fat muthafucka who acted as if they were homies or some shit.

"Nah, you got the wrong one. I'm James, his twin brother. Leo did in fact lose his life New Year's Day after his wedding. Are you a friend of his?"

Leo tried his best to articulate his words in a way people weren't used to. The guard looked puzzled as hell and didn't know what to believe. Anyone would know Leo when they saw him and there was no way he was wrong. Besides, the only sibling anyone knew about was Zan. A twin was never spoken of.

"No, we weren't friends, but I paid attention to him and y'all other brother. In fact, we were about to clean out that unit, because since Leo's death, no one has been around to check on the unit."

Tilting his head to the side, it was Leo's turn to be perplexed. "Why would y'all clean out anything? The storage fee is paid. Isn't the next step contacting the next of kin?"

"I…we…ummm."

The guard couldn't get his lie together fast enough. He and his homies knew Leo more than likely had drugs and possibly more in the unit. They were looking forward to the come up. The guard was cursing himself out for delaying the process from the night before.

"Yeah, nigga. I advise you to quit because it's lights out for yo' ass. I'm not moving shit my brother has in this muthafucka and everything better still be how he left it whenever I return." The truck inched forward, causing Leo to pull his Glock from behind his back. "Where the fuck you trying to go? I'm not finished with yo' scary ass," Leo snapped. "Give me yo' muthafuckin' ID, nigga!"

"Look, man, I don't want no trouble."

"Too late. You knee deep in this shit now. And since you had plans to rob a muthafucka, yo' ass work for me now."

Leo snatched the door to the truck open and yanked the guard out by his coat. Slamming him against the frame, Leo patted him down until he found his wallet. He found the identification card and read the information aloud.

"Mark Pitts, 7336 S. St. Lawrence Avenue, second floor. Don't make plans to disappear because I know exactly where you lay your head. Anytime I come through, you better be there. What's your fuckin' number, nigga?"

"It's (312)-555-0001."

Mark ran his number off quick as hell then dry heaved because he was suddenly sick to his stomach. He was mentally beating himself up and wished he would've kept his mouth closed. Now he was into some shit he wasn't sure how to get out of. Leo was a ruthless nigga, and his brother Zan didn't shortstop either. Mark could only imagine the replica of Leo was a stone-cold killer too.

"One missed call and I will pull up and take out you and everybody else in your family. Your treacherous way of thinking just put you on my marked for death list. Do as I say, and you may get scratched off." Slapping him on the cheek three times, Leo stepped back.

"Keep ya head up, gangsta. All you have to do is follow my lead and you will be able to live life however you wish. Until then, yo' ass is on house arrest for the time being. I'll be in touch."

Leo jumped in the driver's seat of his whip and pulled off. Mark, on the other hand, stood in place because he had shit his pants out of fear. His phone started ringing and he leaned into the truck to answer it.

"H-hello?"

"Get the shiver out ya voice, Markie Mar. No one can help you out of this. So, it would be best to keep this between us. You made a deal with the devil, remember that. It's hot in hell." Leo laughed evilly before ending the call.

"Muthafuckas gon' stop playing on my top."

Leo was breathing heavily as he hit the skyway to dispose Black's body. He knew for sure he didn't want CPD to find his ass. By the time Black was found, it would be springtime. Leo was going to make sure of it.

Chapter 3

J.R. was the designated chauffeur and Blaze appreciated that shit. Since they were already southbound, he dropped Kia off at Staci's first. She got out of the truck without saying anything to anyone. Joe shook his head and got out before she could step foot on the porch. He didn't understand why she had an attitude, but he was destined to find out. Catching up to Kia in a few strides, Joe grasped her arm and turned her toward him.

"Aye, what the hell is your problem?"

"Go home, Joe. I'm not in the mood for this shit. There are major things that need my attention right now. Icy and Staci may want to sweep what Leo has done under the rug, not me. I'm not about to sit back and wait for this nigga to plan a sneak attack to take me out."

"Kia, leave that shit alone for now. Y'all need to concentrate on making sure Staci gets better and out of the hospital. Leave the Leo shit to the guys. We will definitely take care of it."

Joe tried to hug her, and Kia pushed away from him then turned to walk up the steps and into the house. Kia had a hard shield that protected the exterior of her body, but her heart was soft as cotton. She'd never had a man who would outright tell her to sit the fuck down somewhere and play the role of being their woman, not the homie. Joe wasn't about to chase a female that wasn't up for the chase, so he left it alone and allowed Kia to have her way. Leaving Kia standing on the sidewalk, Joe turned and headed back to the awaiting vehicle.

"My bad, y'all. Let's go," Joe said, getting back into the truck. He rested his head on the headrest and closed his eyes as J.R. pulled away from Staci's home.

"Is she cool?"

"Blaze, I don't even know. Kia is going to do what Kia wants to do. We have to find this nigga before she goes out looking for him and gets herself killed."

Icy bit her bottom lip as she listened to Joe's words and the thought of her best friend losing her life scared her to the core. Fishing her phone out of her purse, Icy called Kia, but she didn't answer. She tried again, getting the same results. Kia was in her feelings and Icy didn't like the way she was shutting her out. Being in contact with one another was very important for them for the time being. Without having Icy by her side, Kia was bound to get in trouble some way or another.

J.R. took directions from Bryan and hit the expressway to the city. Blaze made a mental note to compensate him for taking time out of his day to assist them. As they neared Julz's apartment, Blaze's phone rang loudly. He leaned to the side to retrieve it from his pocket and let out a long sigh as he looked at the screen before declining the call.

"Is everything alright?" Icy whispered.

"Amancia keeps calling my phone and I don't know why because I've told her there is nothing happening between us. I believe she's trying to upset you in hopes of running you off. It's fucked up how she's committed to causing drama from another damn country."

"You don't have to worry about Amanda, or whatever her name is, irritating me. I already have what she wants. That's the reason her mad ass probably in Kingston losing her edges. Answer the bitch. What can she do besides beg and cry for your attention? It's on you to entertain that madness or not."

Anger flickered in her eyes, even though she spoke calmly about the situation. Blaze knew Icy was a little upset about the ordeal. His dick got hard from the way Icy's lips pursed. If they were in the truck alone, he would've pulled over and fucked the shit out of her. The text alert brought him out of his thoughts and back to his phone. Amancia went from calling to texting. Blaze unlocked the device, and another came through in a matter of seconds.

Amancia: Avoiding my calls isn't something you want to do, Akoni. Call me back.

Amancia: I wonder if the woman you're with knows you were caressing my silky walls with that long dick of yours. I'll make sure she knows what the deal is because you won't be pursuing anything with someone new. Akoni, you left me once, I'm not sitting back so the shit can happen again. We're connected more than you know.

Blaze ignored the messages and put his phone away. Amancia was on some other shit. He didn't know what she was trying to accomplish, but the hidden message at the end of her last message didn't go unnoticed. One thing for sure and two for certain, he wasn't about to feed into her pettiness. The last conversation they'd had come to mind and Blaze shook it off. Amancia wasn't dumb enough to show up with

her bullshit. He wasn't the same boy she was used to fucking around with back in the day. He could get ruthless if he had to, and she would soon find out how he got down.

Glancing over at Icy, Blaze smiled. He couldn't wait to love on her the way she deserved. The quick trip was a start, but ended abruptly, due to her grimy ex. At every turn, Leo found a way to wipe the happiness from Icy's soul. His days were limited, and Leo had better get right with God because his ass was going to die by the hands of the Jamaican king.

"Would you stop eye fucking me and allow Julz to get out please?" Icy laughed.

Blaze didn't realize the truck stopped. He was so invested in his thoughts that he blocked out everything surrounding him. Even though Icy laughed, it didn't reach her eyes and Blaze didn't like that. He was determined to bring her smile back and make sure it never faltered again. Leo didn't love Icy properly. Blaze had plans to introduce Icy to a new type of love and he could see her being his wife and bearing his children.

"My bad, baby."

Blaze opened the door and got out, then leaned in, pulling the lever to fold the seat. Julz stepped out of the truck with Blaze's assistance. She pulled her coat closed as the cold air attacked her from every angle.

"Thank you so much for inviting me to travel with you and Icy. I really enjoyed myself and it was good to get away from the madness for a few days."

"It was nothing. I'm glad you had fun. Do me a solid," Blaze said in a soft tone. "Be careful out here. Leo is somewhere watching every move y'all are about to make. He's not going to show his face anytime soon, but it's imperative for you to be ready, just in case. Take my number and don't hesitate to call anytime you may need me." Blaze recited his number soon as Julz had her phone in hand.

"I have you locked in."

"Good. Another thing," Blaze smirked. "Give Bryan another chance. That nigga doesn't have any control of Nita's actions."

"We'll see about that," Julz said, blowing off what Blaze said, causing him to laugh at her facial expression. Bryan walked around the back of the truck with Julz's luggage at that moment and that was Blaze's cue to give them a bit of privacy. Bryan stared at Julz without saying anything.

"Do you have something to say, or are you going to just admire me like a creep?"

Bryan smiled. "I just want to say thanks for accepting my apology and hearing me out. Julz, I want this…I want us to work out."

"One day at a time, Bryan. I'll talk to you later. I'm tired and just want to sleep."

Bryan watched as Julz pulled her luggage up the walkway. When she disappeared through the glass door, he got back into the truck. Bryan had never had a woman that was able to tug at his heartstrings in the manner in which Julz had. The intimacy they shared in Aruba was only a fraction of the feelings he felt for her. Bryan was attracted to her drive, her independence and her hustle. Julz was the type of woman a man could build with. Not a woman who constantly held her hand out for a nigga to pave the way for her. Bryan wasn't going to let Nita's jealousy stop him from pursuing the love he knew he endured with Julz. She was going to be his wife and Bryan was ready to fight for her.

***

Icy and Blaze finally made their way into his suite. Icy went into the bedroom while Blaze got comfortable on the sofa. The events of the day had him weary and all he wanted to do was smoke while relaxing. Taking a pack of woods out of the coffee table drawer, along with his rolling tray and a bag of weed, Blaze proceeded to break down what he called his stress reliever quietly.

The trip to Aruba brought a smile to his face as he licked the wood to seal it closed. Images of Icy's creamy folds instantly brought the taste of her love juice to his senses. Blaze glanced in the direction of the bedroom and adjusted his member in his pants.

"Down, boy. Now is not the time. We will see what happens later tonight. We need to relax right now and get some sleep," Blaze spoke lowly.

"What will you see later?" Icy asked, walking in on the tail end of Blaze's conversation with himself.

"Oh, nothing."

"Blaze, who were you talking to?"

He smirked as he searched for a lighter. Once he located one, Blaze sat back against the cushions. The smile on his face got bigger as he licked his lips while undressing Icy with his eyes. Lighting the tip of the wood, Blaze inhaled until a cherry formed on the end then he exhaled, blowing smoke through his nose before responding.

"I was talking to my *dick*. You wanna holla at him?"

Icy's cheeks turned beet red, and her yoni started beating at a rapid pace. She crossed her feet as the sensation intensified in the crotch of the boy shorts she wore. Shaking her head no, Icy backed away from Blaze's gaze.

"C'mere with yo' sexy ass." Blaze took a hit of the blunt as he watched her attempt to retreat back to the bedroom. "Do you think I'm kidding, Icy? Come here."

Icy saw the seriousness in his globes even though they were getting lower by the minute. The cannabis he had consumed was taking effect. She didn't want to start any friction with him, but on the other hand she was too tired to give in to his sexual innuendoes. When Icy didn't move, Blaze put his blunt out and stood to his feet. Icy shifted but his gaze paralyzed her movements, causing her stomach to flutter.

He stood in front of her and grabbed the front of her shorts. Making sure not to break eye contact, Blaze used his thumb to massage her clit. Icy moaned lowly because she knew not to move an inch. Blaze leaned into her body and whispered in her ear.

"Wen yuh start defying me, Icy?" He sped up the movement of his thumb and Icy's mouth fell open in ecstasy. "Wen mi sey cum yah, yuh duh dat shit. There a waah method tuh mi madness."

Blaze's accent sent Icy over the edge, and she came hard. The seat of her shorts was soaked. He grinned as he eased the clothing from her body. Icy didn't fight him on it because she didn't like the wetness that saturated her butt. Stepping out of the shorts, Blaze left her standing in just her sports bra then sat back on the sofa. Icy opened her mouth to snap on him, but his deep baritone put a halt to the rant that was sure to come.

"Cum put dat pussy pan mi face."

Blaze licked his lips as he waited patiently for Icy to follow his command. The inner voice in her mind screamed, *Move, bitch! He's ready to eat!* Moving slowly as she peeled away her bra, Icy stood in front of Blaze and dropped the garment at her feet.

"Lay back," she demanded seductively.

"Nah, I'm good like this. Bring my pussy to me. Sit it right here," Blaze said, resting his head on the cushion of the sofa with his tongue standing stiffly from his mouth.

Icy had never sat on any man's face in the manner Blaze requested. The dominance he presented turned her all the way on and she was eager to try it. She could get used to that freaky shit though. Akoni warned Icy early on about Blaze, but she didn't believe he had it in him, because he was so gentle with her in their past sexual trysts. She was damn sure about to find out, now that he was comfortable with her. Icy placed one foot on the sofa next to Blaze's thigh and being the gentleman he was, Blaze clasped her hand in his to help her keep her balance.

"Mmmm, she smells delectable. Let me see if she tastes as good."

Blaze knew exactly how her nectar tasted, but every time it hit his tongue, there was a different flavor he loved. Licking his lips, he moved his body off the sofa as he positioned his head directly under Icy. He cupped her ass cheeks in his palms and massaged them slowly.

"Sit," Blaze commanded.

Doing as she was told, Icy planted her feet and used his face as a seat. Blaze wasted no time wrapping his soft lips around her engorged bud. She tried standing to her feet when the electric-like current shot up her spine from the pleasure she was receiving. Blaze forced her back into position then sent her into a frenzy as he explored her tunnel with his tongue.

"Oooooouuu shit," Icy moaned, gripping Blaze's locs with both hands. She rocked her hips back and forth, barely breathing from the friction on her growing bud. Sticking his tongue deeply in her hole, Blaze fucked Icy into an orgasm easily.

"B-Blaze, I'm about to cum!"

Without stopping what he was doing, Blaze heard her clearly and was working hard to make sure Icy moisturized his beard. Inserting his middle finger into Icy's asshole, she moaned seductively in his ear as she pushed down so his finger would go in deeper. Her eyes rolled in the sockets before she looked him dead in the eyes with her bottom lip tucked between her teeth. Icy released his hair and palmed both of her breasts while rolling her nipples between her fingers. Her pearl swelled and the pipes burst. Blaze drank every drop of her essence until her well was dry.

"Stop. Stop. I can't take it anymore," Icy whined just as her knees gave out and all of her weight landed on Blaze's face.

Blaze turned his head so he could breathe properly. Icy's pussy was nestled on his cheek, and he could hear her soft snores. He laughed as he lifted her by the waist and lowered Icy onto the sofa. Blaze stood to his feet as he inhaled the sweet smell of Icy on his face. He looked down at his queen and his heart swelled. She was so beautiful. Blaze stood admiring Icy as she slept for a solid ten minutes and the entire time, she was sleeping peacefully in a fetal position.

"Ain't this a bitch," he muttered. "Imagine if I put this dick on her. She'd be in a coma." Cradling Icy effortlessly in his arms, Blaze carried Icy toward the bedroom with a smile. "Knocked yo' ass out," he laughed as he laid Icy on the bed then covered her with the sheet.

***

Blaze rolled over and gazed down at Icy while she slept peacefully beside him. Without waking her he removed her off his chest and onto the pillow. He quietly got out of bed to shower before he left for his appointment. While in Aruba, Blaze secretly talked back and forth with a realtor, trying to find Icy the perfect residence she could call home. He knew how hard it was for her to live in a hotel when she was accustomed to having her own space. Hell, he was tired of being in the hotel as well, but that came with being hands-on in his business. The realtor had three properties she wanted Blaze to see, and he was ready to make his forever lady happy.

After taking care of his hygiene, Blaze sat at the desk and wrote a note to Icy.

Ice,

I had to leave but I'll be back. You were sleeping soundly, and I didn't want to wake you. Plus, I know the orgasm I hit you with had you out for the count. I'll be sure to give you what you really want upon my return. If you decide to leave the suite, please be careful and hit me with your location. Things will get better soon, I promise.

I love you.

Akoni

Grabbing his keys and phone from the dresser, Blaze left the suite and made his way to his rental. As he walked through the lobby of the hotel, his thoughts went to his mother. He hadn't spoken to Kenise in a few days and made a mental note to reach out to her. Blaze wasn't worried about her wellbeing because he watched her every move from his phone and knew she was good. There were times he would witness his mother crying and at that moment he would send her a kissy face emoji to ensure her he was there with her every step of the way.

Once he was seated in the driver's seat, a call came through from the realtor. Blaze answered, letting her know he was on his way. First, he had to pick up Joe because he felt he needed someone else to help him decide on the perfect home for a woman that was perfect in Blaze's eyes. It took thirty minutes for him to pull up to Joe's apartment. His boy was waiting patiently, and Blaze liked that Joe was prompt whenever he needed him to be.

"What up, Loverboy?" Joe laughed.

"I know you ain't talking. The way Kia had yo' ass looking like a sick puppy yesterday."

"Gone with that shit. I was just worried about her doing stupid shit," Joe retorted. "Don't get me wrong, I like Kia a lot, but she don't listen, man."

Blaze laughed as he cruised down the street. "That's what you like about her ass. She don't cower down to yo' wannabe mean ass."

"Whatever."

"Kia is the type of woman a man can't play games with. You have to think about all the shit she's been through. Not to mention, the shit still isn't over for her or Icy. Shit, Julz is in the midst of the bullshit too."

"You don't think I know that? Speaking of the situation, a nigga I used to run the streets with hit me up last night. He told me he knows where that cat Boom is laying his head. I've been waiting to fuck his ass up for the pussy shit he did to Kia. I'm gon' head over there to scope out the spot once I help yo' in-love ass get Icy right."

"Say what you want, hater. Get on my level and maybe one day, you will be in love like me, nigga," Blaze chortled. "Nah, on some real shit, I want to make sure Ice is good when I leave to go back to New York."

"Leave and go back to New York? Nigga, are you crazy? How the fuck you gon' leave her out here by herself?"

"Joe, you know I sent the crew back when the job was over here. I stayed behind because of Icy. It's like, I don't want to leave, but I still have a business to run and money to be made. I'm only going back to sign off on this new contract I received. We will only be gone for a week, tops."

"Who the fuck is we? I'm not leaving Kia to battle Leo's crazy ass by herself. I'm not going. You go. One of us needs to be here to look after them, Blaze."

"I need you on this project, Joe. It's located in Miami——"

"Nah, Blaze. I love what I do with yo' company, but you may as well fire me now, because I'm not going. Leo ain't one to play with. If a muthafucka can fake his own death, have Kia's house shot up, shoot the woman he claimed to love for better or worse, then shoot that same woman in your presence, not to mention almost blowing our asses to smithereens, and running Icy's mama off the road, that nigga ain't gon' stop until everybody is dead! You better tell them folks to send the documents via DocSign and appoint one of the managers to run the company until we put an end to this shit." Pulling a blunt from his pocket, Joe flamed up and continued his rant.

"Do I have to remind you about that nigga's hand in your father's death? Ain't no muthafuckin' way I'll go back to conducting business as if nothing happened and my mama in another country by herself. This nigga knows where she lay her head! Fuck that business, Blaze! That money gon' still roll in with or without you being there! Trust the people on your team. We gotta get at this muthafucka before he succeeds in his mission."

Joe was angry because he thought Blaze was the mastermind in all he did, but he was acting like he didn't know how the streets worked. He made Joe believe he was just as dumb as the white bitch in the movie *Clueless.* There was no way he was leaving Chicago without knowing anything about Leo's plan. Boom was a start and Joe couldn't wait to get his hands on his ass.

"You right, man. I'll make the calls later. Thanks for bringing my ass back to reality. Icy won't be safe even after I buy this house for her," Blaze said, taking the blunt Joe handed to him. "What time you want to check out the information you received?"

"Oh, so now you want to roll with the big dawgs," Joe joked. "You had me worried. Akoni had yo' ass soft as fuck for a minute."

"Ain't shit soft about me, muthafucka. Don't insult my muthafuckin' intelligence."

Joe smiled as he sat back in the passenger seat. He knew exactly what he was doing, and the shit worked. Joe riled Blaze up by reminding him of everything Icy was going through. He wanted his boss to get mad, to become Blaze, the nigga that would tear a nigga's head clean off his body. Joe knew the beast was within Blaze, he just hadn't seen it yet.

"I'm not insulting shit! I need you to get yo' head in the game we're being forced to play. You say Icy is special, right? Treat her as precious cargo, nigga! She is your responsibility now. Protect her at all costs. That's all I'm saying. You from Brooklyn, right? Get in that New York state of mind, muthafucka!"

"Nah, I'm from Kingston, Jamaica!"

"Even better. The best of both worlds. Just leave that nigga Akoni in the rear and bring Blaze to the forefront guns blazing. This is not the time for any type of negotiations. We gotta go hard or go the fuck home. I'm set on go. You with me or not?"

Blaze listened to Joe but didn't utter a word. His jawline clenched as he grinded his teeth. One thing he wasn't was a weak nigga, but Joe had told him just how laid back he'd become since meeting Icy. Protecting her was something he thought he was already doing, but Joe was right, he couldn't leave her sitting like a duck alone.

According to the GPS, Blaze was nearing the first property he was set to look at. When he was notified of his arrival, Blaze turned into the driveway and knew right away he didn't like the home. The structure wasn't what he had in mind. For one, it was a single-level house, and he knew for a fact he had plans to fuck Icy on a carpeted staircase. There weren't any bay windows and that was one of the things he told the realtor he wanted.

"I'm not going to waste my time walking through this one. I can tell it's a hard no for me," Blaze said, stopping his rental.

"What's wrong with it? I think you should take a look."

"Nah, I want a multi-level home. At least two stories."

"Well, I want to see what it's about. I'm looking to purchase some property myself," Joe said. "Once we off that nigga Leo, I won't be able to lay my head in the city. Ain't no telling who is laying in the cut with his ass. I want to make sure I'm straight in the end."

The realtor came out of the house with a smile and both Blaze and Joe admired her from afar. She wore a beige two-piece pantsuit with a white button-down shirt that hugged her voluptuous breasts like a glove. Her hair was bone-straight with a side part and framed her face perfectly. Her caramel complexion beamed in the sunlight as it bounced off her natural features.

"Damn, shawty bad," Joe said to himself but loud enough for Blaze to hear. "I'm 'bout to jump on that. You weren't thinkin' 'bout hollerin' at her, right?"

Blaze cut his eyes at him with a frown. "What the fuck I look like? My bitch bad as hell. Joye ain't got shit on Ice. Yo' ass better think twice about pursuing her before opening that can of worms. Kia's ass is a straight nigga out here."

"Kia is playing games. I'm not interested in entertaining. I'm not the nigga that's about to sit in wait for a muthafucka to act right. My name is Joe, not slow. She better wake the fuck up and get with the program. There are too many prospects out here to concentrate on the one who has no plans of settling down with a real nigga. Joye is about to get this business though."

Joe got out of the car after what he said and made his way up the driveway toward the house, taking in every inch of Joye's physique. His gaze fell to her left hand, not noticing a ring. It didn't mean she didn't have a man, but he was set to find out in the long run. Climbing the stairs, Joe licked his lips as he got closer to the woman before him.

"Hello, Ms. Lady," he said, stopping in front of her.

"Mr. Ottey, it's nice to finally meet you." Joye smiled broadly, batting her eyes. Even though the man who addressed her didn't have the Jamaican accent which swooned her from day one, he was still handsome as ever.

"Nah, you have the wrong one, sweetie. I'm Joe, but it's a pleasure to meet you too. The man you're searching for is behind me." Joe motioned with his thumb over his shoulder. "I'd like to get to know you a little better if you're willing." Joye glanced past Joe at Blaze and he laughed lowly.

"He's not interested. The woman in his life is all he sees. Concentrate on the man who's trying to lay the world at your feet. I'm free as a bird and wanna fly with you."

At that moment, Blaze joined the pair on the steps with a sly smirk on his face. He'd heard Joe spitting game and was intrigued to see how Joye would react to it. Instead of responding, she diverted her attention to the man that would be giving her a hefty commission on the sale, if he signed on the dotted line. However, the words which came from Joe stayed in the forefront of her mind. There was no way she was going to walk away from a man that basically wanted to give her all his attention. She didn't know if he was just trying to lead her on, but she was curious to find out what his motive was.

Joye left North Carolina and moved to Chicago two years prior, escaping the pain and turmoil of her ex. She had to leave all traces of herself behind so he couldn't find her. Calling her family from a burner phone was how she stayed in touch with her parents. Joye knew there was a slight chance of Nard finding her any day. So far, she had been lucky enough to keep her location a secret. Working hard to achieve her goal of becoming a real estate agent paid off and she was making money hand over fist. The downside of it all was the simple fact of not being comfortable allowing a man to get close to her.

"Akoni, I'm glad you could join us. Shall we look at this home and see if you like it?"

"I already know this house isn't for me. But Joe wanted to check it out because he's looking to purchase a home as well."

Joye smiled at Joe before turning on her heels, leading the way inside. Joe watched her ass sway side to side with every step she took. His dick was trying to stand at attention, but his jeans was preventing it at all costs. Entering the home, Blaze didn't move any further than the foyer because he had no interest in the house. Joe, on the other hand, followed Joye around every corner. Thirty minutes later, they were leaving after Joe finally admitted he didn't want the property.

"Okay, well we have two more houses to view. To be honest, there's a third I didn't mention because it's in the same cul de sac of one of the properties, so they are kind of similar in structure. With you guys being friends, it may work for the two of you to live in close proximities of one another."

"We will speak on that once we get there. As a matter of fact, let's check that property out first. It just may be the one I love," Blaze said, walking to his car. Stopping in his tracks he turned to face Joye. "It's not a single-level home, is it?"

"No, it is two stories and beautiful. Follow me and we can be on our way."

"Cool, let me holla at my man right quick."

Joye stared with a puzzled expression as Joe talked lowly to Blaze. She didn't know what was being said but she didn't attempt to move toward her car. Blaze looked everywhere except in Joye's direction as he listened to whatever his friend was saying. Shaking his head, Blaze finally nodded in agreement then opened the driver's door of his car and got in. Joe squared his shoulders and motioned his hand to Joye's car.

"I'm waiting on you, Ms. Joye."

"Waiting on me for what?" she quizzed.

"I'm riding with you so we can start this phase of getting to know one another. Is that alright with you?"

Joye blushed as she nodded her head before allowing Joe to open the door for her. Blaze watched as his boy did everything a gentleman would do for a woman he was courting. But he knew shit wasn't going to be sweet for his nigga once Kia blew up his spot and showed her natural ass once she found out he was fucking with another woman.

Chapter 4

"Mommy, mi nuh ready tuh wake up," Amoy groggily whined as she snuggled deeper under the covers.

"Cum pan, baby. Memba wi a guh visit daddie todah."

At the mention of her daddy, Amoy sat upright fast and was wide awake. Her smile lit up the dimly lit room and it warmed her mother's heart. They hadn't seen nor heard from Leo since the last time he left Kingston to handle business back in the states. It wasn't like him to go so long without talking to Amoy. Avita had been feeling as if something wasn't right for weeks. She prayed every day that Leo was okay.

"Mi get fi si daddie di real?" Amoy asked as she jumped up and down on the bed.

"Yeah. Now, tap all dat jumping before yuh fall an hurt yuhself. Guh inna bathroom an brush yuh teeth. Wi ave a plane tuh ketch."

Avita watched her daughter run out of the room toward the bathroom down the hall. She had already packed their luggage, but still needed to choose an outfit for Amoy to wear for the flight. If Amancia hadn't asked Avita to accompany her to Chicago, she would have never gone on her own. Avita always sat in wait for Leo to come back to them. She thought about calling to tell him she would be bringing Amoy to the states, but she would make that call once they were settled. Even though Amancia was going to the states on bullshit, Avita was ready to have her back.

Years prior when Akoni packed up and left Kingston refusing to go through with the wedding, she cried like a baby for months. There wasn't a man in the village that could get Amancia to be their woman. She didn't want anyone if it wasn't Akoni. She spent all of her days working hard with the younger kids in the village, teaching them to read and write. Not to mention being the good Samaritan who provided food and clothing to the less fortunate. Amancia would do anything she could to keep her mind off the man she deemed the one who got away.

When Amancia confided in Avita about the sexual encounter she had with Akoni, she knew right away her cousin's feelings for him were in full force once again. Too bad Akoni didn't have the same sentiments as Amancia. It was a mistake on her part, for thinking sleeping with him would change his mind about them being together. But there was no telling Amancia that because she was adamant about going to get *her man.*

"Mommy, mi need yuh!" Amoy yelled from the bathroom.

Avita took off running because the urgency in her daughter's voice had her heart racing. Holding her breathe the entire time, she made it to the bathroom to see Amoy combing her hand through her hair. Leaning against the doorframe, she waited for what her three-year-old had to say.

"Mi wa tree ponytails suh mi cya luk pretty fi daddie."

Smiling, Avita wanted to scold her daughter but decided against it. She knew Amoy was excited to see Leo and wanted to look her best. The relationship the two of them had was one Avita wanted from her own father when she was younger. She wasn't going to take that away from Amoy. Leo may not be a full-time father, but he loved Amoy more than anything. Including Avita.

After giving Amoy the hairstyle she wanted, Avita got both of them dressed just as the doorbell rang. Glancing at the clock on the wall, it was a little earlier than the time Amancia said she'd be there so that meant it was the nanny,

Eshe. Avita went to the door and peeked out the window to see who was actually outside her door. She was correct, Eshe was standing in wait.

"Good morning, Avita. I'm so excited about my first trip to the states!" Eshe exclaimed, hugging Avita. "I've been waiting for this experience all my life."

As Eshe stepped inside the house, Amancia's driver pulled into the driveway. It was time to head to the airport. Avita grabbed the luggage while the nanny attended to Amoy. Hurrying to the car before her cousin could get out, Badrick approached to accompany Avita with her bags. A few minutes later, Amoy and Eshe emerged from the house, giving her the opportunity to run back and lock up. Once everyone was settled inside the truck, Amoy started talking nonstop.

"I'm going to see my daddy and I'm so happy."

Amancia looked back at Avita with a questionable stare. She knew her cousin would have a mouthful to say once they reached the private plane. If her uncle knew why they were going to America, he would shit bricks. Amancia conjured up a story about wanting to go on vacation to Chicago just to see what it was like, and she had Avita lying along with her. Now that Avita thought about it, they were going far away from home without knowing a thing about the place they were about to visit.

They had booked two suites. Avita, Amoy and Eshe would share a two-bedroom, while Amancia would be in the connected one-bedroom suite. From the pictures on the website, the hotel was beautiful and not too far from shopping and Millennium Park. Being that it was pretty cold, they already knew visiting some of the sights were going to be impossible due to the weather. According to Amancia, they weren't going to Chicago for fun. She was on a mission to get her man back.

Arriving at the landing strip, everyone piled out of the vehicle, leaving Badrick to handle the luggage. Eshe was amazed as she slowly walked through the aisle trying to find the best seat that would suit her for the long flight. When she found a seat in the center, Eshe melted in the seat with a smile.

"This plane is luxurious and so spacious. Thanks again for allowing me to accompany you all on this trip."

"No thanks needed," Avita replied as she handed Amoy to her. "We will be taking off soon. I'll be in the back talking to my cousin. Do you need anything beforehand?"

Eshe shook her head no as she pulled Amoy's iPad from her tote bag. Placing earphones over her ears, she made sure Amoy was settled in and buckled up. In the meantime, the two cousins sat in the back of the plane quietly as the attendants brought out drinks and snacks. Once the pilot announced they were ready to hit the runway, both women put in their earbuds for takeoff. Once they were safely in the air, Avita was the first to speak.

"What is the plan once we touch down? We don't know anything about America, let alone Chicago. I did a little bit of reading. The city is more dangerous than the villages back home."

"Nothing is going to happen to us. Stop worrying so much. Explain why Amoy believes we're going to see her daddy? I know he lives there, but you don't know the first thing about where he is. At least I have the address to the hotel Akoni is staying in. What information have you obtain to find your no-good ass baby daddy?"

Amancia didn't have a right to talk down on Leo. She was upset about never meeting him and that rubbed her the wrong way. Nonetheless, she had no right to be mad because it wasn't anyone's business who fathered her child. Long as she knew, was all that mattered. It was kind of embarrassing that Avita didn't know anything about Leo's life, outside of him visiting Kingston. She wasn't going to allow it to show in the presence of her judgmental ass cousin.

"I don't have any information. It would be nothing for me to call him up when we settle in at the hotel and I tell him we're there. Stop acting like you know the relationship I have with my child's father," Avita snapped.

"A blind man can see you're the side chick in this…whatever you call what you and him have. That man doesn't give a damn about you!" Amancia chastised her cousin sternly but for her ears only.

"And Akoni don't want shit to do with you either, but you're flying across the world to beg him to give you another chance," Avita snapped back. "I guess both of us are two dumb ass bitches."

Getting up on that note, Avita walked down the aisle to get far away from her cousin. Amancia was quick to throw stones but wasn't sweeping outside her front door in the process. She couldn't wait to see firsthand how Akoni made her cousin look stupid as fuck. Someone needed to slap her off the high horse she was riding immediately.

Avita checked on Amoy before choosing another section of the plane to sit. She listened to "H.E.R. Radio" station on Pandora until she fell asleep with Leo on her mind.

***

The flight was long and very comfortable for Avita. She slept almost the entire commute and was energized. They had about an hour until they landed, and Amoy was becoming restless. She was ready to spend time with her father and Avita hadn't been able to get in touch with him at all. If it took every breath in her body, she was going to reunite her daughter with Leo. Thinking back on the day she'd answered his phone, Avita hurriedly unlocked her phone and went to her notes app. She remembered doing some investigating on the Icy chick and found some lucrative information she planned to use to her advantage.

Avita clicked on the links she'd saved and got to work finding out more about the woman she suspected Leo to involved with. Icy Winters was her name. She was a successful businesswoman who owned a few salons in the Chicagoland area. Winter's Dreamz was the name of her business. By the looks of it, Icy was doing great on her own without the help of Leo. She seemed to be a very strong woman and hopefully, she would be just as strong when Avita paid her a visit to ask questions about the man they were both attached to.

"Avita, I'm sorry about earlier. I shouldn't have taken my frustrations out on you." Amancia interrupted her search, causing Avita to place her phone face down on her lap.

"I'm upset because you have a man who has willingly loved you in his own way and gave you something special. Amoy. A child is the one thing I've always wanted and Akoni is the only man who could ever be the father."

Amancia had tears running down her cheeks as she explained how she felt. Avita stood and moved over a seat so her cousin could sit down beside her. She had a little bit of empathy but not much, because Avita didn't have anything to do with what she and Akoni had going on. In her opinion, her cousin was going on a blank mission which Avita doubted would end well. Akoni had already told Amancia he didn't want anything to do with her, but here they were, on a plane to America so she could get him back.

"There are millions of men in the world who would love to get to know you, Amancia. Trying to persuade Akoni to be with you is only going to hurt you more than you already are."

"I have to fight for what was put in place for us since we were kids," Amancia said as she wiped the tears away. "If he didn't want me, why did he sleep with me giving hope?"

"To be honest, sex doesn't equate to a relationship. You are the one taking it to that extreme. There is this thing called casual sex and you, my dear cousin, experienced it with

Akoni." Amancia rolled her eyes and turned her head away from Avita. "Didn't you say he was involved with someone else?"

"What does that have to do with anything?" Amancia hissed. "I'm less than an hour away from getting my future husband back. The bitch was never part of the plan to spend the rest of her life with him. I was! It was always designed for me to be Mrs. Ottey!"

"Okay, don't bite my head off about it. I'm just trying to remind you of the situation. Things can get ugly, you know."

"Avita, I'm prepared for everything that will come with this. I'm going to make this visit memorable for all involved. Akoni isn't about to fuck me and think he can return to his life in America, then forget who's really supposed to be in his life." Amancia paused as she glanced out the window. "I just hope you have my back through it all, because I've seen many videos on *YouTube.* American women don't fight fair at all."

"I'm with you when you're right," Avita muttered.

"What that mean?"

"We'll deal with it when we get to that point. In the meantime, I need to figure out how I'm going to get in contact with Leo for Amoy's sake."

"Yeah, right. You're looking for Avita. Find the woman and I'm quite sure the man won't be too far behind."

Avita shared her findings with Amancia and decided once they were settled, Winter's Dreamz would be the first place they would visit.

Chapter 5

Icy rested up for two days after returning from Aruba. Her energy levels were at an all-time low and she couldn't figure out why. She had spoken to Sean, along with the other managers of her salons, and promised to come in to touch bases on what was going on. Sean informed Icy of the camera login the tech left after he installed cameras around the shop. Having that protection was something Icy was grateful for. Blaze really showed how much he cared about her wellbeing when he went over and beyond to make sure she and her staff were safe.

Forcing herself out of bed, Icy made her way to the bathroom to shower. Not only did she have to go check on her businesses, but she also needed to visit her mother in the hospital. As she thought about Staci, Icy doubled back because it dawned on her that Blaze was not in the bed with her. She walked out of the bedroom and there weren't any signs of him in the suite. As Icy turned to head back to the bedroom, the door opened.

"Hello, beautiful," Blaze smiled with a bag of food in one hand, and drinks in the other. The aroma from the bags made her stomach growl, reminding Icy that she hadn't eaten since the night before. "I thought you were going to sleep in longer, so I went out to get breakfast."

"Awww, thanks, babe. I slept longer than I wanted, because I must go out to handle business. Not to mention, I have to go see my mother. I'm gonna shower then I'll be right back to eat with you."

Icy hugged Blaze around the neck and pecked his lips. He tried to take it a step further by slipping his tongue in her mouth. Icy stepped back quickly. "I haven't brushed my teeth yet."

"So, it doesn't matter."

"It does to me. I'll be back shortly. Then I'll kiss you until I leave to run my errands."

Blaze chortled as Icy scurried out of the room. Placing the items on the table, he took the opportunity to call his mother while waiting for Icy's return. Going to the app for the cameras he had installed in his mother's home, he watched as she walked across the room for her phone.

"Akoni, ow yuh duh, son?" Kenise asked excitedly. "Mi ave miss yuh suh much."

"Mi miss yuh too, mada. Mi doing fine."

Watching his mother wipe tears from her eyes, Kenise didn't sound as if she was sad, which surprised Blaze. Had he not been looking at the camera, he would've never known because she put on a great act. Blaze knew she was lonely without Duke and he hated that for his mother. Thirty-five years of being with someone, then in the blink of an eye, your soulmate's snatched away. Blaze couldn't imagine the amount of pain his mother felt daily.

"Mada, mi a guh send fi yuh. Mi kno yuh sad without fada an mi nuh wad at fi yuh."

"Mi okay, Akoni. Yuh kno mi nuh wa fi cum tuh America. Kingston a mi home. Mi ave friends tuh kip mi company."

"Eff yuh fine, wah mek yuh crying?" Blaze asked with concern.

Kenise glanced around until she was staring at the camera in the corner of her living room. Smiling as she waved, causing her son to laugh at her gesture. She'd forgotten about the camera until he made the statement about her crying. At that moment, Kenise knew her son could see her every move. Shaking her head, she wiped her eyes one more time.

"Yuh an dem cameras. Mi kno mi nuh fi ave agree tuh ave dem cameras installed. Mi cry cuz mi miss him suh much."

"Mi kno, ma. Tek it one day at a time. It neva gets betta, but it wi eventually become easia tuh deal wid. Believe it or nuh, mi miss Duke too."

The two of them became silent as they thought back on the man both loved in their own way. Icy walked back into the room, catching Blaze's attention. He quickly looked down at his phone to see what his mother was doing since she was still quiet. Kenise was smiling at a photo over the fireplace of her and Duke.

"Ma, di invitation open eff yuh eva wa fi cum wid mi. It wi nuh be permanent, just a couple weeks. Mi ago bi home soon as mi cya. Tap all a dat crying an tink bout di gud times yuh an Duke had together. Him still there wid yuh. Mi luv yuh."

"Mi luv yuh too, son. Chat tuh yuh lata."

Blaze held the phone with a worried expression as he watched his mother go out to the patio. He was about to go to the frame to keep an eye on her, but seeing one of the guards heading out behind her made him feel a little better. The thought of his mother being in Kingston alone and sad made him feel some type of way. Icy's touch changed his mood slightly, causing Blaze to smile.

"How is she holding up?" she asked.

Sighing as he sat down, Blaze steepled his fingertips as he thought about how he and his mother's lives had changed. Even though he had Icy, his mother had no one except security and longtime friends. Kenise wanted to hide her truth from her only child and didn't want him to know how heartbroken she really was.

"She's trying very hard to seem okay, but I know she's not. I've seen her crying countless times on camera." Blaze ran his hand down his face. "I invited her to come to me and she declined my offer."

"Go to your mom, babe. Seeing you in the flesh is what she needs right now."

"Ice, my mother has heavy security. You, on the other hand, don't. I've called my team back in New York to handle things on the business side, for the first time in years, so I can be here for you. Leaving you alone isn't something I'm going to do while Leo is still roaming the streets."

"Whatever will happen to me, will happen whether you're here or not. I would rather you go to your mother than stay here with me. She's more important."

Blaze glared at Icy with fire in his eyes. It was the same look she saw when he was standing toe-to-toe with Leo on their wedding day. Icy knew she hadn't said anything remotely close to what Leo had.

"Mi mada very important tuh me an suh yuh. Neitha one of yuh more important dan di oddah," Blaze snarled. Icy knew he was angry because his native tongue was stronger than it was when he talked to his mother. "Mi ave eyes pan har. Yuh a mi main concern now. Yuh mean di world tuh mi, Ice," he said in a softer voice.

Blaze's accent disappeared instantly. "In a short amount of time, I fell in love with you. The things I've learned about Leo and his motives behind being with you sickens me. Knowing he never loved you angers the fuck out of me. All the shit the coward has done makes me want to snap his fuckin' neck. In the midst of it all, I'm thinking of ways to love you the way you deserve, Icy. This shit I'm feeling is real and I promise you're going to feel it too, if not more."

Icy saw the love in his eyes and it made her heart flutter. She'd never had any man express their love for her sincerely. What she thought was love in the past always came with pain afterwards. With Deron, it was the abuse and the disrespect he had on full display. Icy was never supposed to speak on the many females Deron was parading around without a care.

Then, Leo came into her life at the right time, saving her from the demon who beat her as an everyday chore. Finding out Leo was only on her ass because of what he'd done to her father pissed Icy off to the max. She wanted to end his life in the worse way and couldn't wait until the day he took his last breath.

"Did you hear what I said, baby?"

Icy maneuvered her way onto Blaze's lap and encircled her arms around his neck. Kissing him slowly, he cuffed her ass cheeks in his hands as he kissed her back. When he slid his tongue in her mouth, Icy didn't prevent it. Instead, savored the minty flavor that danced on her tastebuds. She heard every word Blaze recited and she couldn't say she loved him out loud, because she wanted the moment to be special. What she knew as fact was the love he possessed for her was real.

"I heard you."

She pecked his lips a final time before getting up to warm their food. Blaze watched her ass sway the entire time. It wasn't the biggest, but he knew exactly what she had stocked between that muthafucka. The ringing of his phone peeled his eyes from Icy's derriere. When he looked down, the smile fell from his lips. Amancia was calling and he sent her straight to voicemail, but she called right back. Blaze was not in the mood for her bullshit, so he silenced the call once again as Icy walked over with their meals.

"Is everything alright, babe?" Icy asked, sitting the plates down then taking a seat across from him.

Blaze contemplated if he wanted to tell her the truth or just leave well enough alone. One thing he didn't want Icy to think was of him hiding any dealings with Amancia from her. Not wanting any problems, Blaze opted to go ahead and reveal what had irritated him.

"Amancia is still calling my phone. I don't know what she wants, but she won't stop calling."

"Did you strap up when you slept with her?" Icy asked as she put a forkful of hashbrowns in her mouth.

"Of course, I did. Why would you ask that?"

"The only reason I could see a woman hounding a man the way she's doing, is if she is trying to tell you she's pregnant." Icy hunched her shoulders. She didn't appear to be upset. Then again, she could be putting on a façade to keep the peace.

"Nah, that's not even a possibility. I strap up with everyone I've ever laid down with. Until I was introduced to your pussy, that is. I'm not trying to get trapped into being a father with any woman I'm not interested in marrying. So, I know Amancia isn't trying to tell me no shit like that, because she knows I'm not marrying her. That was the reason I left Kingston many years ago."

"The next time she calls, answer. Remember, she threatened to pop up. She just may make good on it. You never know."

"That's not going to happen. She may know what city I'm in, but she won't find me at this hotel. I'm quite sure my mother didn't go that far to give her my exact location. So, she will be searching high and low for my ass."

"If and when she pops up, it would be in her best interest to keep her animosity between the two of you. Her issue is with you and whatever y'all had was before me. I shouldn't be a threat to her."

"You are a threat, Ice," Blaze smirked. "You got all this good dick to yourself, and she wants it. I'll admit, I made a huge mistake fuckin' her the way I did, but that shit didn't mean a damn thing to me. Hell, I was familiar with her and needed some pussy at the time. Blame it on me being a man."

Icy laughed because she knew what he said was true. Hell, she couldn't be mad about what went down, Blaze wasn't her man at the time of their lil fling. Let the bitch try to fuck him again and it's gonna be on. She would be the last woman to suck that meat off the bone.

They finished eating as they talked, then it was time for Icy to get dressed so she could leave. She had plans to come back to the room and cuddle up with her Jamaican king and chill. It was still cold out, so Icy chose a pair of black jeggings, a cream-colored turtleneck, and her tan Uggs to put on. She didn't feel like doing much to her hair, so Icy threw it in a ponytail and grabbed her purse, keys and cellphone before walking out of the bedroom. Blaze was sitting on the sofa smoking a blunt as she approached him.

"You leaving?" he asked.

"Yeah, I'll be back soon as I can," she replied over her shoulder as she eased her arm into the black Moncler jacket.

"Share your location and leave it connected. I want to be able to pinpoint your every move. For your safety, of course."

"Nah, yo' ass just want to be able to see if I'm going where I told you I was going."

"Icy, you have never given me a reason to question your whereabouts. I don't think you would start now."

"I was just kidding, babe," Icy said, tapping away on her phone. "Location is active, daddy." Leaning down to kiss him passionately, she ran her tongue along his bottom lip and sucked it into her mouth.

"You trying to get fucked, huh? Get out before I put this dick in ya life, and you won't be going no damn where." Laughing as she made her way to the door, Blaze's voice stopped her steps.

"I love you."

"Ditto." She smiled as she let the door close behind her.

***

Everything was up to par at the northside salon. Icy was glad because she was really worried about the Maywood location. Sean truly didn't sound like himself when she talked to him when they talked. Icy had just exited at 1st

Avenue when her phone rang with a number she didn't recognize. Letting the call go to voicemail, the person called right back, irritating the fuck out of her. It was too early in the day for bullshit and Icy was in a good headspace. With that in mind she opted not to answer. As she rounded the corner, her phone rang once more, and she jabbed the phone button on the steering wheel and answered with much attitude.

"Who the fuck is this?"

"Is that the way you answer the phone for the man you swore to love 'til death do us part?"

Hearing Leo's voice, Icy automatically started looking in her rearview mirror to see if the nigga was following her. When she didn't see anything out of the ordinary, she concentrated on the road, while her right hand reached into her purse to make sure the Gremlin was in place. She was ready to blow Leo's shit back the moment he pulled up on her. Without answering his question, Icy continued to drive as if she hadn't heard a word he said.

"Bitch, I know you hear me talking to you!" Leo yelled. "That nigga got you thinking you safe, I see. Icy, stop playing with me, yo."

"Or what, Leo? What the fuck can you possibly do to me that you haven't done already?" Icy laughed. "You killed my muthafuckin' daddy, pretended for years to love me, set me up to take a murder charge, and ran my mama off the fuckin' road! Nigga, you did all that shit then went into hiding. Coward ass. Now, who's the bitch?"

Leo laughed. "Yeah, I did all that shit, but hiding is something I haven't done. I've been watching yo' every move. How the fuck you think you almost lost yo' life at the airport? Keep talking, yo' mama would stop breathing today, hoe!"

The threat clicked Icy's crazy button into the on position. She didn't give her brain a chance to think of what to say. "Since you want to play stupid ass scare games, meet me at the Maywood location. I'm on my way there now and I'll be sitting still until you get there. You better bring yo' army because I got some hot shit for yo' pussy ass. You have played with my mama's life for the last muthafuckin' time. Now, you know where I'll be, come see me, punk!"

Icy ended the call and picked up her phone from the cupholder and hit Blaze up. The phone rang and he answered on the first ring. That was the difference between him and Leo's hoe ass, Blaze was always there when she needed him.

"What's up, baby?"

"Leo just called my phone talking crazy. Come to the Maywood salon because he pissed me off so bad I told him where I was headed."

"Icy, you have to learn what to say and not to say, when it comes to that nigga," Blaze said, jumping up from the bed. He grabbed his keys and damn near ran out the suite. "Where are you now?"

"I'm around the corner from the salon."

"When you get there, go inside and make sure the door is locked. I'm on my way. Stay on the phone until you get in the building."

Whipping into her designated parking space, Icy snatched her key out of the ignition and grabbed her purse. She hopped out of the car making a beeline for the door. When she was inside, all eyes were on her as she glanced frantically out the window to see if Leo was anywhere in sight.

"I'm inside. I swear, Blaze, if he shows up, I'm blowing his brains out the back of his head."

"Do what you gotta do. I'll see you in a minute, baby. Stay out of sight. Call me if that muthafucka pull up."

Blaze ended the call and put his foot to the pedal and made a dash toward the expressway. He prayed Leo stalled before going to the salon, because he wanted to be the one to meet his ass at the entrance. Icy talked all that tough cookie shit without thinking, but he believed her when she said killing Leo was going to be her top priority. That was the reason he was breaking all the speed limits to get there. He would take the charge before he ever allowed her to.

Back at the salon, Sean stopped doing his client's hair to see what was going on with Icy. Standing behind his boss, Sean looked out the window to see if he could see what was happening on the outside. Placing his hand on Icy's shoulder, he whispered in her ear.

"What the hell is wrong?'

"Leo called threatening me as I was driving. I told his ass to meet me here and I'm going to shoot his ass if he shows up."

"I got my piece in my bag. If he comes, we gon' kill his ass together. I may have feminine traits, but I'm still a nigga."

The two of them were whispering in hush tones so the clients that were present wouldn't overhear what they were saying. Sean was pissed because Icy had possibly set herself up to be seriously hurt. Leo was crazy and Sean knew firsthand how he could be in the streets. That didn't mean anything to him because he would always be down to protect his good girlfriend.

"That's what I'm talking about. Thanks for always having my back. I called Blaze and he is on his way. In case he shows up late, we already know what we have to do."

"Damn right we do," Sean said, going back to his client.

Turning to walk through the salon, Icy spoke to the stylists and clients as she passed through. Sean kept glancing out of the window to make sure Leo didn't pull up unexpectedly. After about twenty minutes, a car sped into the parking lot and Sean's heart nearly stopped. He took a deep breath when he saw a man that wasn't Leo jump out of the car, walking swiftly to the door of the salon.

"Icy!" Sean screamed, causing Icy to run from the back. "Who is that at the door?"

"Blaze," was all Icy said as she went to open the door for her man.

Hugging her tightly while stroking the back of Icy's head, Blaze couldn't even force himself to let her go. It seemed like forever as the two of them stood by the door in a loving embrace. Sean smiled as she saw how the fine man loved her friend and knew he had her back through thick and thin. Stepping back, Blaze looked into Icy's eyes and saw the fear he hadn't heard in her voice over the phone.

"Let's go to your office," he said, intertwining his hand with hers. "Give me your phone."

Once they entered the office, Blaze took a seat, clicking on Icy's call log after she had given him access. "Is this the number he called from?"

Blaze asked as he turned the phone in her direction so she could see the screen. Icy shook her head yes and sat behind the desk. Blaze didn't waste a minute calling the number back. When Leo didn't answer, he left a message in a voice that was filled with venom.

"Muthafucka, the very next time you want to call *my* woman with idle threats, bring yo' punk ass to the destination. Yo' ass didn't come because you knew deep in yo' heart she was going to have me waiting! I'm gon' be the nigga that ends yo' life. It won't be a sneaky kill, I'm gon' allow you to look me in the face before I blow yo' shit off. Keep hiding, nigga. You never did yo' homework, because I always sniff out the muthafucka I'm looking for. See you real soon, bitch!"

Ending the call, Blaze slid the phone onto the desk as he sat with his leg bouncing at a high rate of speed. Taking his phone from his pocket, he tapped away on his phone as he texted Joe, telling him to pull up at the salon. The day the two of them went looking at houses, they went to the spot where Boom was supposed to be staying. It was a blank mission because there was no one at the residence. Blaze said he would give it some time before they went by there again. Time had passed and it was time to go on another search.

Icy sat nervously behind the desk as she watched Blaze hold a conversation on his phone. The tension in the office was so thick she could feel it on her body. Leo had fucked up threatening her and the man sitting before her was just as tired of the situation as she was. There was no way she would be able to stop him from doing whatever he had conjured up in his mind to do. Something was going down that day, she just didn't know what it was. Icy was too afraid to ask.

"Look, I want you to leave your truck here and ride with me. That muthafucka is hot anyway and I know how much you didn't want to drive it."

"Okay, but you know I was going to see my mother after I went to the southside location."

"Fuck the other salon!" Blaze snapped. "Call the muthafucka you pay to run it and have the conversation over the phone. I need to get you into a whip that nigga knows nothing about!"

Icy snapped her head back because she didn't appreciate how Blaze was talking to her. It felt as if he blamed her for the way Leo came at her. Yeah, she told him where she was going, but that didn't mean he had to speak to her in that manner.

"Watch your tone, Akoni. I don't have a problem with you being mad, but you are taking your anger out on the wrong person. Leo is baiting you in and you're falling right into his trap. Getting under your skin was his motive."

"He wanted my attention and the muthafucka got it! Let's go," he said, standing to his feet. "It's still early and I have plenty of time to do what needs to be done, so you can spend time with Staci."

Blaze left out of the office without waiting on Icy to follow. Snatching her purse and phone off the desk, Icy closed the door of her office behind her as she left. Exiting the hall into the salon, Blaze stood in the middle of the room waiting for her. As she passed him walking toward the door, the newly installed bell sounded. Two beautiful women stood on the other side and Icy opened the door and stood back so they could enter.

"Welcome to Winter's Dreamz. What services are you looking to obtain today?" Icy asked in her business voice.

"I'm actually here to see the owner."

Icy stared at the beautiful, dark-skinned woman who sported a headful of thick healthy hair, that was afroed with tight coils. She had a body a lot of women were paying top dollar to obtain, and she carried it well. Icy's right eyebrow rose slightly at the sound of her accent. She knew right away the woman was of Jamaican descent. Her assumption was confirmed when the other woman's eyes landed on Blaze.

"Akoni? What are you doing here?"

The entire salon became eerily quiet as everyone in attendance tuned in on the drama they hoped would unfold. Icy sensed what was about to happen and didn't want to put on a show in her place of business. She stole a glance at Blaze and his jawline was clenched tightly as he stared the woman down.

"Ummm, I'm the owner. We can step outside to discuss whatever you want," Icy said as nicely as she could. By that time, she knew exactly who one of the women were, but Icy didn't have a clue about the other. She was for sure going to find out.

"No, we can talk right here," the woman snapped. "My name is Amancia——"

"Go the fuck outside like she asked you to do," Blaze said through clenched teeth. "As you can see, she is running a business and you bringing this to her establishment. One thing you won't do is fuck up her money and give these muthafuckas something to talk about."

Amancia didn't budge until Blaze tilted his head to the side and his lip curled into a snarl. She basically pushed the other woman out of the opened door which Icy still had open. Following the women onto the sidewalk, the air was cold and Icy wasn't trying to stand out there talking. Instead, she turned with keys in hand, unlocking the door to the storefront next door to the salon. She had purchased it to expand but hadn't had the opportunity to get things in motion.

"We can talk in here," Icy said as she entered the building, flipping the light switch. Blaze was the last person to enter and he slammed the door behind him, then stood with his legs wide and arms folded across his chest.

"Amancia, do you want to tell me why you're in the states?"

"I told you weeks ago I was coming, Akoni. Don't act like we didn't have this conversation."

"No, you said you were coming, and I told you I wasn't worried about you showing up. If you were looking for me, how did you find your way here? This isn't my establishment."

"She came with me," the other woman said, cutting her eyes at Icy. "My name is Avita. We crossed paths when you called Leo's phone while he was home in Kingston."

The way Avita smirked as if she had one up on Icy was comical. Instead of saying anything right away, Icy gave her the space to get everything off her chest. She was eager to hear what else she had to say on behalf of the relationship she had with Leo's snake ass. Nothing she said would make Icy feel any type of way, but she was ready for the knives she was sure to throw at her.

"Leo and I have been together for the last four years and we have a three-year-old daughter. I had a feeling there was another woman in the states who kept him away for months at a time," Avita said with a smile. "When Leo hadn't come back to me and his daughter when he said he would, I had been calling his phone repeatedly without getting in touch with him. It was a good thing I copied your numbers from his phone and obtained the address to this place. What other way to find my man, than to pay the homewrecker a visit?"

Icy chuckled in Avita's face and wiped the smile off hers. Clearing her throat, Icy stared the woman down for a few minutes, then addressed her accordingly. One thing Icy wasn't going to do was allow the woman to believe she was the one who kept Leo away from his daughter.

"Everything you spoke on, I found out about over a month ago. Not now, nor have I ever been a homewrecker. I was with Leo for five years, and we were married on New Years Eve of last year. The man you are gloating and trying to make me feel bad about, ain't shit. You came to the right place to hear the real from a reliable source. Leo doesn't love anyone but himself. He may genuinely love your daughter because she is the only child he has. But that nigga is not the muthafucka he portrays himself to be. The reason you haven't been able to get in touch with him, is because he was declared dead the day we exchanged vows."

Avita's hand shot to her mouth and a pool of tears fell from her eyes.

"Nah, you can save the tears, hunni. Your baby daddy is alive and well. Leo faked his death and now he is harassing me because he can't let go of the woman that walked away. Maybe now that you're in town, you will give him something safe to do. It will be my pleasure to give you the number to contact him so your daughter can spend time with her father before I end his fuckin' life. It would be in your best interest to never contact me again, if you want to be here to see your daughter turn four."

Icy went into her phone and pulled up the last number Leo called her from and recited the digits to Avita. The woman was sobbing like a baby as she programmed it in her phone. If looks could kill, Icy would've been lying on the floor deader than a doorknob, the way Amancia was evilly peering at her.

"Let me get this straight. You are legally married to Leo, right?"

Icy shook her head no. "The marriage was annulled when Leo was pronounced dead."

"What I'm trying to understand is, how do you know Akoni?"

"See, that's something you should be addressing Akoni about. Whatever y'all got going on has nothing to do with me because it was before my time. Keep it that way and you won't get what you're really looking for."

Amancia turned to Akoni somberly. "How do you know her?"

"Not that it's any of your business, but Icy is my woman. I told you I was involved before you took it upon yourself to get my whereabouts from my mother."

"Ain't this a bitch! Yuh did wid Leo, now yuh wid mi man." Amancia's ranted in her native tongue indicating she was mad. The shit didn't move Icy at all. "We were destined to be together before we knew what marriage was, Akoni. There's no way you can move on with another."

"Amancia, the shit you speak of was put in place by our fathers. I was never down to marry you because I didn't love you. That was the reason I left Kingston back in the day. I wanted to establish a life of my own and not have to live by my father's rules and live off his money. I wanted to find a woman to spend the rest of my life with on my own. Not one chosen for me. I've found everything I want with Icy and there's nothing you or anyone else can do to change that."

"What did you call what we did the night you came to my house in Kingston?" Amancia cried.

"Fuckin'," Blaze said, hunching his shoulder. "That nut didn't mean nothing to me. It was only for one night. Nothing more, nothing less."

Amancia turned quickly in Icy's direction. "You're okay with him sleeping with another woman while with you?"

"Baby girl, he wouldn't dare touch another woman while he's with me. Had you listened when I spoke earlier, you would've heard when I said, that happened before me. Trust when I tell you, Akoni won't give you the time of day again."

"You bitch!"

Amancia charged at Icy and before Blaze could grab hold of her, Icy stepped forward and rocked her shit. Falling to the floor, Amancia held her face in shock and scooted backwards. Avita helped her to her feet and tried to pull her out the door.

"Run up, you get don' up. You're no longer in Kingston, Toto. You're in the Chi, bitch. Get the fuck out of my shit before I fuck you up for real."

"I'm going to leave, but this isn't over. Believe that!" Amancia yelled, rushing out the door.

"Stand in line because there is so many waiting to do some fucked up shit to me," Icy screamed at her back. As she moved quickly toward the door, Blaze grabbed her around the waist before she could step all the way out. "Make sure you're ready for whatever comes your way when you step to me over a big dick nigga."

Icy shrugged out of Blaze's grasp as the car sped out of the parking lot. "I told you what would happen if she came on bullshit. You better tell her ass to check my credentials, because I'm not the one to play with. I slap the fuck outta other people's kids."

Blaze shook his head as he left out of the building and waited for Icy to lock up. Leading the way to his rental, he helped her into the car and walked slowly to the driver's side.

The last thing we need is more drama to add to the bullshit that's already about to come to a head. Blaze thought as he opened the car door and got in.

Chapter 6

Kia was rushing around, trying to get to the hospital to see Staci. Icy and Julz were laying low, or maybe they were in their feelings because of what she said a couple days ago. Kia didn't give a damn, there was shit she needed to do, instead of basically hiding from a nigga that bled just like her. She'd been spinning the block, hoping to see Leo or any one of the pussies, Boom or Pip. Luck wasn't on her side. Kia wasn't giving up though. She made sure her .38 was tucked in her back locked and loaded.

As she gathered her belongings to hit the door, the doorbell rang. No one was home and Kia wasn't expecting anyone to come by the house, she contemplated answering but she needed to leave at some point anyway. Looking through the side window, Kia couldn't quite see who was standing on the porch. With everything that was going on, she was leery about opening the door.

"Who is it?" Kia shouted loud enough for the person to hear her.

"Is Staci home?"

"Who wants to know?" Kia asked irritably.

The two of them were going back and forth as if Kia didn't have anything to do with her life. Pulling her weapon, she slowly unlocked the door and yanked it open. Kia came face-to-face with a beautiful woman who looked as if she was too damn young to even be associated with her aunt. The bitch was bad as fuck, if Kia should say so herself. She could tell her body wasn't natural, but the doctor did a hell of a job sculpting her ass and the thighs matched perfectly. Her nose was sharp as well but enhanced her beauty.

"You don't need that gun," the woman said fearfully as she held her hands up.

"Man, ain't nobody gon' shoot yo' bougie ass," Kia laughed but never put her piece away. "Who the fuck are you and why are you looking for my aunt?" she questioned.

"I'm a long-time friend of hers. We go wayyyy back."

"Bitch, you barely thirty. There ain't no muthafuckin' way you knew Staci Winters back in the day. From the looks of it, you can't be no more than a couple years older than me, and I know for a fact I wasn't chillin' with my aunt at that time." Kia laughed, folding her arms over her chest with the barrel of the gun aimed at the mysterious woman's chest.

"Check it, I'm gon' need you to speak yo' peace and give me a name, before I ruin that beautiful body and face you spent a grip on by riddling yo' ass with bullets. The only way you would remotely be of the same age as Staci is if you underwent a whole facelift. So, name, bitch, and I'm not gon' ask again."

"My name is Julian Mi-Mishap."

Julian almost slipped up by revealing her married name. If she'd done that, she would've been getting zipped up in a body bag before she knew it. Glancing into Kia's eyes to see if she caught on to the slip-up, when she realized she hadn't, Julian continued.

"I've ran out of options and felt Staci was the last person I could come to about the person I've been searching for. Since she's obviously not home, I'll ask you. Have you talked to or seen Kenny? He hasn't been seen nor heard from in weeks."

When the Julian bitch mentioned Kenny's name, the smell of his blood filled Kia's nostrils as if she had killed him moments prior. The day was one she never wanted to think about ever again, but she didn't regret a damn thing about what she'd done. If she could, she would bring his snake ass back and kill him all over again.

"Well, do you know where he is?" Julian asked, breaking Kia's thoughts.

"No, we haven't seen him either. Last month, Staci put a missing person's report out on him. We've been calling him, and he hasn't answered. "What's your relationship with him? Maybe I should be asking yo' mysterious ass if *you've* seen him."

"Kenny is my man and I've been worried about him."

"Hold up! How the fuck is he your man and haven't heard from him in God knows how long, but you show up to his people's crib as a last result? That shit don't sound right. You looking real suspect right now. Bitch, must I make you suck this muthafucka in order to get you to spit the truth?" Kia asked, stepping forward.

"I would never do anything to Kenny. I love him," Julian cried as she backed up until her backside connected with the railing.

"Open yo' muthafuckin' mouth, bitch!"

Julian pursed her lips closed tightly and that only pissed Kia off more than she already was. There was something about Julian showing up on her aunt's porch, asking about Kenny. If she was supposedly around back in the day, who was to say she didn't have a hand in Birdman's murder. Kia wanted to murk everybody involved, and Julian may be the next muthafucka she would have to call the cleanup crew to dump.

"Why are you really here?" Kia snarled, pushing the barrel past Julian's lips. "I'll knock all yo' teeth down your throat!" Pulling the lever back, Kia put a bullet in the chamber and pushed the nozzle further into Julian's mouth.

"Where the fuck is Kenny?" Kia antagonized the woman and wanted to laugh so bad. "You did something to him, didn't you?"

Shaking her head vigorously, tears pooled in Julian's eyes. She couldn't speak because Kia didn't let up on the gun and all Julian could do was look down to make sure she didn't pull the trigger. Raising her hand to touch Kia's, Julian realized she fucked up.

"Touch me and you will meet yo' muthafuckin' maker, bitch!" Snatching the gun from the woman's mouth, Kia smacked her across the head with it, causing her to fall on the porch landing. "Get the fuck up and don't come back! I don't know yo' secretive ass and I don't trust you. If I find out you not who you say you are, I got a muthafuckin' bullet with ya alias written on it. Get yo' ass away from here!"

Watching Julian scramble to her feet and down the stairs, Kia laughed until her stomach ached. She dared not to take her sights off the woman, until she didn't see anything but the tail end of her car disappearing down the street. Turning around to lock up the house, Kia couldn't wait to get to the hospital and ask Staci about the woman named Julian.

Kia jumped in her ride and headed to the leasing office of the condo she was ready to move into. It was time for her to be in her own space again. Plus, Kia wanted to bring a nigga home and fuck loud as she wanted, without worrying about who could hear her moan. She started looking for a place a few days after Kenny gave her the information about the money Birdman left her. So much had transpired that Kia paid for the condo but had yet to pick up the keys. That was where she was on her way to before Julian's suspect ass showed up at Staci's house.

Listening to the song "Truth Is," by Inayah, the lyrics had Kia thinking about Joe and she tried her best to shake the thought. She hadn't spoken to him since the day Kia was injured. Not knowing the details on the incident burned her up too, because she wanted her lick back. Reaching out to Joe wasn't happening. If any information was known, Icy would inform her. Icy called several times and Kia didn't answer. She was sure her sister would've left a voicemail if there was anything of importance she wanted to say.

Kia pulled into the luxury condo parking lot and didn't waste any time getting out. She was excited about getting the keys to her new place. Kia entered the leasing office and the woman behind the desk greeted her with a smile as she stood to her feet.

"Welcome to River West Condos. How may I help you?"

"My name is Kia McKinny. I'm here to pick up the keys to apartment 207."

Tapping on the keyboard, Kia waited patiently for Jennifer, the name displayed on the nameplate on the desk, to finish her search. She walked over to a locked cabinet and retrieved a set of keys. Turning back to Kia, she asked for identification and the lease, which Kia had in hand. After looking over the documents, she handed everything back to Kia, along with the keys to her new apartment.

"These are for you. Welcome. If you'd like, I can go up with you to ensure everything is to your liking."

"That won't be necessary. I already looked around and took pictures weeks ago when I paid the rent for the next six months. I'm sure nothing has changed. I appreciate your offer though."

"Good. Good. My name is Jennifer. Here's my card if there's any issues you may come across. I can be reached here in the office from eight to five." Jennifer sifted through a few folders while Kia waited patiently. She didn't know what else the woman had for her, but she waited to find out. "Were you given the company policy sheet?" she asked.

"I received it, but I haven't had the chance to read through what it entails. I'll be moving in starting tomorrow just to give a heads up."

"That's fine. Will there be anyone helping you with your move?"

"Why does that matter?" Kia asked.

"We have a noise ordinance, and we wouldn't want the rap music to disturb the other residents——"

"In the rudest way possible, no one and I do mean no one, will ever tell me what I can and cannot do in *my* apartment. At twenty-four hundred a month, I can swing from the balcony butt-ass naked if that's what I choose to do," Kia snapped. "Black people aren't the only folks who listen to rap music. I bet your kids are home blasting every song with the word nigga in it, reciting the lyrics with their chest. In case you didn't know, every black person doesn't listen to rap music. Me on the other hand, listens for breakfast, lunch, and dinner. Don't start shit you ain't capable of handling without involving the police. Have a nice day, *Jennifer,* and don't make this hard for yourself or me. I'm with all the bullshit."

Kia left, wondering if she made a mistake moving into the predominately white area. She chose downtown because the hood was no longer safe, after the shit Boom had done to her house. Besides, Kia needed a spot where she could lay low without suspicion after she buried at least one of them niggas. Heading toward the hospital, Kia sang along to every song that played from her playlist.

***

Julian was fuming after she left Staci's house and didn't like the way the lil bitch Kia handled her. If it was anyone else, they would've been dead the minute it appeared to be safe to go about their day. See, Julian had the upper hand because Kia had no clue who she was, but Julian knew Kia better than she knew herself. The interaction between the two was like looking in the mirror for Julian. Kia was a ticking timebomb, just like she used to be in her younger days. It was going to be hell trying to one up the woman she encountered less than an hour prior.

As Julian drove on the expressway, she could feel a knot forming on the side of her head. Touching the spot, Julian looked down at her fingers to make sure a trip to the hospital wasn't needed. Glad there wasn't any blood in sight, she prayed Leo wasn't home because she didn't feel like answering any questions about what happened to her. To be honest, he didn't even know she was acquainted with the very people he was planning on ruining forever. That was a secret she never wanted to get out into the universe, because she was going to handle the shit her way. Julian's mind went back to the past and it was the last thing she wanted, but there was no stopping it.

"Girl, you and Kenny are finally starting a family," Staci gushed after learning she was with child.

"It wasn't planned. If it was up to me, I wouldn't be carrying this baby full-term. My mother is against abortions. How the hell am I supposed to raise this baby, while Kenny's ass is locked up for all this street shit he failed to walk away from? Had he listened, he wouldn't be in the predicament he's in. That's what happens when a muthafucka is trying to live in the shadows of his brother."

"Leave my husband out of y'all bullshit. What the two of y'all have going on in the bedroom has nothing to do with Birdman. We have our own baby to worry about. Icy was definitely made out of love and I think your baby was too. You know we're not going to let you struggle out here."

It had been years since she had laid eyes on Staci. Julian wasn't even around when Birdman was killed, and she was still fucked up behind it. Staci held Julian down just as she promised, but she wasn't there to do the same for her after losing the only man she loved. Kenny was the only person she had after her mother passed away but even then, he barely looked at her twice.

When Kenny got out of jail, their daughter was two years old. His ass had to keep going over numbers in his head about her conception, messing up what they could've truly had together. Once he found out the baby wasn't his, their relationship went from sugar to shit. Kenny stopped coming around, but still did what he had to do as a father, except he couldn't pretend he wanted to be there. Over the years it truly took a toll on her daughter's mental being because she wanted Kenny to treat her like Birdman did Icy.

One day something clicked in Kenny's mind, causing him to snap. He came to the house and demanded Julian to disclose who had fathered her child. Holding her at gunpoint, Julian had no choice but to tell him Birdman was the man she had slept with. The look in his eyes was one she'd never seen before. It was frightening. Kenny looked like the devil himself as he rammed the gun under her chin.

"Birdman is dead and if you don't leave now and never return, I swear you will be next."

Kenny tossed a duffle bag of money at her feet and Julian ran, never looking back until three years later. She met Leo at a club, and it was love at first sight. She was a bad bitch who came back to Chicago to see if she would be able to roam freely without being recognized. Julian never meant to fall in love and get married, especially not to the man who had killed her baby's father. Leo had no clue Julian knew that part of his life either. To him, she was a thirty-two-year-old woman he kept hidden from the world while he fucked any and every female he wanted. In reality, Julian was fifty-year-old Brenda Giles, Kia's estranged mother.

"It's a damn shame I'm going to have to join forces with my husband and kill my only child," Julian said aloud as she exited the expressway, heading to the home she shared with Leo.

Chapter 7

Julz was wrapping up an order when her phone rang loudly on the desk beside her. She smiled, showing all her teeth when she saw Bryan's name on the screen. Since the night they spent in Aruba, Julz tried her best to stay away from him, but he didn't make it easy for her to do. The man sent flowers daily, along with good morning texts, causing her to blush while giving her the energy she didn't know was needed to jump start her day. What broke her down completely was Jamiah FaceTiming her, expressing how much she'd missed Julz. That alone had her and Bryan spending many days together, taking Jamiah out to enjoy herself.

"Hello, beautiful," Bryan said the moment the call connected. "Are you busy?"

"No, I'm just straightening up after a long day of nonstop work. What's up with you?"

"I'm about to leave the center soon. I had a mentoring session with some of the young boys today. I'm in my office and you were on my mind, so I figured I'd give you a call. Plus, it's kind of late and I wanted to know if you received a delivery today?"

"I know you didn't buy me anything. We talked about this, Bryan. It's not necessary because I'm already your woman."

Realizing what she'd said, Julz put her head in her hand without saying another word. She was saved by the sound of knocking. Checking the Ring app to see who was at the door unannounced, Julz could see the UPS worker standing with several packages. She hated when people were allowed into the building without being buzzed in by the person they were attempting to see.

"Bryan——"

"Don't say nothing. Just open the door, Julz."

"Make this the last time you purchase anything else."

"Open the door, woman," Bryan laughed.

Julz did as he asked, greeting the delivery guy with a smile. In total, there were six boxes on a pulley by the door. Julz placed her AirPod in her left ear to free her hands. After all the packages were placed inside, Julz thanked him and closed the door. She reached for one of the boxes, using a letter opener to cut the tape along the seam. Julz yelped when she pulled out a pink Birkin bag.

"No, you didn't! Oh my God! Thank you so much," Julz exclaimed.

"You're welcome. There's more. Carry on."

Opening the packages one by one, Bryan could hear the happiness in her voice, and he loved it. Bryan went all out for Julz. He bought her a pair of Christian Louboutin heels to match her bag, a Mac Pro laptop, a pair of diamond earrings with a matching tennis bracelet, and lastly a small round box of fifteen pink forever roses.

"Thank you so much! There hasn't been a man I've ever dated who knew pink was my favorite color. I love how you pay attention to detail."

"You are so welcome. I will forever pay attention to your likes and dislikes. You are special, Julie."

"Aht Aht! Don't ever call me that hillbilly shit. I haven't been Julie since high school. Put some respect on my name."

"My bad, baby. I will never call you by your gov'ment again. Let me get off this phone and take my ass home. I'm glad I could put a smile on your face."

"Be safe, Bryan. I'll talk to you soon." Ending the call, Julz snapped pictures of her gifts and sent them in the group text to Icy and Kia.

Julz: Come to my house! I need to gush over these gifts with somebody. Plus, we need to catch up.

The text notification pinged immediately.

Icy: OMG! You must've gave Bryan some of that pussy! He didn't hold back at the fuck all! I'm on my way. I just left Blaze.

A few minutes later, Kia chimed in.

Kia: Icy, go home and change your clothes. We're about to hit the club. Julz need to shake her ass and mingle before Bryan lock her down.

Icy: That sounds like a plan. Julz, I'll be there within the hour. We can hit up Insatiable. There's supposed to be a huge party tonight. I heard it on WGCI a few minutes ago.

Julz: I'm down. Let me go in here and get cute. I'll see y'all soon. Oh, how is Staci? I haven't been to see her this week.

Kia: I just left there. We need to talk about some shit that went down today. We'll get into that when we're together. Who's driving?

Icy: I am, of course. My man just copped me an Audi truck. It's time to floss around this bitch.

Kia: You bitches trying to make my ass jealous, huh?

Julz: I'm sure Joe has something up his sleeve for you, Kia.

When she didn't get a reply, Julz assumed Kia and Joe were still at odds. She rushed to the bathroom to take care of her hygiene. It was after seven in the evening, but there was a party at the club, and they would have to get there early to get a seat. It didn't take long for Julz to shower. She got out and wrapped a towel around her body and plugged in the curling iron. As she waited for it to heat up, Julz went to her closet to choose an outfit for the night. Sifting through her clothes, she decided on something simple because it was cold outside. A pair of black high-waisted jeans, a low-cut black blouse and the new heels Bryan gifted her were what she settled for. Julz also made sure to wear the jewelry to set the outfit off. Julz decided to tell Bryan her plans for the night before finishing up her look.

Julz: I'm going to Insatiable with Icy and Kia. In case you call and I don't answer.

Bryan: You know it's not safe for y'all to go out, right?

Julz: We've been sitting back for weeks. We need to go out and have a little fun. Our lives have to keep going, Bryan.

Bryan: Aight. Thanks for letting me know. I appreciate that.

Julz was glad he didn't say anything further. She knew he was concerned, but nothing was going to happen to them in a public setting. Sitting on the side of the bed, she slipped on a lacy bra and panty set. Julz dressed then went back into the bathroom to add big curls to her hair. As she unplugged the device, the sound of a horn beeping continuously outside caused Julz to shake her head. Walking into the bedroom, she slipped her feet into her heels before grabbing her phone from the bed to call the culprit behind the noise.

"Icy, what I tell you about doing that? You're not going to be happy until somebody calls the police on your ass!"

"Stop it, Karen," Icy laughed. "You live in the hood. Ain't no damn police coming to this muthafucka. Bring yo' ass!"

Icy hung up and Julz could do nothing but laugh right along with her long-time friend. Gathering her purse and keys, Julz slipped on a pink furry vest that went well with her outfit and made her way out of the apartment. When she got outside, "Just Wanna Rock" by Lil Uzi Vert was blaring from the speakers. Stopping in her tracks, Julz started dancing like she was already at the club. The passenger door opened, and Sean jumped out to dance with her.

"Ayyeeeee, get it, Sean!"

Sean wore a blue jeaned outfit with a fitted black shirt underneath. His spiked hair was dyed pink at the tips. He looked good and he knew it. Julz loved it when Sean was around for the party. He made the night one to remember with his vibrant attitude, and fun-loving personality. Sean had his arm in the air as he twerked better than most women.

"Fuck it up!" Icy yelled over the music.

Kia pulled up and parked on the street, then joined in on the fun. The song ended, causing them to pile into the truck. Before Kia could get her foot on the runner, one of Julz's neighbors thought it was okay to say something smart.

"This ain't no damn block party! Get away from this building before I call the police!"

"Girl, fuck you with yo' uptight ass! Have that same energy when Main is whoopin' yo ass!"

"Whew, chile! You did not have to serve her like that," Sean squealed while clapping his hands. "Where was the lie though? I can't wait for the weather to break, because babyyyyy, Main gon' be in rare form with the bitches."

"Y'all messy as hell," Julz laughed.

Icy drove out of the lot as she listened to Sean and Kia clown Main and his relationship drama. Heading in the direction of the club, traffic was semi-heavy but nothing she had to worry about. It would still be rather early once they reached Insatiable.

"What did you want to tell us about the hospital visit, Kia? Is my mama alright?" Icy asked.

"First and foremost, Staci told me to tell you two hoes, her words," Kia threw her hands up in defense. "She don't appreciate only seeing one of us today."

"Yeah, she's feeling better." Icy rolled her eyes as she continued to drive. "I'll make sure to go up there tomorrow."

"You better, and you too, Julz! Anyway, I had to smack a bitch at Staci's crib earlier."

"Say what now?"

Icy glanced into the review mirror briefly astonished by what Kia had said.

"Why didn't you call us?" Julz asked.

"I didn't have time for all that. I handled the shit. Now, are y'all ready to listen or not?"

"Go 'head. I have a feeling you've added another dilemma to the shit we already have on our plate."

Kia waved Icy's comment off like it was nothing as Sean turned in his seat to hang off every word that came out of Kia's mouth. Icy may have spoken the truth, seeing Kia allowed the woman to leave with her life. It was nothing for Kia to lay her ass down where she stood, whenever the opportunity presented itself again.

"According to this broad, she hung out with Staci back in the day. She claimed to be Kenny's woman. Talking about she was looking for him and came to talk about his disappearance with Staci as a last resort."

"That don't sound right," Julz said, shaking her head. "She should've come to his family first."

"Same thing I told her ass! Regardless, the bitch lied about who she was, because Staci don't know her. When I run into her again, it's on and poppin'. I'm gon' kill her ass, which I should've done on sight. Instead, I gave her the benefit of a doubt that she was telling the truth."

Icy drove as she tried to figure out who would come to her mama's house pretending to be a former friend. It was time for Icy to find a place and move her mother away from the home her daddy had built from the ground for them. Convincing Staci to leave the only thing she had left of her late husband besides Icy was going to be a challenge, but it had to be done. Icy had to make sure they were safe when sleeping at night. Making a mental note to discuss the move with Blaze later, she checked back in on the conversation.

"What name did this woman use?" Julz asked.

"Julian."

Soon as Kia said the name, Icy swerved a little bit because the name was one she would never forget. She was surprised the shit didn't click in Kia's mind when she heard it. Leo had more people than Icy thought working with him, and that alone was an advantage for them and fucked for her family. The women were in the dark about a lot of things and the shit was terrifying to say the least. The way her adrenaline was rushing, she wanted to kill somebody just for the fun of it.

"Kia, how did you let that name fly over your head? Julian is the bitch who claimed the body at the morgue before we could confirm it was really Leo. She was probably there to kill one of us and you let her walk. She's affiliated with Leo's stupid ass!"

"Oh, shit! The name didn't ring a bell until you just mentioned it! Fuck, that was a missed opportunity, and the shit went right over my damn head."

Icy was pissed off. Kia could've been a victim of a homicide. She was glad nothing happened, but the muthafuckas were playing closely in their faces and getting away with the shit. It was a must for them to tighten up and get the ball rolling on Leo because they were losing at that point. By the grace of God, no one else has been hurt or killed.

"Why would she ask about Kenny? Nobody knew he was missing, outside of family. His whereabouts are for damn sure unknown. Are you sure my mama doesn't know this woman? She knows far too much about my people."

"Staci was adamant about not knowing her. She wasn't under any medication at the time, and I believe her too. This Julian bitch looks a couple years older than us. Staci ain't hangin' with nobody damn near the age of her daughter. She's not even that type of mama." Kia replied. "As far as Kenny, I don't know what was going on with them, but the shit don't sit well with me. Her involvement with Leo gives me a vibe I can't explain."

Icy signaled to turn into the parking lot of the club while tapping the steering wheel. She couldn't get her mind off the target that was placed on her back. It wasn't the time to be afraid. The time had come for Icy to formulate a plan to end everything once and for all. Leo knew Staci was Icy's weakness, and he kept coming for her in the worse way. That shit was about to end.

She lucked up and found a spot close to the entrance. Kia talked Icy into smoking as she put a blunt in rotation. The conversation about Julian came to a halt when everybody noticed how quiet Icy had become. Whenever she wanted to discuss the matter at hand, Kia would be ready to listen. Until then, they were going to have the time of their lives in the club and enjoy themselves. They all needed it.

Icy felt good as she opened the door to her truck. The cold air hit her in the face, causing her body to shiver. She opted to leave her coat behind, so rushing toward the building was her main focus.

"Slow down, Icy," Sean called out behind her.

Ignoring him, Icy moved forward while observing the line that had formed outside the club. There was no way she could stand in the cold for too long, but there wasn't any other option. Icy headed to the end of the line when Kia's voice stopped her.

"Where you going, Ice? We going straight in."

The words Kia had spoken were music to her ears. Icy could hear the murmurs of some of the ladies that were waiting to get inside, but she didn't acknowledge that shit because she wasn't about to be standing with their asses. When Icy got to the door, Kia was talking to one of the bouncers with a smile. Kia knew some of everybody in the city and sometimes it was a good thing, while others not so much. They were ushered inside a few minutes later and there were many people in the club. Kia had sweet talked the bouncer into getting them a VIP section and he made the shit happen. Icy was glad because she really didn't want to be surrounded by people she knew nothing about. Being in the section gave her the ability to enjoy her night with the girls peacefully. The view was spectacular, and the entire club could be seen from where they were seated. Julz wasted no time waving a bottle girl over to order tequila.

"Add another bottle to that. We about to turn the fuck up!" Sean said as he handed over his debit card, then looked down at his phone.

"No, one would be enough. You know our situation, Sean. We have to stay alert."

"I agree with Icy on this one," Kia chimed in. "One bottle is enough for the four of us."

Sean was about to respond when a group of females entered their section. Icy, Julz, and Kia's head swiveled quickly and Icy jumped to her feet once she realized who they were. Sean smiled because he knew Icy's night was about to be better than ever.

"What the hell y'all doing here?"

Shonda stepped forward and hugged her boss tightly. "I've missed you so much. We wanted to see you since you haven't been to the shops lately. Sean called, telling us to come outside and we did just that. We're closing the shops tomorrow because we partying tonight!"

Icy's entire crew from all three locations were present to have fun with her. She didn't mind them shutting down her business for a day. They deserved a break just like she did. With all that had happened, Icy was all for living life to the best of your ability. The world had changed so much that Icy planned to live her life to the fullest for as long as she could. For the first time in months, Icy was smiling in public without Blaze by her side.

After hugs and cheek kisses, the party started, and the club was filling up. The DJ was on the hits, causing the group to finally turn up. Their drinks arrived and Kia poured up the shots. Icy noticed Shonda had sat down with her face buried in her phone. The expression on her face showed what type of mood she was in and also let Icy know something was wrong. Sitting next to Shonda, Icy took a deep breath.

"You good?" she asked with concern.

"Al has been texting nonstop. I've been keeping away from him for weeks, but he doesn't seem to understand I'm done. The last time I was out of the shop, he beat me so bad I was in the hospital for two weeks."

Shonda wiped her eyes, refusing to look at Icy. She was embarrassed because Al hadn't changed, even though Shonda thought he would. Instead, the abuse had gotten worse. She'd promised Icy if he put his hands on her again, she would leave. It took for him to beat her to the point of miscarrying, along with bleeding on the brain, to say enough was enough. Al basically almost killed Shonda before she opened her eyes to leave him alone.

"Why didn't you call me, Shonda?"

"You have your own shit to worry about. Had I listened the first time, I wouldn't be living my life in fear today."

Icy hugged Shonda close as she cried. "We will figure something out tomorrow, okay? For now, dry your face, take a shot, and enjoy yourself. Stop responding to his ass. Fuck Albert James with his punk ass. These niggas need to learn how to let muthafuckas go when their time is up."

"I hear you, Boss Lady. I'm sorry for bringing the vibe down."

"You haven't done anything wrong, so stop apologizing and dance with me."

Beyonce's "Cuff It" filled the club as Icy pulled Shonda from the chair. All the girls stood in the middle of the floor doing the viral *Tik Tok* dance.

"We gon' fuck up the night!" they all yelled in unison.

The song ended and Sean needed to use the restroom. He left everyone behind dancing as he made his way down the steps and into the crowd. It warmed his heart to see Icy having fun again. Moving through the many partygoers, Sean's arm was grabbed from behind and whoever was trying to handle him had a firm grip on his shit. Snatching away, ready to fuck somebody up, he spun around quickly with his fist balled up. Sean came face-to-face with Jamal, better known as J-Rock on the streets. Rolling his eyes, Sean didn't even address his ass before turning back in the direction of the restrooms. Soon as he entered the empty space, J-Rock started talking his shit.

"Why haven't you answered my calls?"

"The real question is, why are you worried about it? Yo' bitch is the person you should be questioning. For a muthafucka who don't want his secret exposed, why the fuck you hounding me? I'm not your bitch. You don't have that right."

"I'm not hounding. I just don't like to be ignored. And what the hell Ariel got to do with us?"

"There's no *us*, nigga. You have a woman, and it would be best for you to talk to her ass, because she got one more time to come to my place of business to look in my face. Keep her ass away from me before I forget I was born a man. Tell that girl the truth, Jamal. You like boy pussy. Why the fuck are you leading her on?" Sean turned his back to piss.

J-Rock strained his neck to watch as Sean pulled his dick out his pants. His mouth watered at the sight of his favorite piece of chocolate. Using Ariel as a cover-up was becoming a harder task to master for J-Rock, because he really wanted Sean to be by his side full-time. He would never get what he wanted because his reputation was too important to live in his truth publicly. The niggas who worked for him would test him at every turn and get fucked up in the process by thinking he was a soft muthafucka. Even having sex with Ariel was difficult because her pussy didn't feel anything like Sean's back door action. Envisioning his male lover during the act was getting old, the shit just didn't make him cum anymore.

"Let me taste that," J-Rock said seductively.

"Come over later. I would hate to blow up yo' spot if somebody decided to enter this bathroom while you bobbing on my shit. You getting sloppy, Jamal," Sean laughed.

The door opened and J-Rock pretended to wash his hands at the sink. Sean chuckled to himself as he shook his pipe and tucked it back in his jeans. The nigga that entered went to the stall, but Sean got a good look at him before he disappeared. He knew exactly who it was, and his heart fluttered with excitement, damn near beating out of his chest. Rushing to wash his hands, Sean had to get out of there before the nigga came out of the stall.

"You good?"

"Yeah, hit me up. I have to get to my girls," Sean whispered then left J-Rock standing by the sinks alone.

Sean couldn't get back to Icy fast enough. He was moving like he was trying to burn a hole in his Balenciaga sneakers. Seeing Boom in the bathroom didn't scare Sean, it put him in protective mode immediately. If he was in the club, that meant Leo wasn't too far behind. Stepping back into the section, Sean focused on Icy until he was close enough to drag her into a corner.

"What's going on, boo?" Icy asked.

"I just saw Boom in the bathroom. Icy, we might have to beat this nigga's ass if he tries something. Leo has to be in the building too."

"Sean, we are going to enjoy the night. Fuck Boom and fuck Leo! I don't give a damn if they're in this bitch!"

Kia could hear Icy's voice over the music and made a dash across the room. When she made it to her sister, the DJ stopped the music and screamed in the mic. Everybody stood still to listen to what he had to say.

"Boom! Long time no see, nigga! Insatiable has missed you and the crew."

Boom waved the DJ off as he blended in with the crowd. Kia surveyed the room, trying to spot Boom and her eyes landed on Joe, standing by the bar with a light-skinned bitch hanging onto his arm. The way he glared at Boom, let her know he was ready to start some shit. The woman was rubbing on his chest and that enraged Kia more than learning about Boom's presence. Whispering in Joe's ear, Kia could tell there was something intimate going on between the two and she didn't like that shit one bit. Icy peeped what Kia was looking at and decided it was time to go.

"Come on. Boom is on the other side of the club, let's get out of here. I'm quite sure Joe has already called Blaze and I don't want to be in the middle of a bloodbath."

"Not until I go holla at this nigga," Kia said, heading for the stairs.

Icy stepped in front of her, shaking her head. "We are not about to entertain these people in this club. Save that shit between you and Joe for another day. He doesn't look too into her anyway."

Icy and her girls made their way to the exit. Shonda led the pack, along with Cerita and Sean. Kia and Julz boxed her in, and the rest of the girls took up the back. Out of her peripheral vision, Icy could see Joe walking in their direction with the bitch close on his heels. She tried her best to keep Kia under control and she took heed and kept moving forward. The crowd dispersed once they realized the coast was clear outside and went to their vehicles. Icy gave Kia the keys to her truck while she hollered at Shonda.

"Call me once you get to your destination. Be careful, Shonda. We will go out tomorrow and get you set up in an apartment. I can't have you running from this nigga a day longer."

"Thank you so much. I truly appreciate you," Shonda said, hugging Icy.

"Go ahead and get in the car. Don't forget to call me."

Nodding her head with a smile, Shonda walked away and headed across the lot. A vehicle entered and stopped behind her car as she reached for the door. The moment Shonda opened the door, the driver in the car riddled her body with bullets then sped away without worry. The shit happened so fast, Icy thought she was dreaming until she saw her friend sprawled on the pavement with blood oozing from beneath her. The sounds of screams snapped Icy out of the trance she was in, and she ran toward Shonda. When she pushed her way through the small space, Icy fell to her knees and cradled Shonda's head in her lap.

"Stay with me, boo. You gon' be alright," Icy talked to her while rubbing her head, not believing anything she'd said as she watched blood fall from Shonda's mouth as she tried to speak. "Don't say nothing. Just keep your eyes open."

Shonda's eyes rolled to the back of her head and Icy slapped her cheek repeatedly until she opened them again. Her heart stopped for a second because she thought she'd lost her friend. Icy knew Al was behind the shooting because Shonda didn't fuck with anyone, and she didn't have beef with nobody except his jealous ass.

"Icy, I love you."

"Shhhhhh. Save your energy and stay with me."

"Al…it was Al," she coughed, spraying blood into the air. "He finally made good on his promise. I'm gonna die, Icy. I can't hold on."

"You have to! We are going to get you a new place. Plus, the ambulance is here. I know you hear the sirens. Hold on a little longer. Squeeze my hand."

Icy rocked back and forth, waiting for Shonda to do just that. When she looked down, Shonda's eyes were closed, and her chest wasn't going up and down anymore. Icy placed her fingers on the side of her neck and let out a loud wail when she didn't feel a pulse. Laying her on the ground, Icy started chest compressions until her arms were tired. Shonda took her last breath while in Icy's arms, but Icy wasn't giving up.

"She's gone, Ice. You have to let the paramedics do their job," Sean sorrowfully said, pulling her up by the arm.

Icy was covered in Shonda's blood and the smell was sickening. Joe walked over and kept looking at the entrance door. Icy wasn't in the right head space for Joe and Kia's shit, but she knew Joe felt he needed to watch over her in Blaze's absence. The woman he was with, stood further back from where they were.

"Look, are you okay?" Icy shook her head no, wiping the tears from her face. "I hit Blaze up and he is on his way. I can't wait around for him, because I have to bust this move. Would you take Joye home for me?"

Icy looked at Joe like he had three heads instead of one. He must've forgot what type of woman Kia was. There was no way the two of them could ride in the same car together with his ass being the common denominator.

"Joe, that wouldn't be a wise thing for me to do. Plus, there's four of us in my vehicle. Order her an Uber and I'll make sure she gets in it. I'm sorry, chancing her and Kia in close proximity is a hell no for me. As a matter of fact, I'll have Blaze take her home."

Joe saw Boom exit the club and walked swiftly toward his whip. Just as he made it, Blaze pulled up and jumped out of his rental. Without a word, he handed Icy his keys and ran behind Joe. Icy didn't have to guess what they were on because she knew. Boom wasn't parked too far from where she stood. Glaring at her, he smirked and pointed his fingers in the gesture of a gun. He motioned as if he pulled the trigger and laughed. She smiled evilly because Boom was fucking with her, but he had signed his own death sentence when he decided to come out to Insatiable to have a good time.

"I'm about to put one in this nigga's head," Kia snarled as she moved in the direction Boom's car was parked.

"No, the fuck you not! Blaze and Joe are on it. I need you to drive my car. I have to do a favor for Joe. Don't say shit. Go to my mama's and wait for me. We'll talk when I get there."

Kia stared the woman down, then checked herself. She didn't have a right to be mad at her because nine times out of ten, she didn't know a damn thing about what her and Joe had going on. She was going to walk away and take shit up with his ass. One thing Kia wasn't for was a nigga trying to pull one over on her. She thought Joe was an outspoken muthafucka who told the truth, but here he was parading around with another bitch, after fucking Kia into submission in Aruba.

"This nigga got me fucked up," Kia said to herself as she climbed in the driver's seat of Icy's Audi.

Chapter 8

Boom was pissed he couldn't get close to Icy. The chick getting shot in the parking lot was bad timing for him. He went to Insatiable because of a dip-off he was meeting up with. When he saw Sean's sweet ass in the bathroom with that nigga J-Rock, Boom knew Icy was somewhere in the building. He laughed to himself when Rock tried to act like he was washing his muthafuckin' hands. Something was going on between the two of them, but Boom couldn't prove the shit. The truth was going to come out sooner than later and J-Rock wouldn't be allowed to bark another day in the streets. Better take his down-low ass to the northside with that bullshit.

As he watched things unfold in the parking lot, Boom took his chance to leave the premises before the cops locked the scene down. Icy, with her fine ass, followed his every move and Boom wanted her to know his eyes her were on her too. He gestured in her direction with a finger gun, and the bitch laughed at him.

Boom climbed in his whip and made his way back to the southside, not noticing he was being followed. He was going to shawty's crib on 86th and Damen so she could suck his dick. He felt bad for having her getting all dressed up, just to tell her he wasn't going to the club. Boom made a mental note to contact her when he was in the vicinity so she could open the door. His pipe hardened as he thought about what he was sure would be in store for him.

Nipsey's "Hussle & Motivation" filled the car soon as he turned on the radio. He hit the expressway, leaving the other cars in the dust. Boom thought about Leo and everything they were going through with the whole Icy situation. To him, Leo was taking things too far because he already had a wife, and was still chasing after Icy because she was with that nigga Blaze. Jealousy was a sickness and it had Leo by the balls because he didn't like to lose. They were safe to do whatever Leo had in mind since Zan was locked up and he was one muthafucka Boom didn't have to worry about while getting the job done. It would be hell to pay if he was rolling in the streets freely.

In the car two cars behind Boom, Blaze couldn't wait to get his hands on the nigga. As they neared the 31st Street exit on the Dan Ryan, he came up with a plan. He looked at Joe and smiled.

"Aye, you got a nail gun in this muthafucka?"

"Yeah, it's in the back on the floor. Why?" Joe asked, puzzled.

"I'm about to force this nigga to pull over. I'm gon' blow out his back tire," Blaze said as he turned to get what he inquired about. He instructed Joe to get on the left side of Boom's whip and let his window down. Joe made sure he stayed parallel with the back of the car. Blaze let off a couple shots, making sure he hit his target. Once he was satisfied, he sat back while Joe slowed down a little. They watched as Boom cruised on the expressway with no worries. Blaze was cussing under his breath because his plan must've faltered. He prayed the shit worked because he didn't want to do a drive-by to kill Boom. He wanted his muthafuckin' ass to see death coming.

As they neared 79th, Boom's back wheel started wobbling. He kept going until they reached 87th and he signaled to get off with his hazard lights flashing. Joe followed suit. There weren't many cars on the street, and it played out in Blaze's favor. Boom made a right turn and pulled into the parking lot of the plaza. At one o'clock in the morning, all the stores were closed. Boom got out of the car and inspected the tire while running his hand over the top of his head. Pushing on the tire, he popped the trunk and buried his head inside.

"Always watch your surroundings, nigga. You got caught slippin'," Blaze snarled as he cocked the Glock he held to the back of his head. Boom lifted up slightly, which caused him to get wacked with the butt of the gun. Hitting him again, Boom fell to the ground. Joe backed his car closer to the trunk of Boom's car and both he and Blaze dumped him in Joe's trunk.

"Let's take this nigga somewhere and get some information out of him. We gon' beat his ass until he gives us something on that nigga Leo."

"I'm with you when you right. This nigga gon' sing like a bird once I put my foot in his ass," Joe laughed. "Since we're over here, we gon' do this shit in the Dan Ryan woods. Then leave his ass stankin'."

Both Blaze and Joe got in the car and flamed up for the ride. They turned the music up just in case Boom decided to wake up from his nap, wanting to cry like a bitch for attention. It took about ten minutes for them to enter the wooded area. Joe drove until he was deep inside the area before he cut the ignition. Pulling his gun from his hip, he went to the trunk and hit the key fob. Boom was waiting with a crowbar in hand. He swung soon as the trunk went up and missed. Joe's reflexes were on point because he punched Boom dead center in the face, and he dropped the tool. Blaze reached inside and grabbed him by the collar, dragging his ass out headfirst.

"Nigga, you must've lost yo' muthafuckin' mind," Joe spat at Boom angrily. "What the fuck were you doing at Insatiable?"

"What the fuck was everybody else doing there? I was trying to have a good time," Boom said humorously.

"Get naked, nigga!" Joe barked.

"I'm not on that gay——" Blaze kicked Boom in the head, causing him to roll over on his stomach.

"You tried it, bitch! Now do what the fuck I told you to do."

Joe stood back fuming. Boom had the audacity to throw that homo shit at him and he wanted to blow his shit back right then and there. He chilled because the nigga was the key to getting to the big fish. The thought of what happened to Kia crossed Joe's mind, heightening his anger even higher. Even though they weren't on the best of terms, her wellbeing was still important to Joe. He would have to address the Joye situation soon, because Kia wasn't going to take that shit lying down. Joe would be ready for whatever though. Boom stood in the frigid cold with his hands over his package as if that was the focal point of the business at hand.

"Check it, where the fuck is Leo?" Blake flat out asked.

"Ion know where that nigga at." Boom lied with a straight face. Blaze reached in his pocket and removed a silencer. Screwing the attachment to the end of his gun, Boom turned to run and was shot in the ass. Joe laughed as he walked in the direction he fell.

"Nigga, where you going? That was just a warning shot. The next one gon' lead you to the light. Now, where the fuck is Leo?"

"Leo got a crib in Glencoe. He is living with a bitch that will kill you on sight named Julian, his wife. He never loved Icy. Leo was using her for the shit he did to her pops. Now, he is going hard to kill her and the whole family, because she stole everything from him when he faked his death."

Boom let everything fall from his lips like diarrhea. The information was lucrative, but Blaze needed more. There were many houses in Glencoe, and he wanted the address. Before he could ask another question, Boom started spilling more without being told.

"Y'all can find Pip on 59th and Loomis."

"Back the fuck up, nigga. What's the address to Leo's spot?" Blaze shot back. Given the address, Joe programmed it into his phone for safe keeping.

"I'm trying to live, man. So, I'm going to tell y'all everything. Leo was behind everything. He ran Icy's mama off the road and he shot up Kia's crib too. He had the detective that arrested Icy to plant the bomb in her car at the airport. Don't go looking for her because Julian killed the bitch a few days ago. Her body must not have been found because I haven't heard anything about it on the news. If Icy gives him the money back and sign his properties back over to him, Leo will leave her alone."

"That shit ain't happening," Blaze laughed. "His punk ass owes her that plus some for the way he played on her feelings. So, he can forget about that shit."

"One last thing," Boom paused. "Leo is set to go to Kingston next month. He said he's going to get what Duke promised him and he is planning to kill yo' mama to get it."

Hearing that flared Blaze's nose. He wasn't prepared for that much information. His mother didn't have shit to do with any of this shit. Duke's money wasn't even in her possession, and she would've been killed for nothing, because Blaze was the one Leo would have to see to obtain the money he was obsessed with getting his hands on. Kenise was sitting on a nest egg, but not enough to lose her life over.

"You told me everything Leo has done, now tell me what part yo' bitch ass played in all this," Blaze snarled. "You ain't innocent by far. I've detected one lie you've told already. What makes you think I believe the other shit you told?"

"I haven't lied about nothing!"

"Bitch, *yo ass* shot up Kia's house after she put a muthafuckin' gun in yo' face!" Joe snapped. "You may not have been at Insatiable to fuck with Icy, but I saw what the fuck you did to her in the parking lot, nigga. And that alone is why you ended up in the back of my shit. Enough of this questioning bullshit, is there anything else you want to tell a couple of real niggas?"

"Y'all gon' let me go, right?" Boom pleaded more than asked.

Both Blaze and Joe looked at one another and nodded their heads yes. Boom rolled his naked body on the snow-covered grass and thanked God for sparing his life. He knew giving up Leo would be his saving grace and it paid off. Standing to his feet, Boom reached down for his clothes to put them on. When he looked up there were three pistols pointed in his direction.

Blaze held one, and Joe wanted to go all in on the snake standing in front of him.

"If you can lie with a straight face, we can too, nigga," Blaze smirked. "Tell mi fada mi luv him. Dance with the Devil when he kills yo' ass at the pearly gates."

Bullets pierced Boom's body at a high rate of speed. His body shook profusely, and he looked like he was dancing instead of dying. Boom fell flat on his back and Joe walked over reloading his clip and emptied it in his face. It had been a long time since he'd ended anyone's life. The feeling of his past life resonated through his bloodstream automatically, making him apologize mentally to the man that saved him from the life he lived back in the day. Joe had to do what needed to be done in order to live on a righteous path. He didn't regret one bullet he sent into Boom's body. There were several more to come and he was ready to end it all or die trying.

Chapter 9

Cherelle hadn't heard from Zan and her nerves were on edge. She tried calling the number he'd called her from, but all her attempts went unanswered. She stopped reaching out because in her mind, the CO's probably shook him down and confiscated the device. Not knowing was the hard part with having a loved one in the prison system. Waiting for communication was the only thing Cherelle could do and she was sitting on pins and needles as the days passed.

Since the incident with Sam, Cherelle stayed at home to be a mother to Zymia and left her brothers to run the everyday business at Zone Out. The dispensary was popular as fuck and doing better than Cherelle ever imagined. Being a business owner was hard work, but she held shit down best she could on behalf of her man. Allowing Zan's hard work to go down the drain was one thing she was not going to let happen.

"Cherelle, get the door for me. I have Zymia in the tub," her mother yelled, bringing her out of the thoughts she'd gotten lost in.

"Okay. I'm getting up now."

Cherelle had been at her mother's for about a week. Being in the house she shared with Zan was lonely as fuck. She couldn't deal with the silence that surrounded her when she was there. Her mother suggested she come to her home for a while and Cherelle took her up on the offer. As she neared the door, she could see a silhouette on the other side of the glass paned window but couldn't make out who it was. The bell sounded again, followed by a series of hard knocks in a rhythm only one person would do. Cherelle almost broke her wrist trying to unlock the door.

"Surprise, beautiful."

Zan smiled, showing all thirty-two of his white teeth. Holding two dozen purple roses, dressed in a black Moncler coat and a beanie. Cherelle jumped in his arms, planting kisses all over his face. Zan laughed aloud at the way she greeted him. It felt good to finally hold her close. When he felt the wetness from her tears, he knew it was time for him to love on his wife properly. With Cherelle's legs still latched around his waist, Zan moved into the house out of the cold. Using his foot, he closed the door behind them.

"Cherelle, who was at the door?" her mother asked as she came down the stairs with Zymia in her arms. "Oh, my God! Is that my baby, Zan?"

"It's me, Ma," Zan said, putting the flowers on the table by the door. "Baby, let me go so I can show my mama some love."

"Nope. I need all the love I've missed out on since January first."

Zan laughed as he tapped Cherelle on her plump ass, then pried her arms from his neck. Once he was free, he gave Charlene a long hug, because he missed her just as much as he missed his wife and daughter. Zymia reached out and touched his face and it melted his heart instantly. Backing out of his mother-in-law's arms, he reached for the baby and she damn near leaped to her daddy.

"Hey, daddy's girl," Zan cooed. "I've missed you like crazy. Have you been a good girl?"

Zymia laughed loudly and cuffed both of Zan's cheeks in her little hands. She gave him the biggest slobbery kiss she could muster up, bringing tears to her father's eyes. The entire time he was away, Zan prayed he wasn't sentenced to life in prison. Not being there to see his daughter grow up was the worst feeling in the world for a man to have. Knowing he wasn't guilty of the charges against him, Zan had plans to fight for his freedom even if it broke him in the process. Sitting on the sofa, Zan continued to kiss and hug on his baby.

"Cherelle, how are the businesses holding up?"

"Better than when you were overseeing them. I put my foot down and got all of your employees working like those kids in the foreign countries. I cut their pay and everything. More money for us."

Zan looked at her as if she had lost her damn mind. He had never underpaid any of his workers and didn't think Cherelle would do that shit either. When she didn't laugh and say she was kidding, Zan cocked his head to the side because he was beyond pissed at the moment.

"Baby, please tell me you didn't do what you just said. That was a joke, right?" Both Zan and Charlene waited for Cherelle to respond.

"I'm just bullshitting. I did go in all your establishments and explained what I expected from each and every one of them and they understood the assignment. I haven't had any problems at all."

"You almost made me mad enough to choke yo' ass," Zan said, shaking his head. "Excuse my language, Mama."

"It's okay, baby. She would've deserved that lack of oxygen for a few minutes. I know you wouldn't kill her."

"Dang, Ma. You just gave him permission to put his hands on me!" Cherelle looked at her mother with a shocked expression.

"Girl, bye. Zan may be crazy, but he ain't stupid by far. He knows the dos and don'ts of being with you. He wasn't locked up long enough to forget." Charlene side-eyed him. "Give me my damn grandbaby so I can spend some time with her. I know you two muthafuckas gon' take her back to that big ass house since Zan is home."

Without waiting, she scooped Zymia up and hurried to the stairs as if they would take the baby away from her. Zan laughed as Cherelle sat next to him on the sofa. She placed her hand on top of his and caressed the back of it with her thumb. Glancing over her husband's attire for a few minutes, it dawned on Cherelle that he had on new everything, from the hat on his head to the shoes on his feet. That shit made her wonder how long he'd been out and who the hell brought clothes along in order for Zan to dress.

"Um, when did you get out?" Cherelle questioned.

"I've been out four days."

"And you're just coming to see me? What type of shit you on?" Cherelle asked furiously. "You had some bitch to pick you up or something?"

"Don't start that shit, Relle. You know damn well ain't no woman out here that can do a muthafuckin' thing for me except Icy," Zan retorted. "To answer your questions, me, Stack, and Smooth took the bus so nobody would know we were out. The less people to know, the better. In case you forgot, my brother isn't dead, and he got a hard-on for my ass. Baby, I had to stay under the radar. As far as the clothes are concerned, the shit been in the closet for the longest. Stop trippin'. I was home alone trying to clear my head. If you don't believe me, check the cameras."

Cherelle did just that. As she watched the footage, she felt bad for coming at Zan the way she had. She saw him plain as day walking around eating, and just lounging around watching television. Watching the full days was something she didn't have to do, because Zan had never lied to her about anything that would jeopardize their marriage. The street shit, yeah, but that was expected with the danger involved.

"I'm sorry."

"You have nothing to be sorry for. I love you too much to do something stupid, like fuckin' around with someone other than you."

Zan pulled Cherelle onto his lap facing him. Smothering her in kisses from her forehead to her luscious lips, he missed the intimacy they shared and was glad to be home to experience the feeling again. There was only so much he could do being they were in her mother's house, but Zan was ready to get his dick wet. He hadn't busted a nut since before he was locked up and it was long overdue. Zan savored the taste of his wife's mouth, then kissed his way to her chest. Lifting her shirt, he pulled one of her breasts from her bra and flicked her nipple with his tongue.

"Cherelle and Zan! Y'all too damn quiet down there!" Charlene yelled from upstairs. "Take that shit to y'all's place of residence because I bet not see no cum stains on my couch!"

Zan put Cherelle's breast back in her bra and pulled her shirt down while looking at the stairwell for her mother. He felt like a teenager sneaking into her house. Cherelle found the whole ordeal funny, but Zan didn't.

"What the hell you laughing for?" He playfully pushed her off him.

"She scared yo' ass and she's not even gonna come down here. That was your opportunity to get a quickie in."

"I wish you nasty bastards would! Respect my shit or get out my house!"

"We not doing nothing but talking, Ma," Zan said, trying to clear the air.

"That's all y'all better be doing. Got me up here screaming and done woke up my baby."

"That's not yo' baby though. She was produced from the very sperm you won't let me release."

Cherelle slapped Zan upside his head with wide eyes. She knew Charlene was about to come downstairs and beat his ass. Moving to the other end of the sofa away from his wife, Zan laughed as he listened to his mother-in-law stomp down the steps with a bat in her hand.

"Say that nasty shit again, Negro!" She raised her arm, causing Zan to fall back with his hands in the air.

"Gone with that crazy mess, Ma. I was just playing," Zan laughed, but hoped like hell she didn't swing. "I'm about to head out anyway. Yo' daughter safe for now."

"Where you about to go?" Cherelle asked.

"I'm going to see Icy. We need to talk about some shit. Is she at the house?"

Zymia started whining, so Charlene left the two to talk for the second time to tend to her. She didn't want to hear anything about what Zan had going on with his brother. The only time she would get involved was if the heat was brought to her front door.

"She moved out of that house, babe. I think she's been staying with Staci. Did you know Staci is in the hospital?"

"No, what's wrong with her?"

Cherelle told Zan what took place and he saw nothing but red. Leo was playing a deadly game with Icy and her family. He knew he had to get to Icy and fast.

"Is my phone here? I couldn't find it at the house."

"Yeah, I keep it with me. It's upstairs in my purse. Let me go get it for you."

Cherelle stood to her feet to get Zan's phone, leaving him sitting in the living room. He hated the fact of being locked up, while Icy had to endure the evil caused by his brother, without him. Zan was ready to do any and everything in his power to get her back to the life she loved living. There was no way Icy was happy with the dark cloud that continued to follow her every day. Cherelle returned with the device and handed it to Zan. He immediately went to Icy's contact information and made the call.

"Hello?"

Hearing Icy's voice, Zan smiled. He had always been her protector since the day he came into her life. After Leo killed the nigga he caught beating her, Icy became the little sister he never had. Everyone thought they were blood related, because the two were just that close. Zan loved her more than the muthafucka who promised never to hurt her.

"I need to see you, Ice."

"Zan?" she questioned.

"It's me, sis." Zan laughed. "Where you at?"

"I'm at the Marriot Hotel downtown," Icy said, giving him the address and room number. "I was going to see my mama, but I'll go after we meet. I can't wait to see you, bro. I've missed you so much."

"Likewise. I'm heading out now. I'll be there fast as traffic allows."

"Okay. Drive safely."

Zan ended the call and stood up from his seat on the couch. Cherelle walked over and hugged him, burying her head into his chest. She didn't want him to leave because she was afraid he wouldn't return. Leo was out for blood, and he was going to go after Zan soon as word hit the street he was released.

"I'll be back. We're going home because I want some of that pussy. Ma already said she would keep the baby."

"I got you. I need you to knock the dust off this thang," Cherelle grinned. Her face turned serious as she palmed her husband's face. "Please be careful."

"You know I'm always sharp when out in the streets. I have no mercy for anybody, not even my brother."

Zan kissed Cherelle passionately and left without saying goodbye. He got in his ride and drove toward the expressway to talk to Icy about all he knew about Leo and his bullshit.

***

Blaze sat in a chair by the window as Icy talked on the phone to Zan, Leo's brother. Before she received the call, he and Icy were discussing how she wanted to purchase a new home. Blaze smiled on the inside because he'd already started the process without Icy's knowledge. While she wanted to protect her mother by moving her where Leo wouldn't know their whereabouts, Blaze wanted to surprise her to start a new life together. The property he had purchased had more than enough room for Staci to move in with them. Blaze was going to convert half of the finished basement into a gym which he would ensure had everything Staci would need to further her rehabilitation process. The doctors had informed Icy that Staci was doing great with her therapy. Blaze wanted her to be able to continue comfortably with an in-home therapist. It would also ease his mind, as well as Icy's, knowing Staci was safe while recovering.

Blaze felt an uneasy feeling as he listened to Icy express how much she missed Leo's brother. To Icy, it may have meant nothing more than that, but Blaze felt as if the call could be a set-up to learn of Icy's whereabouts. His thought process was, how could Icy trust and be so loving to a man whose brother was trying to kill her at every turn? Blaze was ready to stress those very thoughts the moment she ended the call.

"You can't trust shit he has to say," Blaze barked. "Icy, you probably led Leo right to this muthafucka!"

Her head swiveled in Blaze's direction. She didn't appreciate how he was raising his voice, and Icy wasn't about to stay silent and allow him to think it was okay. She had done that enough in her lifetime, but she was no longer that girl.

"Lower your voice," Icy said calmly. "I won't tolerate the verbal abuse I'm experiencing right now. I've dealt with that type of shit in my past and it's a no for me. There isn't a law against speaking your mind, but you will do it respectfully. Especially when you're taking things out of context. Zan is not tracking me down on Leo's behalf. I would bet my life on that. Do you possibly think someone who has been sitting in jail for two months because of his brother, may I add, would turn around and help him get at me? I don't think so, Akoni."

Blaze agreed with Icy about the way he had snapped at her. His intentions were out of pure concern and his anger got the best of him. Icy's safety was what mattered to him the most, and he needed her to understand the type of people that were gunning for her.

"I apologize for the way I spoke to you. I hear all you said about this nigga, but that doesn't change my thought process on what I believe is the plot of him showing up."

"Zan would never hurt me. He has always been there for me. There aren't any hidden agendas behind him coming to see me. If anything, he has something of importance to share and I'm going to hear him out. That is the reason I didn't hesitate giving him my location. You have nothing to worry about, babe. You are welcome to sit in on the conversation. I'm not trying to hide anything from you."

"And I will definitely be right there with you."

Icy got up from the bed shaking her head and went into the bathroom. She loved how Blaze was there at every turn, but he was overexaggerating when it came to Zan. He had his motives all wrong and she understood. That's why she didn't come back with anything more to say. Blaze would see for himself that Zan was team Icy, one hundred percent. There was no reason to argue about a subject she already knew was legit. Blaze's phone chimed with a text from Amancia the moment the door closed behind Icy.

Amancia: It's either you talk to me, or I'll be paying you a visit.

Blaze: Don't play yourself into an ass whoopin'. I have nothing to say to you.

Amancia: I'm pregnant.

Blaze chuckled lowly. Icy called that shit early on. Amancia could say she was pregnant 'til she was blue in the face. It wasn't going to change how he felt because he knew in fact the imaginary baby couldn't possibly be his. Blaze purposely didn't respond. He didn't have time for the childish games Amancia wanted to play.

Amancia: So, you have nothing to say?

Amancia: I'm going to take you for all you're worth! You will help with this baby! I didn't come all the way here to be thrown to the side. You gon' see me, Akoni!

Blaze threw his phone on the bed and made a vow to himself that he wouldn't respond to anymore of Amancia's texts or calls. If she came to Chicago thinking she could convince him she was pregnant by him, Amancia was wrong. She needed to go back to Kingston and figure out who her child's father was, because he wasn't it. Blaze prevented her and Icy from getting into a full-blown fight at the salon, but if she showed up to the hotel, he was going to let Icy release some stress.

He waited a few minutes for Icy to return from the bathroom, then decided to go flame up before Zan made his appearance. The shit Amancia was on had Blaze mad as hell but he wasn't going to allow the bullshit to get to him. As he retrieved what he needed to ease his mind, Blaze went out onto the balcony. The chilly air didn't affect him because all the anger in his body kept him warm. He wanted to calm down so he could hear everything with a sound mind. Blaze didn't realize how long he'd been out in the cold until he heard a knock on the door.

Watching Icy open the door while Zan embraced her in a loving hug, Blaze made his entrance. Zan removed his coat and placed it on the table before approaching Blaze. *Stay cool, Akoni. Give this nigga a chance to explain why he's here for the sake of Icy,* he thought.

"What's up, man. I'm Zan."

Blaze looked down at Zan's hand without shaking it. "Blaze," was all he said.

Icy could feel the tension in the air and it was resonating off Blaze. She gave him a stern look, which didn't change her man's demeanor at all. Icy knew she had to get to the point before Blaze took the meeting to another level. If looks could kill, Zan would've been zipped in a body bag the way Blaze glared at him.

"Look, Blaze, I would be leery too if the brother of a nigga who was after my woman came to see her. I understand your protectiveness, because I feel the same way with Ice. I didn't come here to ruffle any feathers, I'm here to fill my sis in on what the fuck is going on. Hopefully, after I'm finished talking, the two of us can come to an agreement on how to get my brother off the streets for good."

"I'm not trying to get Leo off the streets. I have plans to make sure that nigga eat dirt for the rest of his life. Are you on board with that?"

"Regardless of what you think, I hate my brother for the shit he did. Leo would never get away with putting a hit out on me, lying on me about running an empire I walked away from, and let's not forget all the shit he wrapped Icy up in. So, to answer yo' question, I'm all for killing his ass. I've already asked the Big Dawg in the sky for forgiveness and also told my mama I was sorry the entire time I was locked up. He may be my brother, but the love is lost this way."

Icy stood biting her bottom lip because she heard everything Zan said. Blaze still appeared not to give one fuck. Instead of responding, he hiked his pants up and sat down with his eyes trained on Zan. Turning to Icy, Zan motioned for her to have a seat. He gave her a look that told her he was cool. Icy needed that confirmation from him. The last thing she wanted was for the two Alpha males to tear up the luxury suite she and Blaze were living in.

Icy broke the silence by clearing her throat. Shifting in her seat, she glanced between both men while rubbing her hands down her legs. When she opened her mouth to say something, Zan beat her to the punch.

"I came here to let you know what I found out while behind the wall. The person who was killed was supposedly Leo's twin. That was news to me, because from my understanding, my mother only had two children. I believe it's because dude looked just like his snake ass."

Icy wondered how there was another sibling, and no one knew of him. That was a mystery neither one of them would find out the details about. It was still a shock to know Leo used a blood relative to fake his own death. That showed he didn't give a damn about anybody but himself.

"I also know who the Julian bitch is. She's none other than Leo's wife. I'd never heard of her until Pip answered his phone unknowingly and I heard Leo spilling all the beans. Do you remember the day I was shot outside the trap?" Icy nodded her head, afraid of what she was about to learn. "Leo called that hit. The nigga actually sent somebody to end my fuckin' life."

Just thinking about the shit pissed Zan off all over again. Blaze sat back and sparked a blunt, handing it to him. Leo was a nothing ass muthafucka who that bitch named karma was going to attack full force.

"You need that more than me so I'm willing to share that shit," Blaze said. "If you don't mind me asking, what would make your own brother turn against you the way Leo did?"

Blowing smoke from his nose, Zan handed the blunt back to Blaze. "I told him I wanted out of the game, and he wasn't trying to hear that shit. To be honest with you, I was the brain behind his operation. When I left, Leo didn't know the first thing about the drug game on his own. He had already taken out the one man who had his back. Had he listened to everything Duke taught us, he would've been able to make money hand over fist on his own. But Leo got greedy and now he had nobody to turn to except Pip and Boom."

"He only has Pip because I blew Boom's face off," Blaze said nonchalantly as he inhaled smoke.

"That's what's up. One down and many to go. I want to get at that detective bitch too. I didn't appreciate how she was handling Icy."

Blaze laughed. "According to Boom, Julian took care of her after she didn't kill Icy in the explosion at the airport. I guess everybody you wanted is already taken care of."

"Nah, there's plenty of flesh still out there for my lead to burn through, the main one is my big brother. We all want a piece of that muthafucka, and we will definitely get our turn. Whoever gets their hands on him first, don't kill him. I have a warehouse where he will meet his maker."

Zan thought about the conversation he'd overheard when Julian stepped into the room during the call. There was something about her that told him she really didn't want to hurt Icy. She clowned Leo as if he was a joke.

"Are you sure there's nothing familiar about the Julian bitch, Ice?" Zan asked.

"I don't know that woman. She showed up looking for Staci but got Kia instead. I know she isn't someone we were around growing up because Kia didn't recognize her. After hitting Julian in the head with her gun, Kia let her go. She didn't know the connection between her and Leo until she was telling me the story. I believe Julian is going to come back for revenge."

"You may be right, but I'll bet she won't harm you. There was something about the way she defended you when Leo called you a thief for stealing his money. Julian told him he owed you every dime of that money for the hell he'd put you through. Julian knows more than we think, and I can't wait to put the pieces together." Zan trained his sights on Blaze, dreading telling him Leo's plan to return to Kingston.

"Blaze, I respect you for standing by Icy's side through everything that has gone on. I wouldn't be a man if I told only half of what I know about what Leo has planned. I'm going to be one hunnid with you. He feels like the money Duke promised him is rightfully due. Leo is a greedy muthafucka. He will do whatever, to get what he wants. That includes strong arming yo' mother."

"I'm very aware of Leo's plan to visit my mother. What he doesn't know is that I will be there waiting for him, soon as he tries it. My mother is my everything outside of Icy and I protect her even when I'm not in Kingston. Thank you for telling me, because had I found out you knew of his plan and stayed silent about it, you would be on the receiving end of my wrath. But the way you came through with the information you had, you've earned my trust until I'm shown otherwise."

Zan could respect Blaze. He felt he wouldn't have been able to bring someone into his circle under the circumstances. The trust would've never been there and his hand would always be positioned on his Glock. There was a knock on the door and Zan looked at Blake to see if he was expecting anybody.

"Did somebody follow you here? There shouldn't be anyone poppin' up," Blaze said, going to the bedroom, coming out with his .38 in hand.

"Nah, this ain't on me," Zan clarified as he got to his feet following Blaze to the door with his gun in hand.

Snatching the door open without asking who it was, Blaze came face-to-face with Amancia. Zan stared her down as he tucked his gun because she didn't appear to be a threat. The way the woman and Blaze glared at one another, caused Zan to walk away from whatever that was about. Icy watched him enter the sitting area with a confused expression.

"What's going on?" Icy asked, glancing toward the door.

"Not my business."

Icy took that moment to push up from the sofa. Zan called out to her, but she kept going. When she got closer to where Blaze was standing at the door, she noticed Amancia with her arms folded over her chest. Blaze turned, seeing Icy with a mug on her face.

"I'll explain later."

"How about you explain right now. Why is she here? This is my comfort zone and another female, especially her, shouldn't be anywhere near it."

Trying her best to stay calm, Icy prayed the bitch didn't open her mouth the way she had done when they first met. One thing she couldn't tolerate was disrespect and Icy wouldn't think twice about going back to her younger days of beating a bitch's ass. Zan listened to the conversation as it unfolded and decided to get up, in case he had to hold Icy back. He of all people knew how Icy got down when it came to somebody she cared about. Looked like Blaze fit right into the category.

"I'm here because I needed to talk to my child's father," Amancia smirked as she rubbed her stomach.

"Amancia, gon' with that baby bullshit. Like I told you earlier, I didn't get you pregnant. Stop saying that shit."

"Are you trying to say I impregnated myself? Wake the fuck up, Akoni. It takes two to tango and oh baby, did we not perfect that shit," she laughed.

"We fucked, we came, and I moved the fuck around," Blaze retorted, wiping the smile right off Amancia's face. "Had you done the same, we wouldn't be going through this drama today. You want me and I love Icy. There isn't any room for a third party, because I only have love for one woman in my life. This is it for me," Blaze said, motioning toward Icy.

A tear fell down Amancia's cheek as Blaze words stabbed at her heart. She wasn't going to believe anything he said because they were destined to be together. Icy wasn't going to win the battle. Her baby would win in the end.

"You mean you're choosing her over our child? We were raised as two children of the tribe who would marry and have children long ago. It just so happened, we skipped marriage and produced a child. I love you, Akoni, and going back to Kingston without you and pregnant is an automatic rejection from the family. You know this." Amancia wept.

Icy couldn't stand to watch the pitiful sight of Amancia begging for love any longer. The tears came from a place of hurt by hearing Blaze's true feelings. Deep down, Icy knew Amancia wasn't pregnant, and she was going to prove it. She went straight to her purse and removed one of the three pregnancy tests she was dreading to take on her own. Amancia could still be heard pleading her case, causing Icy to feel kind of sorry for her. Blaze made it clear as day he was with the woman he planned to be with, but she wasn't letting up.

"You can leave now, and I'm being nice about it."

Icy left the bedroom, seeing Blaze leaning against the wall with his arms folded across his chest. She could tell he was trying his best to keep his cool. Amancia kept pushing him though and Icy couldn't for the life of her understand why she wouldn't leave well enough alone.

"I'm not going anywhere until you agree to take responsibility for this baby!"

Blaze reached out and grabbed the collar of her coat in pure anger, causing Amancia to stumble over her feet, hitting the wall. Zan heard the scuffle and rushed over, pulling Blaze back before he could do something he would regret later. Icy moved closer to Amancia, holding out the test.

"Go piss on the stick," she ordered.

"I'm not doing shit! This has nothing to do with you, bitch!"

Icy laughed. "It has everything to do with me. I smell the lies coming from your pores. If I'm wrong, I'll apologize and make sure Blaze takes responsibility. I won't know until you take the test," Icy said nicely. "Now, if you continue to refuse, then I will just have to conclude you're on bullshit and it will give me ample reason to believe you're lying. So, either take the test, or I'ma beat yo' ass! What's it gonna be?" Amancia reached out for the door and Icy smacked her hand down.

"Leaving is no longer an option. Like I said, take the test, or get fucked up!"

Amancia glanced at Blaze, and he threw his hands in the air. "The queen has spoken. I told you there was a woman in my life. It's outta my hands. Yo' tough ass wanted to keep egging shit on, knowing that's not my baby, now you have to deal with shit on her terms. Whatever she does, is on you," he said, before walking away.

Zan couldn't believe Blaze left that woman in the hands of Icy and her cold heart. He may not have known what she was capable of, but Zan sure as hell did. Icy was a force to be reckoned with, especially with all the bullshit she was going through.

"Come on, Ice. Just let her go."

"Fuck that! She's about to prove there's a baby so she can go on with her life. If she is indeed pregnant, DNA will be the next step. As of right now, this bitch has something to prove."

Amancia shifted as she kept her focus on Icy. On one hand, she regretted coming to the hotel. Then again, she did just what she intended, and that was to shake up Blaze's life. He may have acted like he wasn't concerned about the outcome, but Amancia knew he was worried if she was pregnant or not.

Zan took the test from Icy and pulled her behind him. Turning to Amancia, he said, "Take the test and stand on yo' shit, shawty. You say you pregnant, slap it in his muthafuckin' face, then hold his ass accountable. Yo' word ain't shit, they want proof. Stop procrastinating and get the shit over with. In case you didn't know, Icy wasn't throwing threats at you."

"Where's the bathroom?" Amancia asked, snatching the test from Zan.

Icy led the way to the bedroom, while Amancia walked slowly behind her, trying to get Blaze's attention. He had tuned out everybody in the room as he pulled on a blunt.

Standing in the doorway of the bathroom, Icy motioned for Amancia to enter. She tried to close the door and Icy kicked it back open, nearly hitting her in the face.

"You don't have to close shit! All you gotta do is piss, wash yo' hands, and wait two minutes for the results. Simple, right?" Icy snapped. "The last thing you need to worry about is me seeing your pussy. I don't roll that way. I have a big dick nigga sitting out there waiting for yo' lying ass to piss on the stick!"

Amancia opened the package while Icy stood looking like a prison guard on duty. She couldn't wait to see the expression on Icy's confident face when the positive sign appeared on the test. Amancia wasn't lying about being pregnant. A month after her encounter with Akoni, she was experiencing morning sickness, her breasts were tender, and her stomach was getting bigger. She had missed her period and she couldn't forget about the unusual food cravings. There was only one reason she was experiencing all of those things and that was her being pregnant by the man she loved her entire life.

Sitting the test on the counter, Amancia wiped, flushed, then washed her hands. After drying her hands on a towel hanging on the rod, she turned to leave the bathroom. Icy moved to the side to allow her to pass before going into the bathroom to look at the test. The results showed up fast and she got the answer she wanted.

"Get ready to be a stepmama."

Amancia smirked, walking toward the door with her middle finger in the air. Icy didn't appreciate the disrespect at all. All of the anger she held inside came rushing to the surface. Icy reached out and snatched Amancia by her hair and slammed her on the floor.

"Aaaarggghhhh!" Amancia cried out as her scalp burned from the hair, which was removed from her roots. Icy yanked her ass up by the front of her coat, bringing her to her feet before landing a punch to her face. Icy was kicking

Amancia's ass when Zan and Blaze came running into the room. Slinging Amancia around like a rag doll, Icy hit her in her mouth and blood formed on her lip. Amancia wasn't even trying to fight back. Instead, she got a glimpse of two sets of feet from the angle where her head was positioned.

"Get this bitch off me!" she yelled.

"I got yo' bitch," Icy sneered, delivering multiple uppercuts.

Blaze grabbed Icy around the waist with one arm while trying to pry her hand from Amancia's coat. "You gotta let her go, Icy! She may be pregnant!"

"She good," Icy said, punching Amancia in the top of her head.

Zan finally was able to pull Amancia away from the mayhem and took her out of the room. She could feel the left side of her face swelling as tears stung her eyes. Sitting her on the couch, Zan sat across from her shaking his head.

"Look, ma. We don't need the law involved in this shit. Just get yourself together and leave. Icy warned you what would happen, and you still provoked her. That shit might be cool in Kingston, but you gotta know how to fight when you're playing with that type of fire."

"I'm going to the police because I'm pregnant and she assaulted me!"

In the bedroom, Icy struggled out of Blaze's arm and went into the bathroom, snatched up the test, and made a beeline for the door. He caught her by the back of the neck, but not before she hauled the test out the door, hitting Amancia in the back of the head.

"Bitch, you pregnant in your mind because according to that muthafucka, you ain't carrying shit but gas. You better be lucky I can't reach out and touch yo' ass, because I would fuck you up again!" Icy said angrily. "Go to the police, I don't give a fuck. You came here with problems on your mind, and I gave you what you were looking for."

Blaze closed the door to stop Icy's wrath and picked her up, placing her on the bed. He stood before her looking down at her chest heaving in and out. Blaze never wanted his woman to fight on his behalf.

"Icy——"

"I don't want to hear it. I gave her fair warning that she would get her ass beat if she kept pushing. Once she said fuck me, I fucked her up! End of the story. Now, everything between y'all from this point is between the two of you. Leave me the fuck out of it. I suggest you tell the bitch to go the fuck home because she can come up missing in the United States of fuckin' America."

Icy got up, went into the bathroom, leaving Blaze standing in the middle of the room.

Chapter 10

For the past couple days, the same number kept calling Leo and he didn't know who it could be. Julian lay in the bed with a mean mug on her face, because every time the phone rang Leo sent it to voicemail. She knew damn well he wasn't entertaining another bitch with all the shit they had going on.

"It's obvious, whoever is trying to get in touch with you won't stop calling until you answer. Tell the hoe you are back with your wife and it's not safe for her to call again."

"What the fuck you talkin' bout? Ain't no bitch calling me. Hell, I don't even know who the fuck that is. Nobody has this number other than my patnas and Icy. She damn sho ain't trying to get at my ass. Now stop with the assumptions. Plus, I thought I told you not to say shit to me, until you tell me who bust yo' ass upside the head."

"How many times must I tell you I slipped on a piece of ice. Don't you understand? You worried about the wrong shit, Leo. You need to be trying to figure out who's blowing up yo' line."

Julian got up and left the bedroom to get away from Leo's lying ass. He watched her and shook his head at her antics before pulling his phone from his pocket. Soon as he did, it started ringing again. Leo was ready to curse out whomever was calling him back-to-back.

"Who the fuck is this?" The line was silent for a few seconds and that only pissed Leo off more.

"Stop playing on my fuckin' phone if you ain't trying to talk!"

"Daddy, you said a bad word!"

Leo stopped pacing as he heard his daughter's sweet voice. He missed her so much and wished like hell every day he could reach out to Avita, just to talk to them. The shit he started prevented him from doing just that, because he didn't want to involve the only person he loved to be caught up in his shit. Since faking his death, he hadn't been in touch with anyone from his past, except the people that was involved in what he was currently involved in. And nobody outside of them had the number, so Icy was the person who could've given Avita the number to his phone.

I'm going to choke the shit out of that bitch! Leo thought.

"Hey, baby. How have you been?"

"I been good. Me and Mommy came to see you in 'Merica!" Amoy said excitedly.

Leo thought he heard her wrong, because there was no way they were in America. Avita knew better than to take his daughter so far from Kingston to pull up on him. Leo tried his best to calm down because maybe they were in America, they just better not be in fuckin' Chicago. It was too hot for them to be there, especially when he didn't send for them. If Blaze found out, he would for sure use Amoy to bring him out of hiding.

"Did you say you were in America?"

"Yeah. Me and Mama is in Chicago. We came to see you, Daddy. You coming to see me?"

Leo's heart dropped to the pit of his ass when Amoy confirmed his worst fear. Her mother put his lifeline into the inferno, and he was mad as fuck. Not wanting his baby girl to know how upset he was, Leo swallowed all the derogatory shit he had on his tongue for her mammy. It wasn't his daughter's fault her bitch of a mother was stupid. Racking his brain, Leo had to think of a way to see Amoy, because he damn sure couldn't give Avita the address to his house.

Julian knew nothing about them, and he wanted to keep it that way.

Slipping his feet into his slides, Leo made his way to the mancave for much needed privacy. As he walked down the stairs, Julian was coming up. He put a finger up with his free hand and hurried past her. When he was safely in his sanctuary, Leo locked the door before descending the stairs.

"Amoy, I will see you later today. Put your mother on the phone."

He went straight to the bar on the other side of the room and grabbed a shot glass. Taking the bottle of Rémy 1738, Leo filled the glass and downed the liquor before pouring another. Avita was on the other end of the line repeating hello, but he wasn't ready to address her yet. Soon as he opened his mouth, he knew one more shot was needed before he blew his cover by hollerin' every obscenity in the foul language dictionary at her ass.

"Leo, what are you doing?" Avita asked nervously.

"Bitch, wait," he erupted with anger. "Why the fuck would you bring my daughter here?"

Avita was quiet for a moment as she thought about why Leo was so angry. The way he came at her was something he'd never done to her. She guessed being close to his double life did something to him. She didn't give a damn because he still had the job of daddy to attend to. Leo didn't have to hide them anymore, because she knew for a fact he wasn't with Icy anymore. *So, what was the real problem*? was the question on Avita's mind.

"We haven't seen you in a couple months! What the fuck you mean what are we doing here? Your daughter misses you, Leo!"

"That doesn't mean bring your ass here! It's dangerous and you don't know what the fuck I have going on. Did it ever cross your mind I was in the middle of a war or some shit and that was the reason I hadn't been back to Kingston? You already know what happened to Duke!"

"Save the bullshit, Leo! I know all about the stunt you pulled faking your own death. Why would you do such a thing? What if word would've reached me in Kingston and I had to tell our daughter you were dead?"

Leo could hear the hurt and pain in Avita's voice. That shit didn't mean anything to him. All he worried about was his daughter being in danger.

"You wouldn't have known shit about it because it didn't make national fuckin' news! The only reason you know about it is because yo' nosy ass went looking for shit! You do know curiosity killed the muthafuckin' cat, right? You shouldn't be here, Avita! Knowing I'm presumed dead, you know I can't come out to see y'all."

"You have to come! Amoy's really looking forward to seeing you. It would shatter her heart if we leave here and she don't get the chance to spend time with you, Leo."

Leo sat down on a barstool and held his head down. Avita was speaking facts, but he didn't want to be caught slipping with his daughter in his presence. He would never put her in harm's way. Loud knocks could be heard then Julian started yelling like a banshee. Leo tried to mute the phone, but he was too slow because while his wife was yelling on the other side of the door, Avita was in his ear doing the same shit.

"Who the fuck is that?" she asked with much venom dripping off every syllable. "It's not Icy because the bitch left your ass alone and is now fucking on Akoni! How many women are you hiding, Leo? You have every excuse as to why you can't see your child, but you got time to entertain your hoes. Make this shit make sense!"

"Avita, when did you talk to Icy?"

"Come to the Embassy Suites downtown Chicago. Call me when you get here, and I'll come down and we'll talk then. If you don't show up, be prepared to lose all the rights of being a father to Amoy. I don't have time to play your games. I think I've done that enough in the past four years and I'm serious, Leo."

Avita hung up in his face and it only pissed him off more than he already was. To threaten him with taking his seed from him, Avita didn't want those type of problems. She was going to find out the hard way. The side he tried to be oblivious about was the one Avita was about to see in the flesh. But for the time being, Leo was storming up the steps to put his foot in Julian's ass first. He unlocked then opened the door and he was met with a slap to the face.

"Bitch, are you outta yo' muthafuckin' mind?" Leo yelled, yoking her off her feet. "You must've forgotten who the fuck I am? I've let you walk around like Billy Bad Ass and you just ran with that shit, huh?"

Leo slapped Julian repeatedly as he walked her to the nearest wall and slammed her back against it. The more she fought, the tighter he squeezed. Julian's eyes bulged as she clawed at his hands, hoping he'd release his grip. The look on his face was demonic and for the first time since being back with Leo, Julian was scared for her life.

"You don't question me and invade my fuckin' privacy! Your job is to sit back, follow my lead, cook, clean, fuck and suck my dick! I'm the muthafuckin' man around here! You are my wife! Do you hear me, Icy? I will kill yo' ass in this muthafucka!"

Julian stop struggling when she heard Icy's name fall from Leo's mouth. She knew if she didn't fight him back, he would eventually let her go. Her plan worked and Leo allowed her body to hit the floor. Gasping for air, Julian sat there for a few seconds to get her bearings. The minute she caught her breath, she sprang to her feet.

"Nah, nigga, you out of your mind putting your hands on me! I'm not the bitch that's on your mind, but we about to tear this muthafucka up!"

Julian hit Leo with a two-piece and on instinct, he returned the blow. Like she said, they were fighting like cats and dogs throughout the lower level of their home. Julian was hanging with Leo like she was a nigga on the street. It wasn't until he cornered her that he started beating the fuck out of her. Cowering in the corner, Julian protected her face until he stopped hitting her.

"Look what you made me do! Man, let me get out of here before I kill yo' ass up in here," Leo said, rubbing his knuckles. "When I come back, you better have a different fuckin' attitude."

He left Julian sitting on the living room floor and left in a huff. Leo got in his car and backed out of the driveway making his way to the Embassy to see his daughter. He couldn't believe he envisioned Icy while choking Julian. He was about to apologize to her once he realized what he'd done, but she jumped up like the Bionic fuckin' Woman and set him off again.

Icy truly fucked Leo up in the head when she went the extra mile and took everything he'd worked hard for from under his ass. The only thing on his mind when he thought of her was getting his shit back, before killing her and that punk ass nigga she was laying up with. Leo also had a couple homies behind the wall he was going to get to murder Zan and his two stooges in the county. He was ready to clear the streets of all the bullshit. In order to do that, he would have to show his face. And what better way to do that was to get at someone close to Icy. It was time to make her ass cry like the baby she really was. Icy fucked with the wrong nigga and she would pay for everything she'd done.

Leo pulled up to the Embassy and had to circle the block because he couldn't find a spot to park. He found paid parking a block away, then walked back. On the journey, he called Avita so she could be downstairs when he arrived. Leo had calmed down as he entered the lobby of the hotel. The sight of Avita had his dick tightening in his pants. The shit she said on the phone was pushed to the back of his mind until he was face-to-face with her. The way she looked at him displayed hatred. Licking his lips, Leo bent down and kissed

Avita on the cheek. She jerked her head away as if she was burned by his touch.

"Hello, Avita. You're still beautiful, you know that?" Leo smiled as he tried to hold her hand.

"Follow me. Amoy is upstairs upset because she didn't think you were coming."

Turning away from her daughter's father, Avita led the way to the elevators. Leo watched her ample ass bounce in the leggings she wore the entire way. Adjusting his member, he thought about all the positions he would have her in after spending time with his baby girl. The elevator doors opened immediately, and they got on in silence. Avita watched the numbers light up, ignoring Leo's presence.

"You want to tell me when you talked to Icy?"

Avita sighed loudly as if she was irritated by him. "I googled her shop and paid her a visit. I needed to know what relations she had with you."

"How did you know where she was, Avita?"

"She called when you were in Kingston, and I answered the phone. She didn't say anything, then hung up. I saved the number in my phone, along with her business number. That's how I found her since you were being sneaky and shit." Avita spun around to face Leo because she wanted him to see the pain he'd caused.

"You professed your love for me every time you were making love to me! Leo, you lied," Avita cried. "Promising forever with me, came back to Chicago and married another woman, then faked your own death! What type of games are you playing? I'll tell you, a dangerous one! After today, I want you to stay away from me and Amoy. Do you know Icy basically told me she would kill me if I ever approached her again? I want no parts of whatever you have going on and I will protect my baby at all costs."

The doors opened and Avita stepped off, but Leo grabbed her by the waist and kissed the side of her neck. Her knees felt like noodles because she missed his touch. Being close to Leo in an intimate way was her weakness. Avita realized it wasn't love they shared it was just a sexual attraction. Something she could find in another man who would appreciate her worth. Shrugging out of his hold, Avita walked down the hall and opened the suite door with the key card. Soon as she walked in, Amoy came running toward her full speed.

"Mommy, where did you go?" Amoy asked, looking up at her mommy and released her leg quickly.

"Daddyyyyyyy!"

Avita walked further into the suite as Leo swooped his daughter up in his arms. Amoy had a firm grip on his neck and didn't seem as if she would let go any time soon. The sight brought tears to Avita's eyes watching the two of them love on one another. She hated the fact that it would be their last time interacting and she planned to allow Leo to stay long as he wanted. Avita would decide how to break the news to her daughter when the time arose.

"I've missed you so much. Are you staying here with us?"

"I've missed you too, baby. I'll stay until it's time for bed. Daddy has some work to take care of. I promise to come back and see you tomorrow though. For now, let's have some fun and order pizza. How's that sound?"

"Can we watch *Moana* too?"

"Sure can," Leo said, kissing her on the cheek while tickling her. He loved to hear Amoy giggle.

Avita left the father-daughter duo while she and Eshe went through the adjacent door to Amancia's room. Avita heard her come back while on the phone with Leo and figured she'd see how her visit with Akoni went. Amancia was sitting on the side of the bed, holding a towel to her mouth.

"What the hell happened to you?" Avita asked with concern.

"I went to see Akoni to tell him I was pregnant…"

"Pregnant! You left that tidbit of information out of the equation. When were you going to tell me you were with child?"

"Avita, do you want to hear what happened or not?" Amancia snapped. "I didn't say anything because I wanted Akoni to be the first to hear it from me. He wasn't too pleased about the news, saying the baby couldn't possibly be his. Icy was talking big shit and threw a test in my face, demanding I take it. Things got physical and she basically beat my ass."

"Oh, we're going to the police! She assaulted a pregnant woman, and she needs to be locked up!"

Amancia held her head down because she wanted to have Akoni's baby badly. Too bad it was never going to happen. The police wouldn't do anything about what happened on the strength of Amancia not carrying a baby. She was hurt when Icy yelled, "The bitch ain't pregnant." All the signs were there and Amancia knew Akoni would do the right thing and marry her.

"There's no need to do all that. I'm not pregnant. The test was negative. I dodged a bullet anyway because Akoni wants nothing to do with me. He is madly in love with the bitch. He walked away while she threatened me to even take the damn test. Then she whooped my ass like I stole something from her. I just want to go back to Kingston."

Amancia sobbed while Eshe and Avita consoled her. Her cousin may have wanted to leave well enough alone, but Avita wasn't going to let Icy get away with beating Amancia the way she had. Akoni was less of a man to stand by while she did the shit and both of them were going to see her.

"I'll be back," Avita said, heading for the door.

"Where you going?"

"To talk to Leo. I need someone who's familiar with Icy because she's not getting away with this."

Amancia was puzzled. The last she'd heard, Avita didn't know where Leo was, and she hadn't said anything about calling the number she had for him. Standing to her feet, Amancia approached her cousin slowly. She didn't want Avita getting in trouble so far from home. Especially, not with Leo. There was something about him that just didn't sit right with her.

"Don't call him. I'm about to call the pilot so we can leave as soon as possible. It was a mistake coming here."

"I won't have to call Leo. He's in our room with Amoy," Avita said, turning the knob. "Hold off on making that call. I'm not leaving until I beat Icy's ass worse than she did you."

Avita left out of the room, leaving her cousin worried and terrified. Amancia didn't see anything good coming from the situation which was bound to take place after Avita approached Icy. She didn't trust Leo to protect Avita at all. Amancia said a silent prayer for her cousin's safe return, because there was no way she was waiting around to get her ass kicked again.

Chapter 11

Desiree was scrolling through her phone, texting back and forth with her college roommate about coming to Texas. Pria and Desiree met their freshman year at Loyola University, becoming the best of friends. While Desiree majored in business management, Pria was destined to be a doctor. After graduation, Pria left to attend Texas A&M School of Medicine in Houston. Needless to say, Pria was always in her friend's ear about the relationship she had with Leo. After Desiree told her how everything unfolded, Pria was glad he wasn't around anymore. Desiree was beating around the bush, trying to find the words to tell Pria the entire story.

Pria: I'm taking some time away from the hospital to relax for a few weeks. You should come down.

If that wasn't her out, Desiree didn't know what was. She thought about it for a moment before responding. After deciding to pack up and explain her situation when she arrived, Desiree hit her long-time friend with a response.

Desiree: I don't know when you plan to do that, but I can try to be there in a couple days. I need a break from Chicago anyway.

Pria: You are always welcome in my home. Send me your flight info when you get it together. I'll make sure I'm available to pick you up.

That was music to Desiree's ears, and she was ready to pack up any and everything she could to get out of Dodge.

Desiree: Will do. I have some planning to do, and I will keep in touch. I love you, Pria, and thanks for always being there to listen when I vent.

Pria: I love you too, girl. Get here already! We have a lot of catching up to do! Talk to you soon.

Desiree wanted to leave before Leo decided to pop up on her again. The threat he'd dished out to her had been on her mind constantly. Truth be told, she went to Planned Parenthood to get the abortion, but she couldn't go through with the procedure. Desiree had seen the process of an abortion and it was heartbreaking.

Leo had called asking if she had taken care of *her* problem and she lied and said she did. To cover her tracks, Desiree had a friend to ask her cousin who was a nurse, to falsify documents in case Leo wanted proof. The shit scared her because the loving man she had met no longer existed. Since Icy found out about their affair, Leo turned into an evil son of a bitch.

Desiree never meant to take things further than they went with Leo. What started out as an employee going to lunch with her boss to discuss business, gradually turned into sexual hookups. Icy would come into the management office often and Desiree was forced to put up a front while watching Leo love on her. Leo started giving Desiree large sums of money she would've never seen working as his manager alone. The two went on plenty of trips and she loved those times because at the moment, she was his woman. At least it felt that way. Desiree's jealousy surfaced once Leo proposed to Icy. He immediately expected her to tag along and help his fiancée with the planning of *their* wedding. It was hard trying to pretend she was happy for the bride to be, when she was fucking the very man she was soon to marry, any time he came to her. Kia and Julz never hid their dislike for Desiree and sent shots her way whenever she was around.

The jiggle of the lock at her door brought Desiree out of her thoughts. Her heart started beating rapidly as she listened at what was happening in front of her. Desiree knew the person on the other side of the door wouldn't be able to enter because she had a locksmith come and change her locks. She had to prevent Leo from entering her apartment unannounced and it seemed she made the right decision.

"I know yo' ass in there, Desi. Open this muthafuckin' doe!"

Leo's voice boomed through the hall, but he didn't give a fuck. Everybody in the building knew he was the owner and knew better than to interfere. They didn't know if he was there to evict Desiree or what. Minding their business was something they needed to keep doing. Desiree, on the other hand, was sweating bullets standing a few feet away from the door. She had no way of escaping Leo's wrath. He wasn't going to leave, so she didn't have any other options other than to open the door. Desiree's hands shook uncontrollably as she turned the lock. Soon as it clicked, Leo pushed his way into the condo, slamming the door behind him. He held up the key so Desiree could see it with fire in his eyes.

"Why this muthafucka don't work, huh?"

When she didn't respond, Leo's hand was around her throat faster than the speed of light. Backing her into the nearest wall, Desiree could hardly breathe. She clawed at Leo's hands, but that only caused him to squeeze tighter.

"I pay the muthafuckin' bills in here and you had the nerve to lock me out! Are you dumb or stupid, bitch? You thought changing the locks was going to do something, huh?" Leo laughed. "You will forever belong to me. Ain't no muthafuckin' getting out!"

Leo banged her head against the wall, making a small indentation. Desiree had tears falling from her eyes as she struggled to catch a hint of air. She was started to feel woozy, but Leo let her go with one final shove. Heaving to get as much air in her lungs as she could, Desiree felt as if she was dying. Her neck was hot to the touch where Leo's hand once was.

"Answer me! Why the fuck did you change the fuckin' locks?" Leo screamed at her.

"I-I broke my key in the lock. I didn't have a choice other than changing them." Desiree lied once again to get herself out of hot water with the man who stood before her. He didn't appear to believe a word that came from her mouth, but at least he hadn't put his hands on her again.

"Did you take care of that situation?"

"Yeah. I went two weeks ago."

"Where is the paperwork? I need to see the shit for myself."

Desiree was scared to move, so she pointed to the kitchen counter where she left the papers. Leo stalked across the room and rustled through the documents as he read the content. A smile spread across his face as he came back to where Desiree was still rubbing her throat. The way he peered down at her used to make her pussy wetter than the ocean, but at that particular moment, it did nothing for her. Leo ran the back of hand down her cheek, causing Desiree to flinch from his touch.

"I'm sorry for spazzing out on you. When I put the key in the door and it didn't turn, it pissed me off."

"Why did you make me kill my baby, Leo?"

Tears fell from her eyes not because of the baby, but from the fear of Leo. She wanted to see how he was going to spin his actions. Desiree wanted to understand his line of thinking as best she could. Maybe if she made him believe she was hurt about the abortion, he would be guilty enough to give her some pity money to get the fuck out of Chicago.

"Don't start that shit! A baby is something neither one of us need right now. Desi, you know what the fuck I'm dealing with in these streets. If anyone got wind of you being pregnant, you would be the target they use to get to me. Plus, you knew what the fuck it was between us anyway. I have a wife already. You will forever be in my life in some way, shape, or form. I will help you any way I possibly can, long as you stand ten toes down with me."

If Leo thought she was going to continue being his secret lover, he was sadly mistaken. Icy would be a fool if she took him back after what he'd done to her. Desiree regretted pulling the trigger the night of the murder. She had to remind herself that she did it under pressure or better yet, out of desperation of saving her own life. Leo would've for sure killed her if she hadn't done what he wanted.

"I'm going to give you ten thousand dollars today," he said, pulling an envelope from his back pocket. "All you have to do is get in touch with Icy and tell her to meet you somewhere. When she agrees, you will send the location to me, and I'll take care of everything from there."

"Wasn't it enough that you framed her for a murder she didn't commit? What else do you want from her?" Desiree asked.

"I want to see the bitch take her last muthafuckin' breath! If she's not going to be with me, she won't be with anybody! Do what the fuck I tell you to do before you meet her in hell! Call her now!"

Desiree ran to the kitchen to get her phone. Leo was right on her heels to make sure she didn't cross him in the process. Scrolling through the contacts, she hesitated before making the call. The phone rang several times before she got Icy's voicemail. Glancing up at Leo, Desiree left a message.

"Hey, Icy, it's Desiree. I know I'm the last person you want to hear from, but I really need to talk to you. Please give me a call so we can meet up and talk. Any time this week is good with me." She ended the call and Leo smacked her on the ass.

"Good job. Take this money and do something nice for yourself. You in here looking bad. Get your hair done or some shit. You can't be out here looking like what you've been through."

Leo moved closer and wrapped his arms around her waist. Desiree cringed because she knew where Leo was going with his affection. It never failed. In the past she would've welcomed it, but she didn't even know if he could even arouse her anymore. On top of that, his ass had just choked the shit out of her less than thirty minutes prior. Kissing her along the very neck he'd had his hands around, Desiree jerked her head away and Leo gave her a death stare in return.

"Are you refusing me, Desi?" he asked as he pushed his free hand down the front of the lounge pants she wore.

Leo rubbed his thumb over her nub as his middle finger explored her silky folds. Desiree was afraid if her yoni didn't react to his touch, Leo would lash out in anger. She was willing to pretend she was enjoying what was happening, instead of making him mad enough to violate her. Leo was the type of man who didn't take no for an answer. Leo's hand paused as he slowly flicked her clit. Rearing his head back, he looked down at her.

"She's not waking up for me. You been giving my pussy away, Desi?"

Shaking her head no vigorously, Desiree made sure not to take her eyes away from his. Leo inserted his finger into her tunnel, and she closed her eyes as she faked a sexy moan. She envisioned a porn scene she'd recently watched so her kitty would get wet for the monster who was all over her. All Desiree wanted was for Leo to get his nut and leave.

Leo picked her up by her ass cheeks, carrying her back to the living room. He placed her on the sofa and removed her pants before burying his head between her legs. Desiree couldn't fake the orgasm that locked her thighs around his head. Leo was a fuck-up at many things, but eating pussy wasn't one of them. She fed him while holding his head in place as her eyes rolled in her head. The way Leo was pleasing Desiree had her second-guessing leaving the state, but only for a millisecond. She remembered why Leo was putting on a topnotch performance and rode the wave to achieve the nut she needed. Coming up, grinning from ear to ear, Leo wiped Desiree's essence from his face as he stood to remove his pants. Stroking his member in the palm of his hand, Leo sized her up, licking his lips.

"You still taste good as hell. Turn over, and toot that ass up."

Desiree didn't move. Leo must've been out of his mind thinking she was going to have sex with him unprotected. He already forced her to get one abortion, so he thought.

"Aren't you going to wrap that up? We don't want me to have another *problem*." Desiree rolled her eyes.

"You know I don't like using that shit! I'll go out and get a Plan B."

"No, I'm not putting my body through all of that."

Desiree got up and bent over to pick up her pants. Leo grabbed her by the waist, holding her downright as he entered her center. Trying to fight him off, Leo turned their bodies and her head landed in the cushions of the sofa.

"Damn this shit juicy!" he groaned.

Desiree pushed back on his stomach with her hand because he was deep in her womb. Leo slapped her hand down and continued stirring his dick in her kitty. She fought to get away without avail. Violating her, Desiree prayed for him to finish. Leo moaned and groaned, slapping her on the ass as he pulled her into him.

"Ain't no way I can leave this wet shit alone. This is my peaceful place and I love it."

Leo stroked faster, then snatched his wood out of her. Using his hand to turn her head to the side, he stroked his dick until he released in Desiree's face. As long as they had been dealing, Leo had never degraded her in that manner. She had cum coating her skin and Desiree felt dirty. Her phone rang in the kitchen, causing Leo to step back. Desiree used her shirt to wipe Leo's kids off her face, then got up to get her phone. By the time she made it to the device, it stopped ringing.

"Who was it?" Leo asked, standing behind her.

"Icy. I'll call her back."

Returning the call, Icy didn't answer. They were playing phone tag at that point and of course, Leo blamed her for missing the call. She tried several times more, getting the same result.

"Soon as you get a location, hit me up. I'm about to get out of here. When I return, I'll be expecting a key. I'm not about to be knocking on the door to get in. By the way, that pussy still feel like you pregnant. If I didn't see the proof for myself, I would say you were still with child. I'm gon' have to come back before that shit wears off," he laughed as he headed for the door. "Go get your hair and nails done. I want to look you in your beautiful face next time."

With that, Leo left without another word. Desiree called Icy back, but she still didn't answer. She wasn't beating Icy's line down for Leo, she was doing it to warn her to be careful. He was not going to get any information about Icy from her. Desiree planned to be long gone before Leo even thought about coming back to the condo. She looked over at the envelope on the counter and picked it up. As she counted the bills, she smiled because that was her ticket out.

***

After taking a shower, Desiree threw on a jogging suit and a pair of sneakers. She was on her way to the bank to deposit the money Leo had given her. While the water cascaded down her face, Desiree made the brash decision to drive out of the state of Illinois. Her car was paid for thanks to Leo and was in her name. She wasn't looking forward to relying on Pria to chauffeur her around once she got to Texas. Ten thousand dollars wasn't much, but Desiree was going to make it last long as she could. Pulling into the parking lot of the bank, her phone rang. Without looking at the screen, she answered the call.

"Hello?"

"Desiree, it's Icy. What is so important that you're blowing up my phone?"

The animosity in Icy's voice let Desiree know she wasn't pleased to talk with her. Icy had every right to be skeptical about why she was receiving a call from her husband's mistress. It was up to Desiree to let her know she wasn't getting in touch with her for malicious reasons.

"I'm coming to you in peace."

"How the fuck are you calling me in peace? I told you after I bopped yo' ass in my salon to stay away from me. Stop beating around the bush and tell me why you're contacting me!"

"Calm down, Icy. I need you to listen," Desiree pleaded. "I initially called with Leo standing over my shoulder——"

"Bitch, I know damn well you didn't call me for that nigga!"

"Listen to me!" Desiree screamed back. "I was glad when you didn't respond, because he wanted me to set-up a meeting with you and pass the location on to him. Icy, he's planning to kill you and I want no parts of it. I'm sorry you went to jail, but I want to come clean. If you go to the police after I reveal this, I deserve that shit."

"Go to the police for what, and why are you apologizing for me going to jail?" Desiree had Icy's full attention at that point.

"Leo forced me to kill that man and woman outside of the club that night. He held a gun to my head and made me drive your truck. I never knew he was trying to pin that murder on you. I've been on pins and needles this whole entire time because of what I had done."

Icy listened to Desiree and wanted to turn her ass in right then and there. She was still talking, but Icy had tuned her out. Thoughts of how she was going to kill Desiree was floating through her mind. There was no way she was going to allow her to live after setting her up with that nothing ass muthafucka named Leo.

"He threw money at me and told me to get an abortion. I couldn't go through with it because this baby was something made between the two of us. Now, I just want to leave Chicago and raise this baby alone. I never wanted kids, but it happened, and I have to live with my decision. Finding a way out of the state is my only concern. I have to get away from here before Leo kills me."

Bingo! Icy focused on what Desiree was saying at the very end and she was glad for it. She needed money to disappear and Icy was going to help her with the problem she was facing. Closing her eyes, she prayed for God to forgive her for what she planned to do. Either He would forgive her, or He wouldn't. It didn't really matter one way or the other to Icy.

"I'm sorry you're going through that. Leo has put you in a compromising position you didn't ask to be in, and I want to help you get away, Desiree. I swear on my life, if I give you a destination to meet and it's a trap, you will die right along with his ass. Are we understood?"

"Icy, I appreciate you for helping, but I don't think we should meet. What I did was wrong, and you got caught up in the mess and you were innocent. I don't think you're really forgiving me for my actions."

"Girl bye. Didn't you just say you were trying to leave Chicago? I'm not thinking about that murder conviction. I was proven innocent by the court of law. Desiree, you have a baby to take care of and I will make sure you and that baby is straight. Meet me at my salon up north at ten o'clock tonight. I will have fifty thousand dollars for you to leave soon after. Nobody will be out there because it's still cold as hell outside. It's time for you to get from under Leo's spell because his days are numbered. Thank you for the forewarning and I got you. I'll see you later."

Icy hung up and Desiree started crying real tears. She never expected Icy to forgive her and help her out financially. Leo fumbled when he fucked over her. She felt bad about what she'd done to Icy because Desiree knew she was with Leo. The money and good dick made her forget all about that and she got comfortable in the position of being the other woman.

Drying her face with a napkin from her armrest, Desiree grabbed her purse and exited the car to go in the bank to handle her business. After depositing the money, Desiree went home and started packing up the things she was going to take with her to Texas. When she was finished, Desiree stored everything in her car and decided to sleep for a few hours. The drive to Houston was going to be long and she was ready for the journey.

Chapter 12

"Icy, is everything okay?"

Blaze looked at Icy strangely as she entered the suite. Her demeanor was off, because the last time he'd spoken to Icy, she was leaving the hospital with great news. Blaze watched as she toed off the shoes she wore and headed for the bedroom without answering his question. Something was going on and she wasn't sharing with him. Blaze didn't like it.

"Do you hear me talking to you, Icy?"

"I heard you," she said, taking off her clothes.

"What the hell happened from the time I talked to you 'til now? I need you to talk to me, woman!"

"Blaze, do not raise your voice at me. I've told you this one too many times and it's something I'm not willing to tolerate. Nothing is going on, okay?"

Icy went into the closet, then came out with a pair of black jeans and a long-sleeved black shirt. Her gear alone told Blaze Icy was on some type of goon shit and he needed answers. He stood watching her change into the clothes she had chosen, then pulled on a pair of black Timberland boots. When she pulled her hair into a ponytail, Blaze was furious.

"Where are you going?" Blaze asked calmly.

"I'm about to call Kia and we're going to go over the houses I looked at for me and my mama. The doctor said she was progressing well, and in a month or so, she would be able to come home. I want her to be able to enjoy a beautiful home without the worry of someone trying to kill her."

Blaze didn't believe anything she said. It was nine o'clock at night and she was talking about going to look at houses. He didn't believe that shit for a minute and Icy knew it too. Blaze took that opportunity to tell Icy about the home he'd purchased to surprise her and Staci with, hoping his reveal would change her mind about going out.

"You don't have to do any of that," Blaze said, walking up to Icy. "I guess this is a good time to fill you in on my secret. I've already taken the step to make sure you and Staci is straight. I was gonna wait until she was released to spring the news on you, but I see you're trying to have things in motion beforehand."

Icy stared at Blaze to see if he was serious or just saying something so she wouldn't go out with Kia. His expression said it all and she knew her man had gone out and proved his love for her. Leo made sure Icy was good, but his actions were out of pure guilt. Blaze, on the other hand, hadn't done anything to deceive her and the shit he did was based on nothing except love. She felt bad for lying to him by not telling the truth about her plans, but taking care of Desiree was something she had to do, in order to cut the head from one of the snakes that smeared her name through the mud. Desiree could thank Leo for the outcome of her and their unborn child's life being cut short.

"Are you trying to tell me you purchased a home for us, meaning you and I?"

"Yes, I would rather be here with you than New York. I don't have love there. My heart is embedded in the palm of your hand. If that means relocating, guess what? I'm all for it. My forever is with you, Icy. We didn't meet by chance. That shit was meant to happen and I'm not letting you go."

Icy got up from her seat and palmed Blaze's face before kissing him passionately on the lips. Slipping his tongue in her mouth, he deepened the kiss, trying his best to get Icy aroused. Moaning lowly, Icy caressed his locs as her phone rang on the bed. Icy backed away, wiping the gloss from his lips.

"Yeah, Kia," she said when the call connected.

"Bitch, where you at? I thought we had somewhere to be at ten."

"And do. I got caught up with Blaze. I'll be leaving out in a few minutes."

"Make sure you got the Gremlin on yo' hip."

"Never leave home without it. See you in a bit."

"Bet."

Icy had some explaining to do, because Blaze was standing against the dresser with his ankles crossed. She may as well tell him the truth, so he could chew her out or whatever he was going to do. He would have to cut his rant to three minutes because she had shit to do.

"Stop looking at me like that, Blaze."

"You were just talking in code and shit. What else do you want me to do? Where are you going, Ice? And don't lie."

Taking a deep breath while walking to the closet, Icy got her Glock from the lockbox and made sure she had an extra clip. Icy slipped the clip in her back pocket as she walked out. Blaze's left eyebrow rose, and he frowned deeply as he waited for Icy to explain what was going on.

"I'm not going to lie, Desiree called to warn me that Leo is out to kill me. I'm going to meet up with her so she can leave town."

Pondering what Icy said, Blaze didn't believe a word of it. "What you need a gun for, Icy? And who the fuck is Desiree?"

"She was Leo's property manager, who was also fucking the bastard." Icy walked around Blaze, collecting her keys and phone. "Truth be told, I'm going to kill the bitch. Desiree confessed to being the one who committed the murder I was framed for. She may have given me a warning about Leo, but I can't get past the fact of her almost fuckin' up my life behind a nigga. No, I don't want you to accompany me, that's why Kia is coming along for the ride. My location is still active, so you can watch my moves from afar."

Blaze thought about why Icy wanted to get at Desiree and she had valid reasons to do so. He just didn't want her getting blood on her hands. Icy had too much to lose and this shit shouldn't be the reason she got pushed out of her element.

"Allow me and Joe to handle this, Ice."

"Nah, this is my chance to show these muthafuckas that playing in my face is something they shouldn't do. If I get caught, which I doubt I will, you know my account information. Come get me and hire the lawyer who got me off for the murder I didn't commit. I'll see you later, babe. Don't be too mad at me. I have to do this."

Blaze had his eyes trained on the woman he loved every step of the way, but in that moment, he didn't know who she'd morphed into. Icy wore the face of a stone-cold killer and he prayed she would be able to come back from whatever she was setting out to do. As much as he wanted to tie her down to a chair, Blaze had to sit back and let her handle her business, until she hit him up for assistance whenever she needed him.

***

Kia was driving fast as she could without getting pulled over after Icy called, saying she was en route to the salon. She wanted to be the first one there to scope out the area and make sure Desiree wasn't trying to set Icy up. Kia was excited they were finally about to put in work on one of the culprits who had deceived them. Nobody in the equation was safe. It had been months since Operation Icy started. Two months too long, in Kia's mind. She was ready from the start to get revenge but was stopped at every turn. There would be no stopping her after that night, because she planned to keep going until everybody was dead.

Kia picked up her phone to call one of her past dip-offs to ensure he was in place. Icy wanted to shoot the bitch and leave it at that. Kia was going to take things a little further, making sure Desiree's body wouldn't be found for a long time. Renz and Kia had a brief sexual encounter back in the day. He was obsessed with Kia since the first time he was given access to her sweet nectar. He would do anything for Kia, and she knew that. The problem Renz had was Kia didn't reach out to him until she needed something. When the call connected, Renz addressed Kia in a way that made her cringe.

"Where you at, baby?"

"Renz, stop with the baby shit. This is business. I'll be there within the hour. Are you at the spot?"

"I'm here, but let's talk about the compensation side of it all, with yo' sexy ass."

Even though it had been years since Renz was physically involved with Kia, the pictures on her social media page had him gripping his dick in anticipation of sliding inside her walls. When he happened upon her page in the "People You May Know" section, Renz quickly went to Kia's inbox and dropped a message.

For the past two weeks they talked on the phone, catching up on each other's lives. At least Kia knew what Renz had been up to since moving away from Chicago. He still didn't know much about the person Kia was in the present. Renz let her know he was back home for work, Kia listened. A plan formulated in her head when she learned he was a supervisor of a prestigious construction company. Renz reached out at the precise time, because he was in charge of filling the foundation of a new apartment complex on the west side. Kia said all the right shit to get him to agree to help her out. She even took it a step further and allowed Renz to get a taste of her honey to reel him in and the shit worked like a charm.

"You will get the hundred thousand like we agreed. We'll talk about it more when I get there."

"Kia, you know damn well money ain't shit to me. What I want is priceless, baby."

"That's on you. I'm just letting you know the financial part of the deal is stamped in stone. Talking about this is taking my mind off what I have going on. I'm on my way to handle this business and I'll see you when I get there."

"Aight, I'll give you that."

Signaling to get off on the exit ramp, she cruised toward Icy's salon. Kia pulled into the parking lot across the street and shut off her headlights so she could see the entire diameter of the scene in front of her. About ten minutes later, she saw a silver Mercedes parked in front of Icy's business. After scanning up and down the street, Kia called Icy to see where she was.

"Kia, I'm on my way. Are you there yet?"

"Yeah, I'm parked across the street, and I believe Desiree just pulled up. It doesn't look like there's anyone in the car with her and nobody was trailing her. What's your ETA though?"

"I should be pulling up in ten. Have you talked to Julz? I haven't spoken to her since the night we went out." Icy lured the conversation to a different direction because she didn't want to focus on what was ahead for her and Kia.

"I talked to her the other day actually. Julz has been pretty shaken up after what happened to Shonda. That shit was wild and pretty much fucked all of us up in some type of way. Bryan has been there to make sure Julz is alright though," Kia explained. "Oh, his bitch of a baby mama gon' make me pistol whip her ass!"

"What the hell happened? I thought Bryan checked her ass for coming at Julz once before."

"He did! That didn't stop her from causing hell in what Julz and Bryan has going on. She followed Bryan and his daughter to Julz's apartment. *Yo'friend* acted like she wasn't raised in the beat a bitch tribe!" Kia laughed. "When I asked if she beat the fuck outta the hoe, do you know what she said?"

Icy shook her head knowing Kia couldn't see her. The way she was telling the story, Icy could only imagine the steam coming from Kia's nose, even though she laughed. Kia never had to get ready for a confrontation, because her crazy ass was automatically set to go. Waiting a few moments for Icy to respond, Kia continued on when she took too long.

"Julz talm 'bout, *I'm too classy. I let her embarrass herself.* What? All the bullshit that hoe was poppin' outta her mouth should've been lodged in her muthafuckin' throat! I think I need to make *yo' friend* square the fuck up to help her remember what type of bitch she really is. We kicked Julie out of the family back in high school and her stupid ass brought her back."

Icy was laughing so hard, she swerved into oncoming traffic. Luck was on her side because there weren't any cars close enough to cause an accident. Julz was going to give Kia a run for her money whenever she went fuckin' with her about Bryan's baby mama. Icy couldn't wait to witness the show down between the two of them. Slowing down as she turned onto the street of her salon, Icy wiped the tears from her eyes. It was time to get serious.

"Look, get ready. We gotta make this quick. I'm coming down the street as we speak.

"The coast is clear. Desiree is still alone, so it's not a set-up. I was ready to air this muthafucka out. Ya heard me?" Kia said animatedly.

"Shut yo' ass up. Just watch my back because this bitch may not be willing to get in my whip."

"Oh, she gon' get in. Believe that!"

Kia ended the call as Icy turned into the parking lot and pulled up to the side of Desiree's car. Looking down at the duffle bag full of money that sat on the floor of the passenger side, guilt started to set in Icy's mind. Biting her bottom lip, Icy shook the thought away and opened the driver's door. Desiree stepped out as Icy rounded the front of the car with a slight smile on her face.

"I hope you haven't been waiting too long," Icy stated politely.

"No, not really. Do you have the money?"

Icy tried her hardest to hide the aggravation building in her soul. She watched as Desiree peered into her windows looking for the money. Stepping in her line of sight, if Desiree thought it was going to be that easy, she thought wrong. Icy was about to make her work for the fifty stacks she brought along with her. Yeah, she gave Icy a heads up about Leo, but what else did she know?

"Before I even think about giving you the bread you salivating for, I'm going to need a little bit more information about Leo's plans."

"I told you all I know. I haven't spoken to Leo since he threw money at my feet, demanding I get an abortion. I guess you are the only woman he wants kids with," Desiree said, rolling her eyes.

"He can keep hoping and praying on that, because he ain't getting shit out of me. Stop trying to protect his bum ass and tell me what I want to hear."

"I wish I could help you, Icy. I can't because I don't know. All I want to do is save me, and my baby's life, by getting far away from Chicago. Leo is crazy and I have a feeling he will be back."

"And yo' gullible ass gon' let him in. You not leaving here and getting on the road out of this muthafucka. The sacrifices you made for the nigga was top tier. There's no way you're walking away from what y'all got. Now, again tell me everything you know."

When Desiree didn't say anything in return, her silence only pissed Icy off. She could see it in Desiree's eyes, she wasn't ready to leave well enough alone when it came to

Leo. It was time for her to let out a few of his secrets to see how the bitch would react.

"See, Leo didn't give a fuck about me nor you. He killed my father, then fucked me into submission as he kept that information to himself, while he held me close, hoping and praying I never found out about the shit. Not only that, did you know the muthafucka was already married, and has a three-year-old daughter? By *another* bitch, mind you." Icy grimaced.

"I know if he didn't trust you, he wouldn't have taken you along to commit murder. What the fuck do you know? Say nothing and we're going to have a problem."

Taking a deep breath, Desiree shook her head as she looked around the empty parking lot. She turned back to Icy. "Before I told Leo I was pregnant, he came by the condo ranting about how you stole his money. In the midst of that, he received a call from Boom, and I overheard him saying he was going to do something to your mother. He told him to meet him on 65th and Honore. I think that's one of Leo's trap spots. I also know Pip is involved with Leo, and he has a baby mama that lives on Laramie and Lockwood. It's the house on the left with a blue canopy. Other than that, I don't know anything else. I swear."

Icy believed Desiree, but that didn't mean she was getting away scot-free and fifty thousand dollars richer. She did confess to pulling the trigger, which could've landed Icy in jail for life. Some shit was meant for a muthafucka to take to the grave. Too bad Desiree allowed her conscience to get the best of her. Icy's phone rang, and she looked away to see who it was. Desiree took that as her chance to get inside her car and pull off. She didn't like the vibe she was getting from Icy.

"Where the fuck you going?" Icy gritted. "You about to take a ride with me."

"You didn't say nothing about going with you anywhere, Icy. I was supposed to meet you here, get the money, and be on my way."

"I make the rules to this game, bitch. So, what I say goes. Now, get the fuck in my car!"

Desiree didn't move and shook her head no profusely. In a flash, Kia appeared with her Glock raised to the back of Desiree's head, then pulled the trigger. Her body slumped against the car as Icy looked on in shock.

"Don't just stand there, pop the muthafuckin' locks!" Kia snapped throwing a pair of gloves at Icy's chest. "You stood out here debating with this bitch too fuckin' long. You do know the fuckin' pigs will be coming through to patrol this uppity ass neighborhood in about fifteen minutes. Move!"

"You weren't supposed to kill her here, Kia! What the fuck were you thinking?"

"Does it matter? The bitch was going to die regardless!"

Icy put on the gloves, then opened the door to pull the lever for the trunk. Kia was doing shit off impulse without thinking, and Icy didn't like the way she was orchestrating things. Instead of arguing with her, she grabbed Desiree's legs as Kia held her under the arms. After tossing her in the trunk, Kia used a towel she found inside and wiped down the side of the car before blood could drip on the ground. Kia was moving like an expert clean-up person and Icy was in awe. She had never witnessed anyone getting killed in real life. The initial shock of seeing it happen had worn off just as fast as it appeared. Icy was ready to put in work any way she could.

"I'm driving this bitch's car. I need you to get in mine. We can come back for yo' shit because you gon' have to get rid of all the footage from the cameras. No face, no case," Kia smirked. "Meet me on the street, then follow me closely. We have to wrap this shit up before yo' nigga come looking for us. He has called me three damn times in the last ten minutes. That only means yo' ass been ignoring him too."

Kia threw Icy the keys and she took off running across the street. Backing out of the parking spot, she drove out as Kia peeled down the street. Just as they neared the end of the block, the police were turning the corner. Icy kept her cool slowing down a little bit. Once the patrol car was behind them, Kia put her foot to the pedal, tearing ass onto the expressway ramp. Icy's phone was ringing nonstop, but she refused to answer Blaze until she completed the task before her and she was on her way home. Until then, his ass needed to calm the fuck down.

Icy noticed Kia was merging onto the Eisenhower Expressway a few miles into their commute. The confusion was written on her face, because Kia never said anything about changing the plan she had for Desiree's body. The original plan was to lure Desiree to Lake Geneva, shoot her there, then submerge her vehicle into the water. Obviously, that wasn't going to happen, since Kia was heading out west. Icy picked her phone up and it rang in her hand. Seeing Blaze's name, she automatically sent him to voicemail, then called Kia.

"I'm getting off on Independence. There's a construction site I know about and it's the perfect place to dispose our cargo."

"How are we going to do that when we will have to use the equipment to cover the shit? We don't know how to do any of that! You didn't think this through," Icy huffed.

"Icy, I got this, damn! You asking too many questions right now. This shit doesn't need to be discussed over the phone. Wait until we get to the spot. Follow my lead and we gon' be good."

Kia hung up before she ended up cussing Icy out for being an airhead. From the day she learned who her father was, Kia wondered how everyone didn't notice she had every bit of Birdman's DNA running through her veins. Icy was soft as cotton most of the time and only bucked when provoked. Kia wasn't switching up. She always threw the first punch no matter the situation, because she wasn't giving anyone the opportunity to one up her.

Leading the way into the fenced off area on Kostner Avenue, Kia pulled in enough for both cars to enter without being seen. A cement truck was turning as if it was being used, and a dark-skinned guy hopped down with a deep frown on his face. Stalking over to Desiree's car, he pulled on the handle of the door aggressively.

"What is Icy doing here? We don't need no witnesses to the shit I'm about to handle for you, Kia."

"Nigga, relax. Icy ain't gon' say shit. Hell, she's involved right along with us. The body is in the trunk. How long do we have to do this shit?"

"The hole should've been filled hours ago," Renz stated. "It won't be a long process, but we have to get a move on it."

Kia looked down at the hole Renz was going to fill and that muthafucka was deep, deep. She wanted *all* traces of their crime buried and the hole appeared to be wide enough to do just that. Was Renz going to be down for the extra work, was the question.

"Can you use the crane thingy to lower the car into that hole? I need that shit to disappear too."

"That shit is not impossible, but it is extra work for me to do. It will push us back and I don't want to risk that. You're gotta find another way to get rid of the ride. The body, I got you. Everything else is on you."

Kia nodded her head in agreeance, watching Renz walk away. Hoisting himself onto the truck, cement started pouring into the open ground. Icy got out of Kia's car and banged on the trunk for Kia to open it. Renz came over with a large sheet of plastic and placed it on the ground, then lifted Desiree's body onto it.

"Why the fuck she look pregnant, yo?"

"See, you worried about the wrong shit. Pay attention to the job that's paying you," Kia snapped.

"I don't want nothing to do with the missing body of a murdered pregnant woman! Nah, I'm not doing this shit." Renz stepped back but was met with the Gremlin smiling in his face."

"Too late, nigga," Icy snarled. "We here. The cement is flowing, and all you gotta do is throw the bitch in after you wrap her ass up nice and tight. It ain't shit for me to stiffen yo' ass up with the bitch."

Renz couldn't believe Icy was coming at him on some gangsta shit. She was the quietest person he knew back in the day. Everybody knew not to fuck with her off the strength of who her father was. Birdman didn't play about his daughter, and it was known in the streets. If anything, the entire hood looked out for her and Miss Staci when Birdman wasn't around. His untimely death hit the hood hard, but he didn't know that shit turned his baby girl into a fuckin' savage. The way Icy had the tool trained on him, Renz knew he had to do what the fuck needed to be done to get the shit over with. Pronto.

As Renz wrapped the body, Icy glared at him the entire time. The way he stated his concerns bothered her. She knew Kia and Renz had history, but from what she remembered, they were not in touch since he left years prior. Renz was involved, even if he didn't know the particulars of what was going on. Icy had a feeling Renz would be the person to go straight to the cops, leaving his part of the cover-up out of the equation. It took him ten minutes to wrap the body securely in the plastic and that meant he was stalling. Icy placed her gun to the side of his head, pushing it deep into his temple.

"Hurry the fuck up, nigga. You work well with yo' hands messing around with all these heavy machines and it's taking you a lifetime to wrap a bitch up. Stop fuckin' playing with me!"

Kia stood proudly as she watched Icy transform from the woman of concern to a muthafuckin' killa. Renz was beating around the bush, and she was ready to put a bullet in his scary ass herself. There was no need because Icy had that shit on lock. To make matters worse, she looked like she'd done the shit a time or two, but Kia knew it was a first time for everything.

Renz finally finished what he was doing, so Icy backed up and reached behind her, producing a silencer. Screwing the piece on the end of her Glock, Kia wasn't going to stop what needed to be done. Icy may have had the same thoughts as Kia and Renz had to go. The two of them would be the only ones who knew about the happenings of that night. Turning on one another would never happen and they were all they had at the moment. In order to keep both of them out of lock-up, Renzo had to die.

Kia walked over just as Renz threw Desiree's body in the hole. The cement pushed her corpse right under and there wasn't a trace of her left to see. Renz shook his head and said a silent prayer for what he had done. Soon as he lifted his head, Icy embedded two slugs in the back of it. His body joined Desiree's without the added protection, but he met her ass at the pearly gates just the same. The sound of a car door slamming caught Kia and Icy's attention. Kia snatched her tool from her waist, ready to shoot it out with whomever entered the construction grounds. Both of them had their weapons aimed at the entrance, but sighed in relief as they watched Blaze and Joe enter with mugs on their faces.

"What the fuck are y'all doing?" Blaze asked, looking around. "I've been calling for damn near an hour and you not answering had me worried."

Joe went over to the hole and looked down. "Who the fuck is in there?" he asked as a foot vanished in the wet cement.

Icy and Kia didn't say a word, which pissed Blaze off more than he already was. He waited for an explanation as he glared at Icy. Blaze knew what she was going to do, but recruiting somebody other than him to clean the shit up was something he didn't agree with. Icy had just gotten out of a jam she didn't put herself in and now she had actually committed a crime excluding him to keep her safe. The shit was dumb, and he was ready to let her know it. Before he could open his mouth to get in her ass, Icy started talking. She explained everything from start to finish, while he listened to every word.

"The shit y'all did was not smart. I'm glad you read that nigga's body language and got rid of the dead weight though. He was for sure going to roll on y'all," Blaze said. "From this point on, I don't want anybody else involved in this shit unless they are run past me first. We don't have much time to make this shit go away. Y'all lucky this is what I get paid the big bucks to do. Otherwise, we would all be fucked."

Joe had already jumped in the cement truck, adding speed to the flow in order to fill the hole faster. The way he looked at Kia showed how upset he was with her. Kia was glaring at him for other reasons, and it was the bitch she saw him with at the club. If Joe thought she wasn't going to say shit about it, his ass thought wrong. Kia was just going to wait until they finished what needed to be done first.

It took about two hours for the hole to fill completely. Joe made a call and had one of his workers take Desiree's car to one of the chop shops they used. Since he rode with Blaze, Joe got behind the wheel of Kia's car while Icy was led to the other. Kia stood with her hands on her hips as she thought about the audacity of the nigga being in her shit. Didn't he have a bitch waiting for his ass somewhere?

"Get in the fuckin' car, Kia," Joe hissed.

"I know how to drive. You get the fuck out and catch up with Blaze before you be walking."

"Not gon' happen and it's not up for debate. This muthafuckin' place is now a crime scene. Do you really want to be here if the police show up? I don't."

"Go rescue the bitch you were all hugged up with at the club, Joe. You know what? Don't even worry about it. Drop yourself off, then I can go about my night. I'm tired."

Kia got in the car and let the window down before lifting the arm rest, forcing Joe's arm out of the way. After all she'd been through, she needed to flood her lungs with cannabis smoke. Joe started the engine and backed out onto the street. He knew Kia was pissed about seeing him with Joye, she brought that shit on herself though. Long as she wanted to act like she didn't need a nigga, he was going to do what was best for him. Kia made the choice and Joe found another to keep him warm until she was ready.

Chapter 13

Joe pulled up to his home, turned the key in the engine and got out. Kia hurried to beat him to the door because there was no way she was going inside with him. She agreed to get him home and that was all she had for his ass. Joe wasn't having that shit though.

"Give me my keys, Joe! I'm not doing this with you!"

"Pipe all that muthafuckin' noise down outside my crib. I don't need none of these muthafuckas in my business."

Joe unlocked his door, walking in, leaving Kia outside. He wasn't about to beg her to enter, but she could sleep in the car if that's what she chose to do. What wasn't going to take place was her leaving without getting shit off her chest. Joye was a filler for him, all because of Kia and her bullshit. They were going to meet on common ground before the night was over. It was already damn near four in the morning and time was running out. Joe was moving around on three hours of sleep. His bed was calling him.

He was bent down in the refrigerator, trying to get the Italian beef with cheese and plenty of hot peppers dipped well, so he could warm it up when Kia made herself known by slamming the front door. Joe chuckled because she was doing the most for no reason at all. Her attitude matched his and that was the reason they always bumped heads. Kia was head strong, just like Joe. The shit was the formula for disaster, but he loved every bit of it.

When they were in Aruba, Joe thought they were making progress in their courtship. He wasn't looking for commitment because that was when shit turned left. Instead, he was willing to ride the wave of Kia being his girl while they built on things. When she stopped all communication out the blue, that made Joe feel some type of way. He didn't sweat it because he knew shawty was under a lot of pressure with the drama surrounding her family. No matter how Kia felt, he would be there standing beside her 'til the shit was resolved.

As Joe placed his food on a plate, Kia stood in the doorway of the kitchen and cleared her throat. Glancing over his shoulder briefly, he turned back around to put the plate in the microwave. After stealing a few of the peppers, Joe set the timer then gave Kia his undivided attention.

"You want some water or something?"

"Nah, I want my keys so I can go home. I told you I was tired, and you dismissed what I said."

"I did no such thing. It's obvious you have a chip on your shoulder, and what better time to knock that muthafucka off than now. Speak what's on your mind, Kia."

Kia sat down at his table with her hands folded in front of her. Running her fingers through her hair, she let out a loud sigh. "There's nothing to talk about. You got a new thang in ya life and that's all to it. I'm not gon' sit here and spill my feelings about it, because it won't matter, just like what we shared in Aruba didn't. This is what I get for opening up to a nothing ass nigga. Now, give me my keys so I can go get in my bed!"

The timer went off on the microwave, causing Joe to remove his food before addressing what Kia said. Opening the refrigerator once more, he grabbed a bottle of MGD, and a paper towel before taking a seat across from the woman who swore she wasn't bothered. Joe took a bite of his sandwich as he thought about his response. He could lessen the blow by saying the bare minimum, but that wasn't the type of man Joe was. Straight with no chaser was the way he liked to be in every aspect of life.

"See, that's where you have shit misconstrued. What happened in Aruba was amazing," Joe said, taking a swig of his beer. "What the fuck you did afterward was fucked up. I was trying to be there for you after a near-death experience and you shut me out. How do you expect me to play my part as your man if you push me away?"

"First of all, you're not my man."

"Then why the fuck you mad because you saw another bitch on my dick? Make it make sense, Kia! That's what yo' attitude is really about. You thought I was supposed to follow yo' ass around like a sad ass puppy, waiting for you to acknowledge me, but the shit backfired. See, I'm not going to wait for nobody to have time for me. I can always find a bitch to fuck. That's a no brainer. But I want yo' ass and you fighting it. You are the reason you're mad. Own up to that shit!"

"I don't care who you entertain. What I don't appreciate is you leaving the hoe in my presence, then putting my sister in the position to take her home! I could've beat the fuck outta her just because you set her up for failure."

Joe laughed because Kia cared more than she wanted to admit. Fighting a female because she was at the club with him was the thing rachet bitches in the hood did to puff out their chests. Kia was too grown to carry herself like that and he was glad it didn't go down in that manner. Joe watched as Kia stared daggers into his soul while he ate quietly.

"So, what I said was funny to you?" she asked angrily.

"No, but you are. What would putting yo' hands on somebody accomplish? That shit is childish, and you know it." Joe got up to wash his plate. He came back to the table, downing the rest of his beer. "I'm waiting on you to answer the question, Kia. What would you get out of throwing hands with her?"

Ignoring the question as a whole, Kia shot back with a couple of her own. "Who is she, Joe? Did you fuck her? And please don't lie, because that's going to start a whole other argument."

"Lying is not what I do. I don't have no problem telling you who she is. First, I'll answer the question that's really bothering you. No, I haven't fucked her…yet."

"What do you mean yet?" Kia hissed.

"Just what I said. Anyway, Joye is a realtor who helped me find a crib. We've been on a few dates and chilled too. But we have not had sex."

Kia rose to her feet and her attitude was still intact. "Give me my keys! This is the last time I'm going to say it."

"I'm not giving you shit because yo' ass ain't going nowhere."

Joe walked past Kia and went into his bedroom. He went right to the safe he kept in his closet, throwing Kia's keys inside before locking it. Joe took off his clothes, throwing everything in the hamper. When he walked out, Kia was standing in the doorway with a scowl that slowly disappeared when she noticed his dick swinging like a bat with every step he took in her direction. Joe didn't give a fuck about her being mad, he was ready to fuck the attitude out of her system.

Coming face-to-face with her, Joe rubbed his thumb across her bottom lip and Kia slapped his hand away. He didn't let that stop him from taking things a little further. Kia's nipples were standing at attention, so Joe ran his finger across them slowly. When she didn't react to his touch, he rolled the left one between his thumb and index finger until he heard her moan lowly. Joe moved in and covered his mouth with hers and sucked her bottom lip into his mouth. The way her body leaned into him let Joe know she was all in. Using his left hand, he unbuttoned her jeans and ran his hand down her clean-shaven mound. The monkey was smoother than a baby's ass and the shit made his mouth water.

Kia wanted to punch Joe for what he was doing, but fat ma was yelling in her head loudly. *Bitch, don't you dare! It's been too damn long since anybody touched me and I'm tired of yo' shit!* Joe dipped his finger into her honey pot and the dam broke. Her sweet essence ran down her pants leg. Joe released her nipple and pulled her close to his body, while she shook from the orgasm he forced out of her. Kia's head fell to his chest and her breathing was erratic as she gasped for air. Joe strummed her pearl like a guitar string, bringing her to the brink of another explosion.

She didn't know if the heat she felt resonated from her pores or the heat blowing from the vents. All Kia knew was she needed to come out of the coat she was wearing. As she shrugged out of the garment, Joe took that as a sign of her being ready to get naked. Once her coat was off, he lifted her shirt over her head and followed up with helping her release her legs from her pants. When everything was pooled at Kia's feet, Joe lifted her up in his arms to his massive bed.

"We can't do this," Kia panted with her eyes partially closed.

"We can and we will. Now relax and shut the fuck up. I got just what you need and you gon' love it."

Kia leaned up on her elbows to snap on Joe, but he was on his knees between her legs. His breath on her clit sent a shiver down her spine. She almost passed out when he wrapped his lips around her bud. Her hands automatically went to the back of his head and pushed his face deeper into her snatch.

"Fuck!"

Kia moaned as she grinded her pussy into Joe's mouth. He hummed as he sopped up her wetness, not missing a drop. Joe started fucking Kia with his stiff tongue, causing her to grind her pussy harder. He slipped his thumb in her ass, and she bucked like a horse.

"Aaaaah, shit! I'm about to cum. Please don't stop," Kia purred.

Joe looked up and the fuck faces Kia made were sexy as hell to him. The way she begged him to keep doing what he was doing made his dick harder than a brick. The way Kia was panting told him she was on the brink of wetting his face up. Before she could let loose, he backed up off her pearl, joining her on the bed. He pushed her legs back, making her toes touch her ears. Joe entered Kia's warm tunnel and almost screamed out like a bitch. Her cave swallowed his dick like a boa constrictor, tightly.

"Damn, Kia. This how you doing shit? Mmmmmm."

Joe was stuck as he willed himself from releasing his kids into her incubator. One thing he wasn't going to do was go out as a two-minute brother. Joe had too much pent-up energy to waste and not get the full feel of the good shit Kia had laid out on a platter. Rocking back and forth slowly, Joe lifted Kia's leg and brought her foot to his mouth. Sucking her toes one at a time, he swiftly changed the rhythm of his strokes. Even though Kia wasn't able to bring her other leg down, she threw her pussy back with force. Joe threw his head back and allowed Kia to have her way with him. Joe felt his kids racing to the finish line as she fucked him, instead of the other way around. He snatched his dick out to stop the flow. Flipping Kia over on her stomach, Joe pulled her onto her knees and entered her from the back while pulling her hair.

"I'm doing the fuckin' around here, not yo' ass."

"Murder this pussy then, nigga," Kia smirked over her shoulder.

"Say less."

Sweat slid down his back like Joe was in a sauna. Watching Kia's ass ripple in waves as he stroked nice and hard as he spread her cheeks wide, Joe spit down her crack. Inserting his thumb into her sacred hole, he wished it was his meat instead. He knew Kia wasn't ready for that type of action from him. Joe had plans to prepare that muthafucka for entry though. The deeper Joe pushed his thumb into her asshole, the deeper the arch became in Kia's back.

"Ohhhhhh, shit! That feels so good, baby!"

"Oh, I'm baby now, huh? You needed this dick to make you act right, I see," Joe growled, gripping Kia's waist with force. Her pussy was sopping wet, and her juices coated Joe's member, making it easy for him to glide inside with ease. "I'm gon' make you love me, Kia."

"Sounds like you're already head over heels for this pussy. Hit that shit and shut up!"

Joe pulled her head back far as it could go, then leaned forward and kissed her passionately. He hit her with a series of strokes that had her screaming out in pleasure. Kia sounded like she was struggling to breathe and the words she was trying to speak were caught in her throat. Releasing her hair, Kia was finally able to breathe normally. The way Joe was pounding her yoni made her shiver from head to toe.

"Aaaah, yes! Right there! Right there! I'm cummin'!"

Kia's walls clenched around Joe tightly and the oxygen stopped flowing to his brain. His legs locked instantly, causing a Charlie horse to form in his calf. The tingling sensation in his balls was something he hadn't felt in a long time. Something was different about the euphoric nature of the orgasm he was experiencing. Joe couldn't stop his soldiers from going to war, and he hoped like hell Kia was ready to be a mother.

"Got damn this, you pulling this nut out of me! Grrrrrr!" Joe groaned as he emptied his sack.

The word love was on the tip of his tongue, so he bit the side of Kia's neck to stop that shit from happening. Joe's body went limp, causing him to fall onto Kia's back without putting too much of his weight on her. Slowly rolling to the side breathing heavily, the tingling sensation in his legs prevented him from getting up to get a rag. But the swelling of his heart brought on a different feeling for him. Usually when he was finished sexing a woman, it was time for her to go where she paid the bills. That wasn't the case with Kia. Joe didn't want her to ever leave his side.

He glanced over and laughed lowly as Kia snored lightly while lying on her stomach. He planted a kiss on her forehead and snuggled close to her body. Closing his eyes, Joe knew he wanted to be with Kia for the long haul. Hopefully, she would feel the same way when she woke up from the dick coma he had her in.

***

Kia tried to get comfortable as she attempted to move. The strong arm around her waist prevented her from moving an inch. She forgot where she was, until opening her legs made her kitty purr. A smile formed on Kia's face as flashbacks of the night before played in her mind. Snuggling into his body, Kia's nipples hardened, causing Joe to cuff the left one, moaning into her neck.

"You fit just right in my arms," he said, planting small kisses on her shoulder.

"Too bad I have to go." Kia wiggled out of his grasp, getting out of the bed. "Where are your towels? I need to take a shower."

Joe looked like he wanted to say something but decided against it. Instead, he got up and left the room to get what Kia requested. Upon his return, Kia was on the phone going off on someone. Placing the items on the bed next to her, Joe went into the kitchen to make breakfast. Kia's voice rose every second, causing him to pause in the middle of the floor while listening.

"It don't matter where the fuck I am! Go ask the bitch who birthed the child you failed to mention. That explains where you were on the nights you were nowhere to be found. It's cool though. Keep that same energy, nigga."

Stack was trying not to go there with Kia, because she had every right to be mad at him. He didn't think he had to tell her about his daughter, because they weren't exclusively together. Stack knew the outcome would've been the same when it came to Kia, since he was having sex with both women at the same time. Kia made it clear she didn't want a relationship, but was always catching an attitude, and trying to fight any and every woman who looked at Stack wrong. The shit blew the fuck out of him, and he continued to deal with her on the strength of how she was down for him in the streets and the sheets.

"You better stop raising yo' muthafuckin' voice at me, Kia. My seed shouldn't even be a factor, because we're not in a relationship. If I remember correctly, you said we would do *us* with no strings attached. I just so happened to fuck up and produce a baby in the process."

"How the hell was that a fuck-up? You still fuckin' with the bitch!" Kia screamed. "How long you been out, Stack?"

Stack stalled for a brief minute, then answered her question. "A couple weeks, but——"

"My muthafuckin' point exactly! You been laid up playing daddy and thought about my black ass after the fact! If you gave a fuck, you would've been concerned about what's been going on with me! The day you got caught up with the police, my house was shot up by your so-called homeboy. I could've lost my life and you didn't think to reach out to me until now? Fuck you, Stack! Stay wherever the fuck you at, because ain't no coming back to me!"

"I'm not trying to hear all that shit! I was locked up, Kia! How the fuck was I supposed to be of any help to you?" Kia didn't respond and that only pissed Stack off further. "Where the fuck you at? We can discuss this face-to-face."

"We don't have anything to discuss." Kia retorted smartly.

"I went to Staci's house last night and this morning. Yo' ass ain't been there all night! Don't make me come looking for you!"

"I don't care what you did, Stack. You out there looking for me in the daytime with a flashlight, for what?"

Joe was tired of hearing the back and forth going on between Kia and the nigga on the phone. He walked into the bedroom standing in front of her. Kia looked directly at his dick, which was on full display, licking her lips as Stack rambled about God knows what.

"Don't disrespect my shit like that, ma. Hang the muthafuckin' phone up before I break it."

"Who the fuck is that?" Stack's voice boomed through the device.

"The nigga who's about to change her life for the better, nigga. Yo' services are no longer needed."

Joe took the phone from Kia ending the call. Her pussy pulsated at a rapid pace and leaked like a faucet. She didn't have anything to say about what Joe had done, because the shit turned her all the way on. Kia knew Stack wasn't going to go away quietly. Especially knowing there was another man in the picture. The two of them were going to bump heads at some point and Kia didn't know how it was going to play out. The shit wasn't going to be pretty. Joe was pretty pissed because Kia shouldn't have even given the nigga that much attention.

"Let's get something straight," Joe said, sitting next to her. "That was the last time you will address that nigga about what the fuck he has going on outside of you. I was going to take my time going into this shit, but I see there's a pattern with you. It's us or nothing, Kia. I'm a grown ass man looking for a wife. That hardcore, ride or die shit ain't needed over here. I understand the revenge you seeking and I'm all for that. After we end the bullshit, all I expect from you is greatness. You know, making a name for yourself in a legit way, and lovin' on the kid. I'll handle the rest. What I don't do is drama. Stay the fuck away from that nigga before I kill him. He's no longer your concern."

Kia opened her mouth and Joe shook his head no. He grabbed her by the hand, leading her out of the bedroom toward the shower. The only thing she could do was follow his lead while the juices from her yoni ran down her inner thighs.

Chapter 14

"Fuck! This being a businesswoman shit isn't for the weak."

Julz was packing up the last of an order she had to deliver. She had been drowning herself in work to keep her mind off witnessing Shonda's murder. Every night she closed her eyes, the scene played over and over, causing her to have nightmares. Julz picked up a lot of customers in the past couple weeks and she used the nights she couldn't sleep to fulfill orders and be creative. Her mind was sharper than a sharpshooter and Julz embraced it every step of the way.

Without Bryan, Julz didn't know what her state of mind would've been. He stayed by her side as much as he could without being away from Jamiah too long, and Julz appreciated that about him. She wanted to end everything with him when Nia, his baby mama, followed him to her place on pure bullshit. Her first thought was to leave his ass alone, but she didn't go that route because Bryan could only do so much in terms of Nia's actions. They had a long adult conversation about what transpired, and Bryan reassured Julz there was nothing going on between them.

Hell, he was fighting hard in court to get Nia to sign away her parental rights. Jamiah didn't even want to be in her mother's presence, because Nia had become a monster to the little girl. She was doing shit just to get back at Bryan. Everything Nia did was documented and she was not to be alone with Jamiah under any circumstances. Nia wasn't taking it very well because their daughter was the only thing that connected her to Bryan. So, she blamed Julz as the reason Bryan was fighting to keep Nia out of Jamiah's life. The things she had done didn't play a factor, so she said.

Julz sealed the final box for the large order, falling back on the floor. Glancing at her watch, she realized she only had about fifteen minutes before the postal worker would knock on her door to pick up the packages she had to mail off. That was the cost of being the boss. All work, no play at times and she loved when the money hit her account. That was the reason she went hard as she did. She loved to reap the benefits.

Scrolling through her business phone, Julz went to the messages to retrieve the address of her delivery. When she saw it was located in Glenn Ellyn, she groaned loudly.

"Dammit, I didn't plan on driving that damn far!" Julz scoffed as she stood to her feet.

Julz had to get herself together because she had a lunch date with Bryan and was truly looking forward to being in his company. Most of their time together was included with Jamiah which she absolutely loved, but she needed an exclusive date with her man. Intimacy was what Julz needed, and Bryan was making it happen. He reserved a room for the weekend so they could indulge with one another any way they saw fit.

As she brushed her teeth, there was a knock on the door. Julz spit, then rinsed her mouth before rushing out of the bathroom. Peeking through the peephole, she saw the postal worker on the other side.

"Good morning, ma'am. I'm here to pick up your packages," he said with a smile.

Julz ushered the worker inside, pointing to the pile in the middle of the floor. "Leave the three boxes please. Everything else is yours. Make sure the tracking numbers are emailed to me as well."

"Of course."

It took about five minutes or so for them to get all the packages into his cart. Julz thanked him and locked the door, before rushing around to finish getting ready so she could leave the house. Grabbing her phone and keys from the dresser, Julz made her way to the living room. She groaned once more because she would have to make several trips to her car. She lifted the first box and left the apartment. Julz was out of breath by the time she loaded all three boxes, then she ran back inside to get her purse and several bottles of water.

Once she was settled in her car, she downed one of the waters and started her car. Waiting for the heat to kick in, she noticed she needed to get gas. Julz hadn't driven her car in days and didn't realize how low her tank was. She hated pumping gas in the cold, but it had to be done. When the gauge indicated her vehicle was warm enough, she shifted the gear in drive to start her commute.

Pulling into the gas station not too far from her apartment, Julz unlocked the door to get out. She was texting Bryan to let him know she was going to make the delivery and also to share the address with him just in case something went wrong. Julz wasn't paying attention and didn't notice the car that pulled in at the pump beside her. Before she could raise her head, a cloth was placed over her mouth, and everything went black.

***

"The weather is breaking, and crime is at an all-time high. I want each and every one of you to keep your noses clean in these streets. Positivity, excelling in school, sports, or maintaining employment should be the focal point for you all. My worse fear of all time is to get a call that something horrendous has happened to one of you."

Bryan looked around the room at the group of young men sitting before him. He was ending the mentor meeting on a positive note at the center. One would say Bryan was in his feelings about the recent deaths of a couple of minors around the city. The one thing he prided himself in was informing his guys to leave the negativity where it was, in the streets.

"As I say every day, watch the news. It may be painful to hear about everything going on with our youth, but at the same time, it could help you learn what not to do. I want you all to elevate and be great. We have no room for error. Be mindful of the company you keep because it takes a second to become guilty by association. Remember that. So, if you know the environment you are in isn't good for you, get the fuck away! Nothing good can come out of the situation. With that being said, be safe going home. Anyone who needs a ride, holla at me and I got you."

Walking around the room saying his goodbyes and giving parting words to some of the guys, Bryan waited to see if anyone would approach with any concerns or needs. Once the center was cleared, he went to his office and automatically picked his phone up from the desk to see if Julz had called. It was early morning when she texted the address she was headed to for her delivery. Bryan hadn't heard from her since. He'd reached out to her to no avail during the day and she didn't answer, but he didn't think too much about it until that moment. Listening to the phone ring nonstop, Bryan's nerves were on edge.

He turned off the light in his office, locked the door then met with the other mentors, Bryan made sure they were clear about what needed to be done for the end of the day, before heading out for the weekend. He jumped into his whip and made a beeline for Julz's apartment. As he drove, Bryan tried his best not to panic as he listened to the phone ring once more until Julz's voice flooded through the speakers.

You've reached Julz, leave a message and I'll return your call soon as I possibly can.

It shouldn't have taken her hours on end to make the delivery. Bryan felt in his gut, something wasn't right.

"Where are you, Julz?" he said aloud as he sped through the streets.

When he pulled into the parking lot of the apartment complex, Bryan didn't hesitate in getting out. Running up the steps two at a time, he pushed the button with her name beside it continuously. When there was no response to his annoying pushes, Bryan's heart started beating fast in his chest. Slowly walking back to his car, he looked up at Julz's window, hoping she was mad and just didn't answer. That wasn't the case because the blinds hadn't moved an inch. Icy and Kia were going to be worried sick once the news was out that their friend hadn't been heard from for hours. Bryan pulled his phone out and hit Blaze up.

"Yo, B, what's up?"

"Hold on, let me get Joe on the call." Bryan added Joe and waited for him to answer.

"B, what it do?"

Bryan was quiet for a spell, trying to figure out how to lay the news on them. Blaze was impatient than a muthafucka on the other end. He cut into Bryan's thoughts when his voice boomed out with command.

"Bryan, what the fuck is going on, man? Talk to us!"

"Blaze, I didn't know you were on the call. I'm with you, homie. Talk before I pull the fuck up! You cool?" Joe asked with concern.

"Julz is missing," Bryan finally spit out. "She had a delivery to make this morning in Glen Ellyn and I haven't heard from her. We had a weekend getaway planned, she was too excited about it. Now, I can't find her."

"Did she say who the delivery was for?"

"Who are you talking about, Akoni?" Icy asked in the background.

Blaze held his finger up so he could hear Bryan's response. He read the text Julz had sent to him, which only included the address to the client. A name wasn't mentioned in the information provided. Both Blaze and Joe could hear the sadness in Bryan's voice, and they understood just how he felt, because it would've been the same if the shoe was on the other foot. Blaze didn't have a choice but to fill Icy in on what was going on. Putting the call on speaker so she could hear all parties, Blaze cleared his throat as he stalled.

"Babe, have you talked to Julz?"

The way Icy's eyes ballooned then turned into slits scared the shit out of Blaze for a minute. Shaking her head no, Icy couldn't speak. Blaze explained what Bryan knew and she pulled her phone from her pocket, tapping away on the screen.

"Her last location was at the gas station down the street from her house. Bryan, where are you?"

"I'm sitting in the parking lot of her apartment, but I'm on my way to that damn gas station!"

Peeling out of the lot, Bryan sped down the street turning into the first gas station he saw. He knew it was a slim chance of Julz being there, but there may be some clues indicating she had been there at some point. Bryan hopped out with phone in hand, looking around the perimeter. He spotted what appeared to be a purse by one of the pumps. He picked up the bag and noticed a lot of things in it, but there was no wallet. As he was about to walk away, an item on the ground caught his attention. It was Julz's driver's license. Bryan's heart dropped to his ass.

"I found her purse and license," he said into the phone. "Her car isn't here. I hope one of these punk muthafuckas didn't jack her for her shit!"

"I'm on my way," both Blaze and Joe said in unison.

"Don't move!" Blaze barked, ending the call on his end.

"Brah, make a call to get the footage from the gas station! We gon' find her," Joe reassured him.

Bryan called his tech soon as the line was clear, holding the phone for dear life while he took care of business. When he was told the cameras didn't work, Bryan felt defeated. He didn't let that shit be known, instead, he gave the tech the address to run and Julz's number to trace. It took about five minutes for him to obtain a number for the person who lived at the address. The tech told Bryan he would get back with him about any movement on Julz's phone before instructing him to call the number he'd provided. Bryan made the call, doing as he was told.

"Hello?" a woman answered.

"Yeah, I'm looking for the owner of Julz Creations. Did she make it out there with your order this morning?"

"No, I've been calling her all morning and she hasn't responded. I'm pressing charges because she stole my money! I'm tired of these internet scammers calling themselves business owners, when they are actually thieves!" the woman screamed angrily.

Bryan understood where the woman was coming from, but under the circumstances she chose the wrong businesswoman to accuse of being shiesty. Julz was legit as they came, and she had reviews to prove the shit. There wasn't anything fraudulent about her.

"You have the wrong impression this time," Bryan said, defending his woman's reputation. "Julz Creations is indeed a business that Julz take pride in and works her ass off to keep afloat. She didn't rip you off. I can assure you of that. Julz is missing. Your address was where she was headed this morning and she hasn't been heard from since. All I wanted to know was if she made it to you."

"Oh, my God! I'm so sorry. She didn't show up and I was upset, but I truly apologize now since you just gave a back story. I pray she is found safe. I swear, I didn't mean any disrespect."

"It's cool. What was the total of your order? And don't lie."

I ordered a lot of merchandise for my family reunion. It was…" the woman's voice trailed off slightly. "Six hundred seventy-five dollars."

A notification chimed on Bryan's phone, causing him to look at the picture message. There was an invoice with Julz's company logo on top, proving the amount which she had paid. Bryan learned the woman's name was Amira Thomas.

"Thanks for your help. I want to refund your money. Soon as I figure this thing out, I will make sure you receive the items you ordered. If you hear from Julz, contact me directly. What's your source of payment?"

"I appreciate your offer. You don't have to do that. The family reunion isn't until August. Concentrate on finding Julz. Please keep me posted. Remember, the Lord has his arms around her. She will be found."

"Thank you for your kind words. That still doesn't tell me your payment method though. I'm not trying to hear about what I don't have to do. This is something my woman would do if she was unable to deliver. Now, do you have Zelle?"

Amira sighed into the phone and finally broke down and told Bryan he could send money by using her phone number. He thanked her once again before ending the call. He placed the phone in his pocket after sending Amira the money he promised. Getting back into his vehicle, Bryan rested his head on the steering wheel and a lone tear escaped his eye. The hurt he felt in his heart was something he had to get out before his boys showed up. Bryan knew there was nothing wrong with a thug crying, but he wasn't trying to allow anybody to see that shit.

The thought of how he and Julz had come from him almost losing her, then winning back the trust she had in them making shit work. Bryan knew the altercations with Nia were taking a toll on her, but Julz was handling it like a real woman should. The thought of his baby mama had Bryan scrambling for his phone. The last encounter between Julz and Nia got pretty heated, and Nia threw several threats Bryan blew off. Now, the shit had him second-guessing his actions.

The first time he called Nia's phone, it rang without her answering. Bryan tried again and she picked up, then ended the call. The third time, Nia answered with an attitude.

"Why the fuck you calling me, fuck nigga?"

Ignoring the ignorant shit Nia said because she and everybody else knew she was big bad, and Bryan was far from what she described. Instead of getting into a screaming match with her, he decided to stay calm.

"Where you at? I'm on my way to yo' crib."

"Don't waste your time. I'm not there. Me and my man went on a mini vacation."

"Yeah, okay. That don't tell me where you at though."

"You have our daughter, so my whereabouts is none of your business!"

"Where. The. Fuck. Are. You, Nia!"

The line got quiet, causing Bryan to look down at the screen to see if she was still on the line. Then the call dropped. The shit was fishy and Bryan had his tech back on the line to find Nia's location. As he talked, he was informed that Julz's phone wasn't traceable and was probably put in airplane mode so the location couldn't be found. The same shit happened when he tried to trace Nia's phone, and Bryan prayed he wouldn't have to put a bullet in her head, because she wanted to be spiteful.

Chapter 15

Nia was pissed off because she knew Bryan was calling to see where she was, because his bitch vanished into thin air. She paced back and forth across the dirty floor of the abandoned house in Dolton. She was happier than a gay man in a roomful of dicks, until Bryan called questioning her.

Pip came to Nia's house to take her out to eat. She had been messing around with him for a couple of weeks and was really feeling him. When Nia got into the car, Pip said he had to make a run and ended up seeing Bryan's bitch all in her phone at the gas station. Pulling up to the pump right next to hers, Pip soaked a rag with a liquid that had a strong aroma, which caused Nia to cough uncontrollably while lowering the window to air out the fumes. Before she could question what he was doing, Pip jumped out of the car and damn near smothered the bitch. Tossing Julz in the back seat, he instructed Nia to drive her car. Nia spotted Julz's purse and took the wallet, leaving everything else, before snatching up the phone that fell to the ground. Nia wasted no time peeling out behind her man with shaky hands.

The entire ride on the expressway, Nia wondered what Pip's connection to Julz was. There was no way she was fucking another nigga who's dick Nia was sucking. Just thinking about it pissed Nia off. But knowing she would get the opportunity to beat the brakes off Julz made her whole day.

Crossing the room where Julz was tied to a chair, Nia smacked her across the face repeatedly until she came to. Julz's head kept falling forward, then she lifted it up slowly and it fell back as if it was too heavy for her to control. Nia snickered at the sight before her and hit Julz again, just to see her struggle some more.

"Bitch, talk all that shit you were spittin' the other day!"

Julz's vision was blurry, her ears were clogged, and she could barely make out what the woman was saying to her. Every time she tried to open her eyes, they rolled to the back of her head. Julz didn't know what happened to put her in the state she was in. All she could remember was sending a text to Bryan, then everything going black. The feeling Julz was experiencing was one she hoped would never present itself again. She tried to raise her hand to her face but couldn't move. At first, the thought of being paralyzed crossed her mind, until she was able to wiggle her fingers. Julz sighed with relief, and it was short lived when Nia hit her with a strong two-piece to the left side of her face.

"Bryan should've told you I wasn't the bitch to play with! Where that nigga at now?"

Nia took advantage of the fact of Julz being unable to fight back. Julz laughed evilly once she realized who was pretending to be the Big Bad Wolf. A swift punch in the grill wiped the sarcasm right out of her mouth. The taste of blood on her tongue brought her out of the daze she was currently in. Julz spit that shit right in Nia's face, and braced herself for the blows that were sure to come.

"You better kill me after you get ya rocks off, hoe. When I'm able, I'm beating yo' ass to a pulp, before putting a slug or two in yo' muthafuckin' head. Jamiah gon' be straight, because she will call me mama."

"Say less," Nia sneered as she geared up to work Julz over.

Nia was beating the shit out of Julz like it was a recreational activity. Becoming numb to the hits, Julz took every hit with a grain of salt. A revengeful plan was taking over her mind with every blow delivered. Julz refused to cry out in pain though. Nia raised her foot and kicked Julz in the middle of her chest, knocking the air out of her lungs. The chair fell back, connecting Julz's head with the floor.

"Yo! What the fuck you doing?"

Pip rushed into the room with fire in his eyes. Nia bent down to hit Julz again, but Pip swept her off her feet as she fought to get out of his arms. The hold he had on her prevented Nia from completing the task of fucking Julz up in the worse way.

"Calm yo' hot headed ass down! We need this bitch in tip top shape when Leo gets here. That's impossible because you've already beat the shit out of her! Whatever you got against her, deal with that shit on your own time. Not now! When I let you go, sit the fuck down and control yo' muthafuckin' emotions. As a matter of fact, take this blunt and go outside."

Pip took the rolled cannabis from behind his ear and shoved it into Nia's hand. She mugged Julz, still lying on the floor, contemplating if she should run and kick her white ass in the head. The look Pip shot at her made Nia go on outside to release the rest of the stress that was brewing in her system.

The mention of Leo scared the fuck out of Julz. She knew he wasn't going to let her live to tell who kidnapped her. The sudden urge to shit shot through Julz's colon. She had to squeeze her ass cheeks together tightly, while trying to figure a way out. Julz had no clue how much time she had before Leo was due to arrive, but sitting like a duck was something she wasn't trying to do.

Julz winced as she tried to roll over on her side. Pip felt bad to see her in the condition she was in. He grabbed Julz under her arm and pulled her to her feet. Pip sat the chair upright and helped her back into it.

"You good?"

She laughed lowly, thinking, *Do I look good, muthafucka?* Instead of saying those words out loud, Julz just shook her head no.

"I need to use the bathroom. Would you please allow me to do that?" Julz asked with her head down.

Pip checked his pockets as Nia came back into the room. She heard what Julz asked and scoffed. Moving closer to Pip, she looked down at Julz in disgust.

"Piss on yo'self, you musty bitch! Trailer trash white hoe. You should've stayed on the other side of the tracks, because this the type of shit that happens in the hood. You thought getting your body done would make you fit in with us sistas?"

"I see why you mad now," Julz said with a smile. "You jealous. It's no secret that I wasn't naturally born this way, but it fucks you up that yo' nigga love every inch of this store-bought body. That's a you problem. Unless y'all want this muthafucka to smell like pure shit for the duration of my stay, I'd advise you to let me use the bathroom in this nasty ass place!"

Pip whispered something to Nia, and she smacked her lips in response. She went into her pocket and pulled out Julz's phone and handed it to him. Turning to face Julz, he bent down to her level, staring her in the eyes.

"If you try anything, I will kill yo' ass without thought."

Pip motioned for Julz to sit forward so he could untie the knots in the rope. "I can make shit comfortable for you, or this whole ordeal can be yo' worse nightmare. The choice is yours." He licked her outer lobe and Julz cringed. "I've always wanted to feel the inside of a white bitch pussy. Plus, you sexy than a muthafucka."

The pressure of the rope being released caused Julz to flex her wrists back and forth. As she pretended to concentrate on herself, what Pip said replayed in her head. His horniness would be his downfall. Julz was going to make sure of it.

"Come on, so you can take care of yo' business. You lucky I brought tissue with me," Pip laughed as he led her to the bathroom.

Julz entered the room and almost threw up. The bathroom was filthy. There was dirt, grime, and mold everywhere. It was worse than any outhouse she'd ever used at an outdoor event. The smell was horrendous and Julz was scared to even squat over the toilet. Crossing her legs, Julz felt the band of the Apple Watch band touch her ankle and she smiled on the inside. Since the shit with Leo started, Julz never wore her watch on her wrist when she was out alone. She wore it on her ankle in case of an emergency. If something happened to her phone, she still had a way to contact somebody. Julz was glad she thought of the idea because she would be fucked.

"Um, this is gross," she said, scrunching her face up. "What choice do I have? Where's that tissue?"

"It's on the roll. Hurry up," Pip said, leaning against the doorframe.

"Can I have some privacy?"

"Hell nawl! Don't you see that window right there? I can't let you try to escape, buttercup. It's not that type of party. I would hate to have to shoot you in the back of your head. Handle that, so I can get you tied back up."

Julz didn't argue with him because she had to shit for real. If he wanted to stand there, it was on him. Her bowel movements didn't smell like roses, so she knew he would exit stage left soon enough. Lining the toilet with half the roll, Julz sat and dropped three logs simultaneously. The stench was in the air in no time. Pip covered his nose as he glared at her disgustedly.

"Damn! What crawled in yo' ass and died? You stank! That ain't even ladylike. You smell like a whole nigga in this muthafucka. I'm out! Come out when you finish!"

Pip slammed the door and Julz chuckled. *Mission accomplished.* She lifted her leg, going to the settings on her watch and turned the location on. She knew both Icy and Kia could track her moves easily. She sent a message to Icy fast as she could, before Pip decided she was taking too long.

I've been kidnapped by Pip and Nia. Leo is supposed to be on his way. I don't know where I am but get here before he does, because he's not going to let me live. Don't let him kill me, Icy! I turned my——"

The creak of the floorboards was an indication that Pip was on his way back to the bathroom. Julz pressed send in the nick of time and dropped her leg. Pip opened the door with his head turned away. Julz wiped herself, feeling dirty. She needed a shower.

"You done?" Pip asked.

"Yeah," she said, going to the sink to wash her hands after pulling up her pants. Turning the knob on the faucet, nothing happened.

"There's some sanitizer on the counter to the right of the sink. That's all I got," Pip said, looking at her. "I have good and bad news. The good news is you get to live another night. The bad news is you gon' have to stay yo' pretty ass here tonight. I will be with you, but I'll be making a run to drop ole girl off at her crib. When I come back, I'll have some sanitary items for you to clean yourself up with. There may not be no water, but baby wipes will make you feel better. What you want to eat?"

"I'm not hungry. I want out of this muthafucka!"

"Don't be like that, ma. You gon' need yo' energy because I'm getting some of that pussy soon as I return."

Pip licked his lips lustfully. Julz prayed like hell Icy traced her location before his ass got back. To give the nigga something to look forward to, Julz turned while lifting her shirt along with her bra. The forty-two DDs she paid top dollar for was on full display for Pip to see. Caressing her breasts, Julz played with her nipples until they pebbled causing Pip to drool at the mouth.

"Those muthafuckas pretty. They're perky as hell waiting for me to suck the shit out of them. Keep that pussy wet for me. I'll be back to take care of you shortly." Pip winked at her.

"I have to tie you up again though. Wouldn't want you to run while I'm away."

"It's cool. I like that rough shit," Julz said seductively. "Make sure you bring enough dick to the party. If you don't, you die. Deal?"

The expression on Pip's face was priceless. Julz's face stayed stoic, and he didn't know if she was throwing out threats or role playing. Little did he know, she meant that shit with every fiber in her being. Pip smirked as Julz walked over to him with her breasts still on display. Reaching out to get a free feel put a smile on his face.

"No worries. My dick is long, thick, and curves to the left. It will definitely touch every organ in your torso." He grasped her throat tightly as he continued to massage her nipple between his fingers. "Don't ever threaten my life, bitch," he sneered directly in her face.

"That shit just made my pussy leak. I love to be choked, daddy. Kitty purring for you right now. I don't like waiting. Take the bitch home and get back to me so I can ride that dick. What better way to die than after getting dicked down the right way?"

Julz's act of seduction clouded Pip's judgement. He'd fucked up because he had sex on the brain, while Julz had murder on hers. The muthafucka was going to die a slow and painful death. She was going to make sure of it. Pip led her back into the room after helping Julz adjust her shirt. Julz had the opportunity to glance around and spotted a gas can sitting next to a hose across the room.

Is these muthafuckas planning to burn my ass up in here? Julz thought. She immediately closed her eyes and prayed to the man upstairs with her whole heart.

Lord, I hope I'm wrong. While I'm at this point, please forgive me and my people for the sins we're going to commit tonight. You see what's been going on, so give us a pass on this one and the many to come. In Jesus' name, Amen. Julz opened her eyes and Pip was staring at her curiously.

"You good?"

Julz nodded her head yes, then sat in the chair before her. Pip tied her back up, cutting off her circulation. Nia barged in with an attitude the moment she saw Pip so close to Julz.

"I'm ready to go! It shouldn't have taken you this long, Pip."

"Man, go to the car!" Pip growled.

Julz had to antagonize the bitch one more time for the road. "Hey, Nia, I'll be seeing you soon. Whether it's in this lifetime, or in the afterlife, we'll meet again. I owe you for the shit you pulled today. I want my lick back."

Julz blew her a kiss and Pip laughed. The shit was gangsta as fuck and made his dick brick up instantly. Leaving out of the house, Pip listened to Nia bitch about not being able to beat the shit out of Julz. His mind was on the fact that Julz wouldn't live long enough to get back at Nia. He planned to fuck the shit out of her for the rest of the night, because she was going to meet her maker the very next day.

Chapter 16

When Leo got the call from Pip about scooping up Julz, he was set to handle the situation. Eliminating another person close to Icy was top priority, until he couldn't get in touch with Desiree. Leo had been trying to reach Desiree for the past couple days and the bitch wasn't answering. The first thought that came to mind was her tipping Icy off. He was hauling ass to get to the condo to fuck her up. At the same time, he was listening to the phone ring as he waited for the nigga Mark to answer. It was time for him to cash in on what he owed Leo. Soon as the call connected, Mark answered in a shaky voice.

"Y-Y-yeah."

"Gear up, nigga. I need you to head over to Ingalls Memorial in Harvey. Room 319 and smother the bitch. Fuck up and it's yo' ass! Understood?"

"I need to know. After this, will you give me my life back?" Mark asked, scared as hell. "I don't know nothing and I haven't seen shit. Hell, Leo who? I don't know you, nigga." Mark laughed nervously.

"Get the fuck outta my city! If I see you, yo' girl, or those nappy head ass kids ever again, the funeral will be a family affair. Get the job done. Simple as that!"

Bangin' on his ass, Leo pulled into the parking lot of the condos he built from the ground up and jumped out of his whip. He headed straight to the caretaker's apartment and knocked hard as he could. The door swung open, and Leo got straight to the point.

"Bill, my man. I need the keys to unit 410."

Bill's eyes bulged when he saw Leo alive and well. He saw on the news that his former boss was murdered on his wedding day. Now he was seeing him in the flesh with not one scratch that he could see on his body. Bill found his voice and cleared his throat.

"No can do, Leo. You're no longer the owner of this place. You don't have the authorization to enter any of the units."

Leo saw red. The urge to snap Icy's neck was at an all-time high. Her slick ass confiscated every muthafuckin' thing Leo had worked hard to obtain. There was no way he could sit still while the bitch laughed her way to the top on his dime. Icy ran with the narrative of Leo being dead, even though she knew he wasn't going to put her name on every fuckin' thing that belonged to him. Leo pushed the thoughts of Icy to the side and got back to the reason he was at Bill's door.

"Look, I don't give a fuck about none of that shit!" Leo snapped, swiftly pulling his gun and aiming it at Bill's head. "Go get the keys or I'm gon' plaster yo' fuckin' brains all over the entryway. Keep in mind, I'm dead."

Bill backpedaled to the cabinet within Leo's line of vision and retrieved the keys. He didn't want to die over something as simple as keys. The least that could happen was him losing his job. He could deal with that, but losing his life was another issue. He held the keys out within arm's reach and stood still to see what Leo's next move would be. Snatching the keys, Leo turned to leave, before spinning around quickly shooting Bill in both legs.

"Tell yo' new boss her ass is mine. That's the type of shit that happens when you bite the hand that fed yo' fat ass for years."

"Fuck!" Bill cried out as Leo left him bleeding on the tan carpet without worry. The excruciating pain prevented him from moving to call for help. Bill loved the seclusion of having the only apartment on the first floor, until that moment. There was no one around to help.

Leo didn't bother waiting for the elevator. He knew there was limited time before the cops would be at the building once Bill called for assistance. Making it to the fourth floor in record time, Leo inserted the key, barging in after unlocking the door. He checked every room, but there was no sign of Desiree.

"I'm gon' kill this bitch!"

Leo left without locking Desiree's apartment and rushed back down the stairs. He hopped into his ride, speeding away from the scene. Thoughts of where Desiree could possibly be flooded his mind. Leo knew the minute he laid eyes on her, he was killing her ass on sight. Sirens blared as squad cars whizzed past him on the other side of the street. Leo pulled over and watched in amusement.

"You muthafuckas always late," Leo howled. "You can't catch me. I'm the muthafuckin' Gingerbread Man!"

***

Before he became a guard at the storage facility, Mark was a nurse's aide. After Leo's call, he dug deep into a storage bin filled with his old scrubs. He planned to get the job done by hook or crook to save his life. What better way to do it than getting in character to go undetected.

"Mark, where you going?"

"I'm started a new job at the hospital. I told you I wasn't feeling sitting around without a job. I got one now. You're off, so it's perfect. I have a short shift and won't be gone more than five hours. It's a training run."

Mark hated lying to his woman, but there was no way he was going to tell her he was forced out of his job by a nigga on the street. The less she knew the better, because if anything happened to him, she still needed to be around for their kids. Mark was gambling with his freedom fuckin' with Leo, but he didn't have any other options. Going to the police was against the street codes. He would never set himself up to be labeled a muthafuckin' snitch. The task he set out to do was easy as stealing candy from a baby.

He kissed his woman passionately and hugged her a little longer than usual, before leaving her standing in the middle of the living room. Mark jumped into his vehicle and made his way to the expressway. Mark turned the radio on and "I'm Goin In," blared from the speakers as he flared up a blunt to ease his nerves. Lowering the window, he cruised doing the speed limit.

Mark, I thought I raised you better than this. Turn around and go home. Nothing good will come out of what you're about to do.

Swerving into the next lane, Mark jerked the wheel to get out of the way of the eighteen-wheeler that almost took him off the face of the earth. The sound of his mother's voice spooked him. She'd been deceased for the past six years, and Mark heard what she said clear as day. The problem he was having with the message was, he was alive and well and couldn't abort the mission he was appointed to. The shit was a matter of life and death.

The rest of the way to the hospital consisted of Mark rapping loudly along with the artists, in order to push forward without bailing out. The hospital came into view and his nerves kicked into overdrive. He looked at the clock on his dash and it read a quarter to seven. There was no shift he remembered starting at that time of the day. He hoped like hell his plan would get him to the floor he needed to be on without a hitch. Taking a deep breath, Mark sat for a few minutes before he shut the ignition off and made his move.

Entering the hospital through general admissions, he waved at the woman behind the desk, and she smiled waving back. *Yes, I got through stage one.* Mark kept going toward the elevators and pushed the button. A doctor walked up and stood beside him, giving a quick head nod. Mark smiled and waited patiently for the doors to open. The two of them entered the elevator. The doctor pressed the seventh floor, then Mark pressed the button for the third. His armpits were sweaty, causing him to look down to see if it was noticeable to others. The doors opened and Mark rushed out, lowkey checking the room numbers on the wall.

He went down the hall and was relieved the nurses weren't at the station. That gave Mark the opening to get into the room undetected. Leo didn't tell him a name, nor did he send a photo of the person he was supposed to seek out. The woman who was lying peacefully sleeping on her back stirred a little bit. The feeling of guilt tried to takeover Mark's mental, but he didn't allow it in. Instead, he walked across the room and held the woman's nose closed as he covered her mouth. The patient monitor started going off and Mark snatched the plug from the wall. The door opened as he released the woman's nose and a nurse entered.

"What are you doing?" she asked, rushing to check the woman.

Mark ran out of the room, looking for an exit. The nurse started screaming, then sounded an alarm. Panic was what he was feeling as he jogged down the hall in the opposite direction.

"Stop that man! He just murdered the patient in 319!"

Running was Mark's only option at that point. Everyone that tried to stop him from continuing on was punched, thrown into the wall, or shoved out the way. Finally, he saw an exit sign and ran for it. He was out of shape as he huffed and puffed all the way to the ground floor. Mark busted through a side door, slowing his pace. He looked around the perimeter of the parking lot, trying to get to his vehicle. As he turned the corner, Mark was met by four squad cars and about eight officers.

"Hands in the air! Don't fuckin move!"

Mark was fucked and he knew it. He was going to jail for a very long time, because he had a warrant out on him for a charge he obtained for violating probation in Michigan. That was the reason he moved to Chicago, to hide out. Going back to jail was something Mark wasn't willing to do. Holding his hands to his sides, Mark appeared to be surrendering to the cops.

"Get on the ground! Get on the ground!"

Mark moved as if he was going to surrender, then in a swift movement, he reached behind his back and pulled his gun, squeezing the trigger. The officers followed his lead, hitting their target head-on. Mark's body jerked as bullets pierced his upper torso until he fell to the ground. It wasn't until after the mayhem that the officers realized they'd lost one of their own. Mark wasn't going back to jail, but hell had a spot ready for his homecoming.

***

Leo was riding around, trying to figure out where Desiree could've gone, when his phone rang in the cupholder. Turning down the volume of his radio system, Leo didn't look to see who was calling before he answered from the steering wheel. A smile spread across his face at the sound of the little voice on the other end of the line.

"Daddy, I miss you," Amoy said loudly.

"I miss you too, baby. Daddy will come see you tomorrow, okay?"

"Okay. Mommy wants to speak to you."

There was shuffling in the background as Leo drove toward the expressway. Avita sat on the edge of the bed with the phone sitting in her lap. She helped Amoy set up her iPad and placed the headphones on her head. Amancia had left to return go back to Kingston the day before, along with Eshe. Avita stayed behind to get her revenge on Icy, and also to win Leo over to allow her and Amoy to stay in America with him. She was afraid of how Leo would react to her suggestion, but she wouldn't know until she put everything on the table.

"Avita, what the fuck you doing?" Leo's voice boomed from the phone.

"I'm here. I was getting Amoy settled. I heard you tell Amoy you will be over to see her tomorrow. Leo, I need to see you tonight."

"I have shit to do, Avita. It won't be possible for me to come that way until then." Avita went quiet and Leo didn't know what she was going through, but he was for sure going to find out. "What's going on? Did you go back home?"

"No, I'm still in Chicago. Amancia left after visiting Akoni. She abandoned me and Amoy while we were out shopping. I don't know what to do."

Avita decided to lie about why she was still in his city and not back in Kingston. She was also going to take it a step forward and make the story better for her and Amoy. Avita wasn't planning to leave Leo because she felt they should raise their daughter together. She wasn't having it any other way.

"The fuck you mean, she abandoned y'all? Are you still at the hotel?" Leo was pissed because Avita had his daughter in a place she knew nothing about, now she was stranded.

"Yeah, I'm still here, but we have to check out the day after tomorrow."

"Man, this is fucked up. Let me handle some shit and I'll call you when I'm on my way."

Leo didn't wait for Avita to respond and hung up. He was on his way to Dolton, but now he had to figure out how he was going to explain to Julian that he had a daughter. On top of that, there was no way they were staying in that high-priced hotel. His money wasn't long as it used to be, so he couldn't foot the bill for Avita to stay there. Leo had no choice but to take them to his home. He called Pip as he made his way to a bar called Reynold's for a drink to settle his nerves.

"What up, Leo?"

"Everything straight that way?"

"Yeah, I had to take Nia back to the crib. I'm on my way back there now. Julz ain't going nowhere. I made sure she was tied down tight before I left. Do you have any idea what time you'll be there tomorrow?"

"Nah, I had some shit to come up and have to handle that shit pronto. If you have to leave, do that. Make sure the bitch can't get away though. The last thing we need is for her to lead Blaze and Icy back to the spot we're holding her in."

"That won't be a problem. I have nothing more to do. The most I may do is go home to freshen up and get something to eat. Other than that, I want to see how you take care of her ass."

"Bet. I'll check back in later," Leo said, parking across the street from the bar.

Pip ended the call while Leo jogged across the street to beat the traffic. Pulling the baseball hat down over his eyes, Leo walked into the establishment unrecognized. He found an empty barstool and took a seat. The bartender came right over to take Leo's order. After ordering two double shots of Rémy and a Heineken, Leo looked down at his phone which vibrated in his hand. Not recognizing the number, he hesitated to answer, but before the call could go to voicemail, he slid the bar to the right.

"Yeah," he said, nodding at the bartender as she placed his drinks in front of him.

"Leo. I know I'm the last muthafucka you trying to hear from, but I need to holla at you."

Hearing Stack's voice on the other end of the line puzzled the shit out of Leo. Being that he was the reason Stack had to sit in jail for months, he felt there was some funny shit behind his call. Another thing Leo thought about was, if

Stack was out, so was Zan. Curiosity got the best of him, and he wanted to know the nature of the call.

"What do we have to discuss, Stack? And when did you get out?"

"I want to help you get to Kia's ass. The bitch is a snake."

Leo knew how Stack felt about Kia. Before he got knocked, the two of them were basically joined at the hip. Something had to have happened for Stack to be willing to hand her over to the wolves. First things first though, Leo needed to know when the nigga got out.

"How long have you been out?" he repeated.

"I got out a couple weeks ago. No, I don't know what's going on with Zan and Smooth. I'm worried about myself at this point. Kia just did some dirty shit and I want her loudmouth ass dealt with. I heard you were out for blood when it came to Icy and her family, and I wanted in on silencing Kia."

"What she do to you, nigga? Let me find out you mad about her moving on with another muthafucka."

"How you know 'bout that? She been out with this nigga?"

Leo laughed over the music that blared around the bar, because Stack never came off as a simp over a bitch. He was showing a soft side and Leo felt sorry for the nigga. What he wasn't going to do was forget why Stack was locked up. Leo didn't trust any of them niggas, but he had to see where Stack's head was at.

"Who hasn't seen them together? Icy and that punk ass Jamaican, then Kia and the other dude is always together. Enough about that shit, what made you hit me up of all people?"

Stack was quiet for a little bit, which made the antennas on Leo's head stand at attention. It would be nothing for him to kill his long-time friend if he had to, but Leo also knew he needed more people on his team when it came to going after

Icy. With Blaze on her side, getting close to her fine ass was tough.

"Like I said, Kia fucked with the wrong nigga. I've never did nothing for her to stab me in the back the way she has done. I was only locked up for a few months and the bitch moved on to the next muthafucka. Call it what you want, but she's going to pay for that shit."

"Nigga, don't you have a girl and a baby she knows nothing about?"

Leo found Stack funny as fuck. Niggas could dish shit out, but when that same thing was reciprocated back at them, it felt like their chest was caving in. Himself included. He couldn't lie and say Icy being with Blaze didn't hit him where it hurt because it did. The fact she stole everything from him took him over the edge and made him literally hate her ass.

"That means nothing! Are you gon' let me help you get at Kia or not? I can bring her to you, but I won't be the one pulling the trigga."

"I need to make sure this ain't a trap. Is my brother out too, and if so, where the nigga at?"

Stack didn't want to put Zan under the bus, but he was going to let the cat out of the bag, so Kia could get what she deserved. "Yeah, he's out. Zan been sitting low, taking care of his dispensary on Canal. Most of his time is spent at home with Cherelle though. You ain't heard that shit from me."

"Bet. When you get yo' hands on Kia, hit me up and I'll tell you where to drop her ass off. I already got Julz. With her girls missing, Icy gon' crumble. Shit looking good for my plan of revenge," Leo said, tossing back one of his shots. "Oh, Stack, fuck me over and you gon' be the next muthafucka missing in action. That's on my mama, nigga."

Leo ended the call and knocked back the other shot, before ordering two more. Taking a sip from his beer bottle, he looked up at one of the TV screens and saw a breaking story appear on the screen. He read the closed caption fast as it appeared, learning the reporter was outside of Ingalls Hospital. There was red tape closing off part of the parking lot and police were everywhere.

The suspect is identified as Mark Pitts. A thirty-five-year-old male who had extensive warrants in the state of Michigan, was killed after exchanging gunfire with officers. Pitts killed a patient inside the hospital, before shooting a female officer who was pronounced dead on the scene. This is a terrible tragedy for the victim's families, as well as the suspect's. Mental health is becoming out of control all over the world. If you or a loved one is suffering from mental health issues, please seek help. Back to you, Nancy. This is China Lee reporting from Ingalls' Hospital.

"Wasn't shit mentally wrong with that nigga," Leo laughed to himself. "At least he went out strong after completing the mission."

Leo paid his tab and finished his drinks before leaving the bar. He had one more thing to handle, and he didn't know how the fuck Julian would take the news about Avita and Amoy. Either she would accept the shit, or she could push the fuck on. It didn't matter to Leo one way or another. Amoy came before any bitch, including her mama, so Julian would have a choice to make. Hopefully, it would be the right one without any conflicts.

It took Leo less than an hour to get back to the crib he shared with Julian. Entering, it was quiet as hell, and he prayed Julian was either gone or sleeping. Long as she wasn't in the house, that would give him enough time to think about how he would lay the news down to his wife. Leo went into the bathroom downstairs and washed his hands. Julian had cooked and the shit smelled too good to pass up. With the liquor in his system, he was hungry as hell.

The aroma was still in the air, but Julian had put the food away. Leo checked the microwave and there wasn't a plate waiting for him inside. Usually, Julian made sure he was straight when he came home. She must've had a stick up her ass about something. He was sure to find out whenever she showed her pretty little face. In the meantime, Leo took the containers out of the fridge as his mouth watered with anticipation of eating the greens, cornbread, pinto beans with smoked turkey meat, and chicken wings. Loading a plate, Leo hurried and put his meal in the microwave to warm up.

"You finally decided to come home, huh?" Julian asked from the entryway of the kitchen.

"Yeah, I had some shit to take care of. Thanks for the food."

Julian ignored what he said, because her mind was on the news story she'd seen about the incident at the hospital. Julian wasn't stupid by a long shot. She knew the guy who committed the crime was the one Leo threatened a while ago. She also knew Staci was a patient at the same hospital. The name of the person killed wasn't released. Deep down, Julian knew Leo had put a hit out on her former friend's life and succeeded.

"So, you finally went a step further and killed off the mama, huh?"

"What the fuck you talking about, Julian?" Leo asked as he shut the refrigerator.

"You know exactly what I'm talking about. The shit is being covered by every news channel. You killed that girl's mama and, for what? That wasn't even called for, Leo! Don't you think killing her father was enough years ago? If you want to hurt Icy, go after her straight on. Leave her family out of it! It was your fault she gained access to all of your money and your properties. You faked your own death, for Christ sakes!"

Leo cocked his head back as he listened to Julian speak her mind on Icy like she has been invested from day one. Far as he knew, the only thing she could recite about Icy was what he told her ass. Bringing up Birdman and caring about what happened to Staci, gave him a vibe of her knowing more than she ever came forward to share. It seemed like her ass knew them muthafuckas personally, and Leo didn't like it.

"Why does it seem like you're getting emotional about what may or may not have happened to Staci? You didn't know that bitch, Julian. You're not even from the Chi."

"So, she's dead?"

"I don't fuckin' know! What's with the thousand damn questions?"

"You won't listen anyway, so why bother even asking anything more. Karma is riding yo' ass like a bull and when she attacks, I hope I'm nowhere in the vicinity. You are like a ticking time bomb, Leo. Don't think I haven't heard about you having Julz locked the fuck up somewhere. You're going after everybody except Icy! Let me find out you're scared of Duke's son and that's the real reason she hasn't been touched."

"Bitch, you must be smoking dope, talking to me like I'm some type of peon ass muthafucka!" The microwave beeped but Leo ignored it. "Tell me how you really feel and don't hold back. I have a feeling you holding on to valuable information. I'm opening the floor for you to get that shit off your chest right now."

"I've been your wife for years and you don't know shit about me. The reason you're going after Icy is fucked up, because you lied to the woman from day one. You owe her everything she has taken from yo' stupid ass! See, I've been around longer than you think, and the shit is pretty funny too. I know all about you killing Birdman for Kenny's good for nothing ass."

"How the fuck you know about any of that?"

"I have my ways. Walk away from this, because Icy has been harboring anger for old and new and you are right smack dab in the middle. If she's anything like me, you would leave well enough alone. Birdman's blood is flowing through those girls' veins. When they come for you, they're going to come harder than the strongest man in the world."

"What do you know, Julian? You know more than you're saying."

"I do. I'm just not going to reveal the shit because it just may be what you need to save your dumb ass life."

Leo was fuming because she wouldn't come out and reveal what she knew. He took that opportunity to throw his secrets out there. What could she do? Nothing in his eyes. She was lying and hiding shit. He was about to shatter her world by standing on his truth.

"Well, since we have secrets, I'ma let you in on one I was never going to tell you about. I have a three-year-old daughter and she's here. I'm going to let her and her mother to stay here until I can get them safely back to Kingston."

Julian's ears started ringing as she repeated what Leo said in her head. There was no way this muthafucka had a three-year-old and had the nerve to tell her about it. On top of that, he basically told her he was bringing the little girl and her mother to the house they shared. Julian knew damn well Leo had her fucked up. He had taken his plate from the microwave and turned his back like it was checkmate against her.

She remembered the last time they fought and how he got the best of her. The shit was not going to happen a second time. Julian rushed over to where he stood, picked up the plate and hit his ass in the back of the head with it. Food flew in every direction.

"Bitch, you done lost yo' muthafuckin' mind!"

Leo punched Julian in the face, causing her to stumble backward. Leo charged her and they were fighting like two UFC fighters. Julian was never one to back down from a fight, no matter if it was a man or woman. Leo was getting the best of her, but she put a hurting on him as well. They brawled from the kitchen to the living room, turning over furniture and breaking glass wherever they ended up. Julian got away and grabbed the fireplace poker and swung with all of her might, hitting Leo in the middle of his forehead.

Julian didn't check to see if he was okay. She slipped her feet into her shoes, grabbed her keys from the hook by the door and hauled ass out of the house. She hopped in her car and was thankful she had left her purse on the passenger side floor. Julian planned to get a room for the night. There was no way Leo would sit back and forgive her for what she had done.

The only thing on her mind as she drove was making shit right with her daughter and Icy. She hoped they would forgive her for the shit she'd put them through. Julian knew it was time to leave Leo, because there was nothing more in the relationship for her. He didn't have a dime to his name, and she wasn't about to keep shelling out money for a man that didn't have any loyalty for her. He could go back to Kingston with his little family for all she cared.

Chapter 17

"Thank you so much, Fanny. I know it's short notice and if it wasn't an emergency, I would have called."

"Icy, you know I'll do anything for you and my best friend. I wanted to tell you how proud I am of you for stepping up to care for your mama after she expressed how depression was setting in, being in that hospital. I want to thank you."

Fanny hugged Icy close to her chest, and she felt the tears fall onto her scalp. Stepping out of her embrace, Icy wiped the tears from Fanny's eyes with her thumbs.

"You don't have to thank me. I have one mama and I'm gonna love on her while she's here and give her all the flowers she deserves while watching her smell them. My mama is my world. If it wasn't for me getting involved with a nothing ass nigga, she wouldn't be in the position she's in. Now, I have to make shit right, so we can live our lives without worry."

"Icy don't go out there risking your freedom for revenge."

Ignoring what Fanny said, Icy felt the need to tell her what she was going to do. "Take care of my mama until I get back. Julz is missing. Me and Blaze is going to search until we find her. Don't tell my mama, because worrying about me is the last thing I want her to do. If I'm not back in the morning, her nurse will be here at nine, and the physical therapist at eleven. I'll call, so you will know I'm alright. I'll be fine. Birdman has his arms wrapped around his baby girl through all of the turmoil. I'm covered. I love you, Fanny."

I love you too, Ice Baby. Be careful."

Icy showed Fanny where she would be staying for the night, went into her mother's bedroom and kissed her on the forehead before going to find Blaze. The night she and Kia got rid of Desiree, Blaze was pissed at them both, but more-so Icy. He lectured her about the danger she had put herself in, and the consequences she could've been facing had they been caught committing murder. Once he thought he had gotten his point across, Blaze took Icy to see the house he'd purchased. She fell in love at first sight. They stayed at the house that night, then the next morning, went to the hospital to bring Staci home.

It took a few hours to get recommendations for physical therapy and nurse assistants, but they didn't leave the hospital until everything was in place. Staci slept the entire ride to the house. Icy helped her out of the car and walked alongside of her, so she wouldn't fall injuring herself.

"Who lives here, Icy?" Staci asked.

"This is our home, Ma. You will live with us until you get the strength in your legs back. When you're well enough, there's a guest house set up for you behind the big house."

Staci stopped walking and turned slowly to face her daughter. "I can't leave my house, baby. Your daddy had that house built for me, and it's all I have left of him besides you and Kia. I need my house. I'll stay here until y'all do what needs to be done with Leo. I already know that's what your mind is set on. You are making sure I am safe from anything he has planned, because he didn't kill me the first time around. Icy, you have your daddy's blood running through your veins. I've seen a hint of his attitude in you. Kia has his entire persona all the way," she laughed.

The conversation played in Icy's head, making her smile. She was going to make sure her mama could go back home, even if it meant losing her life in the process. Long as Leo was walking around pretending to be dead, Icy's mission was to make sure that muthafucka stopped breathing before he could take another life from her.

"Babe, where are you?" Icy called out as she climbed the last step to the second level of their home.

"I'm in the bedroom."

Entering the room, Blaze pulled a black hoodie over his head. He had on matching joggers, and a pair of black Timbs. His locs were pulled back with a black band. Icy lusted over his ass because he was the epitome of a sexy man.

"Fanny's here. She's downstairs with Mama. I showed her the room she would be sleeping in, and she should be cool until we return. Have you heard from Bryan?"

"I haven't heard from him since we met up with him at the gas station by Julz's house. I know you want to go out and look for her, but we don't know where to start. Have you checked to see if her location is back online?"

"The last time I checked, it wasn't."

Icy walked to her side of the bed and picked up her phone. The notifications on the screen were loaded. Using the Face ID feature, she unlocked her device. Icy went to her text messages, because she had one unread message from Julz. Icy opened the text and started reading it silently.

I've been kidnapped by Pip and Nia. Leo is supposed to be on his way. I don't know where I am but get here before Leo does because he's not going to let me live. Don't let him kill me, Icy! I turned my——"

With shaky hands, Icy went to the Find My Phone app. She scrolled up until she came upon Julz's name. Her phone was still showing up at the last location known, which was the gas station. Icy took a gamble with her friend's watch. She tapped on it and waited for the loading symbol to stop its search. The location indicated Julz was on 151st and Evers. Blaze saw the reaction on Icy's face. It was a mixture of anger and fear.

"Icy, what's wrong?"

"We gotta go get Julz. She sent a text..."

Instead of telling him what the text said, she handed over her phone. Blaze read the message while breathing heavily. He went into the walk-in closet and Icy could hear the locks of his gun case click. There was a few minutes of rustling before he emerged with his gun holster in place over his shoulders. Blaze had two Glock 17s, with extended clips that held thirty rounds each. He was ready for war. Putting two more clips in the pockets designed for them, he threw Icy's phone on the bed.

"Akoni, that message was sent hours ago. What if..."

Icy's voice trailed off because she was afraid to say what she was thinking out loud. She was fearful of her thoughts becoming a reality. Icy sat on the edge of the bed and buried her face in the palms of her hands.

"She's okay, Ice. We're going to get her. I won't try to persuade you to stay behind. As a matter of fact, call...never mind, I got it."

Blaze grabbed his phone from the dresser and paced the room. Icy finally found the strength to stand and put on her shoes as Joe's voice echoed off the walls of their bedroom. Closing the door so her mother couldn't hear what was going on, Icy tuned in on the conversation.

"Come to the new crib. You out here?" Blaze asked.

"Yeah, me and Kia stayed the night. I finally told her about the house. What's up, though?"

"We got a location on Julz. That nigga Pip and Bryan's bitch of a baby mama snatched her up. Bring Kia with you. I'll fill y'all in when you get here. Make sure you strapped, because we have to go in guns blazin'. These muthafuckas won't make it out alive."

"Bet. You called B yet?"

"I had to call you in case you two nasty muthafuckas decided to partake in a game of naked Twister."

"Man, she's been like a jack rabbit around here. I'm not complaining though. I love how she do that thing with——"

"Nope, don't want to hear none of that shit. Save that shit for another day, and make sure you keep it between you and Kia's nympho ass. It's time to set shit off, because these niggas too muthafuckin' comfortable out here."

"Leo thinks he's untouchable and he has no clue he's a millisecond away from being bodied. In the meantime, we'll just send his weak ass crew to him toe tagged."

"Just like that! I'm about to call Bryan to let him know about the new details on Julz. Oh, and for him to explain death to his daughter, because her mammy is a dead bitch walking."

"Wait, what? Never mind, I'm on my way. Kia is dressed and ready to beat my ass for stalling. Even though she could've walked her ass down the street if she was in such a hurry."

"And will. See yo' ass when you get your thumb out yo' ass," Kia snapped as she left the house.

"I'm on my way," Joe laughed, hanging up.

The next call was to Bryan. He answered right away.

"Blaze, what's good?"

"I have news on Julz. I hate to be the bearer of bad news, but she was indeed kidnapped. It's one of the people involved, that's going to blow your mind and piss you off."

"Where the fuck is she? And don't tell me that nigga Leo got his hands on her!"

"Leo was behind the shit, of course. He had somebody else to do his dirty work. It was Pip and yo' baby mama." Blaze paused to allow Bryan to take in what he'd said.

"Nia?"

"Yeah, nigga. Nia. She is going to lose her muthafuckin' life, along with the rest of 'em. Jamiah doesn't deserve this shit, but her mama made a bed she wasn't ready to lie in for eternity."

"Nah, Nia hasn't been a mother to our daughter lately. Her ass not being around won't affect Jamiah's life at all. Nia can come over to see Jamiah anytime she wants, but because her visits have to be supervised, she opted not to do so. That's the reason why I love my daughter with everything in me and makes sure she wants for nothing. I'm the only parent my little girl has."

Bryan expressed his feelings and Blaze listened without interruption. "Enough about Jamiah, brah. She straight. Where is Julz?"

"She's in Dolton. We're about to head out soon. I'm waiting on Joe."

Soon as Blaze mentioned Joe, the doorbell sounded. Checking the app for his camera system, sure enough, Joe and Kia had arrived. Blaze walked to the wall panel and spoke into the intercom as he watched Fanny hesitate to open the door.

"It's okay to open the door, Fanny. It's Kia," Blaze told her, then tuned back in with Bryan. "We're about to head to the location. I sent the address to you, meet us there. Do not go inside until we get there, B! We not trying to fuck this up. One false move and you can lose her forever."

Bryan said he wouldn't go in. Blaze didn't believe a word he said, but he had time to beat Bryan to the location because he was closer. Placing his phone into his pocket, Icy left the room, tucking the Gremlin behind her back. Blaze watched her ass sway from side to side, noticing how wide her hips were. The thought of Icy being pregnant crossed his mind on many occasions. Especially, the day Amancia popped up at the hotel claiming to be pregnant. Icy coming out of the bedroom with a test confirmed his suspicions of him becoming a father for the first time.

Blaze wanted Icy to sit back and allow him and the guys to handle the situation, but he knew it would only lead to being combative with him and going out on her own. His objective was to have her front and back at all times to ensure she wasn't hurt in the process. Blaze couldn't afford anything happening to the woman he loved so deeply.

Descending the steps, Blaze spotted Icy standing in the middle of the foyer, talking to Joe and Kia in a hushed tone. There wasn't a doubt in his mind that Icy was filling them in on what was going on, because Kia's fist clutched tightly at her sides as she listened. Joe glanced over at Blaze while hanging on to Icy's every word.

"See, I told you that bitch wasn't gon' be satisfied until I beat the fuck outta her! Pip or Leo's dick must be made of gold, because one of them niggas got her ass dick dumb. Nia just signed on the dotted line in agreeance to literally give her life to Christ."

"I'm with you when you're right," Icy said to Kia as she took a step back. Facing Blaze and Joe, Icy's eyes turned dark right before them. "I want y'all to know, I don't play about my family. There will be no limitations to the things I do. I'm standing ten toes down 'til the end."

Blaze opened his mouth to speak, but Icy continued on.

"Nope. I don't want to hear shit. I've sat back for months, hiding out so you could see what this muthafucka was going to do. No disrespect, but these muthafuckas about to stop playing in my face. I've been worried long enough and I'm over it. You see my mama in that room depressed because she can't walk without assistance! Now, they have my best friend hemmed up, doing who knows what to her, while we're standing here talking. It's time to get to the action. Let's go. I'm ready to kill a bitch."

Icy left them standing there and walked out of the house. Kia was just as shocked as Blaze and Joe at Icy's mood change. She was a person neither of them recognized. The sweet and understanding Icy was gone. She had nothing on Gena Davis when she played Elizabeth Caine / Charlie Baltimore in the movie, *A Long Kiss Goodnight.*

"Who the fuck was that?" Joe asked.

"Ion know, but let's go so she can get this shit off her chest. We have to move quick because Bryan is probably going crazy waiting for us to pull up."

They all piled into Icy's truck with Blaze in the driver's seat. "X Gon' Give It To Ya" blared through the speakers as they raced to Dolton to save Julz. Icy sat staring straight ahead as she caressed her Glock passionately.

***

Julz had been sitting in the dark, listening to the loud squeaks of what could only be rats. Every second she was in the dump of the abandoned house made her mad. She thought of several ways to kill Pip when he returned and couldn't wait to hear him beg for his life like a bitch. Not knowing how much time had gone by was driving Julz insane. Even though she didn't get the chance to finish out the text, she prayed Icy got the message and was on the road, getting to her location.

Something crawled over her foot, and she screamed aloud before football kicking it against the wall. The shrieking of the rodent after hitting the wall pierced Julz's ears. She had done major damage to the little fucker, because the impact sounded gross. The light came on and Pip entered the room. Julz didn't hear the door open because of the noise the rat and its counterparts were making.

"What the fuck you doing?"

Realizing Julz was still bound to the chair, Pip relaxed. He was still curious about what she had going on. Placing the items in his arms down on a nearby table, Pip started laughing once he saw the rat trying its best to get up off the floor. There was a big splatter of blood on the wall where it had been stabbed by a big nail sticking out of the wall.

"You in here hurting the company I left here with you?"

"Fuck you!" Julz yelled, trying to adjust to the light. Small dots danced in front of her eyes, causing her to blink constantly.

"I plan to fuck you. That's the only reason I'm back in this nasty muthafucka. The jealousy of being a female is why

Nia turned me down for sex. Now, that leaves yo' pretty ass to work this nut out." Pip cupped his dick while walking over to where Julz sat.

"You gon' have blue balls fuckin' with me. I'm not giving myself to you!"

"However you want to do this is fine with me. Talk yo' shit like you were earlier. That shit sounded good as hell and you're going to cash in on it, Big Pussy. It's either you're going to give it to me willingly, or I'm gon' take it. Regardless, I'm getting some of that good shit between yo' legs."

It took Julz a minute to realize exactly what Pip was actually saying. He basically said he was going to take advantage of her. That shit was not going to happen without a fight. Taking off his coat, Pip threw it down on the dirty floor as he walked over and started working to get the knot out of the rope around Julz's left wrist.

"When I free your arm, don't start fighting. I have no problem beating yo' ass."

Julz didn't respond because she had every intention of gouging his eyes out, biting, scratching or whatever she had to do, in order to get way from his sick ass. She knew enticing him was something she'd regret doing, but dwelling on it wouldn't help her get out the bind she was in. She would have to just fight for her life and hope someone came to her rescue before Pip had his way with her.

Julz quietly allowed Pip to untie her. Once she was completely free, Pip ran his hand down the front of her shirt before placing his hand inside, caressing her breasts. Julz smacked his hand, causing Pip to grab her around her throat, swiftly pulling Julz to her feet. He used his other hand to palm the back of her head as he stuck his tongue in her mouth. Julz felt like she would be sick as he explored her mouth while she tried fighting him off. The grip Pip had on her neck became tighter the more she struggled. Julz had to get away so she bit down hard as she could, drawing blood.

"You bitch!" Pip howled, releasing the hold he had on her.

Julz ran toward the door and was snatched backward by her hair. She could feel the hair being snatched from her scalp. Pip body slammed her onto the floor, knocking the wind out of her. Julz couldn't focus on anything around her because the room was spinning from the impact of her head hitting the floor. Pip stood over her delivering blow after blow to her face. Julz felt the moment her nose broke and the blood traveling to the back of her throat, almost choked her to death. She gathered the strength to roll over onto her side and felt a sense of relief, until he kicked her hard in her back.

"Bitch, I told you what would happen if you tried to get away! Then you bit the tip of my fuckin' tongue and split it down the middle!"

"Now you look like the snake you were destined to be, punk muthafucka!"

Pip chuckled as he turned his head to spit out the blood which formed in his mouth rapidly. That wasn't going to stop him from sampling Julz's pussy before he put a bullet in her head. He reached down and grasped her shirt with both hands, before ripping it down the middle along with her bra. Her pink areolas made Pip's dick hard. With her shirt out of the way, he moved to the pants she wore. The moment Pip grabbed the hem of the pants, Julz started kicking and screaming.

"Stop! Don't do this, please!" she cried.

Her entire face felt as if it was on fire. Julz was surprised she could yell out the way she did, because blood was filling her nose to the point she could hardly breathe through her nostrils. Pip was tugging at her pants and Julz was kicking with all of her might to get him off her.

"Bitch, shut the fuck up! You all but threw yo' pussy at me and I'm about to cash in."

He snatched the material off in one pull and Julz was totally exposed. It was hard for her to see through her swollen left eye, but she wasn't going to lie stagnant while

Pip violated her body. She heard his zipper as he lowered it and attempted to get to her feet. He flipped her onto her stomach and started squeezing her ass cheek with one hand, while freeing himself with the other. Pip gripped her waist as he moved his penis against her opening.

"My favorite position, doggystyle. Now the fun begins." Pip spit to the side of him as he spread Julz's cheeks.

"No! No! Let me go!" she screamed loudly, hoping someone on the outside would hear her cries for help.

Pip punched her in the back of the head to stop her from fighting him and drawing attention. They were on a residential street, but there were more vacant houses than occupied ones. He still couldn't take the chance of anyone calling the police, so he had to shut her up. Spotting her shirt on the floor, Pip snatched it up after hitting Julz one more time and wrapped the material around her mouth to muffle her cries.

"Nothing can stop me from fuckin' you long and hard now."

Pip held the cloth in his hand, pulling it toward him. Julz had tears running down her face because the sides of her mouth were becoming raw and dry. Her neck was hurting from the way he pulled it back. Not to mention the wounds she'd already endured beforehand. The tip of Pip's member danced at her opening. Julz forced her body to fall forward as she kicked her foot, catching him in the thigh.

"You like when I beat yo' ass, huh?" Pip hissed as he jerked the fabric with all his might. Julz tried to get out of the hold he had on her, to no avail. Positioning himself behind her like a dog in heat, Pip went in for the plunge. With the tip inside of her yoni, the door to the house was kicked in, sending wood flying around the room.

WHACK!

Pip was hit upside the head, making him fall onto his side. The impact caused Julz to fall as well. When she looked over her shoulder and saw Bryan stomping a mud hole out of his ass, she let out a sigh of relief. Pip was struggling to get away from the bottom of Bryan's boot, but everywhere he moved, Bryan landed another blow. Sending a swift kick to Pip's face, the sound of his jaw breaking could be heard throughout the room.

"You kidnapped the wrong one, muthafucka! Now you gon' die," Bryan yelled as he pointed his gun to the top of his head.

Julz was trying her best to get the cloth from around her mouth. She shook her head no, but Bryan seemed to have blocked out everything other than Pip's bitch ass. Throwing the material to the floor, Julz snatched up her pants and covered herself from the waist down.

"Don't kill him, Bryan!"

Julz's words took Bryan by surprise causing him to look at her as if she was stupid. He couldn't believe she stood before him with a swollen eye, blood dripping from her mouth, and damn near naked, and had the nerve to defend the muthafucka who was behind it all. Bryan was livid and wanted to slap the fuck outta her for even opening her mouth.

"The fuck you mean, don't kill this nigga? Were you not paying attention to what the fuck he was about to do to yo' ass?" Bryan seethed with anger. Gun still aimed in Pip's direction, he stood taller, facing Julz. "The last thing you should be doing is trying to save this muthafucka! Had I waited outside listening to you plead for this nigga to stop a minute longer, you'd probably be in here throwing yo' pussy on him like a real bitch, huh?"

Pip tried to get up and Bryan stomped on his thigh, breaking the bone. Screaming like a bitch, Pip howled as he rolled around on the floor. He wasn't going too far with the pain he was in, so there was no use for him to even try. Pip knew he wasn't leaving the house alive. In his mind, he wished he'd never come back after leaving with Nia.

"Move again and I'm gon' blow yo' shit back!" Bryan growled at Pip. He glared at Julz, waiting for her to reply to what he'd said.

"I know muthafuckin' well you didn't just insult me! I didn't willingly go with this piece of shit! He and your bum ass baby mama drugged me and brought me to this dump. What you walked in on was his nasty ass in the process of raping me! Look at my face! Do that look like I was role playing to get turned on?" Julz snapped. "I don't want you to kill him, because I want to do the shit myself! After this, don't say shit else to me!"

"Julz!"

The sound of Icy's voice echoed off the walls. Bryan took his shirt off and handed it to Julz before the guys entered. She pulled the shirt over her head just as Icy walked in, followed by Kia, Joe, and Blaze. When the two women saw Julz's face, all hell broke loose in the house.

"You punk muthafucka!"

Kia jumped on Pip, beating him anywhere her fists landed. Icy was kicking him in the head, making it bounce off the floor repeatedly. They were fucking him up and the guys let it happen. Soon as Blaze and Joe went to grab them up, both Icy and Kia upped their pistols to end his life. Once again, Julz pleaded for them not to kill him.

"Don't kill him? Bitch, are you slow or stupid? This muthafucka gots ta go!" Kia shouted at Julz. "He kidnapped you, beat the fuck outta you, and God knows what else, but you saving this nigga? You know what? Fuck this shit. I'm out of this bitch!" Kia stormed toward the door.

"Kia!" Julz called out, halting her steps before she could fully leave. "I'm not taking up for him. I just want to kill him myself!"

Kia turned around with a wicked smile. "Tell me something, because I thought you had lost your muthafuckin' mind. You almost made me wash my hands of yo' ass."

"Never that," Julz said, staring down at Pip. "Get his ass up and tie him to the very chair he had me bound to for hours."

While Bryan and Joe roughly grabbed Pip from the floor, Julz headed across the room to the gas can and hose she had been afraid of since she spotted them. Just as she thought, the gas can was full. She didn't know exactly what she was going to do with Pip, but it didn't take long for her to figure it out when she spotted a bottle of tequila, lime and salt in the bag Pip brought in with him. Julz placed the gas can next to the chair and went back to the table for the other items.

"This ain't the time for you to be drinking," Bryan snapped.

"Didn't I ask you not to say shit to me?" Julz snapped back. "Kia, you got your knife on you?"

Kia quickly unhooked he knife from her front pocket and handed it over to Julz, then stepped back. Even though she wanted to help her girl, Kia knew she had to allow Julz to take all her frustrations out on one of the people responsible for what happened to her. She needed the moment to start her healing process.

"You had the opportunity to kill me, but my pussy took up space in your head." Julz laughed as she circled around Pip as she snapped her wrist, releasing the blade in her hand. The grin fell from her face soon as she was standing in front of him. Pacing back and forth, Pip's eyes followed her every move along with everybody else in the room. In one swift movement, Julz sliced his chest twice.

"Aaaarghhhh!" Pip yelled out in agony as his chest burned, as well as the pain in his lower jaw area.

"Shut the fuck up! Talk that tough shit now. You had so much to say when I was tied down and when you were trying to rape me! It's not fun when the rabbit got the gun, is it, bitch?"

Slicing Pip a few more times, Julz was pleased with her cutting skills. She did enough damage so he wouldn't bleed to death, but Pip looked like Freddy Krueger himself stepped out of a dream and attacked him. Icy smiled proudly as she watched Julz put in work. Her friend was taking longer than she would have, but she was enjoying the show.

"Where is Leo?" Julz asked.

She knew a dead man couldn't say shit, so she was going to at least try to get as much information she could before finishing his ass off. Little did she know, Blaze already knew where Leo laid his head. In fact, it was their next move to make after taking care of Pip. So, nobody said a word and just allowed Julz to do whatever she wanted to the nigga.

"If you tell me, I'll spare your life, then make sure you get to the hospital."

"F-fuck you, bitch!"

"Fuck me? Fuck me?"

Julz was mad. The thought of him almost taking advantage of her would forever be etched in her mind. She picked up the bottle of tequila and popped the top. Taking a swig, she flicked her wrist and flung a good amount at his chest.

"Aaaaarghhhh!" Pip cried as he struggled to break out of the restraints. "I'm not telling y'all shit."

"Oh, but you will."

Julz chuckled as she poured more tequila on his open wounds. She felt his shirt was preventing her from hurting him the way she wanted. Walking closer to Pip, she cut his shirt right down the middle, revealing the cuts on his chest. Admiring her demonic work of art, Julz licked her lips and placed the tequila on the floor and picked up the salt. Shaking his head no vigorously, Julz stared him down as she poured a handful of salt into her hand. She held the container out to no one in particular then walked closer to Pip. He used his good leg to kick her in the right knee. Julz buckled, causing both Bryan and Blaze to punch his ass simultaneously.

"Keep your feet to yo'self, nigga!" Blaze said, punching him again for good measure.

Icy closed the door best she could, because if Julz was about to do what she thought, the few people in the neighborhood were going to call the police. Leaning on the door so it would stay closed, Pip let out a sound that mimicked a pig squealing in a slaughterhouse. Julz had smeared salt into his wounds and his ass was bucking like a maniac. His head rolled as if he was about to pass out and Julz slapped him hard.

"I'm gon' ask one more time. Where is Leo?"

"He's…he's going to kill you muthafuckas. That's where he's at!"

Nodding her head, Julz swung the knife so fast, slicing Pip's jaw open, Kia wondered where the hell she pulled it from. She held her hand out for the salt and poured it into the fresh wound. The torture Julz was putting on Pip was very impressive to Blaze. The average woman would be puking her guts out, but the women in the room didn't flinch as he looked around at them. If anything, Kia and Icy seemed like they were waiting for Julz to tag them in, but she wanted to be the one to end Pip's life.

"Fuck! Okay, I'll tell you anything you want to know," Pip said, breathing heavily.

He talked kind of low, but Julz heard him clearly. That's how close she was to him. Pip opened and closed his mouth, but nothing came out. Julz went to pour in more salt and Pip shook his head no, causing her to give him a little time. Bryan was growing impatient and went for his gun.

"Don't you dare! I got this."

"Let her handle her business. I'm kind of enjoying this shit," Joe said, deterring Bryan from pulling his tool.

"Leo has a house in Glencoe…" Pip whispered.

"You have to do better than that. I know I did a number on your jaw, but you got to fight through that shit and tell me what I want to hear."

"Leo has a house in Glencoe with his wife, Julian, 214 Jefferson Avenue is the address. The bitch is just as crazy as he is, so don't underestimate her. He is going to the Embassy Suites downtown tomorrow morning about ten o'clock to pick up his baby mama and daughter. That's all I have," Pip said, closing his eyes taking slow breaths to ease the pain he was feeling. Glancing at Icy sympathetically, he relaxed best he could before he addressed her.

"Icy, I want to give my condolences to you."

Icy's eyebrows rose toward her forehead. "For what?" she quizzed.

"Leo put a hit on your mama. You didn't see the news or get a call from the hospital? She was killed in her hospital room. The nigga who did it was shot and killed by the police."

"I don't know whose mama y'all killed, but it wasn't mine. Nigga fumbled on another play. Stupid muthafuckas. Stop playing with him and kill this bitch!"

"You ain't said nothing but a word."

Julz bent down and inserted the hose into the gas can. After all she'd been though, the thought of Pip and Leo's plans of burning her dead or alive had her livid. She siphoned the liquid through the hose. A little bit got into her mouth, but she spit it out immediately. Icy got a bottle of water from the bag on the table and gave it to Julz to cleanse her mouth. Taking a hefty sip, she swooshed it around before spitting it behind her. Getting back to the task at hand, the gas pooled around her feet as she held onto Pip's head. Getting the hose in his mouth was hard because he kept moving his head left to right covering himself with the volatile substance. The fumes were strong, but Julz was adamant about what she had in play. Blaze stepped forward and held Pip's head steady while Julz inserted the hose into his mouth.

"Hand me that duct tape on the table," Julz yelled out.

Blaze held the hose while she wrapped the tape around Pip's head several times to secure the hose in place. He was drowning before their eyes and Julz didn't think it was good enough. Picking up the tequila, Julz started pouring the content of the bottle around the room.

"What type of shit is this?" Joe asked. "It takes a sick muthafucka to do something like that!"

Pip's eyes were bulging out of the sockets as he fought not to swallow the gas. It was inevitable because after a few seconds, his throat bobbed up and down as he swallowed. His head fell to the side, and he started gurgling like he was about to throw up. Julz didn't give a damn and kept on slinging the liquor throughout the room.

"I'm just giving this nigga a taste of his own medicine. This gas wasn't here by accident. They had plans to burn me in here and now I'm going to beat Leo's ass to the punch."

Throwing the empty bottle against the wall, Julz went back to Pip's pants and took everything from his pockets, finding a book of matches. She watched as he regurgitated the liquid and smiled. Icy couldn't take the smell a minute longer and ran outside.

"Everybody out!"

Julz yelled as she picked up the gas can, leaving the hose dangling from Pip's mouth. She then poured the rest around the room, walls included. Pip looked half dead and that made Julz happy, because now she was going to finish his ass off by sending him to the hottest part of hell. Everybody left except Bryan.

"I'm not leaving you in here."

"You no longer have to worry about me. I was giving it up like a real bitch, remember?"

"Julz, I didn't——"

"Save that shit for the next bitch, because I'm not trying to hear none of it. Either leave or burn with this muthafucka. Either way, I don't give a fuck what you do."

Making a trail to the door, Julz sat the can outside while watching Bryan stand in the middle of the room. After a few seconds of waiting for him to exit, she said, "Fuck it," to herself and struck the match.

Bryan saw a look in her eyes he couldn't describe and made his way out the door, just as Julz threw the match. Fire raced toward Pip and the rats were trying to get away just like his ass. She stood and watched the fire spread rapidly as she took Pip's phone out of her pocket and started recording.

Picking up the can, Julz closed the door with all her might. There was no room in the truck with Icy and Kia, so Joe traded places to ride with Bryan. Flames were coming through the roof and Blaze knew it was time for them to get the fuck away from there.

"What's the move?" he asked.

"To that punk nigga's baby mama house," Julz sassed, handing Joe the can. "Lead the way. The bitch got next."

Julz got into the front seat of the truck and Blaze backed up behind Bryan. She searched Pip's phone, looking for Leo's contact. Julz found the video in the camera roll and captioned it, *'You play with fire, you get burned. RIP PIP.'*

Chapter 18

Kia was pissed when they got to Nia's house and the bitch had packed the fuck up and got ghost. She was antsy as hell on the drive over, because she was for sure going to make good on her word about stomping that bitch's ears together. She didn't know what the hell happened between Julz and Bryan, but her girl wasn't fucking with his ass at all. Kia had her own problems with Joe. He was mad she wouldn't go to the house with him. Kia told him she wanted to go to her apartment to think about her next move.

To be truthful, Stack was blowing her line up the entire time Julz was torturing Pip. Not to mention, he had sent several text messages talking about they needed to talk. Kia didn't feel they had shit to discuss, but she wanted to see what type of bullshit would come out of his mouth. She could've easily called him on the phone, but she wanted to do a face-to-face so she could see the lies as he told them. There was no way she could get away from Joe, had she agreed to go to the house.

Rolling out of bed at nine o'clock the next morning, Kia went into the bathroom and turned on the shower to take care of her hygiene. As she was brushing her teeth, she could hear her phone ringing in the bedroom. Kia groaned loudly because she already knew who was on the other end of the line. The phone stopped ringing soon as she picked it up. There was a missed call from Stack, then the phone sounded again.

"What?" Kia answered, aggravated.

"I'm trying to see what time you coming through?"

"Stack, when I told you I was coming, I meant just that. Seeing that it's not even ten o'clock, I need to get myself together first. Do not rush me to listen to your bullshit, okay? I'll hit you when I'm on my way."

Kia ended the call, then continued brushing her teeth as she reentered the bathroom. She glanced in the mirror and something Pip said about Julian the night before entered her mind. *Leo lives in Glencoe with his wife, Julian, 214 Jefferson Avenue is the address.* Kia rinsed her mouth and called Julz. Putting the call on speaker, Kia applied some facial cleanser on her face just as Julz answered.

"Hey, Kia. What's going on?"

"Shoot me Bryan's number. I need him to get his tech to track down a number for me."

"Humph, I'm glad you were smart enough not to ask me to call that muthafucka." Kia's phone chimed as Julz shared Bryan's contact information. "I have nothing more to say to him. When I catch that bitch, Nia, I'm burying her ass!"

"If you run into her, you better follow her ass while calling me, because I want in on that. How are you doing over there?"

"My damn body and face hurts," Julz started crying. "That nigga punched me like a man. I didn't feel anything until I actually got home. My adrenaline was on an all-time high when I was slicing his ass up. Kia, I look like the fuckin' elephant man right now. I can't believe I did what I did!"

"Those are temporary scars, Julz. You will be back to looking like yourself in a week or two. The good thing about it is, you work from home. If you need me to do some deliveries for you, I will. As far as last night, you did what the fuck you had to do," Kia snapped.

"It's not my physical appearance I'm worried about! He violated me! Kia, he actually penetrated my body," Julz screamed. "If Bryan hadn't come busting through the door, there's no telling what would've happened. Then Bryan had the audacity to say I was ready to bust it open for the nigga, as if I was willing to fuck! He can kiss my ass!"

"Why would he say something like that, knowing what was going on?"

"I told him not to kill Pip just as I said to you and Icy."

"Julz, you have to look at the way I reacted when you said that shit. I'm sure Bryan only responded on instinct at the moment. You may be hurt by what was said, but you have to look at the bigger picture."

"Yeah, okay. An apology and him explaining the shit will be better coming from him. Anyway, I'm going back to sleep. I'll talk to you later."

"Okay, I'm going to come over when I finish taking care of some shit. Don't be too hard on B. Talk to him, Julz."

"Yeah, okay."

Julz hung up and Kia laughed lowly to herself. She knew how her friend could be when she was mad, and Bryan was going to be in the doghouse for a while. He did say some fucked up shit, but Kia understood. She was ready to beat Julz ass herself when she said don't kill him. It was a good thing she explained why before Kia walked out.

Kia washed the cleanser off her face and jumped in the shower. The hot water pouring over her body felt so good. The tension ran down the drain with ease. Kia was going to bask in the moment long as she could because she was going to need to do it all over again before the day was over. After washing her body several times Kia got out and wrapped a towel around her body. She walked into her room and grabbed the shea butter from the dresser. Sitting on the bed, she moisturized her legs, then the rest of her body.

Twenty minutes later, Kia was dressed in a pair of jeans, a hoodie, and a pair of Converse boots. She had gathered her keys, phone and wallet, heading for the door. As she passed the kitchen, Kia grabbed a banana from the fruit bowl and left out. As she waited for the elevator, she shot Bryan a text.

Aye, it's Kia. I need you to have your tech to run this address (214 Jefferson Avenue) and see what can be found on Julian Miller. If there's a number for her, get that to me ASAP

Kia got off the elevator in the garage and hit the locks from her key fob. Jumping in the driver's seat, she got a notification indicating Bryan had hit her back.

Bryan: I got him on it now. Give me a few and I'll have something for you. Have you talked to yo' girl?

Kia: I just got off the phone with her. She's pissed at you. I think you should call her and apologize for what you said to her. It hurt her, Give her time though.

Bryan: She told me not to blow that nigga shit back! How was I supposed to respond to that?

Kia: Don't get aggressive with me. I'm not the one you should be trying to explain that to. I just thought I would put a little buzz in your ear, because you are good for her. I want you to let me know if you get in touch with your baby mama. She violated in the worse way and will have to pay for that shit.

Bryan: I know. I've been calling and she isn't picking up. I'm going by her mother's house later to take Jamiah to see her. Maybe she knows where Nia is. I won't know until I get there.

Kia: Okay. I'll be waiting on your call or text. I have something to take care of.

Bryan: Bet

Kia connected her phone to the Bluetooth and scrolled through her playlist. "Keep Dat Nigga," by iCandy blared through the speakers and she rocked out while pulling out of the garage. Kia turned into traffic and made her way toward Stack's house. She didn't bother calling his ass because she wanted to pull up on his ass unexpectedly.

It took twenty minutes for her to turn down his block. She spotted his car parked in front. Kia found a spot up the street and got out. As she made her way to the house, the door opened. Stack smiled while looking down at the ass of a short female, holding the hand of a little girl. Stack bent down and gave the girl Kia assumed was his daughter a kiss. Seeing the shit did nothing to Kia. If she didn't know about him having a baby and they were still fucking around, her chest would've been tight. That didn't mean she couldn't be petty and blow his spot up though. When Kia walked up his eyes ballooned big as hell, making her smirk. Ole girl was saying something to him, but turned to see what had his attention.

"What up, Trayvon?" Kia smiled. "Hello, how you doing? Tawanna, right?"

"Do I know you?" Tawanna asked with an attitude.

"Nah, but I just found out about you. Cut the attitude because I don't have any qualms with you. That nigga is who I have to address about this situation," Kia said, pointing at Stack.

"And what situation would that be, because I'm the woman in his life for the past five years. I wouldn't call what we have a situation at all."

Kia coached herself to stay calm. Baby girl was poppin' off as if she was checking her and Kia didn't like that. Glaring at Stack, Kia decided to hurt her feelings to put a stop to the lil gloat she thought she had going on. Their daughter couldn't be more than two years old. She was cute and looked more like Tawanna than Stack.

"Five years, huh? Why am I just now finding out about your daughter? I'm not worried about knowing you because the nigga supposed to keep the women in his life from all his wrongdoings. The child is another story. As much time as I've spent with this nigga throughout the years, one would've thought I would've known about a child I suppose he's taking care of and spending time with."

"You didn't need to know shit about my daughter!" Tawanna seethed. "Why the fuck you here?"

"It's obvious the nigga called me to come over. I guess that's the reason he wanted me to hit his line when I was on the way, so he could show yo' ass to the doe. The shit didn't work in his favor because I do as I want and not what I'm told. So, direct that shit toward yo' baby daddy."

"Nah, I'm talking to you!" Tawanna said, dropping her daughter's hand.

"Tawanna, chill out. You don't want to walk up on her. I'll talk to you about this shit later. It's just business."

"It's business, Stack? Since when does who I'm fucking with equate to business? Explain that shit to yo' bitch like she's a two-year-old."

"Come on, man. You doin' too much," Stack sucked his teeth. "You know I called you over here to discuss that shit we gotta take care of."

Stack was talking in circles and lying at the same time. He should've kept it a buck and Kia would've played along, but he wanted to save whatever he had with his baby mama. Taking her phone out of her back pocket, Kia scrolled through her texts while keeping one eye on Tawanna, in case the bitch wanted to run up. She found the thread between Stack and herself, reading his words out loud.

"Man, Kia, a nigga was only locked up a few months and you out here giving my pussy away. That shit foul as hell." Scrolling up, she read another message.

"Whoever told you I had a daughter lying like a muthafucka. After all these years, do you think I'd hide my seed from you?"

"Won't you come through and we can talk about this shit because you owe me an explanation. Shall I go on, Stack? Stop playing on my top, nigga!"

Tawanna ran up on Stack and started hitting him in his chest. Their daughter was screaming at the top of her lungs and Kia felt bad that she had to see her stupid ass parents acting out in front of her. Stack was blocking her fists every time Tawanna swung. He finally had hold of both of her hands and hugged her body tightly. Kia could see his lips moving as he whispered in Tawanna's ear. She shook her head, because the bitch was going to believe whatever she was told. Snatching out of his embrace, Tawanna picked her daughter up and stormed to her car.

"Fuck you and that bitch! You won't be seeing her until I say so, hoe ass muthafucka!"

"Aye, watch that bitch word!" Kia screamed at Tawanna's back. "You don't want me to pull up on Calumet when your daughter ain't around. I'm gon' let you make it on account of her, this time!"

Tawanna stuck up her middle finger and slammed the door after buckling her daughter in the car seat. Kia laughed as she walked up the walkway toward an angry Stack. She could see the steam coming from his nose. His skin was red as hell from the hits his baby mama landed.

"Now, what do you think we have to talk about? If it's us, the shit that just went down is why my strong no stands." Kia stood with her thumbs hooked into the loops of her pants.

Stack ran his hand over the top of his head as he sighed deeply. Kia had added on to the reason he wanted Leo to make her smart mouthed ass disappear. One thing he didn't play about was spending time with his daughter. Hearing Tawanna threaten to take that away from him because of the shit Kia revealed almost made him cry. Instead, he was about to lead her right to the lion's den and her wannabe tough ass wasn't going to see it coming. The nigga he heard in the background had fucked her for the last muthafuckin' time.

"Why would you repeat all that shit in front of her, Kia?"

"The same reason you lied about a whole baby while professing your love for me with the same damn tongue. If you gon' do something, Stack, stand on that shit. You want to be with your baby mama, be with her ass. Looks like she wears the pants anyway. She's mad for the time being. I'm quite sure whatever you said to her had her pussy thumping in her pants. That phony ass outburst was for show."

"You didn't have to go that far though. All you had to do was let her leave and act like the shit was for business."

Kia laughed because he thought she was an airhead. "Stack, since the day you met me, I've been one hunnid about everything I say and do. What made you think I was going to switch up to pacify the next bitch? You got me all the way fucked up. You still with her and want to be mad because another nigga been caressing my walls. The audacity of niggas. I'm out. Go make up with your baby mama, so you can stay the active father you've been behind closed doors."

Kia walked away with her head held high and was yoked up from behind. Stack went to the back of her shirt and snatched her gun from the place where he knew she would have it. Carrying her back to his house screaming and trying to get away, Kia couldn't wait for him to put her down. When they were inside, Stack kicked the door closed with his foot, slamming her head into the wall. She wasn't hurt but she had nothing but murderous thoughts for the man she once laid niggas down with.

Stack tossed her on the couch, and she played the role of being knocked out. He was so eager to get on the phone with Leo to tell him he had Kia at his house, he laid the gun on the coffee table. She peeked out of one eye and saw Stack at the window with his phone to his ear.

"Yeah, I got this bitch at my crib. Do you want me to kill her and call the clean-up crew, or you want to do it yourself?"

"Nigga, you would be the clean-up crew! You can't call them niggas over there to remove her body. They look at her and Icy as family. That pussy got you thinking like you a special-ed student or something." Leo huffed as he thought about what he wanted Stack to do. "Dope her ass up and put her in one of the rooms 'til I get there. You already know she's like one of the killas on our team. Don't take yo' eye off her ass. They got to Pip already."

It was too late because Kia was already sitting up with her gun in hand. She had screwed on the silencer while listening to Stack talk to the opp about killing her. Stack was about to regret turning on the people who held him down throughout his journey in the street. Kia and Zan always made sure his ass ate, just like they did. Leo never gave a fuck about him or anybody else. Stack ended the call and turned around to check on Kia. The phone fell from his hand, because she stood with her gun aimed straight at his head.

"Kia, put the gun down."

"Put it down? Hell nawl, nigga! I just heard you basically asking a muthafucka that's been coming for my family since the end of December what he wanted done to me! I won't drug you, but Leo will find yo' ass in here stiff as a board."

Stack took a step forward and Kia shot him in the knee. He fell to the floor, trying to stop the bleeding. "You crazy, bitch!"

"I'll be whatever you want me to be. What I won't be is dead."

She pulled the trigger again, hitting him in the shoulder. Stack rolled around on the floor as the pain traveled down his arm. He couldn't even raise his other arm because his body was in shock. Kia stood over him with a not-so-loving look in her eyes.

"I want you to know I really loved you, Stack. The secret you held from me was only the tip of the iceberg. You could've come back from that, and we would've still been able to be friends afterward. But, teaming up with Leo just stopped you from breathing. I hope the kiss you gave your daughter lasts for eternity."

"Kia, let's ta——"

One shot to the dome silenced Trayvon "Stack" Diggs forever. Kia took her phone from her pocket and called Zan. She knew he would be hurt by the news, but there was no way she could keep what happened from him.

"Kia, what's up, sis?"

"I need the clean-up crew." Kia's voice shook with every word.

"Where?"

Kia paused and bit her bottom lip before answering, "Stack's house."

A lone tear rolled down her face as she stared down at the man she once loved. Kia exited the house and walked briskly to her car and drove away.

Chapter 19

Zan got out of his truck and stood staring at the sign on the building that read, Zone Out. His dream of being the owner of a dispensary finally came true. Cherelle, her brothers, and cousins really held things down while he was away. Business was booming. The inside of the shop was packed, and people were waiting outside to get in. Everybody and their mama were frequenting his establishment. The numbers spoke for themselves and Zan had to show his appreciation to his customers. Without them, his shop probably wouldn't be shit.

He was running a sale on all of his products, as well as giving the customers an opportunity to spin a wheel to win additional discounts and free items instantly. It took Zan a minute to get through the line leading to the door. He dapped up some of the guys he knew from the hood and kept it moving. Zan was almost at the door when a muthafucka decided to puff his chest out for attention.

"The line is right here. You have to wait like everybody else! We not doing that cuttin' the line shit."

Zan turned to address the situation, not knowing the guy was really talking to him. When Zan realized who made the comment, a young cat named Scooter hit the dude so hard, he knocked him out cold in one punch. As much as Zan appreciated him having his back, what he didn't want was bad press when it came to his establishment. The crowd was recording the dude snoring on the ground making the incident a huge spectacle, prompting Cherelle's brother Byron and a few of the other male workers to come outside.

"Get this nigga out of here!" Zan barked. "If y'all ever see his ass out here again, you already know what to do. The show is over! If I see any footage on social media, don't think I won't pull the fuck up and split yo' wig! The shit won't be pretty either, so don't try me!" Zan flung the door open and took a step inside when he heard…

"That's Zan Miller. He ain't to be played with. Erase that shit, now! He's a stone cold killa. Don't let Zone Out fool you."

Zan walked through the shop to the back as he nodded his way through the customers wandering around. He heard the whispers but didn't pay it much mind. Entering the office, which was technically his, Cherelle was sitting behind the desk looking through a few invoices. Zan stood, admiring his wife's beauty from the doorway.

"Are you going to stand there, or show me some love?" Cherelle looked up with a smile.

"Give me a moment. This is a picture-perfect image I want to store in my mind forever."

"I am your forever."

"You got that shit right. Now, get yo' pretty ass up and show yo' man some love, Boss Lady."

Cherelle rose out of the chair, wrapping her arms around Zan's neck kissing him passionately. He'd rolled out of bed and her side was empty. He got himself together by taking care of his hygiene and getting dressed before Zymia commanded his attention. After spending time with his daughter, Zan got her dressed and took her straight to Cherelle's mother, before going to find the love of his life.

Things had been pretty quiet when it came to his brother. Zan hadn't heard anything about or from him, so he assumed Leo didn't know he was out yet. He'd seen a segment on the news about someone killing a female patient at the hospital where Icy's mother was being cared for. Zan didn't get a call, so he didn't reach out to Icy about it. Alarming her was the last thing he wanted to do.

"You missed me enough to come for me, huh?" Cherelle asked playfully.

"Woman, this is my place of business. You have just taken over. That's something I wanted to talk to you about." Cherelle stepped back with a questionable expression, but she waited for him to say what was on his mind.

"When are you going back to work at the hospital, baby?"

She didn't have to think about her response because she knew the subject would present itself sooner than later. Working at the hospital took Cherelle away from her family for long periods of time. As for running the shop, she was home in time for dinner every night with her daughter and of course, Zan. When he was locked up facing football numbers, the thought of living life without him was constantly on Cherelle's mind.

"Zan, I quit. I like what I'm doing now. It gives me more time to spend with you and Zymia. I may not be bringing extra money into the household, but I love what I do here at the dispensary."

Zan hugged his wife and kissed the top of her head. "Baby, I've always been the breadwinner when it came to our family. Your money was just that, your money. I'm with you in whatever you decide to do. If being at the shop is what you want to do, I'm here for it." Zan stepped back with his finger under her chin.

"Now, let's discuss your salary. There's no way my wife will work for any nigga for free, me included. So, I'm going to hit you with a starting salary of one hundred grand a year with a monthly bonus. How does that sound?"

"What do I have to do in order to meet the monthly bonus goal?" Cherelle asked with a raised eyebrow.

"Oh, that's easy. Keep fuckin', suckin', and making a nigga cum like water and you'll get that shit errrr month," Zan laughed as his phone rang on his hip.

"I do that for free anyway. I'll just put a little bit of spice on it. Maybe I can milk you for a cool five hundred grand more."

"Let me get this, but you got all access to the bank. You gon' be straight for the rest of your life. I'll be waiting for you to snatch my soul though." Zan winked. "Kia, what's up, sis?"

"I need the clean-up crew." Her voice was shaky as hell and Zan knew Kia was a hothead and he hoped she hadn't gone off the deep end killing somebody for unnecessary reasons.

"Where?"

"Stack's house."

Zan immediately made the call, realizing he had hung up on her before asking any questions. Instead, he told his crew he would meet them there. Cherelle knew something was wrong the minute Zan had gone from one call to the next.

"What's going on?" she asked.

"I don't know. Kia needs the clean-up crew. At Stack's spot. I hope she didn't off my nigga for not telling her about his daughter. I'll see you at home later. Don't stay here too long. Those niggas can handle closing down," Zan said as he walked out of the office.

It didn't take long for him to pull up to Stack's crib. Jumping out, Zan damn near ran to the garage that had automatically opened upon his arrival. D-Man was standing beside the van with a grim look on his face.

"Dawg, what the fuck happened to my nigga, and who made the call for the clean-up?"

"I'm going to find out. The call came in to me anonymously and I'm about to beat the pavement to find out."

Zan had to lie for Kia because there was a reason she killed Stack, and he wanted to hear why from her. The last thing he wanted was the streets gunning for her off emotions.

D-Man had tears in his eyes. Zan understood how he felt because his chest was tight too.

"Where is he?"

"He's still in the house. This is the hardest clean-up I've ever had to do. Stack didn't deserve this shit, Zan. What the fuck we supposed to tell Kia? She loved that nigga."

"I'll tell her."

Zan walked toward the entrance to the house with a heavy heart. When he walked into the living room, there were three of his workers standing around Stack's body. Zan noticed three gunshot wounds and the kill shot was a clean shot to the middle of his forehead. Stack was killed instantly because his eyes were still open. Not being able to stomach seeing one of his best friends lying motionless, Zan turned to leave.

"Take his body far out and make sure it's found. His mother deserves to bury her son. Keep this shit to yourselves. This may have something to do with my pussy ass brother. D-Man, I'll hit you up when I find out what actually happened."

Zan left the house and jumped in his whip. Turning the key in the ignition, he picked up his phone and pulled off. Kia picked up soon as it rang.

"I'm so sorry——"

"Not on the phone, Kia. Where are you?"

"I'm at home." She gave Zan the address.

"When the hell did you move?"

"A few weeks ago. He was——"

"I'm on my way, Kia. Calm down and wait for me. We will talk when I get there. Everything will be alright, sis."

Kia held on to the phone as Zan drove on the expressway above the speed limit. He wasn't worried about the law, he worried more about Kia and the condition she was in. A trip that would've taken twenty minutes, was cut to ten.

"I'm pulling up." Zan finally broke the silence.

"Okay. I'm on my way down."

Finding an empty spot, Zan hopped out of the car and made his way toward the door just as Kia stepped out into the cold air. Motioning her back inside, Zan followed Kia to her apartment. Sitting on the couch, Zan took his coat off and got comfortable. Kia sat across from him, but Zan patted the spot beside him.

"Come talk to me. What happened, sis?"

Kia told him about the altercation she had between Stack's baby mama. "When I walked away to leave, he picked me up from behind, carrying me back to the house. I fought to get away, but I really wasn't worried about Stack doing anything to hurt me. I figured he just wanted to get his words out. When we got inside, he hit my head on the wall, and I acted like I was knocked out. That's when I heard him on the phone."

"He got on the phone with his baby mama?"

"No! Zan, he was on the phone with Leo! Stack lured me to his house for your brother. He told him he had me and Leo told him to drug me. I didn't have a choice but to kill him, because he betrayed me in the worse way. He literally was conspiring to kill me, along with Leo. So, I ended his ass first."

Kia broke down after explaining what happened. Zan held her close to him and let her get it all out. Kia wasn't a crier. In fact, she was the strongest female he knew and Zan knew she was hurt for what she had to do to Stack. Kia didn't have a choice in the matter. He always told her to have a kill or be killed mindset, and she protected herself.

"His baby mama knows I was there, Zan. I'm sorry for shooting him."

"You don't have shit to be sorry for. That nigga violated! He knew what the consequences were for fuckin' with family. If you hadn't killed him, I would have if anything had happened to you, Kia. Don't worry about this shit. I'm going to cover this shit up and you won't be tied to it."

"We have to stop Leo, Zan. We are tired of looking over our shoulders. Julz may be scarred for life, Staci is still recovering, I had to move so nobody knows where I lay my head, now Stack is dead. Not to mention, I still need to find out who this Julian bitch is because she is the only person besides Leo that's left. Oh, and that bitch, Nia."

"Whoa! That's a lot to take in. What happened to Julz?"

Kia explained what happened to Julz and filled Zan in on everything else. He sat listening with his jaws clenched tightly. Leo put everybody in the line of fire while his ass sat back safe. Hearing that Boom and Pip were killed lifted the weight off his shoulders because that was less work for him to do. He was going to have to hit Smooth up to pick his brain to make sure Leo hadn't gotten inside his head too. Zan would have no problem sending his ass to hell.

"Damn. I hate y'all is going through all this shit with Leo being behind it all. I'm glad Staci is good because I was afraid to contact you or Icy to make sure she wasn't the person killed at Ingalls the other night."

"To be honest with you, that was a hit on Staci's life. Pip said Leo sent somebody to do the job. I went back to the hospital last night to confirm his story, and talked to one of the nurses that was taking care of Staci. The woman that was killed was in room 319, the same room as Staci. Leo was trying to kill her. Had Icy not taken her home to recuperate, we would be planning her funeral."

Kia's phone rang on the coffee table and Bryan's name was on the screen.

"Bryan, what did you find?" Kia asked.

"Julian Miller is a special type of crazy," he laughed. Kia put the phone on speaker so Zan could hear what was being said.

"She has been married to Leo for years. Her name became Julian Burks seven years ago. On her birth certificate, she was named Brenda Giles."

Kia's ears rang loud and muted out everything else Bryan said. There was no way in hell the woman that abandoned her years prior, was working with the very man that had been turning her life upside down for months. Kia was in the presence of her mama and didn't even know it. She had pistol whipped the bitch and vowed to kill her on sight.

"Go back to her real name," Kia choked out.

"Brenda Giles."

"That's my mama! I've seen Julian. She can't be no older than thirty-five. Nah, yo' people got their information wrong. Tell him to go back to the drawing board because that's not true."

"I'm sorry I had to be the one to bring this to light for you, Kia. The information is spot on. Brenda Giles was born to Shirley and Chaplain Giles, June 12, 1975. She will be forty-seven this year. She had a brother named Chaplain Jr. He died in 1982 at the age of ten, when he drowned playing in the water at North Avenue Beach. Brenda underwent cosmetic surgery and changed her entire appearance ten years ago in the Dominican Republic. She stayed over there for two years, then returned to the states."

Kia received a notification on her phone and opened the picture message Bryan sent. There was a side-by-side photo of the Brenda that Kia knew all too well, then a picture of Julian. The two people looked nothing alike, and Julian definitely looked like she could've been Brenda's daughter. As Kia compared the two photos, she could see the slight similarities of the two images.

"Ain't this a bitch," Kia said with tears in her eyes. "This bitch didn't even try to tell me who she was! She was trying to get close to Staci for that good-for-nothing ass nigga! How the fuck could one blindside their own child?" Kia took a deep breath and chuckled lowly. "You got a number on her?"

"As a matter of fact, I do."

Bryan sent the number via text. Kia already had the address to the crib Julian and Leo were living in, so she didn't need that. She thanked Bryan for the help he provided.

"Kia, I don't know if you heard, but Blaze and Joe went to the hotel and Leo was already gone. His baby mama and child had checked out of the hotel. Blaze went to the house, but he wasn't there either. I found out Leo does have a flight scheduled to fly out in two days. We just don't know where he is at the moment. Call Blaze for whatever plans he has in motion."

"Are you going?"

"No, I have to find Nia. Her mother hasn't seen her. Plus, I want to be here in case Julz needs me. I love her, Kia. I'm not letting her shut me out for something my baby mama did to her."

"She will come around. Give her time," Kia reassured him. "I have to go. I'll keep you posted because I have to call Blaze and my dear mother."

Kia placed the phone in her lap and stared straight ahead. She couldn't believe Brenda pulled a stunt of that magnitude and could've possibly gotten away with it. Zan's mind was going wild as he thought about what he'd heard. Knowing Leo had plans of going back to Kingston, having a conversation with Blaze was a must. Zan decided to call Icy on Kia's behalf since she was still sitting quietly next to him.

"Zan! How are you?" Icy asked soon as she answered the phone.

"I'm good. How's Staci?"

"She's doing alright physically. Mentally, she is fucked up. Time heals all wounds is what I've heard. Hopefully, in due time, my mama will be back to her feisty self."

"Staci will bounce back better than ever," Zan paused. "I was calling because I need to holla at Blaze. Is he around?"

"Um, no. He's out with Joe. Everything okay?"

Zan didn't know how much Icy knew about the situation and it wasn't his place to fill her in before Blaze decided to do it himself. "Yeah, I wanted to talk to him about some business shit. Text him my number and tell him to hit me up."

"Let me talk to her, Zan," Kia said in the background.

"Are you with Kia?"

"I am. Hold on."

Zan handed the phone to Kia and sat listening to her explain everything she had found out about her mother. The words that spewed from Kia's mouth were laced with pure venom. Zan understood why she felt the way she did, because he would be the same way if he was in her shoes. After about fifteen minutes, Kia finished the call. She pressed numbers on Zan's phone, handing it back to him. He listened to the ringing on the other end and looked at Kia in confusion. Before he could ask what was going on, the person answered.

"Akoni Ottey. How may I help you?"

Blaze had no idea who was calling from the unfamiliar number, but he had to treat it as business since he was the boss of his company. He prayed it wasn't any bullshit on the other end, because he had enough to deal with at the time.

"Blaze, it's Zan. Kia dialed you for me. Can we meet somewhere to talk?"

"I've had a lot happen today. I'm on my way to the crib, can this wait until next week? I'm about to get shit together to go home."

"That's what I was calling about. I heard Leo is going back to Kingston and I want to be there when you get your hands on him."

"How you know he's planning on going back to Kingston?"

Blaze didn't like the fact of Zan calling him out of the blue and knowing his brother's moves as well. He felt the shit was a set-up he wasn't about to walk into. He was taught early on that blood was thicker than mud, and there was no way Zan was going against Leo.

"Not the way you're assuming. I can tell you that. I'm not on the team Leo side. Yes, he's my brother, but I'm against everything he has done. Including sending me to the pen for something I had no parts of and was facing a life sentence for."

"I don't trust shit involved with that nigga. Not even you. Icy invited you to the hotel that day and I was against the shit from the start. She trusts you, I don't. Leo is going to die on Jamaica soil, and so will you if you try to save him."

"Blaze, it's Kia. You have the wrong impression of Zan. He's a stand-up nigga. Like Icy, I trust him with my life. The same way I called you about that thing you took care of, Zan had to do the same today. He wants to stop Leo like the rest of us."

Blaze thought about what Kia said. He knew she and Icy meant well when it came to Zan. He just couldn't be too trusting with the nigga, knowing his affiliation with Leo's bitch ass. He understood the shit Zan had to go through, along with Icy. The trust just wasn't in him to have Zan tagging along. After a few moments of consideration, Blaze finally gave in to hear the muthafucka out.

"Bring him to the crib. Zan, I want you to know, I will have gun in hand when you cross the threshold. Don't come to my spot on bullshit, and yo' brother bet not pop up at my place of residence at any given time."

"You got it. I'm gon' need you to show the same respect I've shown you from day one. Hold that aggression for the nigga that counts. The way you love Icy, I love her just as much. Only, mine is on a scale of sibling love. My love doesn't stop there because Kia, Julz and Staci are family as well. I will kill for any of them, no matter who's on the other end of the gun. See you in a minute, nigga. Let that energy subside, because I don't want any unnecessary smoke."

Zan banged on his ass. Blaze was gon' have to share his position in the jungle. Fuckin' with him, they would tear that muthafucka up if the two of them didn't get on the same page pronto.

Chapter 20

Leo was driving on the expressway to Dolton nervously. He had left his charger at the house and his battery died. There was no way for him to reach out to Pip to make sure everything was good on his end with Julz. For some reason, his stomach was in knots. Leo was driving around with no destination in mind since leaving Desiree's crib. Going back home was out of the question, so he decided to stop at a Walgreens to grab a charger, then head out to handle Julz.

The further he got to the south suburbs, the darker the sky became. The thick smoke appeared as if an entire city block was ablaze. Exiting on Sibley Boulevard, traffic was ridiculous in the direction he needed to travel. It was damn near ten o'clock and most of the vehicles were probably heading in the direction of Klubb Karma but something else was going on, because he couldn't go more than three miles an hour without having to stop.

"Aye, man. What's going on 'round here?" Leo lowered his window, asking a random dude walking down the street.

"Some muthafucka set an abandoned house on fire over there on Evers. They just got the fire put out a few minutes ago. They were fighting it for damn near two hours. I heard the fire marshal say it was a gas fire and they found a body inside. I wasn't sticking around to find out. Too many folks missing as is. Shit don't make no sense."

Traffic inched forward enough for Leo to cut through a McDonald's parking lot. Regardless of what he was told, Leo headed toward Evers and ran into a roadblock. By the time he pulled into someone's driveway and got out of his vehicle, a body was being rolled out of the charred house by firemen in full gear. Rushing back to his ride, Leo picked up his phone and willed his phone to power on quickly. He hoped like hell Julz was the person zipped up in that body bag. Soon as his phone lit up, Leo received a video message from Pip. His body automatically relaxed because he knew Pip was good.

Leo opened the message and watched Pip being burned alive. The video was about ninety seconds long, but it seemed like a lifetime. Leo witnessed his long-time friend die while engulfed in flames like old ass furniture. He didn't notice the caption until he was about to close out of the message. When he read what it said, Leo slammed his fist on the dashboard then backed out of the driveway, heading to the hotel to get his daughter far away from there. Pip was the only other person who knew his plans of going to get Avita the next morning. There was no way Pip didn't tell what he knew in order to save his life.

When he made the call for Avita to be ready in the next thirty minutes, she had a lot of questions he wasn't in the mood to answer. He drove in silence and said a silent prayer for his fallen soldiers and made a vow to avenge their deaths. Alone.

Leo pulled in front of Embassy Suites, shaking his head to clear the scene of the fire away. Avita and Amoy stood inside the entrance until he stepped out of his vehicle. Popping the trunk, he walked to help with the luggage. Avita smiled from ear to ear the closer Leo got to the door. Her lips formed a straight line when he bypassed her, scooping Amoy into his arms, kissing all over her little face. She squealed with delight and it warmed Leo's heart. Without acknowledging Avita, he took his daughter to the car.

"You don't see me standing here?"

Ignoring her, Leo made sure Amoy was safely in the seatbelt before giving her another kiss on the forehead. He told her daddy had to talk to mommy and for her to sit tight. Leo closed the door and walked back to the sidewalk where Avita continue to stand with her face twisted up.

"How the fuck could I miss you standing there, Avita? Stop asking stupid ass questions and put yo' bag in the trunk. You lucky I didn't walk up and slap the shit out of you for having my daughter here while yo' ass on bullshit."

"I told you I wasn't going back until your bitch Icy paid for what she did to my cousin!"

"And what the fuck I tell you? To leave Icy to me, right?"

"All——"

"All my ass, Avita! You ain't about that life and you know it. Icy would drag the fuck outta you, then bury yo' ass alive! I don't know why you didn't leave with Amancia. Yeah, I do. You worried about what I have going on with Icy. I told you she's all lovey-dovey with that nigga Blaze, but you knew that already."

Leo placed Amoy's luggage in the trunk and walked to the driver's side of the car. Avita stood watching his every move, but he left her where she stood. A few minutes later, she slammed the trunk with all of her might, pissing Leo off. Avita did the same with the passenger door when she got inside.

"You got one mo' time to slam my shit! I will leave yo' ass on the curb to find yo' own way, wherever you decide to go. You too far from home to be on bullshit, Avita. Stop playing with me, because you're on the verge of seeing a side of me you won't like."

"Daddy, you and Mommy fight?"

The rage that had built up in Leo dissipated at the sound of his daughter's small voice. Glancing in the review mirror, Leo forced a smile for the little girl who held his heart in the palm of her hands.

"No, baby. Daddy's sorry for raising his voice."

"You're sorry for using bad words too, Daddy?"

"Yes, Amoy, I'm sorry for using bad words. I love you. Now, put on your headphones."

"I love you more, Daddy. I'm glad to be with you. Please don't leave me again."

Leo's throat closed up tightly at her words, causing tears to well in his eyes. He couldn't find the right words to say in return, so he just nodded his head slowly. One thing he didn't want to do was lie to his princess. Leo couldn't promise not to ever leave again because what he planned to do in Kingston would shut the entire country down until he was found. It was a get in and out situation or die trying. That was a chance he had to take because Kenise had a whole lot of something that belonged to him, and he was traveling far to get it.

Once he touched down in Kingston, Leo figured he would be able to bombard Kenise, and flee before her body was found. Blaze was a stupid muthafucka if he thought anyone in the village was watching his mother twenty-four hours a day. The best time to catch her was while her old ass slept. While his ass was fucking and sucking on Icy, Duke would have never left his wife open to lose her life like he'd done. Blaze thought his family was untouchable, but Leo proved that shit untrue when he killed two birds with one stone.

The car was eerily quiet. Leo felt Avita staring a hole into the side of his head. He reached to turn the radio on and Avita had the nerve to smack her lips loudly with a deep huff. Turning toward the window, Leo could hear her sniffling while wiping her face.

"The fuck you crying for? It's not my fault you didn't think this shit through. I told you long ago to wait for me…in Kingston! You chose to come here."

"Why did you lie to me, Leo? You said it was about you, me, and Amoy. Then I find out you were with a woman for years and married her! I still wear the ring you gave me promising to make me your wife."

Avita had snot running out of her nose. Leo reached over her as he waited for the light to change and opened the glove compartment, retrieving plenty of napkins. He held the cloth out to her without a care. Avita snatched them from his hand, blowing her nose loudly. Leo thought her rant was over but how wrong he was. Avita was just getting started.

"You have nothing to say, huh?" she asked. "How long did you think you would've been able to live a double life without me finding out? As a matter of fact, what else are you hiding?"

"Avita, you asking questions you really don't want to hear the answers to. Leave well enough alone. Your feelings are already polluting the environment around me. I don't owe you an explanation anyway."

"You don't owe me an explanation? Yes, the fuck you do! I've been your fuckin' secret for years and we share a daughter nobody knows about. Who does that? Oh, your deceptive ass, that's who," Avita cried.

Leo glanced into the rearview mirror to make sure Amoy was still occupied in the backseat. When he was sure she wasn't listening and had fallen asleep, he turned to look at Avita before giving the road his undivided attention. Leo was about to address everything she questioned him about when his phone rang. His quick reaction had him hitting the button on the steering wheel answering the call. He was sure Avita saw *Wifey* appear on the display, so there was no use for him to ignore the shit.

"What up?"

"Don't what up me, Leo. Where the hell are you? I've been calling you since last night."

Avita's mouth opened wide because the woman going off on Leo didn't sound like Icy. Avita wanted to know what else he was hiding, and she was about to find out. Julian, on the other hand, was out of her damn mind calling him to ask where he was, after leaving him unconscious in their living room.

"It doesn't matter where I am. Didn't you leave? Now, I'm where I'm at, it doesn't concern you. When I get back, have yo' shit out of my house!"

"Nigga, what?" Julian laughed. "See, that's where you have yo' bitches mixed up. I've never needed you for shit. When I met you, I had my own every damn thing. You must've forgot, you wouldn't have the muthafuckin' house if I didn't put my name and credit on the paperwork. By law, that house belongs to me! I'm yo' muthafuckin' wife and you out there fuckin' and suckin' bitches in every area code. Hell, you even made it to Jamaica, producing an offspring."

Avita listened with a heavy heart. The man she thought loved her was nothing other than a fraudulent womanizer. She couldn't stop the tears from falling as she listened to the second woman claiming to be Leo's wife. His ass was in these streets being a real polygamist and the shit wasn't even legal in the states. Avita wondered how he pulled it off without getting caught. Julian's voice brought her back to the conversation.

"Shut the fuck up!" she yelled as Leo tried to speak. "You must be with your baby mama. I swear to God you bet not pull up to my shit with your ready-made family in tow. Icy I overlooked, because your freedom was on the line. But this shit right here, nigga, nah find somebody else to do it. Show up and all three of you muthafuckas gon' come up missing."

Julian hung up and Leo was seething with anger because she'd threatened his daughter's life. He had no intentions of taking Amoy anywhere near the house after the way Julian responded to him telling her what he planned. If Leo went to the house, he was liable to kill the bitch. Dealing with Julian would have to wait until he got back from his trip to Kingston. Continuing to drive, he knew it wouldn't be long before Avita opened her dick suckers to call herself checking him.

"I know damn well you're not planning to take me and Amoy to the home you share with yet another bitch."

"I'm not taking y'all there and my marriage to Julian is for show," Leo lied with ease.

"Leo, stop lying so fucking much! I heard what was said and I believe every word. When we get to Kingston, forget about me, okay? You will forever be Amoy's father. Just leave me the fuck out of it. I don't know what you have going on in your life right now, but I refuse to lose my life behind it. There's nothing more I have to say to you. Love on your daughter as much as you can. At the rate you're going, there's no telling how long you will be around before someone kills you for wronging them."

He let everything Avita said evaporate into the air. If she was done, he couldn't change her mind if he wanted to because the call from Julian sealed the deal of him trying to mend anything between them. Avita had him thinking about not being around for Amoy when she graduated elementary school. Hell, Leo wasn't sure he would be around when she turned five. He was presumed dead, but deep down in his soul, he felt his heart wouldn't beat too much longer. Avita had brought a bad omen into his space as she spoke death into his life.

***

In the sitting room of the home she shared with Leo, Julian took a pull of the blunt she held in her left hand, with a glass of wine in the right. She looked out into the yard as she focused on two squirrels wrestling in the grass. Julian had been waiting for Leo to come home with her gun lying by her side all night. She was ready to send her husband to the deepest depth of hell. He was out of his mind dropping the bomb about his bastard child on her like he'd done. After all the shit she had sacrificed to keep his secrets, staying away from her child, killing bitches for him, covering up his fake death, and the willingness to give him money to rise back to the top of the game. Leo still had the nerve to shit on her. Julian had heard the saying, *the person you loved the most, would be the one who did you the dirtiest.*

"It must be God keeping his selfish ass wherever he is," Julian said out loud as she sipped from the wineglass.

The alcohol was working its way through Julian's bloodstream. It had been a while since she'd drank and even longer since she had smoked. Leo had weed rolled in his stash already, so she grabbed one to calm the rage that brewed within her. Thoughts of how she'd ended up where she was in the present day took Julian back in time.

Brenda drove like a bat out of hell toward Birdman's home because Kenny told her that's where he was. He had been gone most of the day and he wasn't on the block picking up money. She had already made the rounds to eliminate the places she knew he wasn't. The lies he told rolled off his tongue smooth as butter. At the time, Brenda was over Kenny's bullshit, and it was at that moment she knew getting to the bottom of his lies was necessary. She didn't bother calling to tell him her whereabouts. Popping up was a better option for her. Brenda didn't think he had another bitch at Staci's home because infidelity was something she didn't tolerate. Brenda was only going there to prove the lie Kenny had told.

She parked in the driveway and hopped out, barely getting her key out of the ignition. She rang the doorbell repeatedly, while tapping her feet impatiently, waiting for someone to answer. When the door opened, an angry Birdman stood with gun in hand.

"Brenda, what the fuck?"

"Where's Kenny?" she asked, trying to look past him into the house.

"He ain't here. Stop all that moving, man! And what I tell you about coming to my shit unannounced? I know Staci didn't know you were poppin' up because she's not even here."

"Let me in so I can see if he's here on my own. If he's truly not here, then he has lied once again. I highly doubt that because Staci's not home to regulate shit, so he can very well be in one of your guest rooms with a bitch! Move, Birdman!"

Stepping to the side, Birdman allowed her to search his home in amusement. Kenny had Brenda's ass going insane and he couldn't wait until she finished so she could feel like the ass she was portraying herself to be in that moment. On many occasions, he had told Kenny to either stop cheating and do right by Brenda or leave her alone, before things got ugly between them. Obviously, the nigga didn't listen.

Birdman knew from the first day he was introduced to her that she wasn't going to be able to handle the stress of being with Kenny. Staci was always Brenda's shoulder to cry on when she called about the issues they were having. Staci tried to give sound advice without telling her to leave altogether. Birdman followed his first mind and stayed out of it. Kenny was a man who had many women, with one whom he gave special attention. Brenda was the one.

"Where is he?" Brenda asked, entering the room after her search. She found Birdman sitting on a barstool at the bar.

"I'on know. I told you he wasn't here when you were outside disturbing my peace."

"'Why is he doing me like this? I've been nothing but good to him. Who is he messing around with? You know exactly who she is, Birdman. Y'all are always together and that's your brother!"

"Not true. He ain't here now, right? I don't get involved in what another man does in his private life. He may be my brother, but I don't sit and listen to anything he does with you or anyone else. Go home and wait for him to return. These questions are for Kenny to answer, not me."

Brenda walked to the other side of the bar and poured a double shot of apple Crown and tossed it back. Birdman watched as she continuously poured her poison without speaking. He took in her beauty and wondered why Kenny could step out on her. Brenda was wasted in no time and that day started something between the two of them inside the home Birdman shared with his wife.

"Damn, I miss Birdman."

Tears slid from the corners of her eyes as she looked up at the ceiling, hoping to see the face of the man she had fallen in love with. Every day after his death, Julian wished she had told him the truth about Kia. She had eighteen years to reveal his paternity, but Julian was afraid of how the news would affect Staci and Icy. Many would think it was bullshit seeming how Julian and Birdman's affair lasted a few years undetected. Guilt ate at her up because she had to continue hanging out with Staci so she wouldn't suspect anything. Kenny going to jail gave Julian the freedom to fuck around with Birdman without worrying about getting caught.

Eleven years later, that same guilt was eating her ass alive with more added to her plate. Had he known he was Kia's father, Birdman would still be alive. Julian held herself responsible for him not being there in the world of the living. A sound outside brought her out of her thoughts. Julian jumped up ready for the battle with Leo, but the doorbell chimed instead. She wasn't expecting anyone, and Leo had a key to enter their home. Julian had no clue who could've been on the other side of the door.

She was slow to react because of the amount of alcohol she had consumed. Heavy knocks echoed through the room and her first thought was the police were there to arrest her or Leo. Her nerves were all over the place, causing Julian to push the gun between the cushions of the sofa before heading for the door.

"Julian, I know you in there! Open the fuckin' door!"

Pausing mid-step, Julian didn't recognize the voice of the woman calling out to her. She obviously knew her and was pissed for whatever reason. Taking a few steps back, Julian decided not to let the person inside her home. The knocks turned into what sounded like kicks causing Julian to make a beeline for her gun. Unable to get back to the sofa in a timely manner, the door crashed open behind her. Julian turned and found herself face-to-face with no other than her daughter, Kia.

"Hello, Julian Miller," she chortled. "Or should I call you Brenda Giles? Wait, maybe I should just cry tears of joy while hugging you tightly, huh, Mama?"

Julian was stuck in place, because she had no clue how Kia figured out she was her mother. She never even thought anyone would be able to find out where Leo lived. Let alone her connection to him. Julian had every intention of contacting her daughter and Staci to reveal herself as well as apologize for her wrongdoings. She couldn't gather her thoughts so she didn't have a rebuttal for the questions asked. Kia walked further into the house with two men standing guard at the door. She kept her eyes on the woman standing before her and actually took in her appearance from head to feet.

"Damn, the doctor who performed your surgery did a good ass job. For a woman who's damn fifty years old, you look better than your twenty-nine-year-old daughter." Kia laughed. "I just want to know, why?"

Julian couldn't find her voice, prompting Kia to slap the shit out of her. "Bitch, say something! Stop standing there like you don't know what the fuck I'm talking about. You owe me that much!"

"Kia, I'm sorry. I never meant to abandon you the way I did."

"Do you think I'm stupid?" Kia asked. "You came to Staci's house and looked me right in the face. That was your opportunity to tell me who the fuck you were. Instead, you were trying to scope out the scene for a nigga that killed my muthafuckin' daddy! How the hell you fuckin' the opp and helping him plan the demise of your flesh and blood?"

"I swear I didn't know how to tell you. That's why I asked about Kenny then explained how I knew Staci. Kia, you hit me with a gun. Had I told you the truth, I would be dead already."

"You're correct. For years I wondered where you were. I've always questioned the reason you up and left me in this fucked up world to defend for myself. That year was hard because not only did I lose my mama, I lost the only man who gave a fuck about me."

Tears ran down Kia's face and she swiped them away quicker than they fell. She seethed with anger and tried her best not to react off impulse. Her mind was telling her to kill Julian and get it over with, but she knew that would be too damn easy. Taking a deep breath, Kia calmed herself enough to speak her mind. Julian stepped back toward the sofa and Kia snatched her by the front of her shirt.

"I had to learn who my father was from Kenny! You lied to me my entire life. Had me hating that man for not spending time with me. I thought he didn't want anything to do with me because that's what you embedded in my head. But the truth was, the muthafucka wasn't even my daddy! I didn't deserve none of that shit! Blame yourself for Kenny's death! His blood is on your hands now, *Brenda.* The lie you told is the reason he killed his only brother. My father!"

Kia was livid. Her hands shook uncontrollably, and she pushed Julian away from her. The little girl Julian had spent all her time with from an infant was now an adult she didn't know at all. Hurt was the only way to describe every word that fell from Kia's mouth. Hearing her say Kenny was dead, Julian knew she had to tread lightly when it came to her daughter. She was a stone-cold killer just like Birdman.

"Please accept my apology. Leo isn't the man I fell in love with."

"I'm not accepting shit! There's no way I can forgive you for the bullshit you were involved in." Kia said, pointing in Julian's direction. "How the fuck you loved a muthafucka who was married to yo' baby daddy's daughter?"

"I didn't know anything about Icy," Julian lied with a straight face.

"You can't convince me you didn't know about Leo's involvement with Icy. The nigga was up her ass twenty-four seven for years. You were probably in on the play from the start. The only reason you are somewhat coming clean now is because the nigga is with his baby mama and three-year-old daughter."

Hearing Kia speak on Leo's daughter got a reaction out of Julian. Her face contorted as if she was possessed. She started breathing heavily and her chest rose and fell repeatedly, while her fist balled tightly at her sides.

"Everybody knew about that lil bitch except me!" Julian screamed with spit forming in the corners of her mouth. "Leo wined and dined Icy while he kept me hidden in the cut. I told him to walk away after she took everything he owned, because he owed her for the deceit that he'd put her through. He wouldn't listen. I tried to help best I could."

"No, you didn't! You could've come to us and spilled the beans on his ass. Instead, you helped him until his people started dying like roadkill. Did it even cross your mind that there was a possibility you would die right along with them?"

Julian laughed. "I'm your mother. There's no way your heart would allow you to hurt me in any way. I love you, Kia. Always will. I've apologized and will continue to do so. We can mend our relationship and get past this."

Kia nodded her head in agreement. "You're right. I won't be able to kill you off the strength of you being my mother. I'm gon' let you make it."

Julian's shoulders relaxed in relief as she closed her eyes and cried. She was not aware of another person entering the residence from the patio. When she opened her eyes and saw Staci standing next to Kia, holding on to a walker, a slight smile formed on her face. The sight of her long-time friend made Julian happy for the first time in years.

"Staci, I've missed you so much!" Julian exclaimed, rushing to hug her tightly.

"I have one question," Staci said, causing Julian to step back grinning from ear to ear.

"You can ask me anything. First, I'm sorry for betraying you. I wanted to tell you about Kia being Birdman's daughter, but I didn't know how you would take the news."

"I'm over that. Kia has always been my bonus daughter since her piece-of-shit ass parents left her out in the streets alone. She won't ever have to worry about me abandoning her." Staci wiped the smile right off Julian's face with the truth. "What I really want to know is, why didn't you kill me?"

The shock on Julian's face was priceless. She didn't think Staci would be able to identify her as the person who ran her down like an animal. There was nothing Julian could say to get herself out of the spotlight, but she was ready to lie her ass off to get out of the situation.

"I-I-I don't know what you're talking about."

"You know exactly what I'm referring to. I stared you in the face soon as the engine of the white Beamer revved in my direction before hitting me."

"Bitches ain't shit," Joe mumbled, glaring at Julian. "How the fuck you claim to love her, but you ran her down like a dog then left her in the street to die?"

"I didn't do shit!"

"Lie again and I'll forget I said anything about not killin' yo ass!" Kia shot back at her mother. I believe you did it because you look like the type who would be dick drunk behind a nigga. Now, answer the muthafuckin' question! What more do you have to lose besides your life?"

"Okay, okay! Leo threatened to kill me if I didn't do as he demanded. Staci means so much to me and seeing her body lying in the street haunts me every day."

"It haunted you so bad that you sat back and waited for a dirty ass cop to place a bomb on my car? That bitch tried to kill me, and you knew about it!"

Julian turned around to an angry Icy. The young woman standing before her had a murderous look in her eyes just like her father. She had seen Birdman furious on many occasions when someone on the street betrayed him. His eyes turned charcoal black when he was about to kill. Julian felt as if she was about to shit on herself. As innocent as Icy appeared, Julian knew she wasn't going to show any mercy.

"You don't have a lie for that shit, huh? Let me guess, you got rid of Cynthia too, right?"

"I know damn well you don't give a fuck about that bitch. She was waiting to hang you out to dry over Leo's dick!"

"Just like your thirsty ass," Icy laughed. "Yo' nigga had his hand in a lot of shit. Starting with the murder of my daddy. Knowing what happened means you're just as guilty of the crime. Kenny already met his fate and is probably still trying to convince the devil he didn't belong in his house. Now, I'm tired of talking about this shit."

"Icy, I'm sorry," Julian cried.

"Don't be sorry, bitch. Be careful."

In the midst of saying the last word, Icy swung her arm slicing a clean cut across Julian's neck. She clutched her throat as she struggled to breathe. It didn't work in Julian's favor because she dropped to her knees with blood dying the carpet red in front of her. Icy walked around the mess, heading for the door.

"Clean this shit up. I'm stressed and need to get back to my man so his dick can relieve me of the pressure."

Staci was shocked at the words Icy spilled. She was at a loss, not knowing what to say. With Joe and Zan's help, they guided her to the car.

"Y'all gotta put an end to this shit. My baby has turned into her father. Leo doesn't stand a chance once Icy gets in his presence. What time are y'all heading out to Kingston?"

"I don't know," Zan spoke up. "We're going to go over the details with Blaze once we get to the house. Did he know where you and Icy were going?"

"No, Icy only told him we were going for a ride."

"He's going to be pissed," Joe sighed. "And the nigga sent me to make sure y'all were cool. I might have to beat his ass behind this shit."

Joe pulled out of the driveway and headed in the direction of Blaze's house.

Chapter 21

The moment Icy entered the home she shared with Blaze, he stood from the stool he sat on going over emails. The splatter of blood on her shirt had his full attention. After making sure Icy wasn't harmed in any way, the questions flew from his mouth.

"What happened? Where is Staci? Where were you?"

"I killed the Julian bitch. That's it, that's all. It's Leo's turn now. What time are we leaving for Kingston? I want my lick back."

Blaze couldn't believe how nonchalant Icy was being. First Desiree, now Julian. She had turned into a woman he didn't know and that wasn't how he pictured his wife. Blaze didn't want Icy getting comfortable taking lives. It was his job to protect her from any and everything. Icy's mood changed in the blink of an eye. Her hard demeanor diminished and the woman he fell in love with was back.

"I want my life back," she wailed.

"I'm going to take care of that, baby."

Blaze pulled Icy to his chest and allowed her to cry it out. The door opened and everybody walked in, witnessing Icy break down. Kia walked up and hugged her cousin from behind.

"Come on, Icy. You need to shower and get some rest. We will find out when we're leaving for Kingston before the night is over. Blaze is going to run the plan by the fellas. In the meantime, we have to make sure you're ready."

Blaze kissed Icy on the forehead and watched her walk slowly up the stairs. Staci was escorted in by Zan, causing Blaze's jaw to flex the further he walked inside his space. He didn't realize how close Staci was to him until she palmed the side of his face.

"The fight isn't with Zander, Akoni. He is nothing like Leo and will forever be part of my family. Your anger is directed at the wrong Miller brother. I need you to concentrate on Leo and the trip to Kingston. I'm against my daughter going, but it is necessary for her to be there. She's turning into somebody I don't know, Akoni. You have to bring my baby back to me."

"I just said that to myself when she came through the door. Staci, Icy is going to Kingston, and she will get a chance to have her way with Leo. I really don't want to involve her, but she's not going to take no for an answer. I promise, she will come back without a scratch."

"She better because the way she handled Julian was kind of scary. She was Birdman in a pair of joggers that hugged all that ass," Staci chuckled. "I had a dream about fish the other night. Is Icy pregnant?"

Blaze ran his hand down his face. "I don't know. I think so, but she hasn't said anything about it. I'll find out for sure when we get back. Deal?"

Staci nodded her head and hugged Blaze before heading toward the spare bedroom. Fanny waited for her so she could get her to bed. Blaze had called her to stay with Staci while they were gone. Once Staci was out of earshot, he glared at Joe menacingly.

"Don't look at me like that, nigga. I followed them like you asked. Where she was going, I didn't know. Hell, she snuck in that muthafucka like Cat Woman. Then sliced the bitch throat fast as lightning before walking off."

"So, why didn't I get a call?"

"Shid, she had it," Joe laughed. "You got her back in one piece. It wasn't like you would've been able to stop her. Icy's inner demons were on full display. Yo' ass better sleep with one eye open whenever you piss her off."

Icy appeared at the top of the stairs with a scowl on her face. Kia was trying to pull her back to the bedroom, but that wasn't happening. She descended the stairs and approached Blaze.

"Ask me why I didn't call, Blaze."

"Baby, this has nothing to do with you."

"It has everything to do with me! My decisions were mine alone. I'm grown and don't need security or somebody clockin' my moves. Julian, Brenda, or whatever she wanted to be called was going to die regardless. Finding out she was the one who hit my mama sealed her muthafuckin' fate." Icy's eyes burned through the man she'd come to love, because he was handling her like she was a weak bitch.

"We have other shit to focus on. Like, how the fuck we gon' handle this pussy ass nigga, Leo."

"I agree with Icy. We have to concentrate on the subject at hand."

Blaze gazed in Zan's direction. Even though Staci told him Zan was nothing like Leo, Blaze still didn't trust him. He'd been waiting on the moment to address his ass.

"Yo punk ass brother will be flying out day after tomorrow. We're leaving bright and early in the morning to beat him there." Blaze paused to see if he could read Zan's body language.

"Okay, nigga, keep going. You act like I'm taking notes to relay back to him," Zan spat. "Let's clear whatever negative perspective you may have about me. Leo is my worse fuckin' enemy to date. The nigga hurt my heart when I thought somebody wiped his ass off the face of the earth. Hell, I was comin' for yo' ass, to be honest. The shit had yo' name written all over it after the way you showed up at the reception. When I found out about all the lies, then facing football numbers to never step foot outside of prison, the nigga's been on my shit list. See, Leo knew who to fuck wit and my family wasn't it. But what he seemed to have forgotten was the Winters is my family too."

Blaze listened to Zan spit his shit and could do nothing but respect the love he had for Icy and her family.

"The shit he has done to make their lives a living hell ends now. So, in case I haven't made myself clear, I'm all in with going to Kingston. That's where all this shit started and it's only right it ends there too. Duke's passing hurt the fuck outta me, then to learn my brother was behind his death left a bad taste in my mouth. Yo' father was a straight up nigga that put us on. If it wasn't for him, we wouldn't have ate the way we did for years. In case you didn't know, everything Duke did was for you. He loved you and didn't hesitate to bring yo' name up. We gon' get justice for Duke."

Blaze walked up to Zan with his hand out. They stared each other down for a few minutes, before embracing in a brotherly hug. Blaze had to put his ill feelings to the side because Zan didn't deserve to take the heat for what Leo had done.

"I apologize for directing that shit yo' way. Icy means a lot to me and it's my job to keep everybody that means her no good away from her."

"Trust, I understand, from what I've seen you are the man for her. Love her accordingly, nigga. You know Leo's story, don't repeat that shit."

"Fo' sho, I'm planning to love her like no other. There ain't a muthafucka out here who would be able to stop her from fuckin' with me."

Tears flowed down Icy's face as she watched the two men she held dear to her heart, squash the imaginary beef they had going on. She got up and went upstairs while everyone else stayed in the living room, planning for what was to come in Kingston. Kia decided to allow the men to talk amongst themselves and followed Icy.

"Blaze, take that woman to the doctor. She's bipolar or schizophrenic. There's no way a normal muthafucka can go from cold to hot like that. To be honest, her ass is scaring me."

Zan laughed at Joe because the expression on his face held nothing but seriousness. He had an idea what was going on with Icy and he felt he should see if Blaze was on the same page as him. Blaze didn't like how Joe was calling his baby something short of crazy.

"Watch ya mouth. Ain't shit crazy about Icy. She don't have multiple personalities or none of that goofy shit you talking about."

"She could've fooled the fuck out of me. You didn't see the change of her eye color before she killed Leo's bitch. The shit was like something out of one of those paranormal movies, brah. She needs a serious evaluation."

Zan was laughing so hard, his stomach ached. Joe appeared to be really scared. "Man, ain't nothing wrong with Icy. I had to deal with that shit when my wife was pregnant. Blaze, congratulations because you about to be a daddy."

***

Icy was sleeping peacefully once Blaze made his way to their bedroom. It took a while for him to get Joe and Kia out of his house before they destroyed everything in sight. Zan told the story of Kia finding out Stack was working with Leo. Joe was fuming because he told her to end the shit with the nigga. Things got heated and Blaze told them to take the noise down the street.

They all had a busy day ahead of them and Blaze was tired as fuck. He noticed their luggage packed by the closet. Blaze watched Icy's chest rise and fall as she clutched a teddy bear in her arms. Not thinking much of it, he went into the bathroom turning the water to the hottest temperature. Blaze removed his clothes, then wrapped his locs in a turban before stepping under the water. The tension in his body ran down the drain relaxing him as the minutes ticked away.

Blaze thought of every possible way to kill Leo, but none of them were good enough for him. By the time he woke up with the sun, he would have the shit figured out.

After washing his body a few times, Blaze stepped out of the shower, wrapping a towel around his waist. He brushed his teeth, gargled mouthwash, then entered the bedroom. His eyes landed on Icy and the teddy bear as he crossed the room. Drying his body, he moisturized his body and climbed in bed behind Icy. Curiosity got the best of him as he eased the bear out for further inspection.

The words printed on the tiny white shirt caught his attention. "Ottey's Love" was on full display. The message made him think of all the love he'd shown Icy throughout the months they had been together. Blaze took it as Icy holding on to the memories they'd shared. Every moment hadn't been peaches and cream, but he had a lifetime to make sure a permanent smile was etched on her face at all times.

Blaze bounced the bear as if it was a baby and it warmed his heart. He'd envisioned Icy carrying his baby and the sight was perfect. He couldn't wait for the day their family went from two to three. Holding the hand of the bear a little too tightly, it spoke to him.

Hello, Daddy. I've been growing in Mommy's tummy for six and a half weeks. You must take me back to Aruba so I can see the beautiful clear waters. I can't wait to meet you.

"Baby."

Blaze shook Icy lightly until she stirred a little bit. Instead of waking, Icy snuggled deeply under the covers. Blaze wanted her to wake up to confirm what he'd heard from the recording inside the bear.

"Babe, wake up. I need you to hear something."

Icy didn't stir because she was exhausted from crying about what she had done to Julian. Her body appeared to be in a relaxed state, but she was actually sitting, happily listening to her father tell her how proud he was of her. It was the first time he had visited her since his untimely death and Icy was ready to spend all the time she could in his presence.

"Icy Shantè Winters, you are so beautiful. You've inherited the looks of your mother and the hustle of your old man. I see you every day doing yo' thang with the salons. It's good to know you didn't get of age and blow the money I left. Instead, you invested that shit! I'm proud of you, baby girl."

"I miss you, Daddy." Icy sniffed. "How can you be proud of me when I've betrayed you——"

"Stop talking crazy! You didn't betray me. That nigga did what he did. The day I was killed, the nigga searched high and low until he found you. Leo watched your every move because he knew the muthafucka you were dealing with at the time. Deron was a ploy, so Leo could save you. He knew for weeks you were going through hell in your relationship."

Icy listened to Birdman fill in the blanks for her. What he said made sense because Deron always had other women, but acted like he loved her. The night Leo came to her rescue was the first time he'd ever taken things to the extreme and put his hands on her. Losing her father clouded Icy's judgement to the point of her accepting his disrespect as love. She felt dumb for not realizing she was being used.

"You better stop blaming yourself. There was no way for you to have known who was responsible for my death. The muthafucka caught me slippin' with the help of my weak ass brother. All Kenny had to do was talk to me. I fucked up by sleeping with Brenda. No, it wasn't a one-time thing. We snuck around for years, and I feel like shit even in the afterlife. Staci didn't deserve what I did. She was always loyal to me. Never giving me reason to doubt her, but I went behind her back, fuckin' with a female she considered a true friend. On top of that, I produced a child in the process. Had I known Kia was my daughter, I would've taken care of my responsibility as a father, not as an uncle. Enough about that shit, it's the past. Now, let's focus on the future."

Icy lowly cried, "No, Daddy. Come back," as he started to fade away. She knew there was more he wanted to say to her. She tossed and turned in her sleep, Blaze realized Icy was having an emotional dream.

He held her and whispered, "It's gonna be okay. I got you," in her ear. His words were unheard because Icy's focus was on her father.

I'm here, baby girl. The moment for me to visit you arrived and I took it. There were plenty times I could've blessed you with my presence, but I think right now was perfect. The stress you've been under isn't healthy for you or my granddaughter." Birdman laughed at the shocked look displayed on Icy's face. "I see all, baby. You better tell that man he's about to be a father. He already listened to the recording in that corny ass bear."

Icy remembered crying, then grabbing the bear for comfort. She never meant to fall asleep, without putting it back in the hiding spot under the bed. She wanted to ask about Blaze's rection, but Birdman started talking again.

"I want to tell you about one rule of the game. Kids and women are off limits when you are getting back at a muthafucka. Desiree fucked up, but she only killed for Leo. She had nothing to do with the charges brought against you." Icy turned away from his gaze. Birdman used his forefinger to bring her attention back his way.

"Hear me out. She messed up talking crazy, then deciding to tell the truth about Leo's warning. It was too late for her, and you eliminated part of the problem. Me personally, I would have told her to disappear and never return. Seeing Kenny do the same with Brenda and she turned up as a whole 'nother person, I'm glad you killed the bitch. Now, Leo will get his karma in Kingston. Speak yo' peace, then allow Blaze and the guys to handle him physically. You have a baby to protect. Promise me you will step back, Icy."

"I love you, Daddy, but Leo will die by my hands."

"No, stand down for me! You have a man who will protect you. Let him do his job!"

"You will be watching, I'm sure. I won't make any promises. Leo has taken so much from me and made my life a living hell in the past couple of months. He won't go to hell thinking I was afraid to touch his ass. I've wished you were here with me on many occasions but wishes don't work in heaven. Thank you for coming to me, Daddy. I needed you more than you know."

"I love you too, Icy. I'll forever watch over you. Continue to take care of your mama. Let her know I love her and I'm saving a spot for her whenever she's ready to join me."

Birdman faded away after kissing Icy on top of her head. Tears slid from her eyes onto the pillow. Blaze saw a small smile appear on her face and decided to let her be until the following morning. Lifting her arm, he placed the bear close underneath and cuddled behind her while cradling her waist. Blaze fell asleep with Leo's death on his mind.

Chapter 22

"So, you're just going to stay close to Amoy?" Avita asked Leo while standing in the doorway of the bedroom. "I've asked you to come talk to me in private plenty of times since last night."

"And I told you there wasn't shit for us to talk about. Act like we're in Kingston. That's when you wanted me to stay the fuck away from you, right?"

Leo was lying on the sofa bed, with Amoy next to him sleeping soundly. Everything he did since they arrived at the hotel, his daughter was right by his side. It was hard being in the same space as Avita because she wouldn't stop talking to herself. Leo wasn't paying her ass an ounce of attention when she spoke her shit. When she didn't respond, he rose from the sofa heading to the balcony, which he knew Avita would follow.

"Why are you going back to Kingston, Leo?"

"Mind yo' business, Avita!"

Leo picked up the blunt he'd left in the ashtray and lit fire to the end. Taking a long pull, he released the smoke through his nostrils as he looked out into the beautiful waters of Lake Michigan. The sun was going to rise soon, and Leo wanted to experience it for the first time. Being in the street doing all he needed to do far as making money, never warranted him to enjoy the beauty of many things in life.

He had a weird feeling in his stomach that morning, but he had no idea what it meant. He smoked in silence, then heard his phone ringing inside the room. Desiree had been missing and he hoped it was her calling because he needed to know where she'd been. Hell, there was no one else for Leo to communicate with, because all his niggas were lined up at the gates of hell. It would be just his luck if it was Julian wanting to argue again. Amoy brought him the phone, rubbing her eyes.

"Daddy, your phone woke me up."

"Go back to sleep, sweetie. I'll make sure it doesn't wake you again."

Kissing her on the cheek, Leo watched his daughter drag her feet back to the sofa bed. Avita was sitting on the bed glaring in his direction and he ignored her. He looked down at his phone and the number was one he didn't recognize. Before he could clear the notification, the phone rang in his hand. Leo was reluctant to answer but he went ahead and did it anyway.

"Hello?"

"Yes, this is Detective Monroe. Is this Sullivan Miller?"

Leo's heart dropped to his ass when the cop used the name he and Julian created for her emergency contact. She had it displayed on the front of her phone as a wallpaper in case something happened to her. Leo cleared his throat nervously.

"This is Sully. What can I help you with?"

"We received a call for a welfare check at 214 Jefferson Avenue in Glencoe, Illinois. Upon our arrival, a female was found inside of the residence. I'm going to need you to come down to the examiner's office and positively identify the body."

"Um, who is the woman?" Leo asked, already knowing the answer to his own question.

"According to the ID, Julian Miller is the victim. Your name and number were displayed on the screen of her phone as I.C.E."

The word victim did something to Leo's feelings. He was so angry at Julian, he didn't even want to communicate with her, and he regretted it. The last time he'd spoken to her, they were shouting back and forth. To learn she was found deceased saddened him. Leo wished he would've pushed her to tell him what she actually knew about Icy and her people when she hinted at it. Now, he would never know the connection between them. Leo wasn't going to identify Julian because he himself were declared dead months prior. He would be going to jail for sure if the police found out he was alive and well.

"I'm out of town and won't be back for a couple days. Can you tell me what happened to her?"

"We're not supposed to disclose this type of information over the phone, but under the circumstances I will. Mrs. Miller's throat was slit. The door was kicked in, so we don't believe she knew her attacker. Is there anyone you can think of who would want to harm Julian?"

"No. My cousin didn't have any enemies that I know of. She mainly kept to herself," Leo lied smoothly.

Leo was pissed, knowing Blaze was behind the death of his wife. He was more eager than ever to land in Kingston. Leo was determined to settle the score eye for an eye. Blaze was going to wish he'd never done what he had done to Julian.

"Thanks for informing me of what happened. I'll try my best to be there soon as I can."

Detective Monroe recited the address to the morgue and Leo pretended to write the information down. Once he finished, Leo ended the call and glanced up to see the sun rising above the horizon. The slew of yellow, orange, and red in the sky was beautiful. The way it danced off the blue of the water as the waves calmly rippled, caused a lone tear to fall from his eye.

"I love you, Julian. Rest easy."

Leo went to the airline app to get them checked in for their flight the next morning. He would be a multi-millionaire before dinner, and Kenise was going to be a distant memory with a weeping son. Leo had plans to leave her body unrecognizable, on full display for whomever to walk in on.

"You want to play, muthafucka. Let the games begin," he said lowly as he sparked another blunt sitting back in the chair.

***

Blaze was in the happiest mood when he woke up. Even though he didn't get much sleep, he was energized to the max. Icy made the rest of his life worth looking forward to just by carrying his baby. That in itself made him want to kill Leo soon as possible. After calling to make sure his plane was fueled and would be ready to take off at the time given, Blaze sent out a mass text.

Blaze: The plane will be leaving within the next two hours. Get up and get ya'selves together, because it's time to get this party started.

Responses started coming in immediately, which Blaze loved, because that let him know everybody was ready to get shit poppin'. Once the last of the bullshit was over, he had plans to make Icy his forever. Blaze made one final call before he went to the bedroom to wake Icy. When he entered the bedroom, she was already pulling socks over her pretty feet while sitting on the side of the bed.

"Good morning, beautiful. I was on my way in here to wake you, but you beat me to the punch."

Icy had on black lounge pants, along with a black crop top. Her stomach was flat as a board, but all Blaze could imagine was the baby bump that would be on display in a couple months. Crossing the room, he wrapped his arms around her waist when she stood.

"Yeah, I want to get this over and done with."

Icy paused the moment Blaze's hand roamed over her stomach. Her father's words echoed in her mind. *You better tell that man he's about to be a daddy.* According to Birdman, Blaze already seen the bear and heard the message she recorded, but he had yet to confirm it. Icy was nervous so she stepped back, looking down at her feet.

"What's on your mind, baby?" Blaze asked with a smile.

"I-I'm-you…" she stammered.

"Icy, how long have you known you were pregnant?"

"I've suspected since we returned from Aruba. I received confirmation a week ago. So much has happened and to be truthful, I didn't know how you would react to the news."

Blaze opened his arms, causing Icy to fall right into them placing her head on his stomach. He kissed the top of her head repeatedly before lifting her chin with his finger. Making eye contact, he stared at the woman that held his heart, while caressing the side of her face.

"Never be afraid to come to me about anything. The love I have for you is here to stay. Starting a family has always been in the line-up of my life. I just wasn't going to allow someone else to choose the mother of my kids. You are the perfect woman to bear my heir."

Blaze kissed Icy tenderly on the lips. Admiring her beauty with a smile, his right hand caressed her stomach as his heart beat rapidly in his chest. Blaze closed his eyes briefly, catching a quick glimpse of Icy holding their child while lying on his chest.

"Hearing I'm about to be a father is the news that has brightened the start of my day. We will celebrate the death of Leo, and the birth of our child as one. There will be no other way to do it. In death, life is born. At least that's what I think the saying was told."

Icy laughed because she didn't think he said that correctly, but she wasn't about to tell his sexy ass he was wrong. Blaze hugged her tightly, then turned her loose to head for the bathroom. He still had to shower and get dressed before they were late arriving to the airstrip.

While waiting for her man to get himself together, Icy put on her sneakers before making her way downstairs to spend a little bit of time with her mother. She tapped on the closed door, lightly waiting for Staci to invite her in. It was early morning and Icy knew her mother was probably still sleeping. She wasn't due to take her medicine until seven. Turning to walk away, Icy heard her mother say come in and she did just that. When she appeared in the doorway, Staci was sitting up against the headboard with the remote in her hand.

"Why are you knocking on a door in your own house, Icy?"

"This may be my house, but I'm going to always give the same respect I give at your house. Your privacy is still yours," Icy smiled. "How you feeling?"

"I'm alright. Therapy is going well. I can't wait until I'm able to walk without that damn walker. The shit makes me feel like a senior citizen and that shit don't sit well with me. I want to get up and go when I'm ready without assistance."

Icy heard the sadness in her mother's voice, but she had a smile on her face, trying to mask the pain. Knowing Staci was working hard to get back to the life she was accustomed to made Icy proud of her. Remembering how she ended up in the state she was in had her blood boiling. Leo had done damage to everyone, but Staci suffered the most out of them all.

"You will get there sooner than you think. When I get back from Kingston, we're going to work on this together." Icy sat on the bed and grasped her mother's hand. "Ma, I'm sorry this happened to you. It's my fault you're not capable of getting around on your own. I'm going to make it up to you. I promise."

"Aht Aht! What you not going to do is place blame where it doesn't belong. We know whose fault this is. Stay focused because you had nothing to do with what happened to me. I would never hold you responsible for something you had no control over. Do you hear me?"

Icy nodded her head yes and squeezed her mother's hand. She was picking at the lint on the comforter, trying to figure out a way to tell her mother the news she'd been keeping to herself. Staci liked Akoni, but they had only been together a few months and she didn't know how she would take what she was about to say. Not to mention, not long before that, Icy had just said I do to Leo's nasty ass.

"Ma, I have something to tell you." Icy never made eye contact with her mother and continued looking down while grasping the comforter into her fist. "Um, you're going to be a grandma."

Standing to her feet, Icy pulled a onesie from her pocket and walked around the bed to hand it to Staci. She watched as her mother unfolded the material. On the front, it read *Granny's first grandbaby.*

"I told Blaze last night your ass was pregnant! I had a dream about fish, and I knew it was you. Congratulations, baby."

"You're not mad at me?" Icy asked nervously.

"Mad for what? You grown! You make your own money, got your own house, and a man that's going to climb the highest mountain to make sure you want for nothing. Long as I don't have to raise this baby, it's all good with me. I am proud of the woman you have become though. Your daddy is up there smiling down at you right now. I wish he was here to help me spoil this baby, because Lord knows I was telling the truth about raising your baby. That don't mean I can't buy him or her whatever I want." Staci and Icy laughed.

"I know Daddy is proud and will always be by my side. He told me to tell you he loves you and will be waiting for you when it's your time to join him."

Staci laughter faded as she looked at her daughter. The tears ran down her face, instantaneously causing her to rock back and forth. Icy knew when she told her mother about the message her father wanted her to deliver, she was going to be emotional. Icy saw firsthand how much her mother missed that man, even after finding out he fathered a child outside of their marriage.

"I'm gon' kick his ass! It's been eleven years and the muthafucka hasn't come to me yet. I'm jealous that you were able to hear him, baby."

Blaze stood in the doorway, watching the two of them embrace. He hated to break up the party, but they had a plane to catch. Clearing his throat, both Icy and Staci glanced in his direction, wiping their tears away.

"We have to head out. Bryan got a call saying Leo changed his flight to this morning. We will still make it to Kingston hours before him, but I had to push the departure time up so I can prep my mother on what's about to go down."

"Blaze, congratulations. I know y'all have to go, but I want both of you to make it back to me. Make this shit quick and easy, but he better suffer."

"Thank you and you already know. That nigga won't come back for what I'm going to do to him. You take it easy while we're gone."

"Boy, bye. Get on out of here with that foolishness. Enjoy your mother. I know she misses you," Staci said, waving him off. "Icy, I love you."

"I love you too, Ma. Since you won't call me, I'm going to make sure to call you every day I'm gone."

Not giving her mother a chance to respond, Icy hugged her and left the room with Blaze on her heels. He'd already brought her purse and phone downstairs and put their luggage in the car. It had been months since she'd seen Leo, and Icy was anxious to grace his presence. It wasn't going to be a very welcoming reunion, but it was going to be a celebration after he took his last breath.

***

Icy went to sleep on the plane soon as they were in the air, right along with Kia. Blaze, Joe, Zan and Smooth were sitting back, smoking and shooting the breeze while listening to music. Blaze half listened to what was going on around him because he couldn't take his focus off Icy as he watched her sleep peacefully with the seat reclined all the way out. He wanted to take her to the back and put her in bed, but that wouldn't be fair to Kia.

"Nigga, are you listening to anything I've said to you?" Joe asked, laughing.

"What you say?"

"Where is Bryan?" Zan passed the blunt to Blaze as they all waited for him to answer the question.

"He changed his mind when he found out Julz wasn't coming with us on this trip. He didn't want to leave her alone knowing Nia is still out there somewhere."

"That bitch vanished into thin air like Casper the friendly muthafuckin' ghost. Hell, her own mama don't even know where she's hiding. I feel sorry for her ass whenever she decides to pop back up. Kia is going to make her wish she was never born."

"Joe, that's on her. She made this shit hard on herself. Kia is yo' problem now. All I know is, Icy won't be out there throwing hands with her. My baby is having a baby and all bullshit is out for her."

"I told yo' ass!" Zan exclaimed, hitting Blaze on the back. "She finally admitted that shit, huh?"

"Nah, not really. When I went upstairs last night, she was sleeping soundly with a teddy bear in her arms. The lil muthafucka started talking when I squeezed the hand by accident, and it told me all I needed to know."

"Congratulations, dawg! That shit is a blessing and I'm happy for y'all. We're all gon' have to make sure she don't run up on that nigga when he step into the trap. The last thing we need is——"

"Don't even finish that shit, Zan. Ain't shit gon' happen to Icy. I'm gon' make sure of that. She's adamant about ending Leo's life, but I can't allow her to do that. She has bodied three muthafuckas and that's more than enough."

"Damn, sis out here handing out death certificates in record time. That's what the fuck I'm talking bout!" Zan saluted in Icy's direction, causing the men to laugh at his reaction. "Tell me this. What's the probability of shorty that came to the hotel poppin' up?"

"Zero to none. Amancia doesn't want any problems with me. There isn't a little bit of chance for her to get with me. She understands that shit now because I involved her daddy in her grown ass business."

"You told her ole man on her?" Joe asked.

"Hell yeah, I did. Amancia hit my line last night and I declined that shit and blocked her number. Knowing I was coming back to Kingston, I didn't want to bring none of that shit to my mama's crib. You feel me? So, I reached out to her father and laid everything out on the table. See, Ayinde don't play when his family name is being smeared into the ground. What Amancia did was lie to him about why she was coming to the states. He was mad when I told him the truth about the lie she told about being pregnant. Ayinde said he would take care of it, and I believe he did."

"That royalty shit comes with consequences, I see. It couldn't be me because I'm a grown ass man and can't nobody tell me shit."

"Joe, shut the fuck up because you ain't royal nothing and I got yo' ass by the balls."

Kia's voice rang out of nowhere, causing the men to clown Joe. He looked down the aisle expecting Kia to be wide awake, but she was still snuggled under the blanket with her arm under the pillow. Joe turned back around, rubbing his hand down his face.

"That don't make no damn sense. What type of woman finds a way to argue in their sleep?"

"A crazy one," Zan laughed.

***

The crew piled out of the SUV, following Blaze to the front door of his mother's home. Icy wondered how a woman could live in such a massive place alone. After a brief second, she understood, because it was the same reason Staci didn't want to leave the house that she and Birdman shared together. It was also why Blaze couldn't convince his mother to move nor visit the states. Duke's presence was still felt throughout, and Kenise didn't want to lose out on that feeling. Instead of using his access to enter the house, Blaze did what everyone else did and rang the doorbell.

When no one approached the door, Blaze went to the app he used to look in on his mother. He saw Bembe walking across the room, and he sighed lowly. Icy rubbed his back gently and Blaze wrapped his arm around her shoulder. The locks on the door could be heard turning, then it was pulled open.

"Bembe, what took you so long to open the door, my guy?"

"I'm sorry, Akoni, I was in the bathroom. I didn't know you would be coming through. Had I known, I would've had the cleaning service come to have the suites dusted. You have plenty of people with you this time around. Anything special taking place?"

Bembe stood to the side so they could enter. He spoke to everyone as they passed while Blaze stood next to him. Motioning toward the sitting room, Blaze waited for Bembe to lock up before responding to what he said a moment earlier.

"No need for all of that. We will get settled just fine. As far as the plans I have in place, I'm going to need you to help us in what we are going to do. Where's my mother?"

"She's upstairs. I'll go get her for you."

"Thank you. Don't tell her I'm here. Just escort her to the sitting room, if you may."

"No problem," Bembe said, hurrying away.

Blaze stood with his hands folded in front of him as he awaited his mother's arrival. When her footsteps were heard descending the steps, everyone stood as if they were about to meet the queen of Zamunda. When Kenise stepped down off the last stair and saw her son, she covered her mouth as she squealed with delight.

"Akoni, wen yuh get here? An wah mek yuh tell mi yuh did coming?" she asked, hugging him tightly.

"Mi want tuh surprise yuh. Plus, mi want yuh tuh meet mi friends, an mi special lady."

Kenise looked around at everyone standing in the sitting area. Her eyes connected with Icy and she smiled broadly. She knew right away that was who her son was courting. The beautiful woman had a glow that Kenise knew oh so well.

"Cum yah, pickney." Kenise gestured to Icy, and she walked slowly toward Blaze and his mother. "Yuh beautiful. Yuh wit pickney, no?"

"Thank you, so are you. I'm sorry, I don't understand what you asked," Icy replied.

"She asked if you are with child?" Blaze beamed.

"Oh, um… yes, I am having a baby."

"Tuh God be di glory! Mi prayed fi years fi be a grandmotha. Tank yuh."

"You don't have to thank me. It is my pleasure to be pregnant by Akoni. He has been nothing but the best man to me. I'm blessed to have him in my life. Thank you for raising him to be the man he is today. I don't know what I would've done if he hadn't come into my life. Praises are all for you, Mrs. Ottey."

Kenise wrapped her arms around Icy as she whispered, "Thank you," repeatedly. "Welcome tuh fi wi fambly."

"I appreciate you having me."

Blaze introduced everyone else to his mother and they were all greeted with a hug. It had been a while since Kenise had a houseful of people over and couldn't wait to feed them. Before she could head to the kitchen, Blaze had her to sit down to explain the seriousness of why he was home. Kenise couldn't believe the man who came to her home often to do business with her husband was coming back to do harm to her for money.

"Duh Leo kno dat yuh ave all di funds, Akoni?"

"No, he doesn't and I didn't tell him because I need him to come here. You are the bait, Ma. Leo will not leave Kingston walking. As a matter of fact, no one will ever hear from him again. Leo has to die and there's no other place to do it than here. I can send you to the village until it's taken care of, if that's what you prefer."

"Mi nuh leaving. Him killed mi husband an him muss pay. Yuh ave mi full support. Tell mi wah mi need fi duh."

Chapter 23

Leo carried Amoy in his arms as they exited the plane after landing in Jamaica. The flight was long and Avita added to his irritation the entire flight because she wanted to nick pick about shit Leo wasn't in the mood to discuss. He tuned her out by putting his earbuds in and going to sleep. Not bothering to wait on Avita, he made his way to baggage claim so he could pick up the rental he'd reserved for his quick stay. The only reason he rented a vehicle was because there was no way he was getting in a car with any of Avita's family members.

He'd overheard Avita on the phone talking to her jealous ass cousin about her father finding out about their trip to Chicago, and she was pissed because that pussy ass nigga Blaze called him. Leo wondered what type of man would call himself telling on a grown ass woman about her whereabouts. Amancia offered to pick them up from the airport, but Leo told Avita she could pick her up, but Amoy was rolling with him. In the end, Avita declined the ride altogether because she wasn't leaving her daughter in Leo's care alone.

It took them forty-five minutes to get out of the airport and into the vehicle. Leo headed straight to Avita's house with the music blasting. He and Amoy was having the time of their lives singing with the tunes, while Avita sat with a scowl on her face. She knew soon as they got to their destination, Leo would be leaving. She wasn't looking forward to him lying to Amoy about coming back later. Avita had a feeling that day would be the last they saw or heard from him again.

Avita was lost in her thoughts and didn't realize the car had come to a full stop until she heard the door slam. Leo had already taken Amoy out and was unloading the trunk. She finally got out and made her way to the door, so Amoy could rush off to the bathroom. She did an about face to retrieve her luggage, but Leo waved her off. Shrugging her shoulders, Avita entered the house. The hot sun had her sweating and the only thing on Avita's mind was taking a shower.

She disrobed, tossing her clothes into the hamper. Entering the bathroom, Avita turned the shower on to a warm setting then stepped under the water. The things she learned on her trip was mind blowing. Bad as she wanted to cry, she refused to do so because it is what it is. Avita loved him more than she should, considering how he was moving behind her back. She never thought he would ever lead her on the way he had, and his actions really left a bad taste in her mouth. To be honest, she didn't want anything else to do with him and his corrupt lifestyle.

Avita grabbed her loofah, adding cocoa butter body wash to it. As she washed her body, her eyes stung, causing her to pause under the stream of water. Willing herself not to cry, Avita took a deep breath. Once she was cleansed from her neck down to her feet, she washed her hair. A gust of cold air startled her a bit, then she knew right away Leo had invaded her space.

"Get out, Leo. I would rather take a shower alone."

"You know I have shit to do here and I'm tense as fuck," Leo said, running his hand over her ass. "You're the only one to relax me."

"You're full of shit! If that was the case, you wouldn't have a wife and ex-wife at the same damn time. Now, for the last time, get off me."

Avita smacked his hand away from her as she tried to get the shampoo out of her hair. She couldn't open her eyes and she felt defenseless because she couldn't see. Without warning, Avita felt Leo's fingers exploring her folds. She hadn't been touched sexually for months and just like that, her pussy had complete control of her mind. Pushing back on his hand, Avita heated up like a sauna.

"Mmmmmmm," she moaned, forgetting all about rinsing her hair.

"All that mad shit you were doing wasn't necessary. All you had to say was you missed a nigga and this dick. Don't worry, baby, I'm gon' get you right."

Leo dropped to his knees, then parted her legs. Lying on his back, he grasped Avita's thighs and forced her to sit on his face. The water rinsed the shampoo out and she was no longer blind. She tried to step away so she could get out, but the hold Leo had on her prevented her from doing so. Instead, he sat up and locked his lips onto her clit.

"Ssssss, shit!"

Her hands clutched the back of his head, and she rode the wave smoothly. Leo squeezed her cheeks together as he slurped all her juices into his mouth. Avita became lightheaded as the most powerful orgasm prepared itself to erupt.

"I'm cumming!" Avita moaned loudly as her eyes rolled to the back of her head.

Leo didn't stop the assault he hand delivered to Avita's creamy center. The taste of her honey was delectable, and he couldn't control the way he shook his entire face into her mound. Avita couldn't hold off a minute longer, she squirted all over his chin and chest, almost losing her balance. Leo broke her fall, then gently sat her on the shower bench.

Avita couldn't focus, between the steam and the euphoric high she was on, she was worn out from the one nut that was taken from her soul. Her yoni was still hungry for more and she wasn't going to deprive herself of what she wanted and needed. Leo placed both of her legs on his shoulders then bent his knees, positioning his pole at her opening. When he slowly entered her, Avita bit her lip and clawed at his thighs.

"Oh, God!"

"Nah, it's daddy, baby. You know how the fuck I get down. Don't try to act brand new to this shit."

The deep thrusts he provided hit the right spot each time. It took seconds for Avita to flood Leo's manhood, pushing him completely out of her love box. He lustfully rubbed his thumb over her bud, and she came for the third time.

"Damn, you were ready to wet me up, huh? I like that shit. That's what I like, always make sure she's ready for me. I love you, Avita."

"I love you too."

Good dick would have a bitch professing her love to the Pope if he was dishing that shit out. The way Leo was making love to her felt different and truly felt like he was taking his time to make sure she was satisfied. For some reason, it felt like this was their final goodbye. Avita tried not to think about any of that as she rode the wave to ecstasy. Leo lifted her up and she wrapped her legs around his strong back. Placing her against the shower wall, he entered her again.

"This pussy is so tight. Damn, she's gripping the fuck out of me."

Leo stepped away for a second before diving back in. Avita knew she was going to have all types of bruises on her back when they finished. The shit hurt so good that she wasn't going to complain. She'd deal with it later. Clasping her hands together at the nape of his head, Avita rode the fuck out of his dick and Leo growled in her ear like a mad dog.

"You gon' make me bust this nut! I'm not ready."

In Avita's mind, she had got off three spectacular orgasms and she was feeling a little selfish now that their tryst was coming to an end. She only wanted to finish him off so Leo could do what he did best. Leave. Bouncing harder, Avita could feel his wood harden with each stroke. It was a matter of time before he let loose. Just as she thought, Leo freed his right arm while still balancing her on the wall. He choked her as he rammed in and out of her pussy. Avita was moaning loudly, not caring if Amoy could hear her or not. Leo was making sure she was satisfied to the max and she wasn't mad at him.

"Grrr, grrr, grrrr," he groaned as he coated her walls with semen.

Avita's secretions slid down his balls with ease and the shit felt good. Leo got what he needed and the tension in his body dissipated soon as his nuts were drained dry. He kissed Avita on the neck before placing her down on the floor of the shower. The water had turned ice cold. He hurried and washed her body again then did the same to himself before helping her out. Avita was tired and ready to sleep.

When she stepped into the bedroom, she didn't bother drying off, she just got in the bed. Before her head hit the pillow, Avita was out like a light. Leo quietly got dressed then went to check on Amoy, before leaving to pay Kenise a visit.

***

Blaze was standing in front of Icy, trying to convince her to go down to the lower level of the house with the others before Leo arrived. She wasn't having it because she didn't want to leave Kenise to encounter him alone. If she wasn't pregnant, Blaze wouldn't have to think twice about her staying, but he didn't want anything to happen to her or their baby.

"It's final. There's no way I'm going to feed her to the wolves. You of all people know what Leo is capable of. He would strong arm your mother in the blink of an eye. He's not expecting me to be here, so it's going to take him by surprise. His plan is going to falter for sure. Don't worry, I have my gun and it's locked and loaded. If I have to use it, I promise not to kill him."

The wicked grin plastered on her face told Blaze not to believe a word she said. Instead, he changed his position and opted to stay close by, just in case he had to beat his ass for going after Ice and his mother. Bembe was already in position to hide in the closet next to the fireplace. Blaze, on the other hand, was going to be ducked off in another across the room.

Blaze glanced at his phone to watch the outside cameras. He noticed a white vehicle turning into the driveway. He made his way across the room with his eyes still glued to the screen. When the car stopped, the door opened, and Leo emerged without a care in the world. He leaned against the vehicle and flamed up a blunt while watching the house intensely.

"It's showtime. Icy, please don't set that man off in any way. Be careful, and smart." Blaze kissed her fully on the lips, then turned to his mother. "Ma, I love you. I trust you will allow him to lead the scene. I'm right here."

"Mi luh yuh too."

Icy and Kenise sat next to each other appearing as if they were having a conversation, with some food Kenise had prepared. There were sweet fried plantains, hot pepper shrimp, and with a side of coco bread. Icy reached for the glass of cold water just as the doorbell sounded. She almost spilled the liquid, so Blaze knew she was slightly nervous. Kenise took a deep breath, before looking over at Blaze for the signal to go to the door. The bell sounded again, and he nodded his head before ducking out of sight. Walking slowly to the door, Kenise turned the knob with a sweaty palm.

"Leo, wah a surprise. Ow yuh duh?" Kenise asked with a forced smile.

Leo didn't respond, instead he surveyed the home over her head. He couldn't see Icy because she was sitting on the sofa out of sight from the doorway. Kenise's smile faltered when Leo pushed his way inside her residence.

"Who's here with you? And don't lie."

Kenise opened her mouth to respond, but Leo's attention was already on Icy. She stood to her feet as they stared at one another without blinking. Cocking his head to the side, Leo's eyes slitted, causing him to appear demonic. That didn't bother Icy one bit because she herself was transforming into that person everyone had come in contact with recently. The nervousness she felt after learning Leo was outside was no longer present.

"The fuck you doing here, Icy?"

Icy's top lip curled into a snarl. "My man is back in Chicago. You don't have a right to question me. But, since you want to be all in my business, I'll fill you in. With all the stress I've been under, Blaze thought it would be a good idea for me to visit Kingston and get to know his mother. Are you satisfied?"

"Why would my muthafuckin' wife need to meet the mother of another nigga? Huh?"

"Pause. I am no longer your wife, Leo. You're dead, remember?" Icy laughed. "See, I didn't wait no time to get that shit annulled. I'm not stupid though, I made sure everything you owned was signed over to me. You knew that already. How about you tell me why you had my mother run off the street?"

Leo noticed the tears that rolled down Icy's cheeks. He had a slight celebration in his head as she fought hard not to break and reveal how weak she was in that moment. Icy's phony hard demeanor was on the verge of crumbling to her feet. Leo was prepared to make her slick ass fall to her knees.

"Icy, I know it hurts like hell to lose both your mother and father. I want you to give my sincere condolences for your loss. You have to understand one thing though, when you play stupid games, you win stupid prizes. Your vindictive ways put your mother in harm's way. It was a brutal sacrifice you will have to live with until it's your time to join her."

Icy was torn while Leo was getting a kick out of taunting her. The smirk on his face only pissed Icy off more than she already was. Kenise had tears in her eyes, while she listened to Leo admit to killing Icy's mother.

"I'm so glad you think killing my mother is a joke. There's nothing funny about taking an innocent woman away from her child!"

Icy cried real tears at the thought of losing Staci, but she was actually thanking God she was still above ground. Holding her head down, Icy pretended to be distraught, adding theatrical effects. The entire time she made sure she kept his shoes in her line of vision. Slowly lifting her head, Icy sniffed then giggled uncontrollably.

"The jokes on you, Leo. Let me tell you how. The woman you put a hit on at the hospital was somebody's mother, just not mine. See, I knew eventually you would try some punk shit like going after my mama. Therefore, I had her discharged to continue healing at home."

Leo's eyes widened in fear but in a millisecond, they were back to normal. Icy peeped it though. She had one up on him and he wasn't too thrilled about that shit.

"Answer me this," Icy's voice trailed off so she could get her wording together. "Did you know your wife Julian was actually Kia's mother, Brenda Giles?"

"No, how the hell is Julian Kia's mother when she was only thirty-five years old?"

"Wrong again, Einstein. Womp, womp. *Brenda* was a forty-eight-year-old mother. She underwent cosmetic surgery and a facelift so she wouldn't be recognized when she came back to Chicago. You never wondered why she always told you to leave me alone? Or when she told you about the money I took was owed to me, for what you had done to my father?"

Realization kicked in as Icy continued to reveal the very thing Leo wished he had gotten out of Julian before she was killed. "Even with Brenda telling me all that bullshit, I still slit her muthafuckin throat for old and new. While I'm confessing, I got rid of Desiree and the baby you never wanted as well. You can thank me later, bitch."

Leo was learning a lot of information he was anticipating from Icy. She had killed Desiree and that was the reason he couldn't find her. With his hands on top of his head, Leo turned his back to them. Icy motioned for Kenise to leave the room while Leo wasn't looking. She eased up and accidentally hit her knee on the coffee table, He spun round fast with his gun in hand. That prompted Icy to pull her weapon from her back, aiming it at his head.

"Where the fuck you going?" Kenise was frozen in place, scared as hell. "Fuck all the rest of that shit you talking about, Icy. Where's my money Duke owes me, bitch? I want every dime of it, now!"

"She doesn't have the money, Leo. Blaze has all access to that money. Not Kenise."

"Shut the fuck up! I'm not talking to you! I will kill this bitch if you keep trying me!"

Leo had yet to look in Icy's direction, so he had no clue she had her gun trained on him. Blaze didn't want Leo dead, so Icy lowered her gun to his knees. He was so fixated on Kenise, he forgot to survey the room. Birdman taught her to always pay attention to her surroundings and she was quite sure Leo knew about that rule as well. But if one was greedy and had money on the brain, all the logical shit went out the window.

With the gun trained on Kenise, Icy watched Leo's trigger finger and knew he was about to shoot her out of spite to Blaze. She couldn't let that happen, because losing his mother would kill Blaze. Never taking her eyes off him, Icy had to move fast.

"Kenise, get down!" Icy yelled as she pulled the trigger twice, shattering both of Leo's knees.

Leo got a shot off and Kenise fell to the floor. Icy's heart felt like it was beating out of her chest as she watched Kenise lying on the floor motionless. Blaze ran across the room and Bembe had his gun aimed on a howling Leo. He kicked the gun away and snatched him up by his shirt collar. The door opened to the lower level and the rest of the crew helped Bembe carry Leo away. Icy focused on Kenise and sighed with relief when she sat up and fell into Blaze's arms.

"Mi tink him shot mi," Kenise cried. "Kill him, Akoni."

Blaze rocked his mother in his arms while checking Icy out from afar. He couldn't tell if she was okay psychologically or not, but he would find out once he tended to his mother. He helped Kenise from the floor then Kia guided her toward the staircase. There were plenty of hands on deck to handle Leo, Kia just wanted to be there for Kenise in her moment of need.

"You okay, baby?" Blaze asked.

Icy whispered, "Yes," and sat down in the closest chair. "I saw him getting ready to shoot her."

"I know. You did good. Your quick decision saved my mother's life. Thank you. I appreciate how you deterred his focus off my mother until you couldn't. Now, the moment you came all the way to Kingston for awaits you downstairs."

"I'm going to sit this one out. Leo is all yours. Don't show any mercy on him. Joining the ladies is a better option for my pregnant ass."

"I couldn't agree with you more. Go upstairs. My parents' room is to the right of the hall."

Blaze kissed Icy on the forehead and hugged her close to his chest. Releasing her, she stepped around him and picked up the plate of jerk shrimp and coco bread from the table. Blaze laughed at the way Icy balanced the items in one hand, while fucking the shrimp up with the other.

"What's funny? Hell, I'm hungry, and the baby don't give a damn about its mama shooting a nigga five minutes ago."

Standing at the bottom of the stairs until Icy turned the corner, Blaze headed for the lower level of the house. Soon as he closed the door, Leo's voice bellowed through the room.

"Nigga, you my muthafuckin' blood! You helped these niggas hoist my ass in the air with chains!"

"You a clown, Jo. Blood don't make us family. How the fuck you think I was going to cross Icy by helping you after what you've done to the both of us? Make it make sense! Leo, you ain't new to this type of shit. We used to fuck niggas up just like this together," Zan laughed.

"The shit you did was clever as hell though. You could've gotten away with it, had you not shitted on so many along the way. You had all this planned out for eleven years! Wow, and the muthafucka who helped you keep yo' shit afloat knew nothing about it. Leo, You ain't smart at all. All the time you had to execute this shit and you failed."

"Fuck you! I killed that bitch ass nigga Birdman eleven years ago! Duke didn't get what he had coming, until he didn't pass the torch to its rightful place!"

Hearing Leo spin a false narrative about his father enraged Blaze. "Let me get this straight. You killed my father because he didn't hand his empire to you?"

"Damn right! I was next in line. Akiel didn't know a damn thing about the game. He was born with a silver spoon in his mouth. I was the nigga working my ass off getting Duke's shit out in the streets of Chicago!"

Walking across the room, Blaze grabbed a samurai sword from the wall. When he turned around, his eyes were black as night. One would've thought he'd morphed into the devil himself within seconds. The plastic crinkled with every step Blaze took as he approached the spot where Leo was hanging.

"Nigga, you a pussy! You need weapons and shit to take care of me," Leo laughed. "Fight me like a muthafuckin' man! Let me down and give me my one for fuckin' my bitch!"

Blaze handed the sword to Joe and pulled his shirt over his head. "Lower that nigga down. Then unhook him. I wanna see if the streets of Chicago taught you anything, other than talking shit."

"Blaze, just kill this nigga," Joe snickered.

"Nah, he wants to fight for something that belongs to me now. I'm going to give him a chance to get his payback."

Joe and Smooth worked together to get Leo out of the restraints, once his feet was on the floor. Smooth gave Leo a quick head nod, but Zan peeped that shit with a questionable expression. He didn't know what the fuck they were up to, but he knew there was a message in the gesture. His eyes were open and if he had to lay Smooth's ass down, he would do it in a heartbeat.

Leo stepped back, squaring up as he moved in a circle. Blaze stood still because Leo wasn't a threat to him. Leo lunged at Blaze, connecting with his jaw. Reaching out, he tried to grabbed Blaze's shirt and was met with an uppercut. Leo's chin clamped shut and the beat down began. Blaze didn't let up as he punched Leo on every part of his body.

"Yo' city ain't taught you shit! This is one of the reasons my father didn't hand his empire to yo' weak ass! The other is because I was next in line!"

Blaze hit Leo so hard, his head snapped back, and he hit the floor hard. Smooth moved fast in Blaze's direction and Joe rocked his ass before he could make it too far. Smooth stumbled to catch his footing but ended up hitting the wall. Leo was lying flat on his stomach, sleeping like a baby. Zan placed the sword on the table in the middle of the room and cracked his neck to relieve the tension.

"I knew yo' ass looked a little flaky," Joe sneered, snatching Smooth to his feet. "You were all in our space while being a fuckin' mole for this nigga!"

"You didn't know shit! Fuck you niggas!"

Joe and Zan put fist and feet on his ass and Smooth balled up like a piece of paper. Zan bent down, grabbing Smooth by the back of the neck, then turned his head to face him. Smooth's face had swollen two times its size, and Zan had no sympathy for him.

"Why, nigga? This muthafucka had you locked the fuck up, and you coming to his aid?"

"A milli is a lot for money and I needed that shit," Smooth muttered through his busted lips.

"Money? You crossed me for money! That shit makes bitches cum, but it just cost you yo' life."

Zan removed his tool from his back and shot Smooth in the back of his head. Standing to his feet, he left Smooth's body right there without an ounce of remorse. Zan was tired of all this bullshit and was ready to end it all. Leo stirred, trying to bear through the pain. His sides were burning because his ribs were broken. Blaze walked around his body and picked up the sword.

"Everything you did to Icy, wasn't worth your life. Had you left her alone, you would've lived a little longer. Don't get it twisted, you were going to die for the shit you did to my family, because I would've still figured out what you and Maven had done. Karma didn't have shit to do with what I'm about to do to you. This is all me. I have no more words for you, nigga!"

Blaze swung the sword, cutting Leo's right arm at the shoulder. The howl Leo let out sounded like a wild animal attacking its prey. Blaze had fire in his eyes as he dismembered Leo one limb at a time. The blood spilled on the plastic and formed a puddle under Leo's torso. His eyes and mouth were open wide. Blaze brought the sword down one last time and Leo's head detached and slightly rolled across the floor.

"Yo' ass is crazier than Icy! Y'all belong together," Joe exclaimed. "Remind me to *never* say nothing else slick to you. I'm sorry for all the shit I've ever said. Nigga, you should get a role in a Jason Voorhees movie or some shit."

Ignoring Joe's wisecracks, Blaze picked up a couple of Leo's body parts and headed for the patio door. Out of curiosity, Joe followed. He tossed the shit in the pond and the piranha's started eating immediately.

"This nigga crazy! Who the fuck keeps thousands of piranhas as pets! Yo' ass worse than Betty White's ass thinking it was okay to feed the alligators in Lake Placid! You better be careful because those muthafuckas gon get big enough to eat yo' ass up!"

"Shut the fuck up, man," Blaze laughed. "Go get that nigga Smooth's body and toss it in there. My babies haven't eaten in months. They're hungry."

Epilogue

Nine months later…

Life had been greater than great for Icy. She didn't have to live in fear of anything bad happening to her family, since everyone involved in her misery was gone. Staci was back to living her best life, one hundred percent healed. It took months for her to bounce back, but she fought hard every day. Icy bought her mother a new car for her determination and will. Staci didn't lie when she said she wasn't moving out of her house. Soon as she was able, she hightailed it back to the home Birdman built.

Kia and Joe were making shit work between them. They had an interior decorating party to get their house just the way they wanted it. It was a lot of fun, until Joye popped up on the scene, trying to check Joe about disappearing on her. Of course, she was the realtor who helped him find the house and knew where he laid his head. But Joye came to the wrong address with drama after the shit they'd been through. She didn't know Kia always wanted the smoke. To everyone's surprise, things didn't go left. Kia actually handled the shit like a woman, then Joye left peacefully. She did threaten to cut Joe's dick off if he ever stepped out on her though.

Julz's business was booming, and she has gotten a lot of business from the customer she was delivering to the night she was kidnapped. Amira was a popular blogger who had over a million followers, including celebrities, on her social media platform. After Julz delivered the order to Amira, she was very pleased with the work that was done on her family's shirts. She shouted out Julz Creations on her page, and it was up from there. Julz came up with lucrative ways to make her company better and it was paying off for her financially.

Bryan never stopped trying to get Julz to forgive him for what Nia had done. That worked in his favor because Julz finally gave in, and they too moved out of the city into a house to raise Jamiah together. Nia still hadn't shown up and Bryan had no problem having full custody of his daughter. He took on the responsibility and it was the best decision he'd ever made, outside of opening the center.

"Damn, who the hell ate a whole bag of apples?" Kia screamed, bringing Icy back to what was going on in her home.

"If you don't stop all that yelling and wake this baby up," Icy snapped. "You know how hard it is to get her to stop crying when Blaze isn't around."

It was Christmas Day and Icy had given birth nine days prior to a beautiful baby girl. She and Blaze named her Akanji Karasi Ottey. She weighed in at seven pounds, six ounces, and was twenty-one inches long. Akanji was a spitting image of her father. The one whose touch gives life, is what Akanji's name meant, and she did that each time she made contact with Icy.

Never in a million years did Icy think she would have the chance to love someone the way her parents loved her. Akanji brought every ounce of joy back into her mother's life and Icy was grateful for the second chance to be happy. The only thing Icy didn't like was how spoiled Blaze had her in a nine-day span.

"I told you to tell that nigga to stop sitting up holding her all damn day. He should be the one here babysitting. Now I have to go out to Walmart and grab apples for the coleslaw."

Julz stopped wrapping presents and stood to her feet. "I'll go with you."

Everyone was meeting up at Icy's to celebrate the holiday. She was being waited on hand and foot while things were getting done by everyone else. All she had to do was sit back and look pretty, since she had a Cesarean and couldn't do much anyway.

"Hurry back, while you fussing. You know Blaze had to fly out to bring Kenise back. You doing too much right now."

"Whatever. Come on, Julz."

As Kia was leaving, Zan and his family was coming in. Icy was glad because she didn't want to be alone. She still got nervous at times, wondering if there was someone else out there that worked with Leo. Blaze told her to stop worrying so much and he would always protect her.

"Damn, Kia. Hello to you too," Zan called out as he watched her storm down the stairs.

Kia raised her middle finger and jumped in the driver's seat of her car. The Walmart was a few blocks away, but she hated driving in the snow. All she wanted to do was finish the sides, sit on her ass drinking eggnog, and sing some carols.

"I could be in the damn she-shed smoking a blunt!"

"Kia, it's your fault because you forgot to buy the apples yesterday. Didn't nobody eat them," Julz laughed.

Kia was quiet while she thought about that shit. "Girl, you shole is right. Oops, my bad. Oh well, I could still be smoking." She turned into the parking lot, and it was empty as hell.

"I know damn well this muthafucka ain't closed! Since when do Walmart close on any holiday!"

Kia was mad all over again as she drove out onto the street. She headed right for the expressway. Julz was puzzled because there was another Walmart five minutes away. Sitting while Kia drove past the exit, she knew they should've gotten off on, she decided to question Kia.

"Um, where you going?"

"They got me fucked up if they think I'm about to keep driving around on a blank mission."

"Who the fuck is they?"

"These suburban ass Walmart owners! I'm going to the city where I know for a fact one of their stores are open."

Julz laughed because Kia was right, you can find plenty of stores open in the city. The suburbs shut down like it was Little House on a Prairie or some shit. It was quiet as fuck before ten o'clock at night. Kia wasn't used to the sound of peace. She pulled into the Walmart on 83rd and just like Kia thought, it was packed. She smacked her lips loudly as she looked around for a space to park.

"These muthafuckas always waiting to the last minute to take they ass to the store!"

It didn't matter what the case was, Kia was going to find a reason to complain about the littlest things. Julz just wanted to get out of the car at that point. Kia sounded like a gnat in her ear. As they circled the huge lot, Kia finally found a spot to park.

"I'm gon' run in here and get these apples. I'll be right back."

Opening the door, Julz spotted a woman with her hood up as if she was having car trouble. She zoomed in closer and realized who it actually was. Julz grabbed Kia's arm just as she was about to get out.

"Bitch, look over there." Julz pointed in the direction of the car.

Kia looked but didn't know why that shit was a concern for her friend. "So, the bitch is stranded. Not our problem."

"Oh, it's *my* problem! That's Nia's ass."

"What you say?" Kia asked, snapping her neck to look at Julz.

"You heard me. I'm about to kick her ass!" Julz got ready to jump out of the car, but Kia stopped her.

"Nah, we gon' play this shit right. You stay in the car. As a matter of fact, get in the back on the floor. I got something for her ass."

"Why I gotta get on the damn floor?" Julz scrunched up her face and asked.

"She knows what you look like, dummy! My plan won't work if she sees yo' white ass. Just do what the fuck I asked you to do. I'm gon' get these apples and then we gon' help this bitch."

"Help her?"

"Watch me work. Trust me."

Kia damn near ran into the store and was back out within seven minutes. Julz was already in position on the floor and Kia was glad she listened. She started her car and backed out of the space and made her way to the aisle where the woman still stood shivering in the cold.

"Excuse me," Kia said, with her window down. "You need help?"

"Girl, yeah. My damn car broke down. I knew the alternator was going out, but I didn't think it would completely shut down on me today! I have to get some gifts to my daughter and now I'm stuck out here."

"I can take you wherever you need to go."

"Man, you're right on time. I have to go home first so I can grab my cellphone. That's why I was standing here, I can't even call nobody."

"It's cool. Get in," Kia said nicely. "Where you live?"

"On 99th and Cottage Grove."

Kia nodded her head because she knew exactly where the bitch lived. She wasn't going to make it to her house, because she was going deep into barely-there trees that lined that street. The business that was right there wouldn't be open, due to it being Christmas. Kia turned the radio on and Megan Thee Stallion's "Hot Girl Summer" came on and Nia started rapping.

"Handle me? Who gon' handle me? Thinking he's a player. He's a member on the team. He put in all the work, he wanna be the MVP. I told him ain't no taming me, I love my niggas equally."

"Let me find out that's yo shit," Kia laughed. "I'm Kia by the way. What's your name?"

"Nia. Nice to meet you. I wish I had a cool ass friend like you in my life. Shit crazy out here. It's hard being by yourself when the father of your child takes her from you."

"I thought you were taking gifts to your daughter," Kia dug into her lie.

"I-I am. Soon as my mama calls and tell me where we're meeting her daddy at."

"So, you spending Christmas alone?"

"Girl, yeah. It's just me at my house. I don't have a man or shit. My lil boo got murdered earlier in the year. I miss his ass so much, even though he got on my damn nerves. Turn right here and go to the end of the block. My house is the last one on the right."

Kia surveyed the area as she slowly went down the one-way street. The majority of the houses were dark as if the families went to relatives houses for the day. There were vacant houses next door and across the street from Nia's. Kia was just going to handle her business swiftly and head out. She parked in front of Nia's place and cut the engine.

"Would you mind parking in the alley because I don't like anyone knowing I'm home. I can go in through the side door."

Nia was looking around like she was hiding. Little did she know, she was with the person that wanted to find her already. Instead of replying, Kia started the car and pulled next to the door Nia spoke of. She said she would be right back and got out. When Nia was safely out the car, Kia screwed the silencer on her gun and jumped out. Julz scrambled to get out of the car, because she wanted a piece of the bitch too. Finally getting out, Kia was on her way back outside. Julz stood looking at her with a scrunched-up face.

"Bitch, get the fuck in so we can go, before I leave yo' ass standing there looking stupid."

Julz got in and Kia hauled ass away from Nia's house and back to the expressway. Kia had gone in, shot the bitch, and left. End of story. Julz could be mad if she wanted, hell, Kia didn't give a damn if she was big mad, the job got handled. Period.

***

The house was filled, and everyone was having a good time. Akanji was being passed around like a hot potato and she didn't like that shit one bit. The one person she wanted had yet to hold her in his arms. Blaze was making sure he was the best host around since Icy couldn't do it. Kenise blended in well with Staci, Fanny, and Cherelle's mother, Charlene. The only difference was her heavy accent. The way she smiled warmed Blaze's heart, because it was still hard for his mother, living without her king.

"Okay y'all. I know I said we weren't opening gifts until five o'clock, but I can't hold off a minute longer. I have to give Ice one of her gifts before all of y'all! Come in the living room please."

"You always trying to outdo somebody. Showoff ass."

"Joe, you sound like a hater right now. Allow my brother to cater to his woman. If anything, you better take notes before you end up living in your mancave."

"I thought you was about to say on the streets, because you were about to get put out right now!"

"Don't start that toxic shit. I'm tired of both of y'all already," Staci said, causing everybody to laugh.

As they all gathered around the recliner Icy was sitting in, Bryan stood next to Kia. Blaze was still stalling, so she had a moment to fill him in on what happened to Nia. Tapping him on the arm to bend down, Bryan obliged.

"I touched yo' baby mama. You may want to put in an anonymous welfare check at 9921 East Cottage Grove so her pretty little face will still be intact for an open casket. Continue to take care of Jamiah. I'm here to step in as Auntie Kia anytime you need me."

"Say less."

Blaze was walking back and forth in front of Icy with sweat beading his forehead. He hadn't told anyone his plans because he wanted it to be a surprise for everyone in their circle. Taking an envelope from his pocket, Blaze tapped it in the palm of his hand.

"Icy, first and foremost, I want to thank you for giving me the one thing I prayed for, and that was a child of my own." Blaze motioned for his mother to give him the baby.

"Akanji is the most beautiful Christmas gift I've ever received, and anyone that knows how I was brought up, those gifts cost a pretty penny." The entire room filled with laughter. "My father tried his best to have my life planned out for me, down to picking my wife at the tender age of five. That shit lasted until I was eighteen when I left home. There was no way that marriage would've lasted, because you can't plan love."

"Ain't that the truth," Charlene chimed in.

"Ice, my baby told me when she was just a tadpole in your stomach, she wanted to go back to Aruba. I put that ass in a coma every chance I got during that trip," he laughed. "I had to take heed to what my baby girl said. With that being said, I have here in my hand a seven-day adventure to Aruba for you. We didn't get to experience Aruba the way we wanted, but we are going to tear it up in four months!"

Blaze handed the envelope to Icy and kissed her on the lips. Icy blushed after Blaze stepped back and opened the envelope. She shrieked so loud when she saw the two first class tickets and the brochure for the resort. She couldn't believe her man had made another trip happen so soon.

"Wait, what about Akanji? She's too young to be without me."

"She will be four months! Ain't nobody gon' hurt that baby. All the love in this room, girl, you worried about the wrong shit. I got my grandbaby," Staci said, rolling her eyes.

"My princess is ridin' out with us. In fact…"

Blaze walked over to the fireplace and picked up a handful of envelopes. Shuffling through the pile, he handed them out by names until everyone in the room had one.

"I know I said this was a gift for Icy, but what would a trip to Aruba be without family?"

"You trying to say you got everybody tickets to Aruba?" Fanny asked.

"Open your envelope and see."

As everyone ripped their envelopes open, Blaze kneeled down in front of Icy and watched in excitement. There were thanks and hugs, being given to Blaze from every direction. He was grateful to be able to give them something for the love they had shown and being there every step of the way for Icy.

"Okay, okay, quiet down. It was my pleasure to do this for you all, but if you know me, there's a method to my madness." All eyes were on Blaze as he dug deep into his pocket, coming out with a black box.

"Oh, my God! I know damn well he's not," Kia gasped with her hand over her mouth.

"Icy, I told you earlier this year that I loved you. That shit was real, ma. I won't go another day without asking you to be my wife. You've earned that shit. My daughter won't be at school being questioned about why her name is not the same as her mother's, because we're all going to be Ottey's around this muthafucka. Will you marry me?"

With tears in her eyes, Icy hugged Blaze around his neck. She pulled back and he wiped the tears away with his free hand. "You know damn well I'm not turning down the opportunity. I was made to love you, and only you. So yes, I will marry you, baby."

The applause and hoots were deafening around the room. Akanji was even celebrating with her parents with a very special wail. Blaze handed the baby to Icy and took the ring from the box. It glistened every time the sun hit the five-carat stone, encrusted in diamonds over a platinum band. He slipped the ring on her finger and kissed his fiancée once more.

"The wedding details will be coming soon. That's the reason y'all got tickets. Merry Christmas, muthafuckas!" Blaze exclaimed. "I love you, Icy. We gon' make this marriage shit look good, baby. It's just me and you for a lifetime."

The End

Follow Me…

Facebook: www.facebook.com/mesha.king1

Facebook Author Page: www.facebook.com/MzMeesh

Instagram: www.instagram.com/author_meesha/

Twitter: twitter.com/AuthorMeesha

TikTok: vm.tiktok.com/TTPdkx6LEW/

Website: www.authormeesha.

Lock Down Publications and Ca$h Presents Assisted Publishing Packages

BASIC PACKAGE	UPGRADED PACKAGE
$499 Editing Cover Design Formatting	$800 Typing Editing Cover Design Formatting
ADVANCE PACKAGE $1,200 Typing Editing Cover Design Formatting Copyright registration Proofreading Upload book to Amazon	**LDP SUPREME PACKAGE** $1,500 Typing Editing Cover Design Formatting Copyright registration Proofreading Set up Amazon account Upload book to Amazon Advertise on LDP, Amazon and Facebook Page

***Other services available upon request.
Additional charges may apply

Lock Down Publications
P.O. Box 944
Stockbridge, GA 30281-9998
Phone: 470-303-9761

Submission Guideline

Submit the first three chapters of your completed manuscript to ldpsubmissions@gmail.com. In the subject line add **Your Book's Title**. The manuscript must be in a Word Doc file and sent as an attachment. Document should be in Times New Roman, double spaced, and in size 12 font. Also, provide your synopsis and full contact information. If sending multiple submissions, they must each be in a separate email.

Have a story but no way to send it electronically? You can still submit to LDP/Ca$h Presents. Send in the first three chapters, written or typed, of your completed manuscript to:

LDP: Submissions Dept
P.O. Box 944
Stockbridge, GA 30281-9998

DO NOT send original manuscript. Must be a duplicate. Provide your synopsis and a cover letter containing your full contact information.

Thanks for considering LDP and Ca$h Presents.

NEW RELEASES

SANCTIFIED AND HORNY
by **XTASY**

THE PLUG OF LIL MEXICO 2
by **CHRIS GREEN**

THE BLACK DIAMOND CARTEL
by **SAYNOMORE**

THE BIRTH OF A GANGSTER 3
by **DELMONT PLAYER**

Coming Soon from Lock Down Publications/Ca$h Presents

BLOOD OF A BOSS VI
SHADOWS OF THE GAME II
TRAP BASTARD II
By **Askari**

LOYAL TO THE GAME IV
By **T.J. & Jelissa**

TRUE SAVAGE VIII
MIDNIGHT CARTEL IV
DOPE BOY MAGIC IV
CITY OF KINGZ III
NIGHTMARE ON SILENT AVE II
THE PLUG OF LIL MEXICO II
CLASSIC CITY II
By **Chris Green**

BLAST FOR ME III
A SAVAGE DOPEBOY III
CUTTHROAT MAFIA III
DUFFLE BAG CARTEL VII
HEARTLESS GOON VI
By **Ghost**

A HUSTLER'S DECEIT III
KILL ZONE II
BAE BELONGS TO ME III
TIL DEATH II
By **Aryanna**

KING OF THE TRAP III
By **T.J. Edwards**

GORILLAZ IN THE BAY V
3X KRAZY III
STRAIGHT BEAST MODE III
By **De'Kari**

KINGPIN KILLAZ IV
STREET KINGS III
PAID IN BLOOD III
CARTEL KILLAZ IV
DOPE GODS III
By **Hood Rich**

SINS OF A HUSTLA II
By **ASAD**

YAYO V
BRED IN THE GAME 2
By **S. Allen**

THE STREETS WILL TALK II
By **Yolanda Moore**

SON OF A DOPE FIEND III
HEAVEN GOT A GHETTO III
SKI MASK MONEY III
By **Renta**

LOYALTY AIN'T PROMISED III
By **Keith Williams**

I'M NOTHING WITHOUT HIS LOVE II
SINS OF A THUG II
TO THE THUG I LOVED BEFORE II
IN A HUSTLER I TRUST II
By **Monet Dragun**

QUIET MONEY IV
EXTENDED CLIP III
THUG LIFE IV
By **Trai'Quan**

THE STREETS MADE ME IV
By **Larry D. Wright**

IF YOU CROSS ME ONCE III
ANGEL V
By **Anthony Fields**

THE STREETS WILL NEVER CLOSE IV
By **K'ajji**

HARD AND RUTHLESS III
KILLA KOUNTY IV
By **Khufu**

MONEY GAME III
By **Smoove Dolla**

MURDA WAS THE CASE III
Elijah R. Freeman

AN UNFORESEEN LOVE IV
BABY, I'M WINTERTIME COLD III
By **Meesha**

QUEEN OF THE ZOO III
By **Black Migo**

CONFESSIONS OF A JACKBOY III
By **Nicholas Lock**

JACK BOYS VS DOPE BOYS IV
A GANGSTA'S QUR'AN V
COKE GIRLZ II
COKE BOYS II
LIFE OF A SAVAGE V
CHI'RAQ GANGSTAS V
SOSA GANG III
BRONX SAVAGES II
BODYMORE KINGPINS II
By **Romell Tukes**

KING KILLA II
By **Vincent "Vitto" Holloway**

BETRAYAL OF A THUG III
By **Fre$h**

THE MURDER QUEENS III
By **Michael Gallon**

THE BIRTH OF A GANGSTER III
By **Delmont Player**

TREAL LOVE II
By **Le'Monica Jackson**

FOR THE LOVE OF BLOOD III
By **Jamel Mitchell**

RAN OFF ON DA PLUG II
By **Paper Boi Rari**

HOOD CONSIGLIERE III
By **Keese**

PRETTY GIRLS DO NASTY THINGS II
By **Nicole Goosby**

PROTÉGÉ OF A LEGEND III
LOVE IN THE TRENCHES II
By **Corey Robinson**

IT'S JUST ME AND YOU II
By **Ah'Million**

FOREVER GANGSTA III
By **Adrian Dulan**

GORILLAZ IN THE TRENCHES II
By **SayNoMore**

THE COCAINE PRINCESS VIII
By **King Rio**

CRIME BOSS II
By **Playa Ray**

LOYALTY IS EVERYTHING III
By **Molotti**

HERE TODAY GONE TOMORROW II
By **Fly Rock**

BABY I'M WINTERTIME COLD 3 | MEESHA

REAL G'S MOVE IN SILENCE II
By **Von Diesel**

GRIMEY WAYS IV
By **Ray Vinci**

Available Now

BABY I'M WINTERTIME COLD 3 | MEESHA

BLOODY COMMAS I & II
SKI MASK CARTEL I, II & III
KING OF NEW YORK I II, III IV V
RISE TO POWER I II III
COKE KINGS I II III IV V
BORN HEARTLESS I II III IV
KING OF THE TRAP I II
By **T.J. Edwards**

WHEN THE STREETS CLAP BACK I & II III
THE HEART OF A SAVAGE I II III IV
MONEY MAFIA I II
LOYAL TO THE SOIL I II III
By **Jibril Williams**

A DISTINGUISHED THUG STOLE MY HEART I II & III
LOVE SHOULDN'T HURT I II III IV
RENEGADE BOYS I II III IV
PAID IN KARMA I II III
SAVAGE STORMS I II III
AN UNFORESEEN LOVE I II III
BABY, I'M WINTERTIME COLD I II
By **Meesha**

A GANGSTER'S CODE I &, II III
A GANGSTER'S SYN I II III
THE SAVAGE LIFE I II III
CHAINED TO THE STREETS I II III
BLOOD ON THE MONEY I II III
A GANGSTA'S PAIN I II III
By **J-Blunt**

PUSH IT TO THE LIMIT
By **Bre' Hayes**

BLOOD OF A BOSS I, II, III, IV, V
SHADOWS OF THE GAME
TRAP BASTARD
By **Askari**

THE STREETS BLEED MURDER I, II & III
THE HEART OF A GANGSTA I II& III
By **Jerry Jackson**

CUM FOR ME I II III IV V VI VII VIII
An **LDP Erotica Collaboration**

BRIDE OF A HUSTLA I II & II
THE FETTI GIRLS I, II& III
CORRUPTED BY A GANGSTA I, II III, IV
BLINDED BY HIS LOVE
THE PRICE YOU PAY FOR LOVE I, II ,III
DOPE GIRL MAGIC I II III
By **Destiny Skai**

WHEN A GOOD GIRL GOES BAD
By **Adrienne**

A GANGSTER'S REVENGE I II III & IV
THE BOSS MAN'S DAUGHTERS I II III IV V
A SAVAGE LOVE I & II
BAE BELONGS TO ME I II
A HUSTLER'S DECEIT I, II, III
WHAT BAD BITCHES DO I, II, III
SOUL OF A MONSTER I II III
KILL ZONE
A DOPE BOY'S QUEEN I II III
TIL DEATH
By **Aryanna**

THE COST OF LOYALTY I II III
By Kweli

A KINGPIN'S AMBITION
A KINGPIN'S AMBITION **II**
I MURDER FOR THE DOUGH
By **Ambitious**

TRUE SAVAGE I II III IV V VI VII
DOPE BOY MAGIC I, II, III
MIDNIGHT CARTEL I II III
CITY OF KINGZ I II
NIGHTMARE ON SILENT AVE
THE PLUG OF LIL MEXICO II
CLASSIC CITY
By **Chris Green**

A DOPEBOY'S PRAYER
By **Eddie "Wolf" Lee**

THE KING CARTEL I, II & III
By **Frank Gresham**

THESE NIGGAS AIN'T LOYAL I, II & III
By **Nikki Tee**

GANGSTA SHYT I II &III
By **CATO**

THE ULTIMATE BETRAYAL
By **Phoenix**

BOSS'N UP I, II & III
By **Royal Nicole**

I LOVE YOU TO DEATH
By **Destiny J**

I RIDE FOR MY HITTA
I STILL RIDE FOR MY HITTA
By **Misty Holt**

LOVE & CHASIN' PAPER
By **Qay Crockett**

TO DIE IN VAIN
SINS OF A HUSTLA
By **ASAD**

BROOKLYN HUSTLAZ
By **Boogsy Morina**

BROOKLYN ON LOCK I & II
By **Sonovia**

GANGSTA CITY
By **Teddy Duke**

A DRUG KING AND HIS DIAMOND I & II III
A DOPEMAN'S RICHES
HER MAN, MINE'S TOO I, II
CASH MONEY HO'S
THE WIFEY I USED TO BE I II
PRETTY GIRLS DO NASTY THINGS
By Nicole Goosby

LIPSTICK KILLAH I, II, III
CRIME OF PASSION I II & III
FRIEND OR FOE I II III
By **Mimi**

TRAPHOUSE KING I II & III
KINGPIN KILLAZ I II III
STREET KINGS I II
PAID IN BLOOD I II
CARTEL KILLAZ I II III
DOPE GODS I II
By **Hood Rich**

STEADY MOBBN' I, II, III
THE STREETS STAINED MY SOUL I II III
By **Marcellus Allen**

WHO SHOT YA I, II, III
SON OF A DOPE FIEND I II
HEAVEN GOT A GHETTO I II
SKI MASK MONEY I II
By **Renta**

GORILLAZ IN THE BAY I II III IV
TEARS OF A GANGSTA I II
3X KRAZY I II
STRAIGHT BEAST MODE I II
By **DE'KARI**

TRIGGADALE I II III
MURDA WAS THE CASE I II
By **Elijah R. Freeman**

THE STREETS ARE CALLING
By **Duquie Wilson**

SLAUGHTER GANG I II III
RUTHLESS HEART I II III
By **Willie Slaughter**

BABY I'M WINTERTIME COLD 3 | MEESHA

GOD BLESS THE TRAPPERS I, II, III
THESE SCANDALOUS STREETS I, II, III
FEAR MY GANGSTA I, II, III IV, V
THESE STREETS DON'T LOVE NOBODY I, II
BURY ME A G I, II, III, IV, V
A GANGSTA'S EMPIRE I, II, III, IV
THE DOPEMAN'S BODYGAURD I II
THE REALEST KILLAZ I II III
THE LAST OF THE OGS I II III
By **Tranay Adams**

MARRIED TO A BOSS I II III
By **Destiny Skai & Chris Green**

KINGZ OF THE GAME I II III IV V VI VII
CRIME BOSS
By **Playa Ray**

FUK SHYT
By **Blakk Diamond**

DON'T F#CK WITH MY HEART I II
By **Linnea**

ADDICTED TO THE DRAMA I II III
IN THE ARM OF HIS BOSS II
By **Jamila**

YAYO I II III IV
A SHOOTER'S AMBITION I II
BRED IN THE GAME
By **S. Allen**

LOYALTY AIN'T PROMISED I II
By **Keith Williams**

TRAP GOD I II III
RICH $AVAGE I II III
MONEY IN THE GRAVE I II III
By **Martell Troublesome Bolden**

FOREVER GANGSTA I II
GLOCKS ON SATIN SHEETS I II
By **Adrian Dulan**

TOE TAGZ I II III IV
LEVELS TO THIS SHYT I II
IT'S JUST ME AND YOU
By **Ah'Million**

KINGPIN DREAMS I II III
RAN OFF ON DA PLUG
By **Paper Boi Rari**

CONFESSIONS OF A GANGSTA I II III IV
CONFESSIONS OF A JACKBOY I II
By **Nicholas Lock**

I'M NOTHING WITHOUT HIS LOVE
SINS OF A THUG
TO THE THUG I LOVED BEFORE
A GANGSTA SAVED XMAS
IN A HUSTLER I TRUST
By **Monet Dragun**

QUIET MONEY I II III
THUG LIFE I II III
EXTENDED CLIP I II
A GANGSTA'S PARADISE
By **Trai'Quan**

BABY I'M WINTERTIME COLD 3 | MEESHA

CAUGHT UP IN THE LIFE I II III
THE STREETS NEVER LET GO I II III
By **Robert Baptiste**

NEW TO THE GAME I II III
MONEY, MURDER & MEMORIES I II III
By **Malik D. Rice**

CREAM I II III
THE STREETS WILL TALK
By **Yolanda Moore**

LIFE OF A SAVAGE I II III IV
A GANGSTA'S QUR'AN I II III IV
MURDA SEASON I II III
GANGLAND CARTEL I II III
CHI'RAQ GANGSTAS I II III IV
KILLERS ON ELM STREET I II III
JACK BOYZ N DA BRONX I II III
A DOPEBOY'S DREAM I II III
JACK BOYS VS DOPE BOYS I II III
COKE GIRLZ
COKE BOYS
SOSA GANG I II
BRONX SAVAGES
BODYMORE KINGPINS
By **Romell Tukes**

THE STREETS MADE ME I II III
By **Larry D. Wright**

CONCRETE KILLA I II III
VICIOUS LOYALTY I II III
By **Kingpen**

THE ULTIMATE SACRIFICE I, II, III, IV, V, VI
KHADIFI
IF YOU CROSS ME ONCE I II
ANGEL I II III IV
IN THE BLINK OF AN EYE
By **Anthony Fields**

THE LIFE OF A HOOD STAR
By **Ca$h & Rashia Wilson**

THE STREETS WILL NEVER CLOSE I II III
By **K'ajji**

NIGHTMARES OF A HUSTLA I II III
By **King Dream**

HARD AND RUTHLESS I II
MOB TOWN 251
THE BILLIONAIRE BENTLEYS I II III
REAL G'S MOVE IN SILENCE
By **Von Diesel**

GHOST MOB
By **Stilloan Robinson**

MOB TIES I II III IV V VI
SOUL OF A HUSTLER, HEART OF A KILLER I II
GORILLAZ IN THE TRENCHES
By **SayNoMore**

BODYMORE MURDERLAND I II III
THE BIRTH OF A GANGSTER I II
By **Delmont Player**

BABY I'M WINTERTIME COLD 3 | MEESHA

FOR THE LOVE OF A BOSS
By **C. D. Blue**

KILLA KOUNTY I II III IV
By Khufu

MOBBED UP I II III IV
THE BRICK MAN I II III IV V
THE COCAINE PRINCESS I II III IV V VI VII
By **King Rio**

MONEY GAME I II
By **Smoove Dolla**

A GANGSTA'S KARMA I II III
By **FLAME**

KING OF THE TRENCHES I II III
By **GHOST & TRANAY ADAMS**

QUEEN OF THE ZOO I II
By **Black Migo**

GRIMEY WAYS I II III
By **Ray Vinci**

XMAS WITH AN ATL SHOOTER
By **Ca$h & Destiny Skai**

KING KILLA
By **Vincent "Vitto" Holloway**

BETRAYAL OF A THUG I II
By **Fre$h**

THE MURDER QUEENS I II
By **Michael Gallon**

TREAL LOVE
By **Le'Monica Jackson**

FOR THE LOVE OF BLOOD I II
By **Jamel Mitchell**

HOOD CONSIGLIERE I II
By **Keese**

PROTÉGÉ OF A LEGEND I II
LOVE IN THE TRENCHES
By **Corey Robinson**

BORN IN THE GRAVE I II III
By **Self Made Tay**

MOAN IN MY MOUTH
By **XTASY**

TORN BETWEEN A GANGSTER AND A GENTLEMAN
By **J-BLUNT & Miss Kim**

LOYALTY IS EVERYTHING I II
By **Molotti**

HERE TODAY GONE TOMORROW
By **Fly Rock**

PILLOW PRINCESS
By **S. Hawkins**

BOOKS BY LDP'S CEO, CA$H

TRUST IN NO MAN
TRUST IN NO MAN 2
TRUST IN NO MAN 3
BONDED BY BLOOD
SHORTY GOT A THUG
THUGS CRY
THUGS CRY 2
THUGS CRY 3
TRUST NO BITCH
TRUST NO BITCH 2
TRUST NO BITCH 3
TIL MY CASKET DROPS
RESTRAINING ORDER
RESTRAINING ORDER 2
IN LOVE WITH A CONVICT
LIFE OF A HOOD STAR
XMAS WITH AN ATL SHOOTER

Printed in the USA
CPSIA information can be obtained
at www.ICGtesting.com
LVHW021815290923
759666LV00001B/58